CRITICAL ACCLAIM FOR *NEW YORK TIMES* BESTSELLING AUTHOR FAYE KELLERMAN

"No one working in the crime genre is better."

—*Baltimore Sun*

"Mystery fans value Faye Kellerman for her superb novels."

—*Washington Post Book World*

"Reading a good thriller is very much like taking a great vacation: half the fun is getting there. Faye Kellerman is one heck of a tour guide."

—*Detroit Free Press*

"Kellerman is splendid."

—*Milwaukee Journal Sentinel*

"Kellerman has become a real pro at setting up crime puzzles, laying on lots of real and fake clues, and keeping everyone guessing."

—*Pittsburgh Post-Gazette*

"It's a credit to Kellerman's storytelling abilities that long after she reveals 'who done it' readers will be frantically flipping pages to find out just how and why."

—*People*

Also by Faye Kellerman

The Ritual Bath

Sacred and Profane

The Quality of Mercy

Milk and Honey

Day of Atonement

False Prophet

Grievous Sin

Sanctuary

Justice

Prayers for the Dead

Serpent's Tooth

Moon Music

Jupiter's Bones

Stalker

The Forgotten

Stone Kiss

Street Dreams

Double Homicide
(with Jonathan Kellerman)

Straight into Darkness

Capital Crimes
(with Jonathan Kellerman)

The GARDEN *of* EDEN

and Other Criminal Delights

FAYE KELLERMAN

NEW YORK BOSTON

Warner Books
Hachette Book Group USA
237 Park Avenue
New York, NY 10169
Visit our Web site at www.HachetteBookGroupUSA.com

Printed in the United States of America

Originally published in hardcover by Warner Books
First Mass Market Edition: August 2007

10 9 8 7 6 5 4 3 2 1

For Jonathan

Contents

The GARDEN *of* EDEN

"The Garden of Eden" is an original Peter Decker/Rina Lazarus tale written specifically for this anthology. It combines my love of gardening with my love of mystery writing. I gave my protagonist, Rina, gardening as a hobby because she's a nurturing person, and planting a garden is a way to give back to Mother Earth. The story deals with the search for the almighty buck when true treasures are found in the most unexpected places.

IT BEGAN AS SOMETHING RECREATIONAL, A way to pass the time pleasantly, but then, as insidious as a burrowing maggot, it turned into an addiction. By six months, every room in the house was a biological testament to Rina Decker's hobby, from the bedrooms and bathrooms to the living room and the laundry room, plants, sprouts, shoots, and cultivars crowding out space once reserved for human inhabitants. Given the dire circumstances, she knew she'd have to act, but the decision was torturous. Which ones merited the honor of being houseplants, and which ones had to be sacrificed for the good of the family?

"I feel like I'm living in the Congo," Decker complained as he sipped coffee at the breakfast table. He was about to tackle the Sunday paper, though he harbored little hope of finishing it. Something always came up.

"What's wrong with the Congo?" Rina countered. "It's foreign, it's exotic . . . Where's your sense of adventure?"

"Sucked out by the miscreants in the streets of Los Angeles, thank you very much. God and Koolaire have given us creature comforts for a reason, Rina. If I wanted to live in a tropical rain forest, I'd pick a more idyllic spot than the San Fernando Valley. The house has become unbearable—way too hot, dripping wet, and teeming with bugs."

"That's because you leave the back door open."

"I leave the back door open because I'm a big guy and I need circulation. Otherwise I drown in my own sweat."

That was true. Peter was six-four, 230 pounds, and in great shape. The bulge of his winter gut usually melted away in the more active summer months. The only hints of his age in the sixth decade were the increasing streaks of white coursing through his ginger-colored hair and mustache. Rina's husband still cut a handsome figure. She said, "I know you need circulation. That's why the ceiling fans are on all the time."

"All they do is blow around the hot air. We need air-conditioning, darlin'."

"Orchids are sensitive."

"So are husbands." The ribbing was good-natured, but there was a lot of truth in it. "Look. I can tolerate the bathrooms. Bathrooms are usually wet and hot. And so are kitchens and laundry rooms. I'll even acquiesce to the living room and den. But I put my foot down with the bedrooms. Even Hannah's complaining. She feels that you've expropriated her space."

"That's ridiculous. There's nothing in her room except a few African violets."

"Fifteen, at last count."

"They barely fill up her windowsill."

Decker took a deep breath in an attempt to harness patience. "Rina, both your daughter and I are glad you found something that taps into your instinct to nurture and that pleases your aesthetic eye."

Rina stifled a smile. "It's my calling, Peter."

"Fantastic!" Decker said wryly. "Everyone should have a passion. Unfortunately, instead of a passion, I have a job . . . a demanding job. I've got to work, which means I've got to sleep. It's either your *Bletilla striata* or me."

Rina saw the desperate look on her husband's face. He

had reached his limit. "I'll clear the bedrooms. I think I have a millimeter's worth of space on a shelf in the laundry area."

Inwardly, Decker chided himself for his laziness. "I know I've been promising to frame the prefab greenhouse." He wanted to add, *The one that's taking up most of the room in the garage so that my vintage Porsche has been relegated to the driveway under a measly cover.* But years of marriage had taught him a little tact. He didn't know why he kept putting off the construction of the greenhouse. It wouldn't take more than a half-day to build it. Maybe, psychologically, he was afraid of what would happen if she had even *more* room for plants. "And I appreciate that you haven't nagged me to build it even though we bought it months ago."

"You work hard and put up with long, long hours. Your time should be your own." Rina was using her best self-sacrificing voice. "That's precisely why I took up gardening. To occupy my time during those long, long hours—"

"All right, all right!" Decker broke in. He covered his face with his hands, then looked at her between his fingers. "Just promise me you won't turn into a dotty old lady like what's-her-name."

"Cecily Eden."

Decker smiled. "Yeah, dotty old Cecily with the eponymous garden. Is Eden really her last name, or did she change it to match her obsession?"

"As far as I know, it's her given last name, and she's not dotty. She's very sharp—a retired microbiologist. She always jokes that she went from growing aerobes to growing Aerides." Rina laughed out loud. When Decker didn't respond, she gently nudged his shoulder and said, "A little inside garden joke."

Decker tried to remain serious but finally gave in and laughed. She was so cheerful this morning. Rina was still his twenty-six-year-old bride, though she had climbed over the forty mark a few years ago. In the past, they had been mistaken for father and daughter, even though he was only twelve years older than she was. Rina had a beautiful complexion, and her hair was still black, although he rarely saw it in its full glory. Traditional Orthodox Jewish convention dictated that married women cover their locks whenever they went out in public. Lately, she'd taken to wearing big straw sun hats and goofy sunglasses.

"You really should see Cecily's garden, Peter. It's magnificent. She has the most unusual plants. The crowning jewel in her backyard is an imported Chinese sacred tree. It's like a magnolia but has these smaller white blossoms with an intoxicating citrus aroma. It's so green and gorgeous. It's from China, it blooms in the fall, just when most plants are fading away."

"I'm sure it's a sight to behold."

Rina clucked her tongue. "How ironic that you're being sarcastic. When we first married, you were the one who communed daily with nature, Mr. Cowboy."

"Yeah, but I never brought the horses into the house. Do you need help with the plants, darlin'?"

Rina stared at him, then broke into a grin. "You want to *garden* with me? That would be great!"

Decker backtracked. "Uh, I meant, do you need help taking the plants out of the bedrooms and into the laundry room?"

Rina smiled to hide her disappointment. "No, I'm fine. It's not exactly strenuous work."

Now she looked dejected. To Decker, gardening meant chopping down trees or hacking away brush, not transplanting cultivars. He took her hand and spoke in earnest. "You know, Rina, it's a beautiful day. How about if you clear the bedrooms of the foliage and bring all the plants outside while I finally build the prefab greenhouse. We can christen it together."

Rina managed a weak smile. He was trying. "You don't have to build it today, Peter. I can cram the plants into the laundry room."

"No, no, no. I'm determined." Decker stood up, a small physical step that signified the morphing of a theoretical idea into action. "C'mon. Hannah's at Julie's. Let's spend some time together outdoors. You garden and I'll build. Afterward, I'll pick some lemons and you'll make lemonade. Then I'll go get some sandwiches from the deli and we'll watch the Dodgers game together. How does that sound?"

This time Rina's smile was genuine. "Actually, it sounds wonderful."

"Great! Let's get to it!" Decker picked up the paper and headed for the compost pile. One Sunday *Times* would make a week's worth of excellent mulch.

Tuesday from twelve to two had been earmarked as Rina's weekly get-together with Cecily Eden, and she couldn't wait to tell her elderly friend about the newly built greenhouse. Rina was pretty sure that, to celebrate the construction, Cecily would insist on giving her all sorts of plants and would spurn any proffered payments. In order to offset this inequity, Rina had come to her friend's house armed with a plate of chocolate-chip cookies fresh from the oven.

As usual, she walked up the driveway to the backyard gate and automatically turned the knob. This time she found it locked. Usually, Cecily left it open when she knew Rina was coming. It was good that the old woman was finally taking precautions. Rina would often scold her: "You shouldn't be so trusting, Cecily."

The old woman would laugh. "At my age, what does it matter? If anyone breaks in, he can take whatever he wants."

Backtracking over the driveway, Rina went around to the front door. Cecily lived in a ranch house built in the fifties, what Realtors called midcentury style. Her kitchen and bathroom still had original tile, and her furniture had lived through enough years to be considered retro. The old woman kept the place spotless. Having worked with germs all her life, she was a stickler for cleanliness.

The structure wasn't much bigger than a bungalow, but the property was over a half-acre. Rina rang the bell, and when no one answered, she rang it again. She knocked but still got no response.

Strange, Rina thought, because she knew that Cecily was expecting her. As she was about to walk away, almost as an afterthought, she gave a quick jiggle to the knob. She was shocked that the door yielded with the turn of her wrist.

The gate was locked . . . but the door was open.

Instinctively, Rina knew that something was wrong. She should have called Peter, but what was the sense of disturbing him at work before she had proof that things were amiss? As a lieutenant, Peter had his hands full of mishap and mayhem. She didn't want to add to the mix unless necessary.

"Cecily?" she called out. "It's Rina. Are you home?"

She stepped inside a tidy living room abloom with spring flowers—roses, lilies, irises, daffodils, tulips, and Cecily's prized orchids. The couch had been upholstered in old floral fabric that looked something like wisteria vines through trellises. Two wicker chairs sat opposite the sofa. The carpet was green; the walls were peach-colored and plastered with botanical artwork—plants and flowers rendered in oil paintings, watercolors, crayon, pencil, charcoal, pastels, every possible drawing medium. Some were good, some were bad, and lots were mediocre. It was hard to enjoy any individual work, because there were so many of them hung chockablock. Still, Rina was always effusive when Cecily presented her latest acquisition picked up at a junk shop or flea market.

I've been collecting them for years, Cecily would say.

Again Rina called out the old woman's name. When she didn't get an answer, she began to worry, although nothing seemed out of place. She walked through the dining room, setting the cookies on the table, and went into the kitchen. Maybe Cecily had been called away suddenly. Rina knew that the old woman had two grown daughters and several grandchildren. Cecily had mentioned them in passing; nothing extensive, but nothing to indicate that the relationships were strained.

"Cecily?" Rina walked through the kitchen and laundry room, then out the back door. "Cecily, are you home?"

It was mid-May, and the garden was in full bloom, a riot of colors and heavy with fragrance. Cecily had divided and subdivided her lot, creating ecosystems and microclimates connected seamlessly by pathways and lanes. She had placed her rose gardens, bulb gardens, and cutting gardens where there was an abundance of sun and some partial shade. Tucked into a back corner was the Zen garden, with a pavilion and a small fishpond covered by barely visible netting that kept out the predators—stray cats, squirrels, raccoons, and herons. The other corner housed her greenhouse. The orchard took up the rest of the space, giant avocados providing shade for aromatic citrus trees. In the center was the rare Chinese sacred tree. A year ago, Cecily and her gardener had built a bench around its trunk. It was one of her favorite spots for reading and relaxing.

It was there that Rina discovered the body.

Gasping, she rushed over and felt for a pulse—for any signs of life—but she knew it was hopeless. There was no heartbeat and no breathing. The pupils were dilated and fixed, her empty eyes brazenly staring into the sun. Still, Rina called 911. Then she called her husband.

The investigator from the coroner's office was named Gloria, a woman in her mid-thirties who had recently come to the profession. Wearing traditional dark scrubs emblazoned with CORONER'S INVESTIGATOR in yellow, she got up from her kneeling position and snapped off her latex gloves. She looked at Rina. "Do you know if she had any health problems?"

Rina shook her head.

Decker said, "Find anything sinister other than the bruise on her left temple?"

"Nope, and the bruise was probably caused by her

falling and hitting her head on the ground. Nothing to indicate blunt-force trauma. She was an old woman. She must have had a doctor."

"Henry Goldberg," Decker said. "He's a cardiologist. I found out his name from one of Cecily's daughters. He's on his way."

"Great," Gloria said. "I think I'm done here. You can go over the body if you want, but I'm feeling that she died of natural causes. If Dr. Goldberg feels comfortable signing off on the death certificate, that's fine with me. That way the next of kin can call up the funeral home, and they can come pick up the body. If not, have the guys bring her to the morgue, and one of our doctors will sign her off."

"No autopsy?" Rina asked.

"Not unless her physician or her children demand it."

"Thanks," Decker said.

"You're welcome, Lieutenant."

After Gloria left, Decker turned to his wife. "What have you been waiting to tell me?"

Rina bit her thumbnail. "It's probably stupid."

"It probably isn't. What's bothering you?"

"Cecily usually unlocks the back gate for me when she knows I'm coming. I tell her not to, but she does it anyway. This time she locked the gate . . . but the front door was *unlocked*. I find that odd."

Decker agreed. "What do you know about her family?"

Rina shook her head. "Two daughters. The elder one is married with children."

"Edwina Lettiger."

"Yes, Edwina, that's the one. I didn't know her last name. Cecily would mention her occasionally, usually in connection with her grandchildren. The younger daughter is Meredith. I don't know a thing about her other than her name."

"Did Cecily ever talk about tension between her daughters and herself?"

"No. Why?"

"Between you and me, I looked around the house. Everything's neat and in place."

"Cecily was tidy. She used to say it came from years of working in a lab."

"Except one of her bedroom dresser drawers wasn't shut tight. A piece of a sweater was wedged between the drawer and the framework. It was a heavy sweater. You know how warm the days have been. Why would she be looking in her sweater drawer?"

"Maybe it's been wedged that way for a long time."

"All the other drawers were shut tight. This one drawer doesn't fit with her image as tidy, does it?"

"Maybe she just never noticed it. You probably wouldn't have noticed it if you hadn't been looking."

"Of course."

Again Rina bit her nail. "What is it, Peter? Do you think I might have interrupted a robbery?"

"Possibly. Someone heard you yelling over the gate, bolted out the front door, and didn't lock it."

"I didn't see anyone."

"That doesn't mean there wasn't anyone. Did you happen to hear a car take off?"

"Honestly, I don't remember. Was the door jimmied open?"

"I didn't find any obvious pry marks, and the lock was a deadbolt. I think if someone was inside the house, he or she got in with a key."

"Or Cecily could have let them in."

"Of course. Maybe I'm on the wrong track totally. Still, I'd like to find out who had a key to her house."

"I'm sure her daughters do." Rina made a face. "I can't believe they'd hurt her. And didn't the coroner's investigator say it looked like natural causes?"

"Sure, it could have been a heart attack. But what if the heart attack was brought on by a bad argument? What if she didn't fall to the ground but was pushed? We have an unlocked door, a locked gate, and a drawer that's askew in an otherwise compulsively neat bedroom. I've been a cop too long not to ask certain questions, and my first one is who has a key to her house." Decker looked at the garden gate. Two distraught women had corraled Gloria, the coroner's investigator. They spoke to her while waving their arms frantically. Decker put his arm around his wife. "Go on home, honey. We'll talk later. Right now it's time to meet the next of kin."

"This is dreadful!" Meredith sniffed back tears. "Just terrible."

"I'm so sorry for your loss," Dr. Goldberg, the cardiologist, told Cecily's daughters. He had shown up five minutes after the daughters. He was in his sixties, a short, slight man with long tapered fingers. "I've handled many patients in my years. Your mother had a wonderful spirit. I think it was her attitude that helped her last this long." He turned to Decker. "She'd had two prior heart attacks."

Edwina blotted her wet eyes with a tissue. Her gaze went from the doctor to Decker. "She gardened because she could no longer rock climb or go white-water rafting."

"Ah," Decker said. He observed the sisters, noting that though there was a strong familial resemblance—both women had oval faces and hazel eyes—they were nothing alike. Edwina, who drove a new 450SL Mercedes, was precise and meticulous in her appearance: dark business suit and heels, clipped and styled blond hair, long manicured nails. Meredith wore a T-shirt, jeans, and sneakers. Her hair was shoulder-length, brunette streaked with gray. She drove an ancient Dodge Dart. They were in their forties, not more than a couple of years apart. "Your mother was very active in the past?"

"Until her first heart attack," Edwina said.

Goldberg said, "The second one came a year later. That was ten years ago. We stabilized her, but at her age . . ."

Everyone nodded solemnly.

"Mom was one of a kind. She did exactly what she wanted to do and always encouraged us to do the same."

"She certainly had a love of beauty," Decker answered. "This place is paradise."

"Mom's version of paradise." Edwina smiled. "I live in a townhouse overlooking the ocean. No grass, no yard, just a terrace with a couple of potted cacti and a stunning view of the waves. That's my version of paradise."

"That's pretty great also," Decker said.

"If there's anything else I can do for anyone, don't hesitate to call me," Dr. Goldberg said. "I must be getting back. I have patients waiting for me."

Edwina's smile was brief. "She spoke very fondly of you, Doctor. Thank you for everything."

"It was a pleasure being her doctor. Again, my condolences."

"Thank you," Edwina answered.

A forlorn Meredith watched while the men from the funeral home loaded her mother into a van. She shook her head as tears leaked from her eyes. "I can't believe she's gone!"

"She was old, Merry," Edwina said. "It wasn't unexpected."

"It's still a shock, Ed! She wasn't hospitalized or anything like that."

"I should start making arrangements."

"What do you mean by 'I,' sis?"

" 'We,' then. *We* need to start making arrangements. I suppose the smartest thing to do would be to contact Mom's lawyer."

Meredith said, "Mr. Mortimer?"

"Yes, Mr. Mortimer. I'm sure Mom had specific instructions. I know she had a will." Edwina handed Decker a business card. "My phone number, if you should need to reach me."

"Why would he need to reach you?" Meredith asked.

"It's a formality, Merry."

"Actually, I do have a few questions, if you don't mind," Decker said. "For both of you."

"What kind of questions?" Meredith asked.

Edwina checked her watch. "How long?"

"Not too long," Decker said. "Who, besides yourselves, has a key to the house?"

"What do you mean?" asked Meredith.

Edwina glanced at her sister. "Why do you ask?"

"Just trying to button down a few details. Anyone other than you two have a key to the house?"

"No." Meredith looked at her sister. "Right?"

"The gardener," Edwina answered.

"He *does*?" Meredith's eyes went wide. "Thanks for clueing me in."

"Mom gave it to him, Merry. I wasn't consulted."

"You didn't approve?" Decker asked.

"I just thought it was weird, but Mom was insistent. She claimed he was here more than either of us." Edwina turned to Decker. "Why are you so interested in keys?"

"The front door was unlocked when my wife came over. Do you know if your mother had anything valuable stashed—"

"Oh, dear!" Meredith shrieked. She bolted toward the house.

Decker ran after her. "Hold on, hold on!" He caught up with her at the bedroom. "Don't touch anything! This could be a crime scene!"

Meredith folded her arms across her chest. "Mom kept cash in one of her dresser drawers. I want to see if it's still there!"

Edwina caught up with them. Anxiously, she asked, "Is it there?"

"I don't know. He stopped me from checking."

"Okay . . ." Decker took out several pairs of latex gloves and handed them to the ladies. "Carefully show me where your mother kept the cash. Please be neat about it."

Edwina slipped on the gloves and went right to the sweater drawer. She opened it with a tug. Meticulously, she rooted through the contents, picking up a stack of folded sweaters and sliding her hand to the back. Her face paled as she shook her head. "It's not here!"

"What do you mean it's not here? Where else could it be?" Meredith bent down, about to check the drawer herself, but Decker stopped her.

"Can I look for the both of you?" he asked. "If a burglary took place, I'd like to prevent any contamination of evidence."

"Yes, yes! Hurry up!" Meredith scolded.

"You two watch me." He went through the sweater drawer. There was nothing inside it but clothing. "Is there any other place she could have put the money?"

"She's always kept money there!" Meredith said. "That was her hiding place!"

Edwina chimed in, "Dammit, I kept telling her to put it in investments! Something that would grow. Mom could be so stubborn sometimes."

"All the time!" Meredith was crying now. "I was *counting* on that money to pay off some loans!" She quickly gasped. "Not that I was thinking about my mother's death to get money!"

Decker nodded but filed her words in his memory bank.

"I know what you're saying," Edwina said. "Losing all that cash is a complete and utter waste!"

"Exactly!" Meredith blew her nose. "Exactly."

"I'm going to check the other drawers now," Decker said. "Watch me, all right?" Twenty minutes of careful searching proved fruitless. He stood up, rolled his shoulders, and shook his head. "How much cash are we talking about?"

"Twenty thousand dollars," Edwina answered.

Decker had to refrain from choking. "Twenty thousand *dollars*? *Cash*?"

"Can you believe that?" Edwina snarled. "It is infuriating! I should have known something like this was going to happen."

Decker looked around. The room overflowed with flowers and plants, dozens of botanical drawings and paintings plastered all over the walls. It made Rina's obsession look moderate.

"Tell me about this gardener," he said.

Meredith was sobbing too hard to talk. Edwina bit her lip. "His name is Lee Kwan. He's about seventy years old. He's small and slight, and Mom has known him for over twenty years. I can't believe he'd ever rob her, let alone hurt her."

"What about the lawyer you mentioned?" Decker asked. "Mr. Mortimer. Could he have a key?"

"It's possible," Edwina said.

"What's the name of the firm?" Decker asked.

"Mortimer, Dratsky, and Farrington," Edwina said.

Decker wrote it down. "Anyone else who might have a key? Think hard!" After both women pleaded ignorance, Decker said, "I'll need to speak with Mr. Kwan. Would either of you have a phone number or address for him?"

Edwina went over to the window and drew back the curtains. "Today's your lucky day, Lieutenant Decker. Kwan's truck just pulled up to the curb."

The man seemed completely confused as to why Decker was talking to him. His dismay also could have been the result of his limited English. Kwan's eyes were moist. "Terrible, terrible. She was nice woman."

Edwina was right: Lee was old and slight of build, but there was muscle and sinew in his body.

"You have a key to her house, Mr. Kwan?" Decker said.

"Yes, I have key. You want the key?"

Decker said, "That would be helpful, thank you. Have you ever used it to get into Mrs. Eden's house?"

"No, I never use it. Why would I use it?"

"Why did Mrs. Eden give it to you?"

"I don't know," Kwan answered. "I never ask. She give me key. I take key. You want it?" He fished it off a sizable key ring and dropped it into Decker's waiting palm. "Here is key."

"Thank you, sir." Decker smiled. "Can you tell me where you were this morning, Mr. Kwan?"

The man's eyes narrowed. "I work all morning. Three houses: one in Porter Ranch, two in Canoga Park. Why you ask where was I?"

"Just routine questions. I need the addresses of the houses."

The gardener stared at him. Then he shrugged and said, "Yes, I give you address. I don't see Miss Eden at all today. Maybe if I do, I can help her. Now is too late. How she die?"

"Heart attack," Decker said.

"Yes, yes. She has bad heart. A couple times she stays outside when it's too hot. I tell her to go inside, but she don't listen. Only laugh. She is very stubborn."

"That's what her daughters told me about her," Decker said.

"See, I tell you the truth."

Spoken with vehemence. He was anxious but probably because he was being probed. Decker handed Kwan a blank piece of paper from his notebook. "Can you write down the addresses of the places you were this morning?"

"Yes, yes."

"Anyone notice you at work?" Decker asked.

"They *see* me," Kwan said. "I don't know if they *notice* me. I'm gardener. Sometimes they see me, they wave. Sometimes no. Only Miss Eden really notice me. Only she take time to talk to me. She ask me about my children. She give me lemonade when it is hot. She pick me flowers for my wife. She ask me questions about her plants. She give me two drawing of orchid from her house because I say I like them. I don't ask for them, she just give them to me." His face grew solemn. "You see big green tree in the back?"

"The magnolia?"

"It is Chinese sacred tree. Once it was against the law to take it out of China. I get one for her because she is special lady. She thank me over and over. We planted it together fifteen year ago when it is fifteen-gallon tree. Now look at it. Just a year ago we build bench." Again his eyes moistened. He scribbled on the piece of paper and handed it back to Decker. "Very special lady. I will miss her."

"You can't search Kwan's house or something?" Meredith shrieked over the phone. "It's been over two weeks since my mother's death, and the money's still missing!"

Decker responded in a calm voice, "I realize you're frustrated, Ms. Eden—"

"I'm a lot more than frustrated," Meredith broke in. "I'm pissed! Just search his house! If you don't find it, I'll shut up!"

"Ma'am, I don't have any cause to search his house. Mr. Kwan was where he said he was—working all morning. All three homes verified his presence. The man doesn't have a record, all his immigration papers are in order, he has a Social Security number, and he's paid his taxes. As far as I can determine, he's a model citizen."

"His lack of record means nothing! The man had a key. He could have burgled the house when my mother wasn't home, and the neighbors wouldn't notice, because he worked there on a regular basis."

"Do you have any reason to suspect that he knew about the money? I mean, as far as you know, only you and your sister were aware that the stash was there, right?"

There was silence over the line.

"Ms. Eden?"

Meredith said, "Well, even if he didn't know it was there, he could have come earlier and seen she was dead. Then, on an impulse, he could have burgled the house and found the money. Or . . . or maybe Mom even told him about it."

"Why would she do that?"

"Because my mother was a senile old woman. I don't know. Can't you just check out his bank account or something like that? See if he made a big deposit?"

"Not without probable cause, ma'am. No judge would issue a warrant." Decker paused. "If you have verification of the existence of the cash, maybe your mother had insurance—"

"No, she didn't have insurance! If she wanted the money safe, she would have put it in the bank."

"Then why didn't she do just that?"

"Who knows and who cares? The bottom line is it's gone. And I know that this Kwan character had something to do with it."

"If you really think that is the case, Ms. Eden, you might consider hiring a private detective—"

The loud click stung his ear. She had hung up on him. Decker stowed the cellular in the inside pocket of his jacket. He shouldn't be talking on the phone and driving at the same time. It served him right for answering the call in the first place. He pulled into his driveway and turned off the motor, still thinking about the missing money. The cash could have been stolen a long time ago. Then he thought about that bit of sweater peeking out from the drawer. The cash might have been gone, but someone had been looking for the stash very recently.

He unlocked the front door and called out Rina's name. He didn't get an answer, but he knew where she was—in the new greenhouse. He walked inside the plastic shed, stacked with exotic plants. "Yo."

She turned around, her face coated with mist. "Hi, there. Can you believe how big my babies have grown in just a few weeks? I know where Audrey from *Little Shop of Horrors* came from."

Decker regarded the orchids, ferns, African violets, and bromeliads. "It's amazing, what you've done. It's beautiful."

Rina beamed. "Thanks."

"Where's Hannah?"

"At a friend's house, doing a science project. She's sleeping over. We could either go out to the deli for dinner by ourselves or have something here, just the two of us."

"What do you prefer?"

"We've got steaks in the freezer. I can whip up a salad and open a bottle of cabernet. Feel like barbecuing?"

"Fantastic." He threw his arm around his wife's shoulders, and together they walked into the kitchen. Their domestic life had seen rare interludes of tranquillity. Decker's older daughter seemed happily married, the boys were doing well in college back east, Hannah was growing up, and Rina was happy with her life. She had been teaching part-time at the local Jewish high school for several years now. A couple of semesters ago, she had started a garden club. Initially, the school had laughed at her but had thrown her and her three students a bone in the form of a dry plot of land that was collecting weeds. Within a few months, the ground was giving forth broccoli, peas, brussels sprouts, carrots, and a variety of lettuces and cabbages. Nobody was laughing anymore.

Rina and her loyal band of followers, now up to five members, had just finished plowing under the dying vegetables to give the ground some nutrients for the fall planting. Right before summer, she had marched into the principal's office and asked to teach an elective class in agriculture next year:

"Kids should know that food doesn't grow in supermarkets."

Yesterday she'd been talking about getting a couple of chickens. Decker didn't know whether she was serious or not.

"I got an interesting call this afternoon," she told him over dinner. "From a man named Arthur Mortimer."

Decker stopped chewing momentarily. "Cecily Eden's lawyer."

"Exactly. Where do you know him from?"

He took a sip of wine. "His name came up when I interviewed Cecily's daughters. What does he want with you?"

"Well, it seems that I'm in Cecily's will."

"Really?" A pause. "Hmmm."

"What does that mean?"

"Nothing," Decker said. "Nothing at all."

"I don't buy that. What's the problem, Peter?"

"The daughters are a strange pair."

"Did they ever find the missing money?"

"The alleged missing money. And no, they didn't find it."

"Why alleged, Peter? Weren't you the one who first noticed the bit of sweater sticking out of the drawer?"

"Yes, that would be me. You know, I did a little research online about the women. Didn't find a thing on Meredith Eden, but I did find out a heap about Edwina, particularly her husband. His name is Garth Lettiger, and he was indicted for embezzlement about five years ago."

"Was he convicted?"

"No."

"So maybe he was innocent."

"If a major firm brings those kinds of charges against you, you're never completely innocent."

"Maybe he was a sacrificial lamb?"

"Maybe the lawyers just couldn't make the charges stick. I wonder if Garth knew about Cecily's money and put his wife up to something."

"Edwina stole the cash from her mother?"

"Maybe she rationalized that it was a loan. She didn't seem shocked that the money was missing."

"You think Edwina *killed* her mother?"

"No, I'm not saying that. There's no evidence that Cecily died of anything but a heart attack. I'm just thinking that maybe Edwina helped herself to the money a long time ago and just never told her mother or sister about it."

"Ripping off her own *mother*?"

"Who better?" Decker sliced off another piece of rib eye. He had cooked it perfectly: medium rare, with a good crust on the outside. "Or maybe Cecily gave Edwina money to help with her husband's legal defense and never told Meredith about it. Or maybe one of them stole the money from under my nose. I wasn't keeping an eye on them all the time."

"That still doesn't explain why the sweater drawer wasn't closed properly. And it doesn't explain why the gate was locked and the front door was open. All that happened before the sisters arrived."

Decker thought a moment. "Then maybe one of them arrived before you did, Nina. Seeing her mother dead, she decided to help herself to the cash. But before she could call in the death, you showed up."

"That's absolutely morbid."

"I've known families who raided the safe-deposit box as soon as the body was declared dead, in order to prevent the IRS from seizing the assets. If Edwina or Meredith had been there before you, it would explain the front door being unlocked, the gate being locked, and the sweater sticking out. I wonder if either of them made any big deposits in the bank lately."

"Could you check that out?"

"I don't know why a judge would give me access. I have no proof that either of them was stealing. Just a hunch." He took another sip of cabernet. "Be careful, Rina. Usually, family members don't like non–family members swiping what they consider to be their inheritance."

"I won't be the only non–family member. Mr. Kwan was in Cecily's will as well."

This time Decker put down the fork. "Huh! How do you know that?"

"Because I asked Mr. Mortimer if I was the only non-relative who'd be there." She swirled her wine. "I keep wondering why on earth I'd be in Cecily's will. I can only conclude that Cecily willed Mr. Kwan and me many of her plants. I'm sure her daughters will be happy to get rid of them."

"That makes sense. Also makes me feel better. It's true. Cecily's daughters wouldn't want them. I'm not sure I want them." Decker shook his head. "Just what we need. *More* plants."

"I've been thinking about that, what I'd do with all of her plants." Rina smiled. "I've come up with several ideas."

"Uh-oh!"

"Don't worry, Peter. Except for the rare ones, I wouldn't keep them."

Decker grinned. "A rare burst of common sense."

"Stop that." Rina sipped her wine. "One of my ideas was to donate them to the Arboretum. We could take a tax write-off."

"Beautiful."

"Or . . . I've been thinking about building a greenhouse at school. What do you think?"

"That's a thought." Decker looked at her with narrowed eyes. "Who's going to build it?"

Rina winked at him. Decker pretended not to notice.

In a brown long-sleeved dress, legs crossed at the ankles, Rina tried to look innocuous and inconspicuous as she sat upright in the chair provided by Arthur Mortimer, Esquire. Lee Kwan sat next to her, dressed in a khaki uniform, his white hair slicked back off his forehead. His face was blank, as were his eyes. He hadn't spoken a word since coming in the office.

Rina regarded the family members, who looked more anxious than somber. There was Edwina Lettiger in her sensible black dress and her husband, Garth, in his black suit. Their twenty-something daughters, Lily and Brooke, were dressed in dark clothing that dramatically set off their long white-blond hair. Tall and lithe, the girls seemed more excited than nervous. Meredith Eden, garbed in a black shirt and pants, sat completely isolated, with red-rimmed eyes and a scowl on her face.

Cecily had planned well for this day, writing a will to avoid probate court. Her instructions were clear. Each of her granddaughters was awarded fifty thousand dollars in cash. The girls screamed upon hearing the news and hugged each other. The rest of Cecily's estate—her house and its contents, all of her stocks and bonds, as well as the remaining cash in her accounts—was to be divided equally between her two daughters.

"Cash" turned out to be a significant wad: three hundred thousand dollars. Both sisters gasped when they heard the amount. With big smiles, they ran to each other and hugged like long-lost lovers. It seemed odd to Rina that Cecily would keep twenty thousand dollars in cash in a dresser drawer when she had so much in the bank and in a brokerage account. She couldn't help but think that maybe the sisters had made up the entire story. But what would be the point of doing that—of pointing a finger at Lee Kwan—if they couldn't file an insurance claim?

Maybe Cecily had kept cash on hand to buy exotic plants or flea-market artwork.

But twenty thousand dollars?

The whole thing was very odd.

The family seemed to barely hear as Mr. Mortimer awarded Mr. Kwan all of Cecily's potted plants and flowers. Nor did they care when Rina was gifted the artwork: all of the paintings, drawings, charcoals, watercolors, and prints that hung on Cecily's walls.

Sixty-three pieces in all. Rina was stunned. Yes, she had expressed an interest in the collection whenever Cecily had presented her latest purchase, but it was just to be polite. Kwan leaned over and whispered to her, "I'm glad she give it to you and not them. You love plant like she did."

Rina loved plants, but not all those *pictures* of plants. What in the world was she going to do with sixty-three framed pieces? But she smiled and pretended to be very grateful.

Kwan whispered, "Any orchid you want? I don't have room for all of them."

"Maybe a few. Are there any pictures that you want?"

He shook his head. "No, I don't have room."

Neither did Rina. After the assets had been distributed, everyone stood up. Kwan said, "I come by next Sunday to pick up the plants."

Edwina was grinning. Inheriting such a large amount of money had lifted her spirits. "You'll have to come by sooner, Mr. Kwan," she sang out brightly. "Meredith and I are selling the house. We have a broker coming by on Saturday to look at it, and I need to get rid of that ugly greenhouse."

Kwan sighed. "Okay, I come by Friday."

"Bring a big truck," Edwina said. "Whatever you don't

take, we're throwing away." She looked at Rina. "Same goes for you."

Rina clasped her hands nervously, still wondering what she was going to do with all those wall hangings. Maybe she could have a garage sale. "If either of you want any paintings from your mother's collection, feel free to take whatever you want before I pick up the pieces."

"Take them all," Meredith said scornfully. "If I never looked at another flower again, I'd be fine. I think Mom loved them more than me."

"In the end, Merry, the old girl came through," Edwina said.

"Minus the twenty thousand," Meredith pointed out. "I wonder what happened to it?"

A slow wave of pink infused Edwina's face. Meredith, already mentally spending the money she had just inherited, didn't seem to notice.

Rina looked at Brooke and Lily Lettiger. "Maybe the girls would want a painting to remember their grandmother by."

Both of them shook their heads. Brooke said, "I loved Grandma, but she was a little extreme."

"Very out there," Lily added.

"If you could pick up the art by Thursday, Mrs. Decker, that would be helpful," Edwina said. "We need to paint the house, and it would be better if the walls were clear."

Decker regarded the sixty-three pieces of art spread out over his living room. "We could give it all to Goodwill and take a deduction."

Rina said, "I think we'd make more at a garage sale."

"Who'd buy any of this stuff?"

Hannah was slowly going through the works. She was twelve now, a decent artist herself, although she much preferred cartooning. "Some of these pieces aren't so bad, Abba. I like this little painting of this white flower."

"Actually, it's a magnolia blossom, and it's very well painted."

"I'd like to keep it."

Decker sighed. "Okay, we'll keep that one, but only because it's small. The rest go!"

"These watercolors look very old," Hannah added. "Maybe they're worth something."

Decker groaned. "I knew this was going to happen."

"What?" Rina asked.

"You're going to keep the entire collection!"

"No, we don't have room."

"Finally, the woman speaks sense."

"However, we shouldn't just junk everything."

"Why not? Sell it, burn it, just get rid of it!" Decker cried out. "If I see one more flower in the house—real or otherwise—I'm going to tear down the place, build a barn, and stuff it with racing cars."

"I'll take this one for my room, Abba," Hannah said, referring to the magnolia painting. "I'll hang it in a corner so you won't even see it."

"You don't like this rose painting, Peter?" Rina held up a thirty-by-forty oil canvas of tumbling pink roses against a dark background. "I think it's pretty."

Decker snarled, "The painting's huge, Rina. Where are we going to put it?"

"How about over the sofa?"

"It's flowers, Rina. I'm sick of *flowers*! And I don't like the frame."

"I agree with you about the frame. How about we take it out of the frame, and then maybe you'll like the picture better." She lifted the painting. "Wow, this is heavy!"

"Don't bother taking it out of the frame . . . just give it away!" But there was no talking Rina out of it. She was already removing the cardboard backing. Within seconds, pieces of paper began falling to the floor.

Lots and lots of paper.

Rina felt her head go light. Of course, she couldn't tell the exact amount of cash. Only that there was a lot of it.

After all sixty-three works had been removed from their frames, the grand total was $11,600, all in Franklin bills.

"It's not twenty thousand," Decker said as he fitted another painting back into its original frame. The living room was an absolute mess. It would take them hours to clean up. His hands were still shaking from counting all that cash.

Rina looked at the rose painting. "Well, we're certainly going to keep this painting now. It's a harbinger of good luck."

"I'll say," Decker agreed.

Rina smiled. "Except we both know, Peter, that we're going to have to give the money back."

"Why? Cecily obviously put it there for a reason. She obviously gave you the paintings for a reason. She wanted you to have the paintings and the cash."

"Peter, we have to give it back."

"They'll just accuse us of stealing from them. They think there should be twenty thousand dollars."

"Peter, we have to give it back!"

Decker sneered. She was right—at least morally right. Under the law, a case could be made for their keeping the cash.

Don't even go there.

"I'll return the cash under one condition."

Rina looked at him. "What?"

"I want those boobs to tell me what happened to the other eight thousand four hundred."

They all met at Mr. Mortimer's office. The atmosphere was friendly, but Decker didn't trust the women or their lawyer. To protect Rina and himself, he had brought his own attorney, a friend from the synagogue named Ernie Garshofsky. Under Ernie's direction, Rena slowly explained how she and Decker had found the money.

"We intend to give it back—"

Decker broke in before Rina could finish. "My wife and I realize there are moral issues about our keeping the cash, even though it was hidden behind a painting that legally belonged to her."

"The painting, yes, but not the money," Edwina countered. "That's obviously where Mom put that cash that we told you about."

"For all we know, you kept eight grand for yourself," Meredith countered.

"I knew this was going to happen," Decker muttered.

Garshofsky said, "We're getting far afield. The Deckers have no intention of keeping the money, even though it's legally theirs—"

"That's not quite true," Mortimer interrupted.

"We don't want to take this silly little matter to court, do we?" Garshofsky smiled. "Lieutenant Decker would just like a couple of questions answered before we return the money to the women."

"What kind of questions?" Edwina asked nervously.

Decker said, "What happened to the other eight thousand four hundred?"

"I don't know," Edwina said.

"On the contrary, I think you do know," Decker said. "You came to your mother's house before Rina arrived, and when you found your mother dead, you took the eight thousand out of the drawer."

"I did not!"

"Then why did you turn bright red when I asked about the missing eight thousand?"

"Edwina, you don't have to say a thing," Mortimer said.

"She does if she wants me to write her a check this afternoon," Decker said. "Otherwise, she can sue and this meeting is over."

"Eddy, why *do* you keep turning red when he asks about the other eight thousand dollars?" Meredith asked snidely. "Why don't you just fess up? You always did have a terrible poker face."

Finally, Edwina said, "Oh, what the hell! What does it matter?" She regarded Meredith. "About three years ago, when Garth was having all those legal problems, I went to borrow money from Mom. She gave me two thousand dollars. That's it! Two thousand dollars. I couldn't believe she'd be that stingy. We all knew she had money in the bank."

"It was her money, not yours," Rina said.

Edwina glared at her. Then she looked away. "I don't know what came over me. I went back and took an additional two grand one day when she wasn't home."

"Oh my Lord!" Meredith cried out.

"I'm sorry. I know it was wrong, but we were broke. We needed the money. The witch just wouldn't budge!" Edwina exhaled. "Altogether, with the loan and what I took, it was about four thousand and change."

"How much change?" her sister asked.

"Okay . . . maybe five thousand total. I'll give you an additional twenty-five hundred dollars from my share of the money that Lieutenant Decker found."

"Whoa, whoa, whoa," Decker said. "As far as I'm concerned, I haven't given you anything yet."

"But you said—"

"We're now up to sixteen thousand six hundred. What happened to the other three thousand four hundred?"

Edwina said, "I swear I only took five thousand at most." Suddenly, she glared at Meredith with granite eyes. "Okay, little sister, now it's *your* turn."

Meredith stared back, but it lacked ferocity. A minute passed and then she gave up. "Just like you, I needed money."

"Right! To sustain your nasty habits?"

"I've been sober for over two years." She burst into tears. "My creditors were breathing down my neck. She gave me *less* than she gave you, for your information! Only fifteen hundred."

"And the rest you helped yourself to?"

"When you're a chemically dependent person, you do crazy things. And who are you to judge, Ms. High Horse, with your sticky little hands in the till?"

"You two have plenty of time to snipe at each other when we're not here," Decker said. "We're still about two thousand short." Meredith looked away and didn't answer, but that was enough for Decker to fill in the blanks. "Okay, you helped yourself, like your sister. So from what I can figure out, it seems you each stole about the same amount from your mother. It's a wash."

Rina said, "Cecily must have found out that either one or both of you were stealing from her. So she hid the money behind the paintings so you wouldn't be able to get to it anymore."

"She obviously forgot about it when she made up the will," Mortimer said.

"Or maybe she wanted you to have it, Rina," Decker said.

"She distinctly left all the rest of her cash to her daughters," Mortimer added.

"It doesn't matter what her intentions were," Rina said. "We're giving the money back."

Decker said, "Before I make out the check, I want to know something. Which one of you showed up right after your mother died, went through her drawer in an attempt to steal the money, but left in a hurry without locking the front door when my wife showed up?"

Rina held up a finger. "You know, Lieutenant, I'd guess that both of them were there and discovered together that the money wasn't in the drawer," she postulated. "Otherwise, each one would have accused the other of taking the cash first. And didn't you think it was odd that they both showed up at the same time but in separate cars when you only called Edwina about the news?"

Decker smiled. "You know? I bet you're right."

Meredith and Edwina exchanged knowing glances but kept silent. Finally, Mortimer spoke up. "I think you've asked enough questions, Lieutenant Decker. And I think you have enough answers. Can I trust you to write a check?"

Decker grumbled as he took out his checkbook. "Do I make out two checks or what?"

Mortimer said, "I'm the executor of the estate. Just one check, and make it out to me."

After they got home, Rina said, "We did the right thing."

"I'm not so sure about that," Decker said. "Why shouldn't we have the money rather than those two vultures?"

"Because she willed me the artwork, Peter, not the cash."

"Speaking of which, how about that garage sale you keep talking about? The frames alone should net us a couple of bucks."

"Sure," Rina said, "but give me a little time. Now that this nasty money business is over, I want to look up some of the names of the artists on the Internet. Like Hannah said, some of the works look old. Maybe a few of them are even worth something."

"Yeah, we're sitting on an undiscovered Renoir."

Rina laughed. "I'm not saying that, but you never know. Cecily had collected for a long time. And even if the artwork isn't worth anything, it doesn't matter. I look at the pictures and I think of Cecily."

"We can't keep sixty-three pieces of junky art, Rina."

"Don't worry. I don't intend to keep most of them. Just

the little magnolia blossom that Hannah loves and our lucky rose painting."

Decker looked at his watch. "I have some time. Give me the names of the artists, and I'll look them up."

"I'll do it, Peter."

"No, *I'll* do it." Decker sat down at the computer. "That way it'll get done. So while I'm going online, get the names you want to look up. Start with the rose painting, if you're determined to keep it."

"It's our lucky painting."

"Not our lucky painting," Decker groused. "We didn't keep the cash!"

She hit his shoulder, then went over to the floral and studied the signature scrawled in the lower left side. "Franz Bischoll." She spelled it for him.

Decker plugged in the name. On the screen came the words: *Did you mean: Franz Bischoff?* Absently, he clicked on the name. His eyes widened. His heart started beating faster. "Rina, could it be Franz Bischoff, with two F's?"

"It could be. Why?"

"Uh, you want to come take a look at this?"

"Why? What is it?"

Decker laughed. "It's a chance for you to say 'I told you so.' And for once, I don't mind."

OPEN HOUSE

"Open House" is another new story penned for this anthology. Real estate in Southern California took a major price jump in 2005, and there were quite a few houses for sale. As I looked at one of the empty homes, my warped mind thought, What a convenient place to dump a body! *I wondered if finding a corpse during a house showing would cool off an overheated market. Probably not in a city that had an attraction called Graveline Tours. It used to take tourists in a hearse to some of L.A.'s most notable crime scenes!*

GEORGINA THOUGHT SHE WAS CLEVER, coming twenty minutes earlier than the start time. Unfortunately, there were others who'd had the same idea. Two couples, plus what looked like a mother-daughter combo, were waiting on the sidewalk, sizing up the competition. This was the second and last showing of a new listing, and the Realtors were going to take offers tomorrow night. There were no lookie-loos here: All those present were out for blood.

This meant that Georgina would have to form a plan. Hers was typically blow and go. Sign in and grab a tear sheet, doing mental calculations about house size versus lot size while giving the place a quick once-over. The living room and dining room were public space, ergo usually in decent shape. If a house had a bad living room, it was probably one step ahead of the wrecking ball. Single-family homes showed their true colors in the kitchen and bathrooms; that and the size of the bedroom closets. She and Derek had lots of junk, so closet space would be a priority. If the place flunked any one of the above, there were still three other houses on her list.

This newest one would go fast because it was priced reasonably and in a good neighborhood. In a hot market, Georgina knew, she'd have to move if she wanted a chance at elusive home ownership. She and Derek had already lost two chances through indecision. The next time,

Georgina swore, if the place was right, passing the kitchen/bathroom/closet test, she wouldn't hesitate.

Finally, a black Mercedes pulled up in the driveway. The listing agent was Adele Michaels, and the ad in the paper said she had sold more than twelve million dollars' worth of real estate this year . . . which translated to three houses in the flats of Beverly Hills. Of course, Canoga Park wasn't Beverly Hills, but some areas in the West Hills boasted multimillion-dollar estates complete with swimming pool, tennis court, and home theater. The two-story English-cottage-style house Georgina was looking at wasn't anywhere close to magnificent, but it wasn't a shack, either. It had three bedrooms, two and a half baths, and sat on a good-size lot with fruit trees and a two-car garage.

The driver's door opened, and out came a pipsqueak of a kid. She looked nothing like Adele Michaels, whose picture showed a forty-plus big-haired blonde with large white teeth. Georgina doubted if this girl was even old enough to vote. The agent had spiky black hair, wore the requisite black suit, and balanced on black spike heels. She rested her sunglasses on the top of her head, then swung a large purse over her shoulder as if she owned the world. To the ten of them anxiously waiting to be let inside, she did.

Obviously, Adele had handed off the listing to one of her flunky neophytes, a house under a million bucks just not worth her time and energy. Georgina rolled her eyes. The flunky fiddled with a ring of keys and then opened the lockbox to the house. Once she'd freed up the front door, she opened it and stepped inside, the faithful gathering of hopefuls dogging her heels in single file. The agent headed straight into the kitchen. From her leather sack—either a Marc Jacobs or a knockoff—she took out a stack of tear sheets and a clipboard that held a pen and a sign-in sheet. She plunked them down on the kitchen counter.

"Everyone sign in, please—name, phone number, and agent, if you have one. This is the last showing, we've already got offers. All offers will be entertained tonight, so if you're interested, you'd better act fast."

First to reach the pen was the mother-daughter combo. Georgina waited her turn to sign in, noting that the living and dining rooms had hardwood floors. The kitchen countertops were tiled. She had hoped for granite, but in this case, she'd make an exception because she *loved* the design of the kitchen. It had been done Tuscan-style, filled with warm golds, and there was a copper hood over the stove. Newer appliances: a side-by-side fridge and a dishwasher.

Things were looking *way* up.

Georgina finally picked up a tear sheet and signed in. Scanning the paper quickly, she saw that the house had twenty-two hundred square feet on a ten-thousand-square-foot lot. This was getting better by the millisecond. The house wasn't going to last through the showing. Immediately, she put in a call to Derek. He picked up on the third ring.

"You have to come now! I haven't even checked out the bathrooms, and already I want it."

"Remember that we agreed not to get swept away in mass hysteria."

"Okay." *Calm,* she told herself. "All right, I'm in the master bedroom. Not so big. We can fit our bed in it. But one of the dressers may have to go." She slid back a mirrored door. "Good-size closet. That'll help . . . Oh, Derek! The master bathroom is marble, with a huge Jacuzzi tub!"

"I'll be right over."

"It's going to go above asking, I just know it! The agent already said they have offers from the Sunday showing—"

"Don't panic, Georgie, we'll deal. And don't do anything until we call up Orit."

"What if we don't get hold of her?"

"I'm sure they're not going to consider offers right on the spot."

"No, that's true." Georgina went back into the kitchen. Oh, how she loved the kitchen. "Derek, the kitchen is just perfect. It's got good appliances and plenty of cabinet space." She opened a drawer. "The cabinets are all on sliders. And it's got a pantry and . . . what's this door? Looks like a broom closet." She yanked on it. "I think it's stuck."

"Georgina, I'm going to hang up now. I'll see you soon."

"Bye." She stowed the phone in her purse and turned to the Realtor. "Excuse me. I think this door is stuck."

The agent ambled over and gave the door a hard tug. "It may be locked." Without another word, she walked away and began to chitchat up a promising-looking young couple.

Little snot, Georgina thought. *And I bet those two don't even qualify.* With determination, she pulled on the handle with all her strength, and the door finally gave way. A large blue plastic garbage bag tumbled out and spilled onto the floor. The tie to the top broke open, and something popped out. It took about a toe tap of time for Georgina to realize what it was.

Then she screamed.

"How long before the coroner's investigators get here?" Decker checked his watch and didn't wait for an answer. "You want to give them a call, Sergeant Dunn? Find out if they'll be here in this century?"

Marge smiled. She had been promoted over a month ago and her new title was a kick to her ears. "I just called the office, Loo. Soon."

They'd been waiting almost an hour. Normally, that would be a good thing. Although they couldn't deal with the body until the coroner released it, Decker and his detectives utilized the time by going over the crime scene. In this case, one thing was immediately clear: The house wasn't the crime scene. The place was spotless. For his effort, Decker found only a couple of fibers that could have been dragged in by someone's shoe and an empty can of soda in the garbage can under the sink. It was possible that they'd lift something off the items or from the body itself.

Marge hung up her cell and rocked on her feet, her five-foot-ten frame swaying from side to side. "Techs should be here soon, Pete."

"To do what?" Decker snarled. "Sweep the floor?"

"They can dust. Check out the drains—"

"Crime wasn't committed here."

Marge shrugged. "An empty house is a good place to lure a victim."

"No spatter anywhere, no wet spots on the floor . . . it's not the crime scene." Decker raked his fingers through his hair, a combination of copper and silver. "I mean, I'm not *positive,* but I'd bet a winning lottery ticket on it."

That was Decker's experience talking: thirty years as a cop, most of them with Homicide, and the last ten as a detective lieutenant.

She said, "Hardly any bloat on the face."

"She's fresh, probably dumped last night. There's no heating inside, and the cool night air probably helped to preserve her."

"The face looks Hispanic, maybe Mideastern."

"Yeah, she's out of her element in this solidly middle-to-upper-class area. The residents are by and large white. She also has a front tooth rimmed in gold. That's not white American dentistry."

"A housekeeper?"

"That's what I'm thinking. It would have been nice if there had been clothes on her. You can tell a lot by a person's clothes." Decker smoothed his ginger mustache. "This isn't some gangbanger's crime. A group of Latinos carrying a body and entering a house would stick out in this neighborhood. This feels like a white man's crime. Some guy screwing the maid, and when she threatened to tell the wife, he panicked. I bet the perp lives nearby and knew the house was empty."

"There's no forced entry," Marge added.

Decker thought a moment. "Maybe it was someone in real estate who had a key to the place. Who's out canvassing the neighborhood?"

"Wanda Beautemps and Lee Wang," Marge said. "Scott Oliver is talking to the people who were in the house when the body was discovered. We got an angry mob out there, Loo. They're furious that the open house was canceled."

Decker smiled. "Go tell the agent that I want a list of everyone who has a key to the place and a list of every Realtor who has shown the house."

"I think it's a brand-new listing."

"Good. That'll make our jobs easier."

"Petechiae in the eyes, deep bruises around the neck that look like finger impressions . . . no overt ligature marks." The investigator was a woman in her fifties named Sherelle Holland. She and her partner wore black uniforms covered by black jackets with CORONER'S INVESTIGATOR in yellow lettering on the back. Sherelle had slid the body out of the blue plastic bag and onto the coroner's white plastic sheeting while the police photographer snapped pictures. "There's a contusion on the right side of her head."

"Blunt-force trauma?" Decker asked.

"No, more like she just hit her head. It's certainly not deep enough to cause her death. There aren't any bullet or stab wounds. Manual strangulation would be the logical guess. There's lividity . . . rigor is just starting to set. Ordinarily, I'd say less than twenty-four hours, but it's cool outside."

"Anything under the nails?"

"At a quick glance, it looks like she fought back. Or maybe the blood is hers." Sherelle started bagging the hands. "We'll clip them. Once we get her onto the table, the doc can tell you more. Any idea who she is?"

"No."

Sherelle shrugged. "Maybe she's a real estate agent. People are getting pretty angry about the housing situation."

"That's a thought."

"Good luck, Lieutenant. You'll need it."

Decker called over a tech from the CSI unit. "You can evidence the garbage bag. Turn it inside out and see if you can't find something. This is desperation time." He signaled to Oliver, who was checking himself out in a full-length door mirror. He was over fifty, with mostly dark hair and a gut that hadn't gone to fat, but he was as vain as a schoolgirl. Decker didn't like Oliver because his own daughter once had. That was way in the past, and Cindy was now happily married to a more age-appropriate guy, but some things remained stuck in one's craw. "What's going on, Scottie?"

Oliver tore himself away from the mirror and walked over to Decker. "Not much. Just calming down a bunch of freaked-out people."

"Did the agent recognize the corpse?"

"Never saw her nor any other corpse in her life. Her name is Sarah, and I offered to take her out for coffee to calm her down after this is all over."

"Out of the goodness of your heart," Decker said.

"I'm just that kind of sensitive guy."

"She's not only young enough to be your daughter, she's young enough to be your granddaughter."

Oliver smiled. "What can I say? Some people can't adjust."

Decker wasn't sure if Oliver was referring to Decker or himself. "Did Margie or you get a list of brokers from her?"

"Not much of a list, Loo. She told me this was only the second time the house has been shown."

"When was the first showing?"

"Two days ago . . . last Sunday." It was Marge Dunn who responded. She checked her notes. "From two to five. Sarah Atacaro, that's the agent for this showing, told us that the only ones with keys were her, her boss, and the owners, who are now in Denver."

Oliver added, "This was Sarah's first time inside the house. She was just helping out her boss, Adele Michaels, who was in San Diego for a wedding."

"Get Michaels on the phone. We need to talk to her."

"I already did," Oliver told him. "She's en route, and the cell reception was iffy. For what it's worth, she told me she'd checked out the house yesterday afternoon in anticipation of today's showing, and she was adamant that there were no dead bodies anywhere. I think it would have been something she'd remember."

"Did she specifically remember checking out the broom closet?"

"She said she checked out everything."

"All right. Then, assuming her information is correct, that would mean the body was placed no more than a day ago. Did any of the neighbors see or hear anything?"

"Nothing that would point us in the direction of the murderer."

"I doubt the killer just stumbled on the house. He must have known that the house was going to be empty between Sunday and today."

"Someone in real estate."

"That's what Marge and I have been thinking. We have pictures of our vic now. Why don't you show them around? Maybe someone's housekeeper didn't show up for work. And if the two agents were the only ones with a key, let's recheck the doors and windows for pry marks. Maybe we missed something because this wasn't the crime scene, and as sure as hell, the body didn't walk in on its own accord."

The cigarette smoke didn't bother Decker, but Marge was less tolerant and kept fanning her face. Eventually, Adele Michaels got the hint and stubbed out the butt with her foot. They were in the house's backyard outside the kitchen door. The body was gone, but a pall remained.

"I don't know what more I can tell you guys. The body wasn't here yesterday afternoon." Adele's voice was deep and hoarse. A face-lift had stretched her leathery skin over cheekbone implants. "I checked every closet and cabinet. I turned on and off every tap, flushed every toilet, and opened and closed every window. The house was in tip-top shape."

"And you have no idea who she is?" Marge asked again.

"No, for the tenth time. I don't know who she is. Why would you think I'm holding back on you?"

"Just trying to prod your memory," Decker said.

"There's *nothing* to remember!"

"And you're sure that no one besides Sarah Atacaro, the owners, and you has a copy of the key?"

"Positive."

Marge said, "What if someone made a copy from your key and you didn't know about it?"

"*Two* sets of keys besides the owners in Denver, guys: Sarah and me. And both sets are accounted for. You think I'd allow someone access to *my* listing without *my* permission? This hasn't gone to caravan. The house is going to be sold in a couple of days, body or not. It's a fair price." She paused and looked Decker up and down. "Are you in the market?"

Decker smiled and shook his head. "What about Sarah's key? Could she have left it on a desktop or in her drawer—"

"Not a chance! She'd guard it with her life." Adele was losing patience. "Can I go run a business now?"

"Just bear with me for a couple of minutes. You said this was the second time you've shown the house."

"Yes. The first time was on Sunday. When can I start letting people see the place again?"

"Not today," Decker said. "We're still dusting inside. You're probably a good judge of character after dealing with lots of different people all these years, right?" Adele looked at Decker with suspicion on her face. She was short and very thin. There was well over a foot of difference in height between the two of them. "I mean, that's your job, to read people, correct?" Decker said.

"What are you getting at, Sergeant?"

Marge said, "I'm the sergeant, he's the lieutenant."

Decker said, "You can probably tell serious buyers from those who don't belong. Maybe you remember someone from Sunday who looked like he or she didn't belong? Take your time before answering."

"I need a smoke," Adele said. Before she pulled out her cigarette, Decker was there with the match. She blew out a plume of vaporized tobacco and wrinkled her brow—as best she could wrinkle her brow. Botox was doing its job. The agent sighed. "The place was a mob scene."

"How about right before you were ready to lock up?" Decker said. "Anyone walk out of the place with you?"

The agent paused. "Now that you mention it, there were a few people hanging around. You know, trying to sweet-talk me into looking at their offers. One couple in particular . . . wait, wait . . . there was this young guy . . . I almost locked him in the house."

Decker nodded. "Could you describe him to a police artist for a sketch?"

"Yes, I think I could. And I might even be able to do you one better. He might have signed my sheet. I don't know if it's his real name and phone number, but it's better than what you've got right now."

"What we've got is nothing," Decker said.

"That's why what I've got is better."

Over the phone, Medical Examiner Dr. Charles Angelo told Decker that he had extracted scrapings from under the nails. "I'll try to get the material into the lab sometime this week. How long the lab takes to get you a genetic profile is anyone's guess. They're backlogged over a year."

"Maybe you can put a rush on it?"

"I can try, but you haven't even ID'd the vic yet, let alone have a perp to match it to. This isn't going to be high priority."

How right he was. Decker said, "Do the best you can."

"I do have other news for you. The vic was pregnant."

Decker cursed silently. "How many months?"

"It wasn't an embryo, but it wasn't as far along as a

fetus, either. Maybe a little over three months. Interesting to see if the genetic material under the nails matches to the father of the baby."

As he passed out copies of the composite drawing, Decker regarded the sketch and winced. It featured a nondescript man in his thirties. Adele had told the police artist that he had a young face but a receding hairline; dark eyes, thin lips, average build. She remembered that he had a mole over his right eyebrow, and that was about the only distinguishing mark on him. Decker supposed he should stop bitching. Every little bit helped.

The detectives were sitting in the conference room in the Devonshire division of the LAPD. Five of them around the table, drinking cold coffee while comparing notes. Not much to talk about, but still the theories abounded.

Decker said, "So this is what I think happened. This guy came in on Sunday, looking the place over, acting like a prospective buyer. That way he could open and close the closet doors and look around without arousing any suspicion. He waits until the agent has locked up, then surreptitiously unlocks the back door. Then he pretends that he didn't know she was about to leave and says something like, 'Hey, wait for me!' They walk out together. She's not going to go back and check all the doors. She just assumes he was entranced by a toilet or something. So they just walk out together. Then he comes back on Monday night to dump the body."

"But the agent came on Monday afternoon and checked out the closets," Marge reminded him. "I'm sure she locked all the doors, Loo."

"Maybe he came through a window?" Oliver suggested. "The agent would check the doors but not the windows."

"I like that," Decker said. "You'll notice I'm using 'he' for the murderer. It could have been a she. It's just a pain in the ass to say 'he or she' every time."

Wanda Beautemps spoke up. She was in her fifties and the newest member of Homicide. "If he was looking for a place to dump the body, then are we thinking that the girl was already dead on Sunday?"

"Not necessarily," Decker said. "The deputy coroner thinks that she was murdered about twenty-four hours before we found her, which would put her death sometime on Monday."

"So he finds the dump spot before he kills the girl?"

"Perhaps," Decker said. "That would imply premeditation. We're checking everyone on the sign-in sheet, but so far we don't have a hit. Adele's description to the police artist is the best we have so far. If anyone identifies the guy, don't go over and confront him. Don't even talk to him. Let's just identify him, find out who he is, where he lives, where he works. He could be a completely innocent schnook. Let's try to avoid a lawsuit." He looked at Lee Wang. "Are we anywhere close to identifying the vic?"

Wang checked his notes, written in a sloppy hand. He always claimed his Chinese handwriting was much better than his English penmanship, except that Lee was a born-and-bred American. "Nothing from our canvassing yesterday. I've been checking Missing Persons in the Valley—LAPD. That's been a fat zero. I haven't checked Burbank or San Fernando or Simi or the city. I'll keep working on it."

"Good," Decker said. "Go out and canvass the area for this guy. And good luck."

"Matthew Lombard," Marge said. "He's thirty-one and lives about four miles away, married with two kids. He works as a junior lawyer at a downtown firm."

"You canvassed four miles from the house?"

"One of the clerks at the local 7-Eleven says Matthew comes in every day for coffee and a doughnut before he goes to work. He said it *could* be him. The face, he wasn't so sure, but the mole, maybe. The guy doesn't have any kind of a sheet."

"All right, Margie, this is what I want you to do. Go get a black-and-white snapshot of him, put it in a six-pack, and see if Adele can pick him out. You can probably pull something off Google—yearbook graduation picture, something like that."

"Not a problem. Some of the search engines have a 'show me an image' feature. No privacy anymore. Not that anyone wants privacy, judging from the moronic reality shows on TV."

"That's for certain. You tell the grocery clerk to keep quiet?"

"I told him if he didn't, I'd check out his green card. I don't think we have anything to worry about."

The interview room had a table and four chairs. Adele Michaels sat on one side, Detective Scott Oliver across from her. She was playing with her pack of cigarettes, looking nervous. Oliver laid the photo spread—six front-face pictures, five stooges and Lombard, matched for age, race, size, and features. It took the real estate agent approximately twenty seconds.

"That's him!" Adele hit the black-and-white of Lombard. "That's the guy I almost locked in the house. He kept asking me questions."

"Thank you, Ms. Michaels," Oliver said.

"Do I get to pick him out of a lineup now?"

"No, ma'am. As far as we know, the man hasn't done anything wrong except stay too late at your open house. If you see him again, don't mention anything about this, okay?"

"Why would I see him again?"

"Maybe he was a legitimate buyer." Oliver shrugged. "Or . . . not accusing anyone, but sometimes people who do nasty things enjoy returning to the scene of the crime."

"No chance of that," Adele said. "Body or no body, the house sold."

"After going through the recent Missing Persons files in the Valley, San Fernando, Burbank, and Glendale, I came up with a dozen possibilities," Wang told Decker. They were sitting in the Loo's office. Decker was in his chair, Wang standing over the desk. "Unfortunately—or happily, for the families—nothing panned out."

Decker said, "Sure it wasn't denial?"

"They showed me pictures of their daughters. They didn't appear to be our vic, but if you want, I could bring them in and show them the body."

Decker thought a moment. "Why put them through something that awful when you're pretty sure it's not their loved ones? Besides, you still have the city MP to check out."

"I'll start on those this afternoon."

Wang was about to leave when Marge walked into the room, dusting a speck of dirt off her black jacket lapel. She wore beige pants and had on flat shoes with rubber soles. "That's what I love about dark colors. They never show dirt. Lord only knows why I put on light pants. I'm just asking for trouble. Do I smell coffee?"

"I just made a fresh pot," Decker said. "Help yourself."

Marge walked over to the table and poured coffee into a paper cup. Decker always provided fresh coffee for anyone who walked into his office. It made him popular with the rank and file. "Lombard works at a large firm, one of those chichi downtown places that have a million names, like Cratchet, Hatchet, and Patchet." She checked her notes. "The actual name is Frisk, Taylor, Pollin, Berman, and Pope. They have almost fifty partners. Lombard isn't one of them."

"How long has he worked there?" Decker asked.

Marge put down her coffee and flipped through her notepad. "I don't know if I have that . . . Oh, here we go. Five years. Stable guy."

Decker raised his eyebrows. "Way back, I was a lawyer for about six months."

"I didn't know that," Wang said.

"It's something he doesn't advertise," Marge said, "but it makes him handy around the PDs."

Decker smiled. "The point is, when I started out in law, it was well known that ambitious people don't stick around in big firms if they don't make junior partner by year two or three."

Wang said, "Maybe Lombard's just not that ambitious."

"Or maybe the firm offered other benefits, like a certain lady," Decker said. "Did you talk to anyone in the firm to see if our vic worked there?"

"That was my next step," Margie said.

Wang said, "If we start showing a postmortem picture of our victim, we're going to arouse interest at the firm. Are you worried about Lombard bolting?"

"It's always a possibility." Decker thought a moment. "Body's still in the crypt?"

"Unless corpses can walk, I would say yes," Wang answered.

"Wise guy," Decker muttered. "Okay, let's do this. Put a little makeup on her, fix her hair, and dress her. Then have someone take another picture of her gussied up. Do you think we could convince someone in Human Resources at Cratchet, Hatchet, et cetera, that she's still alive?"

"Pshaw, Loo, nothing's impossible," Marge said. "This is Hollywood!"

The young clerk's brown eyes first squinted, then widened with surprise. The HR office of Frisk, Taylor, and friends was tucked into a corner of the fifteenth floor in a twenty-three-story chrome and glass building. The firm took up not only floor fifteen but sixteen and seventeen as well, anonymous corridors of Berber carpeting and white walls. Sitting in his little cubicle, the clerk studied the picture, his eyes traveling from the picture to Marge's face. "Is that Solana?"

Marge played along. "Yes, of course."

"She doesn't look so healthy."

The clerk's comment gave Marge a better ruse than the one she had originally invented. "That's why I need to see her. She's a diabetic."

"I didn't *know* that. It wasn't on her medical form when she applied for the job." The clerk suddenly looked suspicious. "Why are you talking to *me* instead of Solana?"

A logical question: Luckily, Marge was good at thinking on her feet. "Our pharmaceutical company has come out with some very important new drugs, and she was one of our subjects. But she hasn't shown up for the last couple of days. I tried calling her at home, but no one answers. She put this place down as her employment. I hoped I might catch her here, but I don't know what department she works in."

The clerk gave Marge a strange look. Then he reluctantly checked his files, jotted down some numbers, and picked up the phone. Marge could hear the voice mail kicking in—Solana's voice.

The victim had a voice.

The clerk said, "Hi, Solana, it's Jack from HR. Can you give me a call when you get in?" He hung up. "She's not at her desk."

"Can you call someone else to find out if she's even at work? We're a little concerned."

He sighed heavily but cooperated. This time he actually spoke to a human on the other end of the line. "Hi, Terry, it's Jack." He smiled and dropped his voice. "Yes, I'm in, what do you think? Do you want me to bring the wine?"

At this point Marge cleared her throat. Jack looked

miffed and held up a finger. “Okay, I’ll do the reds, let Randy do the whites . . . Right, right, right. Okay, it’s a deal. Terry, before you hang up, I’ve got someone from . . .” He looked at Marge.

“Taykell and Company Pharmaceuticals.”

“Someone from a drug company looking for Solana Perez. Do you know where she is? . . . I did call, and all I got was voice mail. Do you know if she’s in today? . . . Of course I’ll hold.” He glanced at Marge. “Someone’s hunting her down.”

“Thank you very much.”

“You’re welcome. I can’t believe she actually let someone take her picture when she looked so awful. The poor thing is as white as chalk.”

“She wasn’t feeling very well.”

“You know, she should have listed her illness on the application. Our health insurance has to know— Hi . . . oh? For how long? Okay. Okay. Okay, I’ll see you Thursday. Bye.” The clerk exhaled. “She hasn’t been at work for three days.” He frowned. “Do you think something’s happened to her?”

“Yes, I think something’s happened to her,” Marge said. “I’d like to see her personnel records.”

Again Jack frowned. “Those are confidential.”

Marge drew out her shield. “Don’t make me get a subpoena.”

The clerk’s mouth dropped open. “You’re police? Why didn’t you just say so in the first place?”

“Because if Solana was here, I could just talk to her, clear up this mess, and you’d be none the wiser. But she isn’t here and hasn’t been here for three days. That’s why I’m asking for her records.”

"What did she do?"

"She didn't do anything, Jack. It's what was done to her."

Jack whitened several shades. "Oh my God! That picture! Is it . . . Is she . . ."

"I'm afraid so."

Jack quickly excused himself and made a mad dash down the hallway. Marge heard some retching and hoped he had made it to the bathroom in time.

The Homicide group was stuffed into Decker's office. Lee Wang, Wanda Beautemps, Marge Dunn, and Scott Oliver were devouring several takeout pizzas. Decker was wolfing down one of his wife's famous roast beef sandwiches. It was past seven, and they all had appetites worthy of a pack of hyenas. "First thing we've got to do is positively ID our victim as Solana Perez. What do we know about her?"

Marge said, "No husband, according to her application. She's from a border town in Texas. Her parents are Ana and Jorge Perez, but contacting them has been hard. There's no address or phone number. Nothing in Texas directory information. Scott and I are thinking that she's from immigrant parents."

"That's not good," Decker said. "We've got to get the body ID'd. Let's bring someone from her office down to the morgue."

"Not Lombard," Oliver said. "He'll deny knowing her, if he's smart."

"No, not Lombard, or any other lawyer, for that matter. I don't want anyone charging the department three hundred and fifty an hour. Round up a secretary." Decker looked at Beautemps and Wang. "Lee, set something up at the crypt, say around ten tomorrow. Wanda, you go to the firm and find someone who knew Solana and can identify her. The two places aren't too far apart. You should be in and out in an hour, especially if Lee sets up the body for camera viewing beforehand."

Wang said, "I was going to work on the city's Missing Person files. I only got through a quarter of them this afternoon."

"You can do that afterward. Besides, it won't be necessary if we get a positive ID." Decker turned to Wanda. "If you don't get a positive ID, you help go through the MP files in the city."

"No problem," Wanda answered.

"Great," Decker said. "Now, if our body is Solana, it's really tempting to jump to conclusions about Lombard, but let's keep an open mind. We know Solana is missing. And we know that Lombard was in the house where the body was dumped. We know that Solana and Lombard worked in the same department."

"You forgot to mention that our vic was three months pregnant and he's a married guy," Oliver put in. "Ask the guy for a blood test. We can see if he's the father."

"Even if Lombard is the father, it doesn't mean he killed her," Decker said.

Marge said, "Everything's circumstantial except him showing up at the house two days before some poor devil finds our body stuffed in a closet. With that, Lombard's painting a nice picture for the DA."

"Sure would be nice to find where the vic was killed," Oliver said.

"Funny you should think of that, Scottie," Decker said. "I just got off the phone with Solana's landlord. He's meeting me at her apartment in forty minutes."

Marge asked, "Where did she live?"

"Reseda. Who wants to join me?"

There was resounding silence.

"Okay, let me rephrase that. Who's on call?"

"I think that would be Oliver and me," Marge said.

Wang stood up. "Thanks for dinner, Loo." He looked at Wanda. "See you tomorrow at ten."

"Wait, I'll walk you out." Wanda threw away her paper plate and picked up her purse. "See you tomorrow."

After they left, Decker spoke to Oliver. "You look like you swallowed quinine."

Oliver sighed heavily. "I was planning to meet someone for drinks. She's gorgeous and in her forties. You'd approve."

"Don't start, Oliver. I outrank you."

"I'm serious, Pete. I'm trying to act somewhat age-appropriate."

Marge added, "Especially because forty now seems young to him."

Decker smiled. "All right, Oliver, go on your date. Margie and I can handle this. If the apartment turns out to be the crime scene, I'll page you."

"I'm suspicious when you're too nice."

"Nah, don't be fooled. It's part of my persona as the benevolent dictator."

Decker and Marge accompanied Irv Fletcher up a flight of outdoor steps. The apartment building was an anonymous white box with sparkles in the stucco. The landlord was in his late seventies, short, slight, and bald, but with a spring in his step. "Her rent wasn't due for another week, so I had no reason to contact her."

"Good tenant?" Decker asked.

"The best kind: the one who pays her rent on time."

Decker had a thought. He still had Solana's postmortem picture in his pocket. "Did you know her well?"

"Never met her. Everything was done through an agent."

So much for the quick ID. At the top of the stairs, Fletcher fished out a ring of keys. "You think something happened to her?"

"Maybe," Marge said. "She hasn't been at work for the last couple of days."

As they got closer to the apartment, a faint stale smell wafted through the chilly air. "Here we go . . . number eight."

"Do you mind if I open the door?" Decker asked. "Fingerprints, you know."

"Sure, sure." Fletcher handed him the master key. Decker put on a pair of latex gloves, inserted the key into the lock, and opened the door. He groped around the wall until he found the light switch. It turned on two floor lamps, bathing the tiny living room in soft light.

A couch decorated with lacy pillows, and a coffee table, a chair and an end table, a set of bookshelves that held more DVDs than paperbacks, discount furniture, cheap but serviceable. The same space also held a dinette service for four and moribund flowers in a vase set in the middle of the table, dropping dead petals. The water stank of rotten eggs.

Marge and Decker exchanged looks. Marge said, "Mr. Fletcher, would you mind waiting outside?"

"Sure, sure. You mind if I sit in my car? It's a little warmer in there."

"No, sir, not at all. We'll be down in a bit." Decker walked around and peered into the kitchen, an out-pouching of the living area. It appeared clean and tidy. He went back into the living room and studied the floor, slowly walking toward the lone bedroom. Before he opened the shut door, he crouched down and stared at the joint where the jamb met the floor. "Looks like some blood here, mixed with hair. Our victim had a contusion on the side of her head."

Marge said, "He was dragging her out and bumped her head on the doorjamb."

Decker nodded. "I don't see any smear tracks from the wound. He came back and cleaned up pretty good. But not all that good, if he left this. I'll have the techs luminol the area tonight." He got up from his squat and opened the door.

The room was orderly. The bed had been made; the nightstand held a lamp and a book. Framed photographs lined the dresser. Decker pointed to a pretty young woman with long flowing hair and full red lips. A glint twinkled in her brown eyes. She appeared around twenty. Decker took out the postmortem photograph. It was the same woman, but the two snapshots couldn't have looked any more different.

Marge sighed. "Well, it looks like we've ID'd our victim."

"And most likely found the crime scene." Decker pointed to a corner of the room, at a blotch of something rusty brown. He bent down, sniffed it, and made a face.

"Blood?"

"More like excrement." He stood back up. "Since she was choked, we wouldn't expect to see a lot of blood. But victims piss and shit as they die. We'll have the techs dust for fingerprints and take a look at this splotch under the scope."

Marge said, "What should we do with Lombard?"

"We've got a witness who tells us he was in the open house that Sunday. And we know he worked with Solana. That doesn't mean there was a relationship."

"We could probably find that out easy enough. Should we bring him in?"

"Not yet. First let's see if the techs can put him in her apartment by finding his fingerprints. In the meantime, Margie, he gets his cup of coffee from the same convenience store every day. Tell the store clerk to pour Lombard a cup from the dregs. Then, after he takes a sip, the clerk should offer him a fresh cup. When Lombard throws his cup away, you move in. Let's get his DNA. If he's the father of the kid, he can't very well deny a relationship."

It took little time for Decker to learn about Lombard's affair with Solana from several of her coworkers. Office gossip was rampant, though no one had anything damning to say about Solana other than she was having an affair with a married man. Lombard's fingerprints were on file, a requirement of his state license, and they matched dozens of prints found in Solana's apartment. Though the DNA profile hadn't come back, Decker decided it was time to bring in the young lawyer for questioning.

Dunn and Oliver caught up with Lombard during his lunch break—two hours at the Marquis Club, a posh private organization that catered to the downtown white-shoe firms and the multimillion-dollar corporations they represented. The young lawyer was accompanying the bosses. His job was to take notes and say nothing. The detectives waited until Lombard was done with his official business and discreetly moved in. The young lawyer reacted without dramatics. Wearing a black suit, a white shirt, and an ice-blue tie, Lombard was an average man in all respects, the only distinguishing mark being the mole over his right eye. The nevus was a dark, round spot, serrated at the edges and flush with his skin. At a quick glance, it resembled a bullet hole. After he made excuses to his bosses—an emergency at home—he willingly came down to the station house without a peep of protest.

Once in the interview room, Decker expected Lombard to lawyer up. Instead, the man sat stoically in his chair, waiting for the cops to make the first move. Oliver and Marge were behind the one-way mirror.

Decker said, "You know why you're here?"

"You tell me."

"We're investigating the murder of a woman named Solana Perez."

Lombard nodded. A moment later, a single tear leaked from his right eye. He quickly blinked it away.

"How long were you two involved with each other?"

Without a moment of hesitation, Lombard answered, "A while."

Decker tried to hide his surprise at the admission. "Could you be more specific?"

Lombard rubbed his eyes. "I didn't kill her."

"That's not what I asked you, Matt. I asked how long you two were involved with each other."

"Two, three years."

"A long time."

Lombard didn't answer.

"Did you know she was pregnant?"

There was a pause. Then the lawyer nodded. "She told me."

Again he had talked freely. Decker gave himself a microsecond to collect his thoughts. "Solana told you she was pregnant with your child?"

"Yes, she told me."

"How'd you feel about that?"

"Surprised."

"Just surprised?"

"It wasn't planned."

"Since you're married with two kids, I could imagine it wasn't planned."

Lombard said nothing, exhibiting none of the usual bodily reactions that most suspects had. No sweating, blushing, random movements, or fidgeting. It was as if his nervous system had shut down.

Decker said, "How'd you feel about her condition after the surprise wore off?"

"Maybe a little nervous . . . maybe excited."

"Excited?"

Lombard shrugged.

"Did you tell your wife?"

"No."

"Did you intend to tell your wife?"

Again Lombard shrugged. "I don't know what I intended to do. I was thinking long and hard about it. I was at a crossroads. Then Solana . . ." He paused. "I don't want to talk anymore. Am I under arrest?"

"So, here's the story, Matt, and it isn't looking very good for you. Your mistress is dead, and you, by your own admission, know that you're the father of her unborn child. We've got forensic evidence that puts you in her apartment. We've got an eyewitness who puts you in the house where we found the body."

For the first time, Lombard reacted. "Where did you find the body?"

"You dumped her there. Why don't you tell me?"

"I didn't dump her anywhere. I have no idea where you found the body. For all I know, you could be lying. I know that's what you people do. And I know it's legal."

"I'm not lying."

Lombard became still. Then he slumped in his chair, a defeated man.

Decker said, "Matt, you're a married man with two kids. Now you've got a love child on the way. That could cause all sorts of problems—with your work, with your wife, with your life. You wanted Solana to have an abortion. You offered to pay for it and her medical expenses and even a little extra cash to boot. But she refused—"

"I didn't kill her."

"You didn't kill her?"

"No."

"You're the father of her unborn child, you were at the crime scene, you were in the house where the body was found, but you didn't kill her."

"I don't know anything about a crime scene, and I don't know where the body was found. I loved Solana. I would never hurt her. I would never force her to get an abortion."

"She was killed at her apartment, Matt. We've got your fingerprints all over the place."

"Or course you do. I was at her apartment dozens of times." A pause. "She was murdered in her apartment?"

"You tell me."

"I can't tell you, because I didn't murder her. I certainly wasn't at any crime scene, unless you count me going over to her place to look for her when she didn't show up at work."

"Yes, Matt, I'll count that."

"I didn't know it was the crime scene. Everything looked pretty much in order when I was there. But I knew something was wrong. She wouldn't just disappear without telling me."

"So if you suspected something was wrong, why didn't you go to the police?"

"I don't know why I didn't. Maybe I was scared because I was afraid that something had happened to her. Maybe I was confused. I loved Solana, but I also have a wife and two kids. You can think what you want, but I didn't kill her."

"You didn't kill her."

"No."

"If you didn't kill her, do you have any idea who might have killed her?"

"Don't ask me that."

"Why not?"

"I'm not going to answer that."

"So what's going to happen when you're asked the question on the witness stand?"

"I'll plead the Fifth."

"That's going to look bad for you, Matt."

"I suppose it will. I think I should call a lawyer now."

"That's up to you."

"I know that. The interview is over."

And that was that. Still, Lombard had admitted the affair. He also had admitted being the father of Solana's baby. Adele had put him at the open house, but there was nothing specific to tie him to the actual murder. Since DNA banding charts took months to get back, Decker had yet to receive a profile for Lombard. But even if they found trace amounts of Lombard's blood at the apartment, that would be meaningless, since he had acknowledged being there many times. He could always say he nicked himself shaving or cut himself . . .

Nicks and cuts.

Decker mentally slapped himself on the forehead. There had been material found underneath Solana's fingernails, and Lombard's face was free of scratches. Decker wondered about other areas of the man's body and decided to try the most obvious first. "Now, I'm not going to ask you any more questions—"

"You can't ask me any more questions," Lombard said. "I already asked for a lawyer."

"You know, it would be really good for you if you rolled up your sleeves."

"What?"

"I'm not asking you to do it, but if you happen to do it, I'd like to take a look at your arms."

"What are you doing? You're not taking my blood, are you?"

"Of course not," Decker answered. "All I'm saying is

that if you roll up your sleeves of your own volition, I would like to take a look at your arms." Lombard was silent, his eyes locked with Decker's. "You don't have to do it. Completely up to you. But an innocent man has no reason not to cooperate."

"Innocent men have no reason to be charged with crimes they didn't commit. Still, it happens all the time."

"Your cooperation would be duly noted," Decker said.

"You shouldn't be asking me anything after I asked for a lawyer."

"I haven't asked you a thing. I've just said that if you did it, it would be convenient for me to look at your arms."

Lombard shook his head. "You're out of line." Still, he rolled up his sleeves. His forearms were covered in dark stiff hair; the undersides were pale, with prominent pulsing veins.

"Thank you," Decker said. "Will you excuse me for a moment?"

"I have a cell phone. I'm calling my lawyer."

"Sure. I'll be back in a minute." Decker closed the door to the interview room and went into the chamber where Oliver and Marge had been watching. From the one-way mirror, Decker saw Lombard picking up his cell only to stow it in his pocket. He sagged in the chair, his hands in his lap, his chin almost touching his chest. Then he closed his eyes. Lombard was on automatic pilot. It was clear to Decker that he was involved, but in what way? The lawyer hadn't exhibited any agitation that Decker would expect from a guilty man.

"What now?" Dunn asked.

"We have a strong circumstantial case, but not beyond a reasonable doubt. Certainly we can get a warrant to search his house. Maybe we can turn up some bloody clothes or something that puts her DNA on his clothes, or . . ." Decker thought a moment. "Or even better would be something that put his DNA on her body."

"The body was nude, Loo," Oliver reminded him. "Someone had cleaned her up."

"Well, she had a full head of hair. Someone at Mission Road must have combed through it by now."

"They did," Marge said. "We checked. The loose hairs that they pulled were consistent with her own hair."

"There was matter under her fingernails. Lombard's arms were clear, but I couldn't check his back or his legs. We need a DNA profile from the scrapings."

"The labs are backlogged."

Decker frowned. "Anyone on good terms with a DNA geneticist who does private testing?"

"I know someone who works for Biodon," Oliver said.

"Him or her?"

Oliver smiled.

"Good terms with her, Scottie?"

"She never complained."

"Take her out to dinner on the department. Impress upon her the need for speed."

Oliver grinned. "I know a great bistro with a dynamite pinot noir. Quiet, dark, a good place to conduct business."

"What place is that?"

"Geraldo's."

Marge said, "That place is around seventy-five a person, Scott."

"I know. I take my job very seriously."

* * *

The woman who answered Decker's knock was around five foot eight, with a full bosom and curves. Her hair was strawberry blond, and a sprinkling of freckles dotted her nose. She wore faded denim jeans, a long-sleeved cotton blouse, and a red bandana around her neck. Her eyes went wide when Decker showed her his badge.

"Police?"

"Yes, ma'am. Are you Laurie Lombard?"

"Yes. What do you want with me?"

"Who said I wanted anything with you, ma'am?"

The woman went silent. Decker produced the search warrant. "This says we're allowed to come inside your house and search it. We also have separate documents for your car and your husband's car."

"You can't come in here now. My husband's at work."

"He doesn't have to be home for us to execute the warrant. But you can call him if you want."

Laurie said, "I'm calling my lawyer, that's what I'm doing."

"It's up to you, Mrs. Lombard. But we don't have to wait around for either one of them to get here." Decker turned to his detectives. "Let's go." He gently grazed Laurie's shoulder as he sidestepped around her.

Laurie stared as a stream of official interlopers invaded her private space. "I was just about to go out."

"You can't use your car, ma'am," Marge Dunn told her. "We have to search it. It may be impounded."

"But I have to pick up my children at school!"

"Not at ten-thirty in the morning."

"But what if you're not done?"

"Call a taxi."

Decker said, "Oliver, go over her car first. First of all, the body had to get from the apartment to the house—"

"Body?" Laurie interrupted. There was panic in her eyes. They darted from person to person. "What body are you talking about?"

Decker didn't answer her and went on with his instructions. "If her car interior is clean, you might as well let her have access to it. I'll do the bedrooms, Lee and Wanda can do the rest of the house."

He marched down a small foyer that led to a series of bedrooms. The first belonged to her sons, two beds separated by a nightstand. The bookshelves were repositories of trophies from Little League, toys, CDs, DVDs, and an iPod.

The next room was Matt's office. His bookshelves actually held books. It was neat, clean, and dusty, as if it hadn't been used in many months. Decker suspected that Matt had been doing some of his take-home work at Solana's apartment.

The master bedroom was in the back and was about twice as large as the other two. It had an enormous walk-in closet. Laurie's clothing took up three-fourths of the space, relegating Matthew's portion to one shoe rack and a couple of poles for suits. It would have been easiest to start on Lombard's side, but that wasn't the focus of Decker's attention. Instead, he began by looking at Laurie's sneakers. Solana had been strangled, meaning there probably wouldn't be big puddles of blood to step in. But Solana did have a big scrape on her head that had bled, and Decker remembered the rusty blob in the corner of the room. The murderer might have stepped in something.

Laurie had decided that Decker was in charge, so she addressed her pleas to him. "Please, Detective, I've got a house to run. I have to get groceries for dinner."

"You might think about doing takeout tonight . . . with delivery." There was a pair of athletic shoes hidden in the back recesses of the closet. Hands encased in latex gloves, Decker pulled out the shoes and studied them. Suede and leather top, with dirty gray laces that had once been white. He sniffed the tops: They smelled of dishwashing soap. The bottoms gave off a slight foul odor. Lucky for him that today's athletic shoes were made with a topographical map's worth of grooves and ruts. Decker could see specks of brown crud lodged inside one of the furrows. It could have been dirt, it could have been dog turd, or it could have been human waste. He turned to Laurie.

"The police have chemicals that can pick up tiny, tiny droplets of human matter—blood, waste, urine, skin. And there are scientists who can get an entire DNA profile from these tiny droplets. What do you think about that?"

Laurie opened her mouth, then closed it.

"Would you mind taking off your scarf for me, please, Mrs. Lombard?"

Her hands flew to her neck. Then her mouth tightened and her chin jutted out in an expression of defiance. "I don't have to do anything for you."

"I'm afraid you're going to have to come to the station house with us."

"I'm not going to talk to you."

"That's your choice. But before I do the tests on this material that's stuck inside the treads of your shoes, you might want to tell me your side of the story. You see, we're already doing tests on the human skin that was found under Solana's fingernails. And I suspect that you have scratches underneath your scarf. You might think about cooperating now, while there's still a question mark. Because once this shoe is tied to Solana's DNA, and the human material under Solana's nails is tied to you, there won't be room for negotiating anything."

Laurie's bottom lip began to quiver.

"But sure, call up your lawyer, if you want." Decker shrugged. "Did you call your lawyer?"

Slowly, Laurie shook her head.

"Well, if you want your lawyer, now's the time to call him or her."

"Him," she whispered.

"You can't tell me anything, if you want your lawyer. You know that. So I guess the powers that be won't hear your side until your lawyer wants us to hear it."

"And if I don't want a lawyer?"

"Well, you've watched enough TV to know the drill, Laurie. You've got to sign a card saying that you were offered a lawyer and you didn't want one. Then you can talk to me."

There was no reaction from the woman. For a brief moment, Decker thought that she might lunge at him and try to wrest the shoes from his grip. Then her mood turned as gray as her skin tone.

"Bitch!"

"I'm sure she was . . . carrying on with a married man with two children."

"You don't know the half of it!"

Her nostrils flared with anger. It was easy to see how this big-boned woman could choke the life out of Solana, drag her into a car, and stuff her into a closet.

"I'd like to hear it all, Laurie. So let's go down to the station house. We'll sit and have a cup of coffee together, and you can tell me all about it."

"Do you have French-press coffee?"

"Uh, no, but I'll see what I can do."

"How'd you know it was she and not he who did the choking?" Oliver asked Decker. "Matt was acting pretty guilty, if you ask me."

"Guilty because of what had happened, not because of what he'd done. Initially, it was nothing more than a gut feeling. When the preliminary DNA of Solana's nail scrapings came up female, I had no doubt in my mind what had happened." Decker took a sip of his coffee. "She killed his mistress, then set him up to take the blame."

"How did she get inside the open house unless he left a door open for her?" Marge said.

"They originally had gone to the open house together, just as it was closing, and they had a long list of questions to ask the agent. Then Laurie suddenly claimed that she had a headache and had her husband handle it. But not before she'd unlocked a window so she could come back in. In the meantime, Matt had bombarded the agent with enough questions that Adele would be sure to remember him."

"And Laurie knew that her husband's fingerprints would be all over Solana's apartment," Oliver said.

"Right."

"Do you think Matt knew that his wife had done it before she confessed?" Marge asked.

"Definitely," Decker said. "All his talk about taking the Fifth—not to protect himself but to protect his wife."

"She kills his girlfriend and tries to set up her husband. But he still takes the Fifth," Oliver said. "What an idiot."

"He felt guilty, Scott," Marge said.

"I repeat: What an idiot."

"Solana's parents are coming in tomorrow from Texas by bus," Decker said. "They want to take their daughter back to Mexico and bury her there, but they don't have a lot of money."

"We're taking up a collection," Marge said.

Oliver grimaced, then took out his wallet and opened it. "I've got a five."

"You've also got a twenty." Marge plucked it out of his wallet. "We're trying to raise two hundred to give her a good church burial in a decent coffin. Pete and I offered to drive them to their town in Mexico."

Decker said, "I figured I could use a little practice with my Spanish."

"That's how you two want to spend your days off?" Oliver was incredulous.

Marge said, "We've been thinking that maybe afterward we'd go to Acapulco."

Oliver's ears perked up. "Now you're talking my language. Do you know Spanish, Margie?"

"Not really. What about you?"

"*Sí, no,* and *Usted cuesta mucho dinero*."

Decker smiled. "Coming with us, Scottie?"

"Us?" Again Oliver was surprised. "You're going to Acapulco *with* us and *without* your wife?"

"Rina's going to meet me there. We've decided to turn it into a mini-vacation. You two will be on your own."

Marge winked at Oliver. "You come and help split the driving, I'll be your wingman when we hit the bars."

"You've got a deal."

"But don't go too far, Pete," Marge said. "We'll need someone Spanish-speaking to plead his case after he's been arrested for a drunk-and-disorderly."

"You wound me," Oliver said.

"Not as much as you wound yourself," Marge said.

"And not as much as Solana Perez was wounded." Decker shook his head in disgust. "The capacity of human beings to inflict pain on one another is just astonishing."

"At least we got her a modicum of justice," Marge said. "Until the next one." She gave her words some thought. "And there always is a next one."

"Speaking of which . . ." Decker handed them a detail sheet. "Lee and Bontemps just caught this case. They could use some help."

Marge and Oliver let out a collective moan.

"Aw, quit your bitchin'," Decker said. "Crime may make us cynical and ugly, but it's how we earn our paychecks. It's a nasty job, but someone has to do it."

BULL'S-EYE

"Bull's-eye" features Peter Decker and his daughter Cindy dissecting a perplexing shooting of an unpopular drill instructor at the Los Angeles Police Academy. It required a visit to the academy, a fascinating place within spitting distance of Dodger Stadium. I was surprised to learn that many of the academy facilities were funded by Jack Webb of Dragnet *fame. This story is the first time that Cindy Decker appears in a professional capacity. Father and daughter have a few issues to work out as they edge toward solving this baffling case.*

C*razy broad!* HOLSTETTER KEPT HIS FEELings in check, his face impassive, as Sergeant Rigor talked and talked . . . trying to break him, break them all. He knew all the others felt that way, too, even the girls—uh, women. Martinez was always calling Rigor a fascist, MacKenny rolling her eyes whenever she lectured. Even Decker despised Rigor, said she suffered from a bad case of queen-bee syndrome, whatever that was.

Rigor wasn't a particularly big woman—around five-six or -seven, medium build, brown hair clipped close to her scalp, one step below a crew cut. Psycho eyes that took you in and spat you out.

Holstetter realized he was beginning to slump. He straightened, hoping Rigor hadn't noticed.

"Gettin' tired, Holstetter?"

"No, ma'am, no!"

Rigor's eyes drilled into his. "Sure? I wouldn't want to tire you out."

"No, ma'am, no!"

"Maybe you and your troop should take a run up the hill—say, five, ten miles. Sound good?"

Holstetter could feel the anger rising around him, his fellow cadets silently cursing him. His momentary lapse in posture had cost all of them. Still he remained expressionless. "Yes, ma'am, yes!"

"Great!" Rigor said with mock enthusiasm. "Tell you

what, Holstetter, I'll even run with you." She lifted a finger. "But first things first."

She addressed her charges. "You people think you're making progress? You got *miles* to go—I mean *light-years*—before you're even fit to call yourselves trainees."

She glared at them. "I can't stress brainpower enough. You're going to need every cell in your less than adequate craniums when you're out on the streets. Those bad guys out there . . . tell me about the bad guys, Baldwin."

A burly African American answered in a deep voice: "There's more of them than of us."

"See, folks?" Rigor announced. "Baldwin's actually learned something! There are way more of them than of us. And they got no morals. They got nothing holding them back, nothing to prevent them from turning you into a colander. Why did I bring up a colander, Martinez?"

"Because it's full of holes," a young Latina said.

"Excellent, Martinez. My job here is to prevent any of you from turning into a colander. Got it?"

The group answered in unison, "Yes, ma'am, yes!"

"That's good. I'm glad you understand. Because this is what I wanna do. You get good shooting practice here, but I don't think it's enough. So you know what I'm gonna do for you? I'm gonna take you out on Saturday—voluntary, of course. We're going to run a bit, train a bit, shoot a bit. Not here. At another range . . . to get you used to different situations and circumstances. So you don't get to thinking that Mr. Scumbag is always directly in front of you, twenty feet away, just waiting to be shot at. You gotta train all over the place!"

The sergeant stared at her cadets in their regulation blue sweats, her eyes scanning the names sewn on the shirts: Darwin, Holstetter, Baldwin, Martinez, Jackson, McVie, Decker, MacKenny . . . all of them so damn young!

"This extra target practice is my idea, not part of the academy program. So you don't have to sign up. But let me say this. You can go into the streets two ways: prepared or unprepared. I'm willing to give up my free time to prepare you. I don't need you to be grateful. But I do need you to be good cops."

Rigor held up a sign-up sheet. "This'll be waiting for you in my office. Anyone asks you what it means, just tell them it means a fun-filled Saturday with Sergeant Rigor. You sign it or not—up to you."

She turned to Holstetter. "Cadet, how 'bout you and me leading the way now?"

"Yes, ma'am, yes!"

"Fall into rank!" Rigor shouted, and the troop shuffled into place, one long line, two abreast. She nodded to Holstetter, and they began their uphill jaunt. Holstetter had to pump hard to keep up with Rigor's stride, his breath quickening, leg muscles contracting, as he concentrated on his step.

Sadistic bully!

"What can I say? It's cruel and unusual punishment. But who am I complaining to . . . or, rather, to whom am I complaining?"

Peter Decker smiled at his daughter. "If you want to be technical."

Cindy laughed and sipped her coffee. "Three months

out of college and I'm already talking like a Valley Girl! What would my lit professor say?"

"Probably that you should have stayed in graduate school."

"Wasting my time and your money," Cindy said wryly. "Anyway, I know I've been griping nonstop for the last half hour."

"Oh, you took a couple of breaths," he said.

She grinned at her father, showing a crescent of white, even teeth. She was a fine-looking girl, Decker thought—well-sculpted face, big brown eyes, white skin paprikaed with freckles, and a mop of red hair. He had never seen her in such fine physical shape. *The Police Academy'll do that for you,* he thought.

"I'm not unhappy, Dad. I'm just venting. I can vent to you, can't I?"

"I"m honored."

"The classroom courses are a snap. As far as the physical training goes—well, yes, I *am* exhausted. But it feels terrific to be forced to go that extra distance, knowing your life may depend on it, propelling yourself until it hurts. Because out on the street, when you're giving chase to a criminal, there's no time limit."

Her words were straight from some instructor's mouth, he thought. Still, they were even truer today than they had been in his time. He was glad Cindy was taking them seriously.

Decker stretched his long legs under the table. "You're right about that," he told her.

Again Cindy grinned at him. "Like you need me to explain this to you."

Decker took a bite of his onion bagel. "We're not talking about me, we're talking about you." He chewed a moment. "You haven't said much about your classmates. Found any friends?"

"Sure. It's a nice group. Some of the guys are a little . . . heavy-handed."

"They give you a hard time?"

"They give everyone a hard time. They come down like he-men in hand-to-hand combat. They get a charge out of hurting people. No big deal. You just fight back hard."

"Exactly. Just make sure you do it calmly, not out of anger. They hassle you in other ways?"

"Like harassment? No. Not overtly. The academy doesn't put up with that. One of the first lectures we got was the 'No harassment, no racism, no discrimination' speech. You know—that 'Cops come in only one color: blue' thing."

"That's good. What about the women in your group?"

Cindy shrugged. "Ordinarily, I don't think I'd have a tremendous amount in common with them. But we're going through such an intense experience together, there's some bonding. Two of them—Angelica Martinez and Kate MacKenny—come from cop families, too, so we've had similar childhood experiences."

"Like never having a father around?"

"More like we're just now beginning to understand the pressure our fathers must have been under. And we haven't even made it onto the streets yet! So much to learn in six months. It's overwhelming." She shrugged again. "Oh, well. One day at a time."

"That's the right attitude. How are your instructors?"

"Some are better than others. Controlled Substances is okay. Report Writing—now, there's a real snoozer.

Evidence is great—really interesting. I'm going to make a great detective!"

Decker laughed.

"Our Combat Wrestling instructor is a woman—Sergeant Peoples."

"Don't know her."

"Our Firearms instructor is also a woman—Sergeant Rigor. Well named—she's a maniac."

Decker's face was immobile. "Lynne Rigor?"

"You know her?"

"Yes. Known as a crack shot. Why do you say she's a maniac?"

"She's obsessed with training us . . . making us do extra work on weekends. She believes in training us at different sites, getting us involved in different situations. We start this Saturday."

"So it's mandatory?"

"Voluntary mandatory. The way she set it up, we really don't have a choice."

Decker frowned. "Well, I guess a little extra exercise can't do you much harm."

"She's also taking us shooting at an off-campus range."

"What? That is the most ridiculous thing I've ever heard!"

"It's not that bad."

"Taking twenty green kids to a range is a recipe for disaster. You've had, what? All of two months' worth of firearm experience?" He scowled. "I wonder if her superiors know."

"Dad, please don't interfere."

"But it's dangerous—"

"Being a cop is dangerous."

"At least get your normal training first. Cynthia, I'm not shielding you against a mean instructor. I'm trying to prevent trouble for the lot of you. At least let me talk to Lynne, find out what she has in mind."

Cindy looked at him calmly. "How would you respond if your daddy butted in?"

Decker started to say something, stopped, and then said, "Is Rigor planning on doing simulation exercises with firearms and blanks?"

"Maybe. I don't know."

"I don't want you to participate."

"Dad!"

"Cindy, accidents happen, especially when the exercises aren't well thought out."

"So what do I tell her? 'Sorry, Sergeant. Dad says no'?" She leaned forward. "How would it look if I bowed out, not only in front of her but in front of my classmates? I'd be branded as a quitter—a chicken. Nobody would want to partner with me. And they'd be right."

Decker knew she spoke the truth. He closed his eyes and said nothing.

"I'll be extra-careful. Okay?"

Decker opened his eyes, nodded. "All right."

"You don't look happy."

Decker pushed his bagel away. "I'm not, but I trust you."

"Thanks. That means a lot to me." She touched her father's hand. "I'll be fine. And I'll call you Saturday night."

After several go-rounds, Angelica Martinez finally found a space in the parking lot of Bootles Outdoor/Indoor

Shooting Range. She, Cindy Decker, and Kate MacKenny were fast becoming friends—all of them sticking together, even if the glue wouldn't hold forever. Martinez killed the motor, got out along with the other two, and stretched. Below the lot sat the shooting range, a flat area of scrub sandwiched between endless waves of hillside. Loud pops broke through the whipping wind. Dark clouds hovered above like a steel plate. "Wow, are my legs sore!" she said.

"Ten miles uphill will do that to you," Kate answered.

"Aren't you sore?"

"Beyond sore," Kate said. "More like into rigor mortis. I hate that woman."

"That should be her nickname," Cindy said. "Rigor Mortis. We'd all like to see her dead!"

The young women laughed. Kate pushed wisps of blond hair off her face. "Man, what I wouldn't give to do target practice on Rigor!"

Angelica said, "You'd have to wait in line—behind me."

Rigor had lit into Angelica earlier in the morning. Just tore her apart for no apparent reason. Cindy thought Angelica had handled it extremely well, had brushed it off and moved on. But apparently she was still brooding.

It was biting cold. Cindy rubbed her hands, looked at the complex stretched out below. Built for competition as well as target practice, Bootles had several types of outdoor courts, all of them ending in tall steel-plated backstops and ground baffles to catch stray bullets. In the center was a glassed-in tower where a range officer was giving instructions over a PA system to a group of rifle shooters. For protection, the outdoor ranges were walled in by twenty-foot sandbag berms. Beyond them were miles of knolls filled with chaparral and California scrub oak. The indoor-range building sat at the foot of the parking lot.

"Where are all the others?" Kate asked.

"I brought us through a shortcut," Cindy explained. "My dad lives about twenty miles from here, so I know a couple of tricks. They'll be here soon. Maybe we can even earn a few brownie points for being the first ones here."

"Rigor'll probably just accuse us of trying to show her up," Kate said. "God, I detest her."

"Everybody does," Cindy said. "Baldwin's ready to—"

"Man, he don't hate her as much as Holstetter does," Angelica interrupted. "She rides Holstetter any harder, she's gonna need reins and a bit!"

Standing erect, Cindy didn't dare sit or lean against the wall, even though Rigor was seated, drinking coffee. Couldn't appear weak, even if her feet were killing her. At least it was warm here in the commissary—stifling, as a matter of fact. So much so that someone had opened the window for circulation.

First the morning run, then the hours of calisthenics, then the ten-mile uphill jog, and now two hours of target practice. Cindy was cranky and hungry, looking at the food in the vending machines but not buying. She and Kate had agreed not to eat, wanting to show Rigor they had iron stamina. And so the two of them stood with about a half-dozen other cadets, waiting for an empty slot, listening to a female range officer instruct the pistol shooters in the glassed-in lanes below.

A strong icy draft whooshed through the open window, chilling Cindy's hands but keeping her awake, clear-thinking. Her eyes focused on the range, studying the trainees who were shooting. Angelica was in Booth 8, her body taut with concentration. At the given signal, she let go with a volley, missing most of center target. At that point Angelica was clearly frustrated. After she had disengaged her weapon, she shoved it into her harness, yanked out her earplugs, and stomped out of the booth and out of sight.

Rigor made a tsk-tsk sound and instructed Cadet Jackson to take Angelica's place. To Cindy and Kate, Rigor said, "Girl not only has an impulse problem, she can't shoot her way out of a paper bag."

Cadet Jackson entered the booth vacated by Angelica. Cindy sighed inwardly, stuck with Rigor for at least another ten minutes.

Rigor suddenly pointed to a couple of empty chairs. "Why don't you two have a seat? This isn't boot camp."

Cindy hesitated, then parked herself, hoping her relief wasn't too obvious.

"You both come from cop homes," Rigor commented. "I don't know your father, MacKenny, but I know yours, Decker."

Cindy said, "Yes, he's been around the LAPD for a while."

"Earned quite a name for himself."

"He's a hard worker."

"Probably never home when you were growing up—right?"

"He was home when it was important to be home," Cindy said calmly.

"Apparently not. Your parents are divorced, aren't they?"

Anger swelled inside her. Intellectually, Cindy knew Rigor was testing her, trying to crack her. "Yes, they are divorced," she said, hoping her voice wasn't too tight.

"Must have been problems at home."

"I was young when they divorced, Sergeant. I try my best not to dwell on the past. It's counterproductive."

Rigor nodded. "Got all the answers, don't you?"

Cindy tried a small smile. "Wish I did."

Rigor stood, went over to the coffee machine, and dropped some coins into the slot. "How do you take your coffee?"

Cindy started to rise. "I'll get it, Sergeant—"

"Just answer the question, Cadet Decker."

"Black," Cindy said. "For both of us."

Kate smiled appreciatively.

"Only got two quarters left," Rigor answered. "You two can share." She reached into the coffee slot and took out the steaming paper cup. She turned around, then suddenly jerked backward as if blown by a huge gust of wind. Black jets of coffee flew upward as Rigor's head cracked against the cement floor, blood spurting from her temples.

Kate screamed. Cindy raced over and pressed her palms to Rigor's head in an attempt to stanch the blood. Moments later, several other classmates were at her side. "Get help!" she shrieked to Kate. "Call nine-one-one."

Kate tore out of the room.

An eternity passed. Even as Cindy waited, she knew it was bad. Her fingers could feel a dying pulse, slower and slower, weaker and weaker, until there was no pulse at all.

* * *

By the twentieth time Cindy had to tell it, the story took shape. It went something like this.

Rigor was standing at the machine, getting them coffee—no, she had gotten the coffee. She turned to face them—*them* being Kate and her. Then she suddenly jerked backward and fell to the floor. They both heard this awful crack as her head hit the cement. Blood was spewing from her head.

Where did the bullet come from?

Out of nowhere.

Bullets don't come from out of nowhere, Ms. Decker.

Rational thought dictated that it had to have come from the open window. It couldn't have penetrated the walls because they were concrete, and no bullet holes were found. The door to the hallway had been closed, so it couldn't have come from there. It didn't come from inside the commissary, because the only people there had been Sergeant Rigor, Kate MacKenny, and herself.

Remember seeing anyone out the window?

No. Not a face, not even a fleeing figure.

The inquiries lasted past dinnertime—for Cindy and Kate, for everyone in the commissary, for everyone in Rigor's class, everyone at the range. And when the police were finally finished there, Rigor's superiors took her cadets back to the academy for more questioning.

Suspicion hung heavily over the group like a cloud. Woe to anyone who wasn't in public view when the shooting occurred. Luckily for Cindy, she had Kate and the others to back her up. And vice versa. But there were a few cadets who had been off by themselves—Baldwin, Holstetter, Angelica.

Academy officials took away their guns for testing. They grilled everyone over and over, usually starting with Cindy. She'd been there, been the first to do something. No matter how often she went over what'd happened, they looked at her as if she'd done something wrong!

Did you move the body, Ms. Decker?

No. The only thing she did was apply pressure to the wound, trying to stop the bleeding.

Are you sure?

Of course she was sure! Why didn't they believe her? She was getting firsthand interrogation experience, she realized—but from the wrong side.

The hours passed, and the story became rote, her words mechanical, devoid of the emotion they had held in the beginning.

Finally, the last interview was wrapped up. Stay close to home in case other questions come up, Cindy was told. Report to the academy on Monday. No classes. The group would be suspended until this tragedy was sorted out.

It was almost midnight when Cindy left the interview room. The worst was behind her, she figured—until she saw her father waiting for her. His face was impassive, his cop face.

Tears came to her eyes. Fiercely, he whispered, "Look down! And when you look back up, make sure your eyes are dry."

She did as she was told, happy to follow him and his unambiguous orders.

They walked through the long hallway of the old stucco building, past window after window of academy athletic trophies. Her father nodded to familiar faces as they walked along. He didn't touch her, didn't talk to her, until they were out of the building and in the parking lot.

Decker restrained himself from hugging her for fear of breaking her bones with relief, simply asking, "Are you all right?"

"I'm . . . yes, I'm . . ."

"I knew I'd worry once you hit the streets." He smiled grimly. "But I see you're giving my heart attack a jump-start."

Cindy hugged herself tightly. "That wasn't my intention."

"All that matters is that you're in one piece."

"At least physically."

"Right now physically is all I care about." He ran his hand over his face. "Come home with me. I'll drive you back tomorrow."

She nodded, followed her father to his reconstituted Porsche. Usually, he tore out of parking lots. Tonight he drove slowly, methodically. Neither of them spoke.

He passed up the freeway signs, headed into the dark hills of Chavez Ravine, the serpentine roadways rising and falling at regular intervals. Small bungalows lined the tarry asphalt, dots of light emanating from a few windows. He drove deeper into the area.

Cindy was puzzled. "Where are we going?"

Abruptly, Decker pulled the car over to the curb, turned off the ignition, and slumped down in the driver's seat.

Cindy's heart leaped. "Oh, my God! Dad!"

In a calm voice, Decker said, "I've been shot, Officer. You've got to radio it in. Where are we?"

Cindy was shaking, blind with anxiety.

Her father sat up, ran his hand through his hair. "I asked you a question. Where are we?"

Cindy's mouth fell open. Her father was okay. More than okay. He was *testing* her. After all she'd been through today, he actually had the nerve to *test* her. Spontaneously, she erupted into tears.

Decker waited, doing nothing to comfort her. Then he started the car. "You need to think with your eyes as well as your brain," he said.

"How could you do this to me after what—"

"That's especially when you must be on your guard." He handed her a tissue. "When you've been through hell and back and you're zonked out, bone-tired, hungry, and frazzled. Because that's when you're ripe for a slipup. What you need to do is stop, take a deep breath, and make sure your brain's working. The life you save may be your own."

Feeling betrayed, she dried her eyes and said nothing. But as they rode on in silence, she realized she was looking at street signs.

"Want to talk about it?" her father asked finally.

"You didn't have to come down and rescue me, you know." Weakly, she asked, "Are they planning on expelling us?"

"Don't know. They've got to sort through the details first."

"You know the details?"

"I'd like to hear them from you."

Cindy told the story yet another time. "Rigor was uniformly disliked," she added when she'd finished. "Everyone made comments about wishing she were dead."

"Including you?"

"Including me. But Dad, no one took them seriously. I don't know what they've told you, but I don't believe any of us murdered her."

"Angelica Martinez was angry with her, stomped off the range—"

"She was frustrated."

"She was alone when the shooting occurred. And this Holstetter guy. Rigor really had it in for him. Dressed him down whenever she could. Isn't that true?"

"Yes, but I can't believe . . ." Cindy paused. "Holstetter's a jerk—but he's no murderer. Besides, it'd be incredibly dumb to kill her there, out in the open."

"It wasn't in the open. No one saw anything. You didn't see a thing, and you were standing about five feet from her."

Cindy was quiet for a moment. "Guess my powers of observation need a little honing," she said.

"Tell me the story again."

"You're kidding."

"No. Go on."

Once again, Cindy recited automatically: Rigor walked up to the coffee machine, put money into the slot, got the coffee. As she turned to face them, something jerked her head back.

Decker interrupted. "Did you hear anything? You've told me what you saw. Did you hear anything?"

"No."

"You were standing above a shooting range, Cindy," Decker said. "You had to have heard the range officer's instructions. You had to have heard gunfire pops."

Cindy bit her lip. "I suppose I did. But at that point, they were just background noise."

"A gun firing close enough to hit her. No glass to deaden the sound. You should've heard something louder than background noise."

She thought, then shook her head.

"Close your eyes for a moment. Picture yourself back there . . . right before Lynne turns around."

"Okay," she said resignedly.

Decker spoke soothingly. "She's about to turn around. Right as she's doing it, her head jerks back. Do you hear anything that corresponds with Rigor's movement?"

Cindy shook her head. "No . . . no."

"Bullet just comes flying through the window?"

"I suppose. All I hear is that awful crack of her head smashing against the cement floor. I run over to her and put my hands on the wound, trying to—"

"Which way did she land? Faceup or facedown?"

"Face . . . faceup."

"How would you explain that?"

Cindy stared at him. "What do you mean?"

"If she landed faceup, how do you explain the crack in her forehead?"

A long pause. "I don't know."

Decker said, "Rigor cracked her forehead, but she fell faceup. The people who were questioning you were thinking that you had to have flipped the body over."

"But I didn't! I swear I didn't move her."

"Could be the impact of the bullet spun her around, threw her face against the wall, and smashed her forehead. Then she bounced off the wall and fell backward, faceup. They question you any more, you tell them to take a look at the back of her head. Should be an indentation there as well."

Cindy rubbed her eyes. "You know, they kept asking me if I'd moved the body. I kept telling them no. I didn't understand. I've got a long way to go, don't I?"

"To get where?"

"To get where you are."

"Talk to me after twenty years." Decker paused, then said, "You plan on shooting someone in the head, where do you aim?"

"I've never thought about it." She shrugged. "Between the eyes, maybe the back of the head. Shoot when they're not looking."

"Bigger surface area. Less likely to miss. Rigor was shot in the temple, right?"

"Yes, she was. What's troubling you?"

"I'm not sure." Decker licked his lips. "You didn't see anyone out the window, you didn't hear a corresponding pop when Rigor dropped. She was hit in the temple. It's odd—sounds like a stray bullet, almost. But Bootles is one of the safest ranges around. I don't get it." He tapped the steering wheel. "Maybe they'll get a match from someone's gun. Let's hope it's not your friend Angelicas's."

"Impossible!"

But Decker was dubious. He'd seen much weirder things in his life.

Cindy said, "What are you doing tomorrow?"

"Working on the new house. Why?"

"Thought maybe you and I could go back to the firing range."

"It's not my jurisdiction, honey." When Cindy did not respond, Decker gave in. "Okay," he said. "A quick trip."

"Thanks, Dad."

They rode in silence for the next ten minutes. Then Decker said, "I love you. Just wanted to say that."

Cindy didn't speak, longing to cry to release the heavy knot of tension in her throat. Instead, she forced out, "Love you, too. So we're on for tomorrow?"

"It's a deal."

Again Decker jerked the car to the side of the road. "Where are we?"

Fighting off fatigue, Cindy stammered out the location. Decker nodded, then guided the Porsche onto the 110 Freeway North. She glanced at her father's stoic face, then kept her eyes fixed on the roadway, taking in everything, looking at the world from an entirely different perspective: a cop's perspective.

Parked in Bootles' gravel lot, Decker hung up his cell phone and looked at his daughter. "Your friend Angelica is off the hook. The bullet came from Holstetter's gun."

"But he didn't *do* it," Cindy insisted. With that pronouncement, she climbed out of the Porsche and slammed the door.

Decker slowly got out of the driver's seat. "Obviously he did, Cynthia."

"Well, I don't believe it."

"That's another issue entirely." He tightened his jacket collar against the freezing wind. The sky looked as uninviting as the barrel of a gun. He caught up to his daughter. "What is it you expect to find here?" he asked.

"I'll know when I find it." Cindy stopped. "Where is Holstetter now?"

"With the local police. They're talking to him—"

"No one's that stupid! Not even Holstetter."

"Cindy, why are you snapping at me?" Decker rubbed his hands together. "I'm cold, and I'm getting very grumpy. Let's get out of here, get some coffee or something."

"Has he admitted to anything?"

"I don't know."

She pointed ahead. "How about a hike?"

Decker stared at her. "And what do you possibly hope to find?"

She stared back. "Dad, I've been reliving that moment over and over. It's plaguing me. My eyes weren't more than inches away from the window when Rigor fell. I didn't see anyone."

"You weren't looking. You were focused on Rigor."

"I didn't hear a shot. You thought that was very odd, remember? Can we take a short walk? I just want to see if it's possible to shoot from up there in the mountains into the commissary window."

Decker looked at the hillside. "More than a short walk. I'd say about a half, maybe three-quarters, of a mile."

"It'll warm us up."

"Cindy, it's hard to hit something half a mile away."

"Typical bullet range for a nine-millimeter is close to a mile."

"I know the statistics. I'm talking reality."

"Please?"

God, Decker thought, *she's worse than I am.* "C'mon," he said.

They groaned as they trudged up the rocky hillside. The cold was seeping through Decker's shoes, into his feet. But Cindy wasn't complaining, and he'd be damned if he'd be out-stoicized by his own daughter.

Panting hard, they reached the top, the frigid wind cutting them to the bone. A few minutes later, they were standing above the firing range.

"You can see the commissary window from here," Decker said, pointing. "But you can't see *in* it." He paused for a moment. "Holstetter was angry with Rigor, wasn't he?"

"Very much so, but—"

"Where was he when the shooting went down?"

"He said he was just walking around."

"Around the range?"

"Yeah. He was waiting for a lane to open up."

"Someone should have seen him, then. At least right after Lynne was shot. But he wasn't seen for at least ten minutes afterward. So what does that say, Cin?"

"That Holstetter was far away. Like, off the grounds."

"Like, possibly up here. And he didn't want to tell anybody that he'd left the grounds without permission, giving Rigor a legitimate reason to kick him out of the academy."

"But Dad, even if he was up here, it doesn't mean he shot her—through a window—half a mile away."

Decker frowned. "Guys usually don't cool off by walking around and ruminating," he said. "They *do* things. They act. If I were really ticked off at Rigor, I'd have gone straight into target practice and pumped out a few rounds."

"The range was crowded yesterday," Cindy pointed out. "We had to wait for booths . . ." Her eyes widened. "Target practice," she echoed, and turned to her father. "If he couldn't work off his frustration that way, because the booths were full, why not come up here and shoot at trees?"

She was excited now. "A stray bullet, Dad—you said that yesterday."

"Cindy—"

"The wind could have deflected the bullet, carried it through the window!"

"Not if he was shooting in the opposite direction, toward the mountains. Even *this* wind isn't strong enough to do that."

"Or maybe the bullet was deflected by a tree and then carried by the wind," Cindy said. "And Holstetter didn't say anything about it because he didn't want anyone to find out he was shooting. First thing we were taught is never, ever discharge your weapon without a reason! Doing so is grounds for expulsion. Rigor was real big on that rule. Make sense?"

Grudgingly, Decker admitted it made some sense.

"If he was doing target practice, he had to be aiming at something," Cindy reasoned. "Maybe the building; hence the bullet. Although that would be pretty stupid."

"More than likely, if he was up here, he was aiming at trees," Decker said.

"So let's start looking for bullet holes in tree trunks."

Decker stared at her.

"Dad, even if Holstetter tells the truth now, they aren't going to believe him, because he didn't come clean yesterday. He's going to be accused of murder. We're here already. What's another hour or so?"

"An hour or so of freezing weather is called torture," Decker said, but he started looking. Because the kid was right.

* * *

Sipping coffee in a drab, windowless room, the buzz of cops surrounding her, Cindy prayed that someday she would be a part of all this. She was waiting for her father to finish making his statement to the officers in charge. He was taking a lot longer than she had, she thought—but then his observations carried a lot more weight than hers.

A half hour later, her father emerged. She stood, her eyes questioning. He put an arm around her shoulders and said, "Let's go."

"What are they—"

"When we're in the car."

They walked quickly to the Porsche. As soon as she was buckled in, Decker gunned it out of the parking lot. He put the heater on.

"Did Holstetter admit to discharging his weapon?" Cindy asked.

"With a murder charge thrown in his face, it was the first thing he did admit," Decker said. "But at that point, he had a credibility problem. No one was listening to his story."

He paused and appraised his daughter. "He owes you big, Cindy. You saved him jail time. On the basis of our statements and the physical evidence we recovered, the DA's going to plea-bargain down to involuntary manslaughter. Holstetter will probably just get probation and community service. But his career as a cop is dead."

Cindy nodded without speaking.

Decker said, "You carry a gun, you take the responsibility that goes with it. Holstetter didn't, and it cost a life. If there's a moral here, it's 'Don't play with firearms.' "

"Still, I feel sorry for him," Cindy said. "He didn't mean to do it."

"I know," Decker said, "but Rigor's still dead." He turned down the heater. "A stupid, stupid tragedy. Not a moment has gone by that I haven't been thanking God. You were two feet away from Rigor when she was hit."

"Yes, I—" Cindy abruptly changed the subject. "Did you tell them our theory of the bullet trajectory? About the scrape marks on the two tree trunks and the deflection angle that led right toward the window?"

"Yes."

"What did they say?"

" 'Highly unlikely' was their response . . . something like that. Still, they must have given it more weight than they let on, because they *are* planning on reducing the charge." He smiled. "It didn't hurt that we found six other bullets in the tree trunks that also matched with Holstetter's gun. It gave him some mileage in the truth department."

They rode in silence for a while. Finally, Cindy said, "Our group . . . do you think the academy will take us back?"

"I don't think the academy subscribes to collective punishment. Why wouldn't they take you back—all of you except Holstetter? But they'll be watching you like hawks."

"Fair enough."

"More than fair." Decker waited a beat. "Cindy, listen to me carefully. You only have one obligation on this earth."

"What's that?"

"To take care of yourself. Promise me."

"I'll do my best."

"Not good enough."

"It's all I can give you right now, Dad."

Decker didn't say anything. Instead, he abruptly pulled onto the freeway shoulder.

Cindy grinned. "Piece of cake. Westbound 118, about to hook onto 405 South. Any other questions?"

"None," her father said. "That's it. Class dismissed."

A WOMAN *of* MYSTERY

"A Woman of Mystery" explores the past coming back to haunt the present, a favorite theme of mine. Although we are not controlled by our own histories, we are the sum total of our experiences. How we handle our personal histories says a lot about who we are. This story also offers a tiny glimpse into Rina Lazarus's past.

As a student, Eve Miller was different—not odd but distinct. And because Rina Decker was an experienced teacher, she knew this intuitively, although she could have pointed out several objective reasons why she thought Eve unique.

First off, the young woman's working knowledge of the Bible was far better than most of Rina's first-year Introduction to Judaism pupils. Although there were gaps in Eve's knowledge, she knew the stories of Genesis and Exodus by heart and could even quote passages from memory. More impressive, she was familiar with the later sacred texts, specifically the Prophets.

Second, Eve didn't embrace the religion with the typical zeal found in born-again Jews—the ba'alei tshuva—whom Rina generally taught. On the contrary, Eve appeared hesitant to commit to the Orthodox ways. She asked probing questions and analyzed Rina's explanations. Eve seemed unsure about her spirituality, so it didn't surprise Rina to find Eve lingering about after class one evening, waiting for the others to leave.

Maybe Eve had been working up her courage. After all, she was young—early twenties, whereas most of the other pupils were closer to thirty. She was fresh-scrubbed and pretty, with short blond hair that had been layered to expose gold-studded earlobes. Her complexion was soft, her cheeks had a natural blush. Her lips were full, and her eyes were iridescent green. She dressed neatly and conservatively: black slacks, white shirt under a crewneck sweater, flats on her feet. She was on the tall side, five-six or -seven. Her notebook was always tidy, her handwriting legible and neat.

The class was officially over at nine P.M., but there was always a barrage of last-minute comments that stoked protracted discussion. It heartened Rina that her students were so enthusiastic that they rarely noticed the time. But eventually, she did have to put a stop to the after-hours dialogues. Rina did have a life. Still, she always felt a pang of guilt when she announced that it was time to go home.

And even after she dismissed class officially, there were students who had just one more question or one last comment. How could she cut them off at such a crucial time in their religious development? In reality, there wasn't any pressing need for her to rush home. Her sons were almost young men and certainly didn't require physical care. Hannah was only six, but she was sleeping soundly by nine. And Peter could always find a way to occupy himself. Still, Rina valued her private time with her husband. As a police lieutenant, Peter worked long, hard hours and she never took her husband for granted.

Yet here was Eve, lingering, ill at ease, judging from the tapping of her left foot. Her arms were folded across her notebook, which she was pressing to her chest. Her expression was tense. Rina knew the young woman needed to talk. It took twenty minutes for the other students to file out. Finally, it was just the two of them.

Rina stacked the loose papers spread across her desk. She smiled. "Hi, Eve. Is there something I can help you with?"

"You look busy."

"Not at all." Rina pointed to an empty chair. "Please. Have a seat. What's up?"

Eve sat and placed her notebook on her lap. She licked her lips. "I don't know where to start." Her voice was a whisper.

"How about if you begin at the beginning?"

"That's just it, Mrs. Decker, I don't . . ."

A pause. Rina said, "Don't what, Eve?"

"I don't know the beginning." Another hesitation. "I don't know the beginning or the end." She locked eyes with Rina. "I don't know anything, because I don't know who I am." She held back tears. "I mean that literally. I have no memory of the past."

Slipping under the covers, Rina enjoyed the warmth of the blanket, the softness of the pillow beneath her head. She looked over at Peter, then took his hand. "I'm not a neurologist," she said, "but I don't think it's anything like a brain tumor. Eve's mental acuity is fine. At the risk of sounding psychobabbly, I'd say maybe it's some kind of dissociative state."

"Very psychobabbly." Decker marked off the page of his book, placed it on his nightstand, and turned off his reading lamp. He ran his fingers over his ginger mustache. "She needs to be checked out medically, Rina. And as soon as possible."

"Absolutely," Rina agreed. "I told her that."

"And what did she say?"

"She insists her problem isn't physical. She's sure that her memory loss means she's escaping something psychologically painful."

"So why doesn't she see a shrink?"

"She's too scared."

"Pretty swift insights, Rina," Decker said. "To me, it sounds like a bad movie. Are you sure she's not snowing you?"

"Maybe." Rina gave her husband's words some thought. "But why would she want to do that?"

"For attention."

"I don't know, Peter. She seems so genuinely upset." Rina paused. "For the moment, can we assume that her amnesia is legitimate?"

He shrugged. "Sure."

"How would you go about searching for her true identity?"

"How would I do it?" Decker smiled. "I'd send her to a psychiatrist, let him or her do all the work."

"I meant as a detective."

Decker lifted his eyebrows. "I can see you're determined to suck me into this. Okay. First tell me what you think."

"For starters, she sounds educated."

"Why?"

"Her use of language. Her syntax and vocabulary."

"Some college?"

"I think so."

"Does she remember going to college?"

Rina shook her head. "Her personal slate is blank, Peter. Except for her name. She thinks her actual name was something similar to Eve Miller. Also, she told me she liked the name Eve because Eve was the first woman."

"Also the first person to commit sin."

"She's aware of that fact."

"Yet she doesn't know how she picked up her knowledge of the Bible?"

"No. Just that she knows it in the same way she knows how to work a calculator or read a book. She says that was why she came to my class in the first place—to hear me speak on Jewish laws and customs. She felt it might trigger something."

"And?"

"Nothing. The Jewish rituals are foreign to her." Rina turned over on her side to face him. "My guess? She had some kind of religious upbringing, like a churchgoing family."

"A college-educated person with a religious upbringing," Decker said. "But you don't think she's Jewish, because although she knows Bible, Jewish customs are alien to her."

"Exactly."

"So if she isn't Jewish, what religion is she?"

"My first thought was Catholic. But I think that most Catholics are taught more catechism than Bible." She looked at Decker for some kind of confirmation.

He said, "Beats me."

She sighed. "I'd say that she could have been raised as a fundamentalist Christian, maybe Baptist or Evangelical."

"Amish?"

Rina thought for a moment, then said, "She seems too worldly."

Decker nodded. "And she came to you for help . . . to find out who she is?"

"Someone must have told her that my husband is a police detective. Maybe she figured I was in a position to help."

"So why didn't she go directly to the police?"

"I told you, Pete—she's scared."

Decker rubbed his jaw. "On the professional side, it's a snap to plug the name 'Eve Miller' into the Missing Persons Network."

"A good place to start."

"You think so?" Decker smiled at his wife in the dark. Rina was anxious to help, but there was always a flip side to do-gooding. "You know, once I start this process, I'm going to find out things. Does she know she may learn information that could be very disturbing to her? Does she know that once the facts are out in the open, she can't take them back? And do you know that you may get blamed for everything if this turns into a mess?"

Rina took in his words. "Why don't you talk to her?"

"How did I know that was coming?"

"Because you're prescient," Rina answered. "Just hear her story. Then you can make an informed decision."

"Suddenly you're out of the picture?"

"I'll bring her in."

"You bet you'll bring her in. And I'd like you to stay during the interview."

"Don't you think it would be better if you talked to her in private? You'd probably get more out of her."

"Rina, the woman is disturbed, possibly a nutcase."

"I don't think so."

Decker shook his head. His wife was so naive. "I'll need a witness during the interview. Tag, you're it."

"It wasn't like I woke up one day and didn't know who I was. It was more . . . gradual."

Silence.

Decker nodded encouragingly. "Go on."

Eve wrinkled her brow. "It was like I was returning from a deep sleep. Things drifting in and out, then slowly coming into focus. I found myself in a strange apartment." She looked down and took in a deep breath. "I must have ordered lots of take-out food, because there were empty pizza boxes, Chinese-food cartons, empty McDonald's wrappers."

Eve was pale, and her hands were shaking. Rina took her hand. "You're doing great," she said. The young woman gave her a grateful smile.

Decker persisted. "And you didn't have any ID on you?"

"No, sir."

"No traces from your past?"

"Nothing. Even the clothes in my closet had been recently purchased. The price tags were still on."

"You don't remember buying them?"

"No, sir."

Calling him "sir," Decker noted. Respectful. "You must have had money to buy food and clothes."

"Yes, I must have had." Eve averted her eyes. "I don't have anything now except what I earn from my job."

"You work?"

"Yes, sir. I do invoicing for Anya's Accessories. It's a midsize manufacturing company. They make all kinds of small leather goods, things like wallets, key holders, belts."

"She's been working at Anya's for three months," Rina added. "They love her down there. She's already gotten her first raise."

That was Rina—everyone's mother, Decker thought. He said to Eve, "You've worked there for three months. And how long have you had the memory lapse?"

"As far as I can tell, I've been like this for around six months."

"So what were you doing before you got your job?"

"Trying to adjust." She let out a mirthless chuckle and clasped her hands tightly. "That's a joke. How do you adjust to something like this? But the will to survive is great. I needed to live. And to live, I needed money."

The will to survive is great. To Decker's ears, she sounded as if she was quoting somebody. "How'd you manage to get a job, Eve?" he asked. "You had no ID—no driver's license, no Social Security number, no credit cards, no past job history. Most companies ask for references. How'd you fool them?"

Eve bit her lip and remained silent.

"Did you invent a job history?" Decker asked. "Maybe even pay someone for bogus ID?"

Eve looked up at the ceiling. "Are you going to arrest me?"

Rina stepped in. "Eve, you came to me to discover the truth. If you still want that, you have to tell Lieutenant Decker everything."

There was a long pause. Then she said, "I was a person with no identity. I knew I had to survive. I knew I had to be somebody—to have a name and an ID. I went to one of those gigantic bookstores that have information on everything—on how to disappear, on how to reinvent yourself to avoid creditors or irrational ex-boyfriends . . ."

"Go on."

"I followed the procedure step-by-step. You go to a

county registrar's office and look up death certificates of people who would have been your age. Then you pretend you're that person and apply for a birth certificate, saying you lost your original one. I found the name Eve Miller and decided to use it because . . . I don't know, it sounded familiar. Then, once I had a birth certificate, I got a Social Security number and a passport."

Pretty savvy for such a young woman, Decker thought. What was she running from? "Why not a driver's license?" he asked.

"I don't have a car, sir."

"But you know how to drive."

"Yes, sir, I do."

"Why'd you get a passport? Were you planning on going somewhere?"

Eve opened and closed her mouth. "I really don't know why I applied for one. I just thought I should be prepared."

Prepared for what? Decker wondered.

Eve shook her head. "I wouldn't blame you if you didn't believe any of this. It sounds wild to my own ears. But I'm telling you the truth."

Decker scribbled more notes. "You do invoicing. What software do you use?"

Her answer was immediate: "QuickBooks."

"What other programs do you know?"

"Microsoft Word. I can also do spreadsheets." She smiled, allowing herself a bit of crowing. "I think that's why they hired me. I was versatile with the computer."

"How'd you learn to use a computer?"

Eve hesitated and blinked back tears. "I don't know." She wiped her eyes. "You can't imagine what this feels like! I'm sure something . . . traumatic must have happened to me. But I don't know what. Please help me!"

"You need to see doctors, Eve—a medical doctor and a psychologist. They can help you more than I can."

"I know that, Lieutenant Decker. And I swear I will get medical help. But first, I need to know who I am. Can you help me?"

Decker closed the door to his office and handed his wife a Styrofoam cup of coffee. "No Eve Miller popped out of the Missing Persons Network computer," he said.

"That would have been too easy." Rina took a sip of coffee. It had been three days since Peter interviewed Eve. "It took you all this time to find that out?"

"I was working on the problem from several other angles. Because once I get started, I find it hard to stop." Decker sat down in his desk chair. "During the questioning, she kept talking about how 'the will to survive is great' and about 'the need to be prepared.' Something like that. You remember her saying those words?"

Rina frowned. "Vaguely."

Decker smiled. "See, that's why I take notes. If I had to trust my memory, more felons would be walking the streets. Anyway, her language set off warning bells. She was acting as if she were running from something. So I began to punch the permutations on the name Eve Miller into some of the crime databases. I'd start with Eve Miller, then Eva Miller, then Ava Miller, and so on."

Rina's stomach lurched. "Is she wanted for something?"

Decker took in a breath and let it out. "Eve Miller isn't a wanted woman, but Ava Mueller is."

"Ava Mueller." Rina bit her lip. "She's German?"

"Yes, Ava Mueller is German, and not a nice one. During World War Two, Ava Mueller was a Gestapo guard at the Ravensbrueck labor camp. I took the liberty of calling up the Holocaust Center to find out about the camp's history. It was basically divided into two sections—subversive women detained by the state and Jewish women in captivity. There was a universe of difference between the two camps—their living quarters, their clothes, the treatment, the food. Namely, the non-Jewish contingency had edible food, whereas the Jewish unit survived on turnip soup and moldy bread. Ava worked as a guard in the Jewish bunkers. Afterward, she was wanted for Nazi war crimes because she was considered to be personally responsible for the deaths of over three hundred women."

"Oh my God!" Rina blurted out. "Do I even want to hear the rest?" Though sickened, she knew she had to listen. "Go on."

Decker heaved a sigh. "I asked the center if it had any postwar records on Ava Mueller. One of the librarians told me that Ava had somehow made it into the States using false papers, and had disappeared. This was about 1949."

He finished his coffee and continued, "Thirty-five years later—in 1984—one of Simon Wiesenthal's Nazi hunters in New York got a tip on Mueller's whereabouts. She was now a doting grandmother, living a quiet life as a Mennonite in Indiana. Makes sense. The vast majority of Mennonites are either German or of German heritage. Many of them speak Palatine Dutch, a German dialect. And religious sects are very forgiving. They also tend to be isolated, generally don't mix much with the secular world. What better place to hide?"

"I'm sorry, Peter, but I don't see the Mennonites randomly welcoming in a former Nazi."

"I'm sure Ava Mueller didn't tell them about her past. Or maybe she had some Mennonite relatives. Lots of people, present company included, have a skeletal relative or two in the closet. For me, it's Great-uncle Ray, the Alabama Klansman."

Rina smiled. "And I have Great-aunt Bessie the Stalinist. Even on her deathbed, she insisted that Josef meant well. He was just misguided."

Decker let out a laugh, then the room fell silent. Rina tried to break it but couldn't find the words. Finally, she said, "What happened after Ava Mueller was discovered?"

"She, her husband, and her family left the conclave and were lost again." Decker shrugged. "Maybe this time they ventured into the city. If so, Ava's granddaughter, Eve, or whatever her name really is, would have been about five or six. If the family had chosen to settle in a more urban neighborhood, then Eve would have gone to a more urban school and learned things like how to operate a computer or how to drive. That scenario would explain why Eve knows the Bible so well—her early upbringing—and why she also has some contemporary skills."

"This is all just speculation."

"Of course." Decker tried to be gentle. "But it does help explain some things." He formulated his thoughts. "Suppose, as a girl, Eve didn't know about her grandmother's dark history."

Rina nodded.

"Then let's suppose that around six months ago, as an adult, she discovered her grandmother's evil past and was horrified by it. Suppose she confronted her grandmother and demanded answers. You've implied that Eve is a deep thinker and doesn't accept explanations by rote."

"Yes, that's correct," Rina said.

"What if her grandmother tried to rationalize her behavior, tried to make Eve understand Ava Mueller's state of mind. Maybe she spoke about how the will to survive is great and how you had to be prepared. Maybe Grandma gave her details on how she disappeared and reinvented herself. To me, that would be logical. Because I never bought the story of Eve going to a bookstore and carving out a new identity by reading texts. It just sounds too rehearsed, too . . . TV."

" 'The will to survive' . . . 'be prepared' . . ." Rina thought for a moment. "Eve was subconsciously parroting her grandmother's words."

"Not only parroting her words—reliving her story."

"But Peter, if Eve was horrified by her grandmother, why would she take on her name and story?"

"Because this time, Eve decided to reinvent Grandma as a good person, a kindly person who not only likes Jews but wants to learn more about them. It's no accident that she showed up at your class, Rina. And it's no accident that she chose to confide in you."

Rina felt weak. "How do we break it to her?"

Decker shook his head. "We don't. Even if it's true, neither one of us is equipped to deal with it. Eve needs to find a psychiatrist who's familiar with these kinds of traumas. Then we tell the psychiatrist what we found out, and leave it up to his or her professional judgment." He grinned at her. "Which was what I suggested in the first place."

"I know, I know." Rina managed a tepid smile. "Thanks for helping."

"Are you okay? You don't look well."

"I don't feel well. I know you told me this could happen. I was forewarned." She sighed. "Unfortunately, I wasn't forearmed."

Eve had eagerly agreed to an initial round of therapy—six sessions, one per week. During the first session, the psychiatrist started the slow process with an intake and history, leaving Eve unsatisfied. She needed her identity now! She needed hypnosis! But the doctor refused to rush the therapy.

So she dropped him and went to someone else—not a psychiatrist this time, but a hypnotherapist. As far as Rina was concerned, he was not qualified to handle Eve's delicate situation, and she wanted no part of it. But Eve begged her to accompany her to the appointment, and Rina relented.

As the session progressed, Eve broke into tears, sobbing bitterly. But she divulged little except to say that her name was Sarah Miller. Twenty minutes later, Rina insisted the hypnosis be stopped. Eve was too emotionally wrought to go on.

Afterward, Rina walked her home, staying with her until Eve/Sarah insisted she was all right. The next day Rina went to check on her, but it was too late. There was no answer at the door. The apartment was empty. The young woman had packed up and left.

Decker had not expected easy resolution, and Eve's behavior came as no surprise to him. Rina hadn't expected much, either, but still, she was sharply disappointed. For months, neither of them talked about Eve. Then one night, just as Rina was drifting off to sleep, Decker said out of the blue, "I wonder what she's doing. Whether she really has any memory of what happened."

Rina turned to face him. "I'd hate to think of her flitting around in one confused mental state after another," she said. A pause. "Maybe she's gone home to make peace with her grandmother."

Decker said, "How would you feel about that?"

Rina didn't answer right away. "I don't know. It's a terrible position to be in, to love a woman who once was a monster. Still, even though Ava Mueller would be an old woman now, perhaps even frail, she has innocent blood on her hands. She ought to be held accountable for her actions."

Decker ran his finger over the rise of Rina's cheekbone. "Maybe that's why Eve came to you in the first place."

"Why?"

"To see if you, as a Jew, were capable of forgiveness."

"There's nothing to forgive. Eve didn't do anything wrong. Even my parents, who are camp survivors, don't believe in collective guilt."

"Not to forgive her, to forgive her grandmother. Could you have done that if Eve had asked you?"

Rina thought about it, then slowly shook her head. "No, I couldn't have forgiven Ava Mueller, because I'm in no position to grant that forgiveness. The only people who can do that are long since dead."

"I know. But it's sad to think of Sarah going around with this burden. Do you think she'll ever make peace with her guilt?"

"I don't consider guilt a burden," Rina answered. "To me, guilt is the police department of the human soul. No offense, Peter, but cops can be pains in the neck. But think of how bad we all would be if they weren't around."

"Maligning my profession?" Decker laughed.

"Not at all. I'm complimenting it."

"Yeah, right! Let's go to sleep."

She kissed her husband good night and then stared up at the darkened ceiling. As her mind free-associated, Rina thought not of Sarah Miller but of a crime more than half a century old, and of those lives taken prematurely. She said a prayer for the deceased, and her words comforted her. As she fell asleep, Rina wondered if Sarah Miller would ever find words to comfort herself.

The STALKER

"The Stalker" deals with the double-edged sword of idolization and adoration. This is a case of obsession and compulsion gone horribly wrong, until it reaches its terrifying conclusion.

IT WAS HARD FOR HER TO FATHOM HOW IT all went so sour, because in the beginning the love had been sweet. The roses and candy that had been sent for no occasion, the phone calls at midnight just to say "I love you," the amorous notes left in her mailbox or on the desk at work, his stationery always scented with expensive cologne. The many romantic things that he had done during their courtship were now a thousand years old.

Somewhere buried beneath rage and hatred lay the honeyed memories. Julian telling her how beautiful and alluring she was, how he loved her lithe body, her soft hazel eyes and silken chocolate-kissed hair. Bragging to his friends about her rapier wit or whispering in her ear about how her lovemaking had made him weak-kneed. The last compliment had always been good for giggles or the playful slap on his chest. How she had blushed whenever he had raised his brows, had given her his famous wolfish leer.

The evening of his proposal had been the pinnacle of their fairy-tale romance, starting off with the Rolls-Royce complete with a uniformed driver. The chauffeur had offered her his arm, escorting her into the back of the white Corniche.

The most fabulous night of her life. And even today, steeped in righteous bitterness and bottomless hostility, she would admit that this sentiment still rang true.

There had been the front-row tickets at the theater. The

play, *The Fall of the House of Usher,* had been sold out for months. How he had gotten the seats had only added to Julian's aura of mystery and intrigue. Following the drama had been the exclusive backstage party where she had met the leading actors and actresses. They were all renowned stars, and she had actually *talked* to them. Well, truth be told, mostly she had gushed and they had murmured polite thank-yous. But just *being* there, being part of the crowd . . .

She had thought herself in a dream.

And the dream had continued. After the play had come the elegant candlelight dinner in the city's most expensive restaurant. Julian had preordered the menu—a peek of what was to come. But that evening she had mistaken his controlling nature for élan and confidence. He had arranged everything, starting with the appetizers—beluga caviar accompanied by blinis and crisp cold vodka. Next came a puree of warmed beets served with a dollop of sour cream and a sprinkle of chives. Then a salad of wild greens, followed by a lemon sorbet to clear the palate. All the courses enhanced with the appropriate wines.

She always remembered the feast clearly. So real. If she thought about it long enough, she'd wind up salivating.

The delectable beef Wellington dressed with pungent, freshly ground horseradish, accompanied by boiled red potatoes and julienne carrots and celery. And the desserts! The most sumptuous pastry cart. To complete the evening's meal, a deep, full-bodied sherry aged over fifty years.

They had eaten and eaten, and afterward their stomachs had bulged to dangerous proportions. So he had suggested a ride to the lake. They had walked the banks in bare feet, small wavelets spilling liquid silver over their toes and onto the shore. How beautiful he had looked that night, his fine sandy hair slightly disheveled by a rippling breeze, gentle blue eyes full of longing and love. At the perfect moment, he had wrapped his arms around her waist. Strong, muscular arms in perfect proportion with his hard, well-worked body. During the kiss, he had slipped the diamond on her finger.

It had been pure magic.

That night she felt as if she had died and gone to heaven. Looking back on everything that had transpired since, she wished she had.

Subtle changes, barely noticeable at first. The catch in his voice when she came home a few minutes late . . . the questions he had asked.

What happened?

Who were you with?

Why didn't you call, Dana?

She explained herself, but he never seemed satisfied. She brushed off his nosiness and irritation. It was because he cared.

Then there were other things. The lipstick in her purse placed in the wrong zippered compartment, her clothing drawers in disarray even after she distinctly remembered folding her sweaters neatly. Finally came the strange clicks on the extension when she talked to a girlfriend or her mother.

No, it couldn't be, she would tell herself. *Why would Julian want to listen in on my boring conversation?*

Yet the clicks continued—day after day, month after month. At last she summoned her nerve and asked him about it. At first he had waved her off as imagining things. She took him at his word because the clicks seemed to suddenly stop.

But they returned—occasional at first, then once again at frequent intervals.

He'd been eavesdropping: Of that she was sure. She was puzzled by his odd behavior, then angry. He was violating her privacy, and that was inexcusable. Another discussion was in order. Despite his initial denials, she knew he was lying. So she pressed him.

Her first mistake. He exploded, raising the phone upward, yanking it out of its jack, and heaving it against the wall.

"*Goddammit, Dana!* If *you* wouldn't tie up the phone so long, *I* wouldn't have to pick up the extension to see when you finished your conversation."

Tears welled up in her eyes; her ears were shocked with disbelief. She stammered, "J-Julian, why didn't you just ask me to get off the phone?"

"I shouldn't have to *ask* you; you should goddamn *know*." He was breathing very hard. Suddenly, he lowered his voice. It became quieter but not any softer. "A wife should know what her husband wants. And where's your consideration, for God's sake? What kind of a *wife* are you, anyhow?"

Stunned, she turned on her heels to leave. He caught her arm, spun her around. Spittle at the corners of his mouth, red angry blotches on his face. His fingers clamped around her arm like an iron manacle. And his *eyes*! They had turned into hot pits of violence. She shrank under his scrutiny. His voice so whispery it was sepulchral.

"You don't . . . *ever* . . . walk out on me, you hear?"

Paralyzed with fear, she hadn't been able to respond. When Julian repeated his demand a second time, the threat in his tone even more menacing, she somehow managed a nod.

It was the first of many incidents. The slightest insult—real or imagined—sent him into fits of uncontrollable temper and rage. Though he never actually hit her, his demonic eyes were enough to cause her to cower. She didn't dare tell anyone the truth. Sinking faster and faster into a quicksand pit of despair and loneliness, she knew she had only two options: to die or to escape.

Her defection was quick and complete. One day when he was away at work, Dana simply packed up her meager belongings and left. For six months, she hid under many aliases and assumed identities. As expected, he caught up with her. But six months was a long enough time for her to recover her ground. She boldly marched into the lawyers' offices. A few months later, Julian was served divorce papers along with an official restraining order. She knew that the order had little enforcement or protection power; a weak remedy akin to the Dutch boy plugging up the dike by putting his finger in the hole.

So she took precautions. Every time Dana got into or out of her car, she scanned her surroundings, looking over both shoulders. Keys gripped in her right hand, Mace locked into the fingers of her left hand, she always made it a point to walk quickly from her car to her destination, her head pivoting from side to side, her ears and eyes alert, attuned to the simplest of nuances, perceiving imminent danger out of seemingly innocuous events.

"Terrible to live like this," Dana muttered angrily to herself, "but what is the alternative?"

Dana knew Julian was possessed, just too crazy to be dealt with. Maybe it was because the wound was so raw. She hoped that things would get better after the divorce. Julian was no dummy. Surely he'd come to his senses and realize that his obsession was no solution for either of them.

The day their marriage was declared legally over, things became even worse. First came the midnight tapping on her door. Then the rattling of windows and the unexplained jiggling of doorknobs. One night, after weeks of having been mentally tortured by his lunatic hovering, she drew up enough strength to investigate. In a wild burst of energy, she threw open the front door only to witness an eerie dark landscape of streets and trees and houses, all devoid of human intrusion.

A portent of things to come. He always seemed to disappear just out of fingertips' reach.

The sounds continued, so Dana moved—and moved and moved. But he always seemed to find her. Not that he ever showed his face directly; Julian was too much the coward for that. Still, she was aware of his presence *wherever* she went, *whatever* she did. He appeared as furtive shadows and distant ghosts.

And always at night.

Sometimes she could swear she actually saw him, her fleeting phantom. At these times she'd run down the street, cursing his name. People thought her crazy.

And Dana felt as if she *was* going crazy. Because no matter how hard she tried, she failed to catch him. Julian seemed to fade into the mist until nothing but air was left behind. Nerves frayed, Dana couldn't eat, and her weight dropped dangerously low. Fearful for her sanity, she remained housebound except for essential errands. In desperation, she bought a guard dog, a German shepherd that abruptly died one day from food poisoning. She bought another dog. The second canine, Tiger, was killed by a vicious hit-and-run motorist, the vehicle throwing the dog twenty feet into the air, breaking every bone in its body. The driver, of course, was never caught.

In the animals' martyrdom, Dana finally found an inner strength. Something erupted inside Dana's soul when she carried Tiger's carcass, lovingly wrapped in a warm blanket, to the vet. Nobody should be able to get away with this.

So she began to fight back. At first, she carried a knife in her purse. When she learned that carrying a concealed knife was a felony, she switched over to a gun. Concealing a revolver was just a misdemeanor, and she could live with that. With her last spare dollars, she purchased an unregistered .32 Smith & Wesson on the black market. Then she began to learn how to use it. Weekly visits to the shooting range became daily visits. Developing her accuracy, her reflexes, her eye. Six months later, she felt as if she had parity with the bastard.

She felt *empowered*!

Just try anything now, Julian. Just try *it.*

If he dared to make a move, so would she.

She was ready.

Frequent moves during the last year did little to enhance Dana's job résumé. After months of rejection in her trained field of social work (who wanted a therapist whose own life was in shambles?), Dana gave up on employment in counseling. Determined to beat her spate of terrible fortune, she managed to land a job as a sales representative for a small family-owned medical supply company. Her job necessitated lots of travel, visits to hundreds of doctors' offices and hospitals scattered over the Southern California area.

To Dana's surprise, she loved her work. Her hours were her own, and she liked working with people. The unexpected bonus was *Julian*. The son of a bitch had been able to prey upon her when her routine consisted of driving to and from the market. But with her on the road most of the time, traveling from office to office, the bastard just couldn't seem to keep up with her schedule. It was too hard for him to stalk over wide distances.

As a traveling salesperson, Dana was meticulous about the care and upkeep of her car. So she was surprised when her Volvo—usually as reliable as a dray horse—stalled on the freeway.

Of course this had to happen at night.

Quickly, she pulled the car over to the side, shut off the motor, shifted back to neutral, and tried again. The engine kicked in but knocked loudly as she drove. Then the motor started smoking.

By her calculations, she was still some twenty miles away from home. Immediately, she pulled the car off the freeway, hoping to find a twenty-four-hour service station. But as Dana peered over the deserted ink-washed streets, she decided that getting off the freeway had been a bad idea. Better to be in a trafficked area. She'd phone the AAA from a freeway call box.

Though Dana had only traveled around six blocks, she had abruptly lost her sense of direction. She made a couple of turns, her car bucking at each shift of the wind. Abandoned and fearful, she felt swallowed up by urban decay.

The engine heaved a final hacking cough before dying. Again Dana tried to breathe life into the machine. Though the motor turned over and over, wheezing like an asthmatic, it refused to kick in.

Suddenly, Dana was aware of her heartbeat.

She had been on the road for over three hours, coming back from San Bernardino. She knew she was somewhere in downtown Los Angeles but wasn't exactly sure where. She had taken the Los Angeles Street exit from the Santa Monica Freeway. During the day, Los Angeles Street held small shops and open-air stalls of discount apparel. But late at night, as the hands on Dana's watch approached the witching hour, the streets were ugly and desolate.

She didn't panic, though. Her .32 was in her glove compartment. She inserted the key into the box's lock, turned it to the left, and then the door dropped like a drawbridge. She picked up the hard-packed metal. Moonlight struck her eyes as she examined her reflection in the nickel-plated steel. Without thinking, she realized she was fixing her hair.

Well, that makes sense, Dana. Primp and preen so you'll look attractive to all those rapists.

She let the gun drop to her lap and tried the engine for a final time. The motor spat out rapid clicks that sounded like rounds of muted machine-gun fire.

She yanked the keys out of the ignition and threw them in her purse. Exhaling out loud, she rooted through the glove compartment until she found the box of bullets. Little compact things. For a minute she fingered them like worry beads, the slender pellets picking up sweat from her hands. Then she loaded the gun. Checking the safety catch, she stowed the revolver inside her jacket.

Dana got out of the car.

She shut the door, securing the car with the beep of a remote. Forget about fixing the damn engine. Just walk back to the freeway, find a roadside phone, call a taxi, and get the hell home. She'd worry about the Volvo in the morning.

If it was still there in the morning. The neighborhood was rich with car thieves and other bad actors.

Don't even think about it.

The sky was foggy, moonlight glowing iridescent through the mist. It was good that there was a moon out tonight, because the streetlights offered little illumination. Just tiny spots of yellow blobs looking like stains of dog piss.

First things first, Dana thought. *Find out where you parked so you can direct the AAA back in the morning.*

She had stalled in the middle of a long, deserted block. Nothing much in the way of immediate landmarks. The street held old two-story buildings fronted with iron bars and grates. As Dana's eyes swept over the street, she noticed a few vacant lots between the stores, breaking up the rows like a giant smile missing a couple of teeth.

Most of the buildings were in disrepair. Some of them had bricks missing from the facades; others had their surface stucco pocked by bullets. All the structures were heavily graffitied. The shops were chockablock retail outlets. Dust-covered windows displayed kitchen supplies and tool chests sitting next to boom boxes, CD players, and television sets. Dresses and jackets were strung on clotheslines across the ceiling, the apparel looking like headless apparitions. Nothing distinct about any of the shops. No names stenciled onto the doors or windows, and the signs above were illegible in the dark.

Just get home and worry about it later.

Warding off the willies, Dana hurried toward the nearest street corner, hearing footsteps echoing behind her. Though wrapped in a wool jacket, Dana realized her legs, encased in thin nylon, were freezing. Her feet, shoved into hard leather pumps, felt like ice blocks. Looking over her shoulders, eyes darting about, she jogged stiffly to the corner, heels clacking against the sidewalk.

No street signs.

Where was she? And where the *hell* was the freeway? She couldn't see in the dark, couldn't make out any elevated roads of concrete. Dana knew she hadn't driven very far from the freeway. Damn thing had to be around here someplace.

A distant shriek made her jump. Who or what had made that noise? A victim's cry for help? Someone whooping for joy? Maybe it was just a night owl.

Heart racing, she realized she was breathing too fast.

Don't panic! Dana instructed herself. *Use your brain!*

No, she couldn't see the freeway. But she could hear it. A soft, distant whooshing of cars passing by at high speeds.

Follow the noise. She turned left at the corner.

Walking toward the sound, making sharp taps on the pavement. Her hands were numb, frigid fingers stuffed into her pockets.

Another turn. She couldn't be far from the on-ramp now.

Her footsteps reverberating, trailing her like Hansel and Gretel's bread crumbs.

Clack, clack, clack, clack . . .

The blast of a motorcycle shot through the air. Dana stopped, jumped, brought her hand to her chest. She took a deep breath and pressed on. A turn right, then a turn left. Passing one store after another, her stride quick and efficient.

Clack, clack, clack, clack . . .

Another block. More stores. A disquieting sense of sameness . . . stillness.

A ghost town.

Then the strained rumbling of a semi going uphill.

Freeway noises.

Yet the sounds were as distant as before. Was she walking in circles? Toward the noises? Away from the noise? She was disoriented, lost, and scared.

A chill ran down her spine. She spun around, her eyes catching a glimpse of a shadow.

Or did they?

She was seeing things.

A turn to her left, something darted out of sight.

Her imagination playing head games.

Stop it! she ordered herself.

She began to sweat, clay-cold fingers now slippery wet. She rubbed clammy fingers on her skirt. Looked all around.

Go back to the car!

Where was the car?

Moisture poured off her forehead.

She turned around, heels going clack, clack, clack, clack . . .

Noises followed her.

She stopped cold in her tracks.

Silence.

She continued on, then heard the foreign noises again.

Little pat-pat noises. Rubber-soled shoes—like rodents scurrying in the attic.

Again she stopped.

And so did the noises.

What to do! What to do!

Julian!

Son of a bitch!

This time he was going to get her.

Or so he thought!

She willed herself to breathe slowly, rubbed her hands together.

She took a few steps forward.

Clack, clack, clack, followed by pat, pat, pat.

She stopped walking.

So did he.

She pivoted around.

Nothing to see. Nothing to hear. A quiet night except for the rapid inhalations of her own breathing. Slowly she made out distant echoes.

A few more steps.

She stopped, jerked her head over her shoulder. Saw nothing but dewy air.

Kept walking.

More footsteps behind her.

She started running.

So did he.

Footsteps keeping pace with her, *stalking* her. Louder, harder, closer. Panic seized her body.

Don't turn around. Don't let the bastard see your fear.

And then the absurdity hit her.

Your fear?!

You're letting the bastard make you feel *fear*?!

Slowly, her right hand reached for her revolver, icicle-hard fingers gripping the butt of the gun.

With shaking hands, she retracted it from her jacket.

This is for you, you *bastard*!

No more!

Trembling so hard, she almost dropped to her knees.

No more, no more, no more!

End it all, Dana!

Right now!

Here!

At this moment!

No more running!

No more hiding!

No more *fear*!

Skidding to a stop, she swung around on her heels, gun grasped in a professional two-handed hold.

Shouting, "Freeze, you filthy *bastard*!"

But he didn't freeze!

Immediately, the air spewed forth hot white lights. Like bursts from firecrackers, except it wasn't the Fourth of July. Deafening shots ringing in the air, exploding in her head!

Still, the bastard kept coming at her!

Falling at her!

His mouth open—frozen into a horrific silent scream.

Blood pouring from his gullet.

Crying out as he lunged helplessly toward her, hitting her chest, knocking her backward. A dull thud as he hit the ground facedown. Dana could hear the crunch of facial bones smashing against the hard pavement.

Dana screamed—a helpless siren that was heard by no one. Staggering to keep her balance, seeing tiny pinpoints of light.

Don't faint, she pleaded with herself. *Don't faint!*

Breathing hard and deeply, eyes intently focused on the corpse lying at her feet. Her fingers were still gripped around a trigger.

A simple death wasn't enough for the years of abuse he had inflicted on her.

Aiming the barrel toward the crumpled body.

Pressing the trigger harder and harder.

Take *that,* you slimy bastard!

Take *that*, and *that*, and *that*!

But the gun refused to spit fire.

Jammed!

But how could that . . .

Then her brain spun into overdrive as her eyes noticed the reason why.

The safety catch was still on.

The gun hadn't jammed.

The gun never went off!

Then how did she . . . how could . . .

Eyes drifting upward from the body to the erect figure in front of her.

Julian!

A smoking gun at his side. An evil smirk on his face.

In the still midnight mist, his soft-spoken words screamed derision inside her head.

"Just can't survive without me, can you, Dana?"

He started walking toward her.

"Gun can't help you if you don't have the guts to use it. And you don't have the guts, do you?"

His mocking smile widening as he came closer.

"Lucky for you, I was around. Otherwise, you'd have been turned into hamburger by Mr. Shit over there."

Julian kicked the body, moved another step closer to her.

"Speak, my love," he crooned. "A simple thank-you would be sufficient."

Tears pouring from her eyes, streaming down her face, Dana whispered out a sob-choked thank-you.

Julian's expression softened, but his smug smile remained.

"I'll always be around for you, Dana," he whispered. "Always. Because I love you. I can't escape you, Dana. And you can't escape me, either."

She nodded.

Julian fell to his knees. "It's never too late, my beautiful lover. Come back to me. Come back to where you belong."

He stood, then raised his arms, ready to accept her embrace.

She raised her arms.

Unlocking the safety, she pumped six rounds of fiery lead into his body.

He died with the smirk still on his face.

At the eulogy, Dana spoke of his extraordinary valor. How he had saved her from a sick and deranged man with evil on his mind. Through molten gunshots and powder-choked air, in a moment's flash of unthinking selflessness, he had risked his life to save hers. Managing to squeeze off enough rounds to end her attacker's life before succumbing to his own mortal wounds. And because of his superhuman act, her life was spared while his own life had ended. His years . . . cut short . . . in his prime . . . just because of one man's treacherous deeds.

The funeral was crowded. His mother cried bitterly. His sisters wept and wept. It seemed that all the neighbors had come out to pay their last respects. Everyone attending the ceremony knew his history. Yet they were all more than a little puzzled by Dana's flowery words, her effusive commendations and praises.

And so it came to pass that Eugene Hart, a twenty-two-year-old felon with a long and notorious history of brutal violence and rape, was put to rest with a hero's burial.

MUMMY *and* JACK

with Jesse Kellerman

"Mummy and Jack"—an acid fable centered on a peculiar mother and son—is the product of my first collaboration with my son, Jesse. A novelist as well as a playwright, Jesse has infused the story with his own unique brand of dark humor, a trait shared by his father and mother. This just goes to show that a twisted mind can be a genetic endowment.

WHEN I WAS SMALL, MUMMY WOULD say, *if ye're a good boy, then I will tell ye a bedtime story.* But now she cannot because she is too sick. The time has come now that I must take care of her and not the other way around. I must do things for Mummy. I must get Mummy her medicine and buy her spirits. I must bring Mummy her supper every night. Yet she is not yet so sick and old that she cannot tell me what to do. She has her opinions.

Lately, this has become more of a problem because I want (and she wants me to also, I think) to court a lass or two, and I must bring the lass home to have a proper introduction. Sometimes Mummy makes this very difficult. Her opinions. They are very strong opinions. I am, however, a proper-raised gentleman, and I have been educated in the way that makes me respect Mummy even if her opinions are extremely particular and particularly strong. I always do my best to make her happy.

Sometimes I do wish for a bedtime story, though.

A couple of weeks ago, I decided to go out for a stroll at night. I groomed my mustache. Mummy likes my mustache, and she tells me that I look very right and handsome. I like it when I please her. I straightened my freshly starched waistcoat, then I took my cane, my cloak, and some other things. I did not think it was late in the evening, but Mummy heard me opening the door.

Jack! she called to me.

Yes, Mummy? I said like a good boy says.

Jack, where are y'goin'?

I am goin' for a walk, I said.

It's too late in the night, Jack, she said.

It's not so late, Mummy. I thought of mebbe gettin' a bit of air . . .

Don't go, Jack! she said. She was almost screaming at me from the other room, and her voice was like a very sharp knife. *Don't leave me here, Jackie!*

Her voice made me hurt quite bad. I thought that maybe she was going to die if I left her alone. All of a sudden I got frightened. So I went to her room to make sure that she was well. When I peeked my head through the door, I could see that she was surrounded by a big pile of pillows (pillows I bought with money that I had earned for her) looking like a fat white man hugging her tight. She was sitting up in bed and maybe even crying a little. It hurts me when she cries with her voice so little and full of pain. Especially because she looks so weak, with her thin bones and white hair.

Please don't go, Jack! she begged.

I will come back soon, Mummy, I said. *I am goin' to bring some spirits. I'll bring y' back a pint.* (I knew that Mummy likes an occasional pint and she would be happy if I offered to bring her one.)

Oh, would ye, Jack? That would be so nice . . . so nice.

I will come back soon and bring ye a pint, Mummy, I promised.

Oh, but not a pint. Bring us some red wine, Jack, she said. *Port, if you will, Jackie. That makes me bones very warm.*

Right, then, Mummy, I answered. *Some old red port.*

Thankee, Jackie, said she, gratefully.

I left the house and walked around for a bit. After some time, I was very far from where we lived. I was not certain where I was, although I thought I might be in Whitechapel. I wanted to hear my mummy's voice telling me a bedtime story, and feel her giving me wet kisses on my forehead. There was a big clock striking the late hour, and I thought that I would get Mummy her wine and maybe a pint for myself. (Because it was a very soggy night and I wanted to warm my bones.) Afterward, I would go home and go to bed.

Instead, I came upon a lass out walking. She was very short and stout, and she had an ugly smile, but she looked like she wanted to be my friend. I thought that because she walked up to me and said, *Allo, sir, how are ye?*

I said, *I'm fine, thankee. Why are you here so late at night?*

She began to laugh, like a horse throwing its head back and sniffing the air. I could see tiny blue lines in her fat neck where her blood was. It was not a pretty neck, although I have seen pretty necks: long, stretchy white necks, like swans gliding in the lake in the park. I touched the stiff edge of my collar and waited for her to talk again. Her face was dirty, and the sleeve of her dress was ragged, like it had been chewed.

I know ye want to buy me a nip o' gin, sir, she said. *Will ye buy me a nip?*

Since I had to go get some wine for Mummy, and the lass seemed nice enough, I told her I could buy her a nip.

Oh, you're a good boy! said the lass.

(Of course, I know I am a good boy, because Mummy tells me that all the time. I try very hard to be a good boy for her.)

What's your name, sir? she asked.

Jack, I said.

You're a good boy, Jack, said the lass. *My name is Annie.*

It is an honor to meet you, Annie, I said. Lasses like that, when I talk courtly. Annie liked it, and she laughed again.

Come on, then, she said. *Let's get us a drop!*

I went with Annie to a pub and bought Mummy's port. Annie wanted a gin, and so I bought her a nip. She was thirsty, and she took the whole glass at once. I thought her gulping a bit common and lower-class, but when she asked me for another, I bought it for her. Then she asked for a third.

I've not got any more money, Annie, I said.

Oh, my! she said. *Well, then, I shall have to find another man to buy me a nip. Because it is a cold, damp night.*

No, Annie, I said. *Don't go.* (Because I was starting to fancy her.)

Well, sir, I don't want to go because ye have been so nice to me. But I am very thirsty. Then she laughed again.

I thought that Mummy would be very thirsty by this time, so I decided that I should go home. But I still fancied Annie.

I said, *Annie, can I ask ye to supper? I can give you a bit of gin that I've got back at home.*

Annie smiled at me with a big brown rotted smile. *It's too late for supper, but I can give ye a bite if you want, sir.*

No, thankee, I said for I was not hungry. *Why don't ye come for supper on Friday, then?*

Oh, sir, said Annie, *that would be quite nice.*

I shall come to get ye, Annie.

Thankee, luv, she said. *Come to get me here.*

Cheers, I said, then left and headed toward home. The whole walk home, I tripped over rats running beneath me in the fog. The misty air was like a big fish swallowing the street. I wanted to be home and to hear a bedtime story before I went to sleep. But when I did get home, Mummy was asleep. I put the wine in the cupboard and went to bed with no bedtime story (which made me feel quite lonely).

The next morning I told Mummy that I had invited a guest for supper for next week.

Who's that? she asked.

A lass, said I.

Jack! Why are ye bringing lassies home? she scolded me.

She wanted to meet ye, Mummy.

It's not proper to bring lassies home! she yelled. *Not proper at all!*

Then I remembered the port and brought it from the cupboard. While I poured her drink, I said, *She is nice, Mummy.*

Mummy drank a bit. Then she drank a wee bit more and smiled. She said to me, *Well, I must meet her if ye think she is nice, my Jackie.*

She is nice, Mummy, I said.

She had another nip and said, *Mummy can tell ye if she is a proper lass or not.*

I said that was why I wanted Mummy to meet her.

Good boy, that y'think of your mummy. You were raised a proper gentleman, my Jack.

I was very happy when she said this. There are times that Mummy makes me very happy. Even if she has her sharp opinions.

The following week I walked out again and found the pub where Annie was supposed to be. She was not there, and I waited for her. The barman tried to give me drinks, but I did not want to drink anything.

Get out if you're not goin' to be buying somethin'! he yelled. *You're in a pub, you fool.*

I am waiting for a lass, I answered.

Who, then, are ye waitin' for? he asked me.

Annie, said I.

What Annie? said the man.

Jest Annie is her name.

Ye can wait outside, then, said the man.

I waited outside near the door. Annie came, but she was late. She almost did not see me. She almost walked through the door without saying hello. But I took her on the elbow, and that got her to turn around.

Allo, Annie, I said.

Allo, mate, she said. *Buy me a slug, will ye?*

I looked at her, and she stared back as if she did not know my face.

Ye are coming for supper, then? I asked.

Supper? Why would I come with ye to supper? she asked.

I thought she was playing a game. *Annie, ye said ye'd come the night to supper with me,* I explained.

Buy me a nip o' gin, and I'll come to supper with ye, she said.

All right, then, Annie. I'll buy you a nip.

We went inside. I bought her a gin and then a few more. She was soon very happy to come to supper, although I was no longer so certain she should come. She was tipsy, and Mummy does not think it proper for a lass to be tipsy.

I tried to tell her that, but she laughed in my face. Still, she followed me all the way to home. I opened the door, and Annie walked in behind me. *Annie,* said I, *do ye know any bedtime stories?*

Aye, she answered. *I know every story every man wants to hear. But first I want a nip o' gin.*

I told her soon, after supper. Mummy could not lay the table, being so sick. So I put the cutlery out. Then I took dishes and gave them to Annie.

Lay the dishes, please, Annie, for I must go to see how Mummy is getting on. Then I went to see Mummy.

She was waiting for me. *Is that lass here?* she asked.

Yes, Mummy, she's here, I replied. *Do ye want to eat with us, or shall I bring ye something in bed?*

I think I'll eat with ye, Mummy said. *Bring me to the table, my Jackie.*

I lifted her up and brought her to the table, and Annie was sitting there. She had not yet laid any dishes.

Did ye not lay the table, girl? asked Mummy.

Annie looked at Mummy with bleary eyes and did not say anything, which I thought was very rude.

I brought to the table a piece of cold beef, bread, and water.

Ye said you'd give me a nip, Annie said.

Annie was not behaving the way I thought she would with Mummy present, but I gave her a bit of gin anyway. Then she was quiet for a minute. Mummy ate a few bites of beef and bread. Then she said to Annie, *What're y'called, lassie?*

Annie Chapman, ma'am.

Annie Chapman, said Mummy. *Where did ye meet my Jack?*

Annie drank and did not say a word. But my mummy

continued, *Jack is a good boy, Miss Annie Chapman. Do y'know that?*

Aye, ma'am, answered Annie, *he's a good boy.*

He was not always such a good boy, said Mummy.

Annie looked up from her nip. *How's that?*

Once, when he was a wee lad, he tore up all my linen, Mummy said, coughing and cackling. *Do ye remember that, Jack?*

Yes, I said. I was a bit embarrassed.

Said Mummy, *I was quite cross with him when he was young because he ruined everything. He was a little terror, my Jackie. A terror and a tearer. Jackie the Tearer. But now look how handsome he has grown up to be.*

Aye, Annie answered.

Do ye like his mustache? asked Mummy.

I do, said Annie.

Then Mummy et a bit more. Annie did not have any bread or beef, but she took another glass of gin. After a while Mummy turned to me and said, *Jackie, take us to bed, will ye?*

I carried her to her bedroom once again. Before I left, she whispered loudly to me, *Jack, I donna like the lass. She is not for a proper-raised gentleman like you.*

Oh, Mummy, I said. I was disappointed, but Mummy was sick, so I tried to hide it.

She does not smile like a young lady. Tonight she did not smile at all, Jack.

I have seen her smile, Mummy. Sometimes she smiles at me.

Mummy shook her head. *She does not smile big enough, Jackie. Not big like a bright young lassie is meant to smile!*

I listened to her words. They were not nice words, but they were proper. *Do ye think so, Mummy?*

I do, she replied.

Then what shall I do with her?

I donna care. Just get her away and come back to me, Jack.

I knew she was right. She is right always. *Ye are clever, Mummy.*

I jest want to save me boy from bad lassies, Jackie.

Ye love me, Mummy?

I do, Jackie, said Mummy. *You are my babe.*

I was so happy to hear her say that. I knew what could make her happier. I gave her a kiss on her head full of white hair and told her I'd be back soon.

I took the cutlery and the dishes to the cupboard and stowed almost everything away. *Come on, then, Annie,* said I. *It's time to take ye back home.*

Give another nip o' gin, luv, she cried.

We've got nothing to give ye, Annie, and so let's get a go.

Oh, but for a bit of gin!

Back in the pub, Annie, I said. *Let us go back to where I found ye.*

Aye, luv! she cheered.

We walked a bit. Then I said, *There's a nice pub over here, Annie.*

Where? Annie asked. *I donna see nothin'.*

It was true, because the street was dark and the place was very still.

Annie, said I, *Mummy said ye don't smile big enough.*

I cannot smile when I've got no drink in me, she answered.

I think ye should smile bigger, I said.

She pouted. *Then why don't y'make me smile bigger, luv.*

I can, Annie, I can, said I.

And then I made her smile the biggest smile she ever had.

When I got home, Mummy was asleep, so I could not tell her about Annie's big smile. I took off my clothes, which were quite wrinkled from walking home in the mist and fog that swallows up everything like a big fish.

The next morning I did not tell Mummy, because I wanted to keep it all a surprise for her birthday, which is very soon. She will know when I tell her. She will see what a good boy I am. And then maybe she will tell me a bedtime story. Perhaps even a bedtime story every night.

But tonight I shall go for a walk again and get my mummy a wee bit of port for her spirits. I do it because it makes her so happy to have her spirits. It is often hard to make Mummy happy because she has so many sharp opinions. But I try and try. I do it all because I love her.

BONDING

"Bonding" is probably the most disturbing tale that I've ever written. My very first short story written for a Sisters in Crime *anthology, it provides a stark contrast to Peter Decker and Rina Lazarus's supportive parenting style, something that I repeatedly emphasize in my novels. I wanted to write something radically different from my first novel,* The Ritual Bath, *and I suppose I did just that.*

I BECAME A PROSTITUTE BECAUSE I WAS bored. let me tell you about it. My mother is a greedy, self-centered egotist and a pill-popper. I don't think we exchange more than a sentence worth of words a week. Our house is very big—one of these fake-o hacienda types on an acre of flat land in prime Gucciland Beverly Hills—so it's real easy to avoid each other. She doesn't know what I do and wouldn't care if she did know. My father doesn't hassle me 'cause he's never around. I mean, *never* around. He rarely sleeps at home anymore, and I don't know why my parents stay married. Just laziness, I guess. So when my friend came around one day and suggested we hustle for kicks, I said sure, why not.

Our first night was on a Saturday. I dressed up in a black mini with fishnet stockings, the garters lower than the hem of my dress. I painted my lips bright red, slapped on layers of makeup, and took a couple of downers. I looked the way I felt—like something brought up from the dead. We boogied on down to the Strip, my friend supplying the skins, and made a bet: who could earn the most in three hours. I won easily; I didn't even bother to screw any of the johns—just went down on them in a back alley or right in their cars. I hustled seven washed-out old guys at sixty bucks a pop. Can't say it was a bundle of yuks, but it was different. Jesus, anything's better than the boredom.

The following day, after school, me and my friend got buzzed and went shopping at the mall. I took my hustle money and bought this real neat blouse accented with white and blue rhinestones and sequins. I also saw this fabulous belt made of silver and turquoise, but it was over a hundred and fifty dollars, and I didn't want to spend *that* much money on just a belt. So I lifted it. Even with the new electronic gizmos and the security guards, stealing isn't very hard, not much of a challenge.

Let me tell you a little about myself. I was born fifteen years ago, the "love child" of a biker and his teenage babe. I think my real mother was, like, twelve or thirteen at the time. I once asked my bitch of a mother about her, and she got *reeeallly* agitated. Her face got red, and she began to talk in that hysterical way of hers. The whole thing was, like, too threatening for her to deal with. Anyway, I was adopted as an infant. And I never remember being happy. I remember crying at my sixth birthday party 'cause Billy Freed poked his fingers in my Cookie Monster cake. Mom went bonkers—we hadn't photographed the cake yet—and started screaming at Billy. Then he started crying. God, I was mad at Billy, but after Mom lit into him, I almost felt sorry for the kid. I mean, it was only a cake, you know.

Once, when I was around the same age, my mom picked me up and we looked in the mirror together. She put her cheek against mine as we stared at our reflections. I remember the feel of her skin—soft and warm, the sweet smell of her perfume. I didn't know what I'd done to deserve such attention, and that frustrated me. Whatever I did, I wanted to do it again so Mom would hold me like this. But of course, I didn't do anything. Mom just stared at us, then clucked her tongue and lowered me back onto my feet with an announcement: I'd never make it on my looks.

Well, what the hell did she expect? Beggars shouldn't be choosers. It's not like someone forced her to adopt me. The bitch. Always blaming me for things out of my control.

Did I tell you Mom is beautiful? Must have slipped my mind. We forget what we want to, right? Mom is a natural blonde with large blue eyes and perfect cheekbones. I've got ordinary brown hair—thin, at that—and dull green eyes. It's been a real bitch growing up as her daughter. Mom turned forty last year, and she treated herself to a face-lift—smoothing out imaginary wrinkles. Now her face is so goddamn tight, it looks wrapped in Saran. Her body is wonderful, long and sleek. I'm the original blimpo—the kind of woman that those old artists liked to paint. I'm not fat but just really developed. Big boobs, big round ass. My mother used to put me on all these diets, and none of them ever worked. I finally told her to fuck herself and gorged on Oreo cookies. Ate the whole package right in front of her, and boy, did that burn her ass.

She gave me this little smirk and said, "You're only hurting yourself, Kristie."

"I'm not hurting myself," I said. "In fact, I'm enjoying myself!"

Then she walked away with the same smirk on her face.

She once went to bed with this guy *I* was sleeping with. Can you believe that? Happened last summer at our beach house. I caught the two of them together. Mom got all red-faced, the guy was embarrassed, too, but I just laughed.

Inside, though, I felt lousy. I felt lousy 'cause I knew that the guy really wanted to fuck her all along and was just using me as a stepping-stone.

You might ask where the hell was my dad when all this went down? I told you. He's never around.

My friend and co-hooker came down with strep throat today and asked if I could service her regular johns. I said sure. So I go to the room she rents. It's a typical sleaze-bucket of a place—broken-down bed, filthy floor, and a cracked mirror. Who should I see in it but my *father*? I turn my face away before he sees me. To tell you the truth, I barely recognize his face. Then I realize that he must have gotten a lift, like Mom, 'cause his skin is also like stretched to the max.

I'm shaking—half with fear, half with disgust. That dirty son of a bitch. Doing it with teenage hookers. Then I remember a few years ago. How he eyed my friends when we sat around the pool. How he strutted out of the cabana wearing red bikini briefs and shot a half-gainer off the diving board. My friends were impressed. He popped through the water's surface, a strange expression on his face.

It was lust.

I sneak another glance in the mirror.

He holds the same look in his eyes now.

What the hell do I do?

I think about running away, but I know my friend will be real pissed. Jesus.

My dad.

I can't screw my dad!

Then I think to myself, *My mom screwed* my *guy . . .*

But this is something different. He's my dad.

'Course, he isn't my dad by blood . . .

And it's been a long time since I've seen him . . .

The thought starts to excite me. Yeah, I know it's real perverse, but my whole family is perverse.

And at least it isn't boring.

I take a quick hit of some snow from the vial I wear around my neck. Man, I need to be buzzed to pull this one off.

I'm real excited by now.

I drop my voice an octave—I can do that 'cause I have a great range—and tell him to can the lights. He starts bitching and moaning that he likes to do it with the lights on, and where the fuck is my friend. I tell him my friend has strep and it's hard to give head with your throat all red and raw, and if he doesn't want me, fine, he just won't get laid tonight.

He cans the lights. The only illumination in the room comes from a neon sign outside that highlights his semi. It's a good-looking one, and it turns me on even further. But I stay well hidden in the shadows of the room.

I wonder what he'll think of my body after laying Mom all these years. Maybe he'll think I'm too fat, but the minute he touches my boobs, his you-know-what becomes ramrod-straight. I let him bury his head in my chest, kiss my nipples. I give him a line of coke, then I take another snort. My face is always hidden.

I ask him what kinds of things he wants to do, and he says everything. I say it will cost him two fifty, and he gets suddenly outraged. A real bad acting job. I know what he makes, and he could buy all of Hollywood if he wanted to. Anyway, by now he's too excited to argue, and five fifty-dollar bills are slapped into my wet hand. I do whatever he wants as long as he can't see my face.

When it's over, I tell him I have a surprise for him. He's lying in bed now, smoking a joint. Still naked, I saunter over to the light switch, then suddenly flip it on. The cheesy room is flooded with bright yellow light. We both squint, then he sees me. It takes him a moment, then I see his tanned, tight face drain of all its color. His eyes pop out and he begins to pant. His skin takes on a greenish hue and he runs for the toilet. I hear him throw up.

Afterward he cries in my arms. But we both know it's not over.

Dad came home at eleven tonight. Mom and he start fighting. They always fight, did I tell you that? Probably why Dad started staying away. Anyway, it's the first time I ever remember Dad coming home in like twenty years or something. I'm no dummy. I know what the sucker has in mind, and that's okay by me. After all, I'm not really his daughter by blood, you know.

He comes into my room at around two o'clock. I make him pay, and no shit, he agrees. Man, I know you're gonna think I'm sick, but I gotta tell you. My dad's all right in the sack.

This goes on for the next month. If Mom suspects anything, she doesn't say a word. Then a strange thing happens. Life is weird—very weird. A real strange thing happens.

We fall in love.

Or something like it.

We consider all the options. The first is running away

and giving me a new identity so that we can marry. The idea is discussed, then tossed in the circular file. Dad makes a couple a million buckeroos as a TV producer, and no way he could make that kind of money outside of L.A. Neither of us likes poverty.

We consider having Dad and Mom divorce and I'd live with Dad. That's out. California has stiff community-property laws, and the bitch would get half of *everything*!

There's only one option left.

First off, I gotta tell you that neither one of us really feel guilty about our decision 'cause: A, I'm not my dad's real daughter; and B, Mom has had this coming for a long time.

Way overdue.

We plan to do it next Saturday, right after she comes home from one of her parties. She's usually pretty sauced and hyped and has to pop some downers to get to sleep. We figure we'll help her along.

She comes in at two A.M., surprised that I'm still up. I say I was having trouble sleeping and offer to make her some hot coffee. She nods and dismisses me with a wave of her hand. Like I'm a servant instead of her daughter doing her a favor. I lace the java with Seconal. Halfway through the drink, her lids begin to close. But she knows something is wrong. She tells me she's having trouble breathing and asks me to call the doctor. I act like I'm real worried and place the phony call. By the time I hang up, she's out.

Both Dad and I are worried. She only drank half a cup, and we wonder if it's enough dope to do her in. Dad feels her pulse. It's weak but steady. A half hour later, her heartbeat is even stronger. Dad says, "What the hell do we do now?" I think and think and think, then come up with a really rad brainstorm.

I get ten tablets full of Seconal, crush them in water, and suck the mixture into my old syringe. Did I tell you I shoot up occasionally? When the boredom is just too much. I haven't done it for a while, but I keep the syringe—you know, just in case the mood hits me. I shoot the dope under her tongue. It's absorbed fast that way and doesn't leave any marks. A friend of mine told me that.

Dad feels her pulse for a third time. Squeezes her wrist hard. Nothing. *Nada!* We celebrate with a big hug and a wet kiss, then wash the cup and wipe the place clean of fingerprints.

A half hour later, Dad places a panic call to the paramedics.

God, I'm a great actress, carrying on like Mom and I were like bosom buddies.

"Mommmeeeee," I wail at the funeral.

Everyone feels sorry for me, but I don't accept their comfort.

My dad has his arm around me. He pulls me aside later on.

"You're overdoing it," he tells me.

"Hell, Paul." I call him Paul now. "I lost my fucking mother. I'm supposed to be upset."

"Just cool it a little, Kristie," Paul says. "Act withdrawn. Like someone took away your Aerosmith records."

I sulk for a moment, then say what the hell. He's older. Maybe he knows best. I crawl into this shell and don't answer people when they talk to me. They give me pitying looks.

The detective shows up at our door unannounced. He's a big guy with black hair, old-fashioned sideburns, and acne scars. My heart begins to take off, and I say I don't answer any questions without my dad around.

"Why?" he asks.

"I don't know," I respond. Then I ask him if he has a warrant.

He laughs and says no.

"I'm sorry," I say. "I can't help you."

"Aren't you supposed to be in school?" he asks.

"God, are you crazy?" I say. "I mean, with all that happened? I can't concentrate on school right now. I mean, I lost my *mother*!

"You two were pretty close, then."

"Real close."

"You don't look much like her," he remarks.

I feel my face changing its expression and get mad at myself. I say, "I'm adopted."

"Oh," the detective says. His face is all red now. "That would explain it."

Then he says, "I'm sorry to get personal."

"That's okay," I say, real generous.

There's a pause. Then the detective says, "You know, we got the official autopsy report back for your mother."

I feel short of breath. I try to keep the crack out of my voice. "What's it say?" I ask.

"Your mother died of acute toxicity," he says. "Drug OD."

"Figures," I say calmly. "She had lots of problems and was on and off all sorts of drugs."

He nods, then asks, "What kind of drugs did she take?"

Then all of a sudden I realize I'm talking too much. I tell him I don't know.

"I thought you two were close."

I feel my face go hot again.

"We were," I say. "I mean, I knew she took prescribed drugs to help her cope, but I don't know *which* drugs. Our relationship wasn't like that, you know."

"Why don't we just peek inside the medicine cabinet of your house?" he says.

I shake my head slowly, then say, "Come back tonight, when my dad is home. Around eight, okay?"

He agrees.

Paul has a shit-fit, but I assure him I handled it well. By the time the detective shows up, we're both pretty calm. I mean, all the drugs found in her stomach came from her own pills. And then there was the party she went to. I'm sure at least a half-dozen people remember her guzzling a bottle or two of white wine. She loved white wine—Riesling or Chardonnay.

My mother was an alcoholic. Did I tell you that?

The detective has on a disgusting suit that smells of mothballs. It hangs on him. He scratches his nose and says a couple of bullshitty words to Paul about how sorry he is that he had to intrude on us like this. Paul has on his best hound-dog face and says it's okay. Now I understand what he meant by not overdoing it. Man, is he good. *I* almost believe him.

"Sure," Paul says to the detective. "Take a look around the house."

I think about saying we've got nothing to hide, but don't. The detective goes over some details with Paul. My mom had gone to a party by herself. Paul didn't go 'cause he wasn't feeling well. At around three in the morning, he got up to get a glass of milk. I was asleep, of course. He went downstairs and found my mother dead.

"Where'd you find your wife?" the detective asks.

"On that chair right there."

Paul points to the Chippendale.

The detective walks over to the chair but doesn't touch it. He asks, "What'd you do when you found her?"

Paul is confused. He says, "What do you mean? I called the paramedics, of course."

"Yeah," the detective says. "I know that. Did you touch her at all?"

"Touch her?" Paul asks.

The detective says, "Yeah, feel if the skin was cold . . . see if she was breathing."

Paul shakes his head. "I don't know anything about CPR. I figured the smart thing to do was to leave her alone and wait for the paramedics."

"How'd you know she was dead?" the detective asks.

"I didn't *know* she was dead," Paul says back. His voice is getting loud. "I just saw her slumped in the chair and knew something was wrong."

"Maybe she was sleeping," suggests the detective.

"Her face was white . . . gray." Paul begins to pace. "I knew she wasn't sleeping."

"You didn't check her pulse, check to see if she was breathing?"

"He said no," I say, defending my dad. "Look . . ." I get tears in my eyes. "Why don't you leave us alone? Haven't we been through enough without you poking around?"

The detective nods solemnly. He says, "I'll be brief."

We don't answer him. We stay in the living room while he searches. A half hour later, the detective comes back carrying all of Mom's pills in a plastic bag. He says, "Mind if I take these with me?"

Paul says go ahead. As soon as he leaves, I notice Paul is white. I take his hand and ask him what's wrong. He whispers, "Your fingerprints were on the bottle."

I smile and shake my head no. "I wiped everything clean."

Paul smiles and calls me beautiful. God, no one has ever called me beautiful. Want to know something weird? Paul's a much better lover than he is a father. We make it right there on the couch, knowing it's a stupid and dangerous thing to do, but we don't care. An hour later we go to bed.

The fucking asshole pig comes back a week later with all his piglets. Paul is enraged, but the pig has all the papers in order—the search warrant, the this, the that.

Paul asks, "What is going on?"

"Complete investigation, Mr. James."

"Of *what*!"

"I don't believe your wife's death was an accidental overdose."

"Why not?" I ask.

Paul glares at me. The detective ignores me, and I don't repeat the question.

"What do you think it is?" Paul asks.

"Intentional overdose."

"Suicide?" Paul says. "No note was found."

"There isn't always a note," the detective responds. "Besides, I didn't mean suicide, I meant homicide."

My body goes cold when he says the word. The pig asks us if we mind being printed or giving them samples of our hair. Paul nudges me in the ribs and answers, "Of course not," for the both of us.

Then he adds, "We have nothing to hide."

Now I'm thinking that was a real dumb thing to say.

They start to dust the Chippendale, spreading black powder over the fabric. Paul goes loony and screams how expensive the chair is. No one pays attention to him.

He stalks off to his bedroom. I follow.

"What are we gonna do?" I whisper.

"You wiped away all the prints?" he whispers back.

I nod.

"They've got nothing on us, babe." He inhales deeply. "We'll just have to wait it out. Now, get out of here before someone suspects something."

I obey.

All the pigs leave about four hours later. They've turned our home into a sty.

Paul is becoming a real problem. He's losing it, and that's bad news for me. When I confront him with what a shit he's being, he starts acting like a parent. Can you believe that? He fucks me—his daughter—then, when he's losing it, he starts acting like a parent.

Yesterday he didn't come home at night. That really

pissed me off. I reminded him that we were in it together. That pissed *him* off, and he claimed the entire thing was *my* idea and that I was a witch and a whore. Man, what a battle we had. We're all made up now, but let me tell you something, we watch each other carefully.

Real carefully.

They arrested me this morning for the murder of my mother. They leave Paul alone for now. Apparently, whatever they have is just on me and not him.

To tell you the truth, I'm kind of relieved.

I'm left waiting in this interview room for about an hour. Just me and the detective. Finally, I say what I know I shouldn't say.

I say, "How'd you find out?"

"Find out what?" the detective answers.

"About my mom being murdered and all."

His eyebrows raise a tad.

"You mean, how'd I find out you murdered your mom?"

I know it's a trick, but what the fuck. I don't care anymore. I nod.

"Did you kill your mom, Kristine?"

He asks the question, like, real cool, but I can see the sweat under his armpits.

"Yeah," I admit. "I offed her."

"How?" he asks.

"I laced her coffee with her own Seconal," I say. "When that didn't do the trick, I injected her with more. That finished her off."

"Where'd you inject her?" he asks.

"Under her tongue."

He nods. "Smart thinking," he says. "No marks." Then he pauses and adds, "So you're a hype, huh?"

I shake my head. "Recreational," I say.

"Ah."

"So how'd you find out?" I ask again.

"Two other things set an alarm off in me," the detective says. "The autopsy report showed bruises on the inside of your mom's right wrist. Like someone squeezed her."

"Maybe someone did," I say.

The detective says, "Yeah, like someone was feeling for a pulse. Yet your dad denied touching her."

I say, "Maybe she was playing a little game with one of her lovers."

"I thought of that," the detective says. "She went to a pretty wild party. But then the bruises would have been on both of her wrists."

I don't say anything right away. Then I say, "You said two things. What was the second?"

"Your mom had loads of Seconal in her body, along with booze and coke. She also had just a trace amount of heroin. Too little, if she actually shot up a wad."

"My needle," I say. "I forgot to clean it."

"It's hard to remember everything, Kristie," the detective says. "I found it when I searched the house the first time, but I couldn't take it with me for physical evidence because I didn't have the proper papers. I waited a week until I had the search warrant in hand, then took it. We analyzed it, found traces of Seconal and heroin. People don't normally shoot Seconal. You should have dumped all your evidence."

"I never was too good at throwing things away. Mom

used to yell at me for that. Called me a bag lady, always keeping everything."

I sigh.

The detective says, "Also, we powdered your mom's meds and found they had been wiped free of prints. If your mom had committed suicide, her prints would have been on the bottle."

"I should have thought about that," I admit.

"Well, you did okay for your first time out," the detective says. "The marks on the wrist were a giveaway. Started me thinking in the right direction. You—or your dad—shouldn't have squeezed her so hard. And you should have used a fresh needle. And gloves instead of wiping away the prints."

He leans in so we're almost nose-to-nose.

"Close but no cigar. You're in hot shit, babe. Want to tell me about it?"

"What do you want to know?"

"Why'd you do it, for starters?" he asks.

" 'Cause I hated my mom."

"And why did your dad help you?"

"What makes you think my dad helped me?"

"The bruises on your mother's wrist were made by fingers bigger than yours, Kristie. It was your father who felt for the pulse, even though he emphatically denied touching her."

"You can't prove who made those bruises," I say.

The detective doesn't say anything. Then he sticks his hands in his pockets and says, "It's your neck. You could probably save it by turning state's evidence against your dad."

I don't say anything.

"Look," he says. "I understand why you offed your mom. She treated you like shit. And your dad offed her so he could marry his girlfriend—"

"What girlfriend?" I say, almost jumping out of my seat.

"The cute little blond chickie that was on his arm last night."

"You're lying," I say.

He looks genuinely puzzled. He says, "No, I'm not. What is it? Don't you get along with her?"

I feel tears in my eyes. I stammer out, "I . . . I don't even know her."

"Don't cotton to the idea of your dad making it with a young chick?" he asks.

"No," I say.

"Why's that?"

I blurt out, "Because *I'm* his girlfriend. We're *lovers*."

I hear the detective cough. I see him cover his mouth. Then he says, "You want to talk about what happens when you turn state's evidence?"

I shrug, but even as I try to be real cool, the tears come down my cheeks. I say, "Sure, why not?"

Old Paul is on death row, convicted of murder along with rape and sodomy of a minor.

Me? I'm in juvie hall, and it ain't any picnic. The food is lousy. I'm with a couple of bull dykes, and everybody steals. So I can't make any headway in the money department. A couple of gals here say they were raped by their fathers, and they wanted to kill their mothers, too. They talk like we have a lot in common. I tell them to leave me alone. Sometimes they do, sometimes they don't. But it's cool. I'm beyond caring what the hell happens to me. Just so long as I don't die from boredom.

All that attention. It was really exciting.

I've got to get out of here.

They assigned me a real sucker for a shrink. An older man about my dad's age who gives me the eye.

I mean, he really gives me the eye.

The other day he told me he was going to recommend my release to the assessment board. He says I have excellent insight and a fine prognosis.

The other day he also asked me why I became a hooker.

I mean, what's on *his* mind? I wonder.

Yeah, I have insight.

And I know what's on his mind. And I'll do what I have to in order to get out of here.

I need freedom.

At least juvie hall was a new experience for a while.

Just like killing my mom and fucking Paul.

I hate to be bored.

DISCARDS

"Discards" is one of my more complex short stories and features my very first private detective, Andrea Darling, a young woman of whom I'm quite fond. Los Angeles is blessed with mild weather, a calm blue ocean, and breathtaking natural terrain. But what happens to the unfortunates who live in the shadow of the "beautiful people"? The Bible emphasizes that a society is judged by how it treats its widows and orphans. What does that say about a town whose existence is fueled by narcissism and celluloid illusion?

BECAUSE HE'D HUNG AROUND LONG enough, Malibu Mike wasn't considered a bum but a fixture. All of us locals had known him, had accustomed ourselves to his stale smell, his impromptu orations and wild hand gesticulations. Malibu preaching from his spot—a bus bench next to a garbage bin, perfect for foraging. With a man that weather-beaten, it had been hard to assign him an age, but the police had estimated he'd been between seventy and ninety when he died—a decent stay on the planet.

Originally, they'd thought Malibu had died from exposure. The winter has been a chilly one, a new Arctic front eating through the god-awful myth that Southern California is bathed in continual sunshine. Winds churned the tides gray-green, charcoal clouds blanketed the shoreline. The night before last had been cruel. But Malibu had been protected under layers and layers of clothing—a barrier that kept his body insulated from the low of forty degrees.

Malibu had always dressed in layers even when the mercury grazed the hundred-degree mark. That fact was driven home when the obituary in the Malibu *Crier* announced his weight as 126. I'd always thought of him as chunky, but now I realized it had been the clothes.

I put down the newspaper and turned up the knob on my kerosene heater. Rubbing my hands together, I looked out the window of my trailer. Although it was gray, rain wasn't part of the forecast, and that was good. My roof was still pocked with leaks that I was planning to fix today. But then the phone rang. I didn't recognize the woman's voice on the other end, but she must have heard about me from someone I knew a long time ago. She asked for *Detective* Darling.

"Former detective," I corrected her. "This is Andrea Darling. Who am I talking to?"

A throat cleared. She sounded in the range of middle-aged to elderly. "Well, you don't know me personally. I am a friend of Greta Berstat."

A pause allowing me to acknowledge recognition. She was going to wait a long time.

"Greta Berstat," she repeated. "You were the detective on her burglary? You found the men who had taken her sterling flatware and the candlesticks and the tea set?"

The bell went off, and I remembered Greta Berstat. When I'd been with LAPD, my primary detail was grand theft auto. Greta's case had come my way during a brief rotation through burglary.

"Greta gave you my phone number?" I inquired.

"Not exactly," the woman explained. "You see, I'm a local resident, and I found your name in the Malibu Directory—the one put out by the Chamber of Commerce? You were listed under Investigation, right between Interior Design and Jewelers."

I laughed to myself. "What can I do for you, Ms. . . ."

"Mrs. Pollack," the woman answered. "Deirde Pollack. Greta was over at my house when I was looking through the phone book. When she saw your name, her eyes grew wide, and my oh my, did she sing your praises, Detective Darling."

I didn't correct her this time. "Glad to have made a fan. How can I help you, Mrs. Pollack?"

"Deirdre, please."

"Deirdre it is. What's up?"

Deirdre hemmed and hawed. Finally, she said, "Well, I have a little bit of a problem."

I said, "Does this problem have a story behind it?"

"I'm afraid it does."

"Perhaps it would be best if we met in person?"

"Yes, perhaps it would be best."

"Give me your address," I said. "If you're local, I can probably make it down within the hour."

"An hour?" Deirdre said. "Well, that would be simply lovely!"

From Deirdre's living room, I had a one-eighty-degree view of the coastline. The tides ripped relentlessly away at the rocks ninety feet below. You could hear the surf even this far up, the steady whoosh of water advancing and retreating. Deirdre's estate took up three landscaped acres, but the house, instead of being centered on the property, was perched on the edge of the bluff. She'd furnished the place warmly—plants and overstuffed chairs and lots of maritime knickknacks.

I settled into a chintz wing chair; Deirdre was positioned opposite me on a love seat. She insisted on making me a cup of coffee, and while she did, I took a moment to observe her.

She must have been in her late seventies, her face scored with hundreds of wrinkles. She was short, with a loose turkey wattle under her chin; her cheeks were heavily rouged, her thin lips painted bright red. She had flaming red hair and false eyelashes that hooded blue eyes turned milky from cataracts. She had a tentative manner, yet her voice was firm and pleasant. Her smile seemed genuine even if her teeth weren't. She wore a pink suit, a white blouse, and orthopedic shoes.

"You're a lot younger than I expected," Deirdre said, handing me a china cup.

I smiled and sipped. I'm thirty-eight and have been told I look a lot younger. But to a woman Deirdre's age, thirty-eight still could be younger than expected.

"Are you married, Detective?" Deirdre asked.

"Not at the moment." I smiled.

"I was married for forty-seven years." Deirdre sighed. "Mr. Pollack passed away six years ago. I miss him."

"I'm sure you do." I put my cup down. "Children?"

"Two. A boy and a girl. Both are doing well. They visit quite often."

"That's nice," I said. "So . . . you live by yourself."

"Well, yes and no," she answered. "I sleep alone, but I have daily help. One woman for weekdays, another for weekends."

I looked around the house. We seemed to be alone, and it was ten o'clock Tuesday morning. "Your helper didn't show up today?"

"That's the little problem I wanted to tell you about."

I took out my notebook and pen. "We can start now, if you're ready."

"Well, the story involves my helper," Deirdre said. "My housekeeper. Martina Cruz . . . that's her name."

I wrote down the name.

"Martina's worked for me for twelve years," Deirdre

said. "I've become quite dependent on her. Not just to give me pills and clean up the house. But we've become good friends. Twelve years is a long time to work for someone."

I agreed, thinking: Twelve years was a long time to do anything.

Deirdre went on. "Martina lives far away from Malibu, far away from me. But she has never missed a day in all those years without calling me first. Martina is very responsible. I respect her and trust her. That's why I'm puzzled, even though Greta thinks I'm being naive. Maybe I am being naive, but I'd rather think better of people than to be so cynical."

"Do you think something happened to her?" I said.

"I'm not sure." Deirdre bit her lip. "I'll relate the story, and maybe you can offer a suggestion."

I told her to take her time.

Deirdre said, "Well, like many old women, I've acquired things over the years. I tell my children to take whatever they want, but there always seem to be leftover items. Discards. Old flowerpots, used cookware, out-of-date clothing and shoes and hats. My children don't want those kinds of things. So if I find something I no longer need, I usually give it to Martina.

"Last week I was cleaning out my closets. Martina was helping me." She sighed. "I gave her a pile of old clothes to take home. I remember it well because I asked her how in the world she'd be able to carry all those items on the bus. She just laughed. And oh, how she thanked me. Such a sweet girl . . . twelve years she's worked for me."

I nodded, pen poised over my pad.

"I feel so silly about this," Deirdre said. "One of the

robes I gave her . . . it was Mr. Pollack's old robe, actually. I threw out most of his things after he died. It was hard for me to look at them. I couldn't imagine why I had kept his shredded old robe."

She looked down at her lap.

"Not more than fifteen minutes after Martina left, I realized why I hadn't given the robe away. I kept my diamond ring in one of the pockets. I have three different diamond rings, two of which I keep in a vault. But it's ridiculous to have rings and always keep them in a vault. So this one—the smallest of the three—I kept at home, wrapped in an old sock and placed in the left pocket of Mr. Pollack's robe. I hadn't worn any of my rings in ages, and being old, I guess it simply slipped my mind.

"I waited until Martina arrived home and phoned her just as she walked through her door. I told her what I had done, and she looked in the pockets of the robe and announced she had the ring. I was *thrilled*—delighted that nothing had happened to it. But I was also extremely pleased by Martina's honesty. She said she would return the ring to me on Monday. I realize now that I should have called my son and asked him to pick it up right at that moment, but I didn't want to insult her."

"I understand."

"Do you?" Deirdre said, grabbing my hand. "Do you think I'm foolish for trusting someone who has worked for me for twelve years?"

Wonderfully foolish. "You didn't want to insult her," I said, using her words.

"Exactly," Deirdre answered. "By now you must have figured out the problem. It is now Tuesday. I still don't have my diamond, and I can't get hold of Martina."

"Is her phone disconnected?" I asked.

"No. It just rings and rings and no one answers it."

"Why don't you just send your son down now?"

"Because . . ." She sighed. "Because I don't want him to think of his mother as an old fool. Can you go down for me? I'll pay you for your time. I can afford it."

I shrugged. "Sure."

"Wonderful!" Deirdre exclaimed. "Oh, thank you so much."

I gave her my rates, and they were fine with her. She handed me a piece of paper inked with Martina's name, address, and phone number. I didn't know the exact location of the house, but I knew the area. I thanked her for the information, then said, "Deirdre, if it looks like Martina took off with the ring, would you like me to inform the police for you?"

"No!" she said adamantly.

"Why not?" I asked.

"Even if Martina took the ring, I wouldn't want to see her in jail. We've had too many years together for me to do that."

"You can be my boss anytime," I said.

"Why?" Deirdre asked. "Do you do housekeeping, too?"

I informed her that I was a terrible housekeeper. As I left, she looked both grateful and confused.

Martina Cruz lived on Highland Avenue south of Washington—a street lined by small houses tattooed with graffiti. The address on the paper was a wood-sided white bungalow with a tar-paper roof. The front lawn—mowed but devoid of shrubs—was bisected by a cracked red plaster walkway. There was a two-step hop onto a porch whose decking was wet and rotted. The screen door was locked, but a head-size hole had been cut through the mesh. I knocked through the hole, but no one answered. I turned the knob, and to my surprise, the door yielded, screen and all.

I called out a "hello," and when no one answered, I walked into the living room—an eight-by-ten rectangle filled with hand-me-down furnishings. The sofa fabric, once gold, had faded to dull mustard. Two mismatched chairs were positioned opposite it. There was a scarred dining table off the living room, its centerpiece a black-and-white TV with rabbit ears. Encircling the table were six folding chairs. The kitchen was tiny, but the counters were clean, the food in the refrigerator still fresh. The trash hadn't been taken out in a while. It was brimming over with Corona beer bottles.

I went into the sole bedroom. A full-size mattress lay on the floor. No closets. Clothing was neatly arranged in boxes—some filled with little-girl garments, others stuffed with adult apparel. I quickly sifted through the piles, trying to find Mr. Pollack's robe.

I didn't find it—no surprise. Picking up a corner of the mattress, I peered underneath but didn't see anything. I poked around a little longer, then checked out the backyard—a dirt lot holding a rusted swing set and some deflated rubber balls.

I went around to the front and decided to question the neighbors. The house on the immediate left was occupied by a diminutive, thickset Latina matron. She was dressed in a floral-print muumuu, and her hair was tied in a bun. I asked her if she'd seen Martina lately, and she pretended not to understand me. My Spanish, though far from perfect, was understandable, so it seemed as if we had a little communication gap. Nothing that couldn't be overcome by a ten-dollar bill.

After I gave her the money, the woman informed me her name was Alicia and she hadn't seen Martina, Martina's husband, or their two little girls for a few days. But the lights had been on last night, loud music booming out of the windows.

"Does Martina have any relatives?" I asked Alicia in Spanish.

"Ella tiene una hermana, pero no sé dónde ella vive."

Martina had a sister, but Alicia didn't know where she lived. Probing further, I found out the sister's name—Yolanda Flores. And I also learned that the little girls went to a small parochial school run by the Iglesia Evangélica near Western Avenue. I knew the church she was talking about.

Most people think of Hispanics as always being Catholic. But I knew from past work that Evangelical Christianity had taken a strong foothold in Central and South America. Maybe I could locate Martina or the sister, Yolanda, through the church directory. I thanked Alicia and went on my way.

The Pentecostal Church of Christ sat on a quiet avenue—an aqua-blue stucco building that looked more like an apartment complex than a house of worship. About twenty-five primary-grade children were playing in an outdoor parking lot, the perimeters defined by a Cyclone fence. The kids wore green-and-red uniforms and looked like moving Christmas-tree ornaments.

I went through the gate, dodging racing children, and walked into the main sanctuary. The chapel wasn't large—around twenty by thirty—but the high ceiling made it feel spacious. There were three distinct seating areas—the Pentecostal triad: married women on the right, married men on the left, and mixed young singles in the middle. The pews faced a stage that held a thronelike chair upholstered in red velvet. In front of the throne was a lectern sandwiched between two giant urns sprouting plastic flowers. Off to the side were several electric guitars and a drum set, the name Revelación taped on the bass drum. I heard footsteps from behind and turned around.

The man looked to be in his early thirties, with thick dark straight hair and bright green eyes. His face held a hint of Aztec warrior—broad nose, strong cheekbones and chin. Dressed in casual clothing, he was tall and muscular, and I was acutely aware of his male presence. I asked him where I might find the pastor and was surprised when he announced that he was the very person.

I'd expected someone older.

I stated my business, his eyes never leaving mine as I spoke. When I finished, he stared at me for a long time before telling me his name—Pastor Alfredo Gomez. His English was unaccented.

"Martina's a good girl," Gomez said. "She would never take anything that didn't belong to her. Some problem probably came up. I'm sure everything will work out and your *patrona* will get her ring back."

"What kind of problem?"

The pastor shrugged.

"Immigration problems?" I probed.

Another shrug.

"You don't seem concerned by her disappearance."

He gave me a cryptic smile.

"Can you tell me one thing?" I asked. "Are her children safe?"

"I believe they're in school," Gomez said.

"Oh." I brightened. "Did Martina bring them in?"

"No." Gomez frowned. "No, she didn't. Her sister brought them in today. But that's not unusual."

"You haven't seen Martina today?"

Gomez shook his head. I thought he was telling me the truth, but maybe he wasn't. Maybe the woman was hiding from the INS. Still, after twelve years, you'd think she'd have applied for amnesty. And then there was the obvious alternative. Martina had taken the ring and was hiding out somewhere.

"Do you have Martina's husband's work number? I'd like to talk with him."

"José works construction," Gomez said. "I have no idea what crew he's on or where he is."

"What about Martina's sister, Yolanda Flores?" I said. "Do you have her phone number?"

The pastor paused.

"I'm not from the INS." I fished around inside my wallet and came up with my private investigator's license.

He glanced at it. "This doesn't mean anything."

"Yeah, that's true." I put my ID back in my purse. "Just trying to gain some trust. Look, Pastor, my client is really worried about Martina. She doesn't give a hoot about the ring. She specifically told me *not* to call the police, even if Martina took the ring—"

Gomez stiffened and said, "Martina wouldn't do that."

"Okay. Then help us both out, Pastor. Martina might be in some real trouble. Maybe her sister knows something."

Silently, Gomez weighed the pros and cons of trusting me. I must have looked sincere, because he told me to wait a moment, then came back with Yolanda's work number.

"You won't regret this," I assured him.

"I hope I don't," Gomez said.

I thanked him again, taking a final gander at those beautiful green eyes before I slipped out the door.

I found a phone booth around the corner, slipped a quarter in the slot, and waited. An accented voice whispered hello.

Using my workable Spanish, I asked for Yolanda Flores. Speaking English, the woman informed me that she was Yolanda. In the background I heard the wail of a baby.

"I'm sorry if this is a bad time," I apologized. "I'm looking for your sister."

There was a long pause at the other end of the line.

Quickly, I said, "I'm not from *inmigración.* I was hired by Mrs. Deirdre Pollack to find Martina and was given your work number by Pastor Gomez. Martina hasn't shown up for work in two days, and Mrs. Pollack is worried about her."

More silence. If I hadn't heard the baby crying, I would have thought Yolanda had hung up the phone.

"You work for Missy Deirdre?" Yolanda asked.

"Yes," I said. "She's very worried about your sister. Martina hasn't shown up for work. Is your sister okay?"

Yolanda's voice cracked. "Es no good. Monday, *en la tarde,* Martina husband call me. He tell me she don' work for Missy Deirdre and she have new job. He tell me to pick up her girls 'cause Martina work late. So I pick up the girls from the school and take them with me.

"Later, I try to call her, she's not *home*. I call and call, but no one answers. I don' talk to José, I don' talk to no one. I take the girls to school this morning. Then José, he call me again."

"When?"

"About two hour. He ask me to take girls. I say jes, but where is Martina? He tell me she has to sleep in the house where she work. I don' believe him."

It was my turn not to answer right away. Yolanda must have been bouncing the baby or something, because the squalling had stopped.

"You took the children yesterday?" I asked.

"I take her children, jes. I no mind takin' the kids, but I want to talk to Martina. And José . . . he don' give me the new work number. I call Martina's house, no one answer. I goin' to call Missy Deirdre and ask if Martina don' work there no more. *Ahorita,* you tell me Missy Deirdre call *you*. I . . . scared."

"Yolanda, where can I find José?"

"He works *construcción.* I don' know where. Mebbe he goes home after work and don' answer the phone. You can go to Martina's house tonight?"

"Yes, I'll do that," I said. "I'll give you my phone number, you give me yours. If you find out anything, call me. If I find out something, I'll call you. Okay?"

"Okay."

We exchanged numbers, then said goodbye. My next call was to Deirdre Pollack. I told her about my conversation with Yolanda. Deirdre was sure that Martina hadn't taken a new job. First of all, Martina would never just leave her flat. Second, Martina would never leave her children to work as a sleep-in housekeeper.

I wasn't so sure. Maybe Martina had fled with the ring and was lying low in some private home. But I kept my thoughts private and told Deirdre my intention to check out Martina's house tonight. She told me to be careful. I thanked her and said I'd watch my step.

At night Martina's neighborhood was the mean streets, the sidewalks supporting pimps and prostitutes, pushers and buyers. Every half hour or so, the homeboys cruised by in souped-up lowriders, their ghetto blasters pumping out body-rattling bass vibrations. I was glad I had my Colt .38 with me, but at the same time I wished it were a Browning Pump.

I sat in my truck, waiting for some sign of life at Martina's place, and my patience was rewarded two hours later. A Ford pickup parked in front of the frame house, and out came four dark-complexioned males dressed nearly identically: jeans, dark windbreakers zipped up to the neck, and hats. Three of them wore ratty baseball caps; the biggest and fattest wore a bright white painter's cap. Big-and-Fat was shouting and singing. I couldn't understand his Spanish—his speech was too rapid for my ear—but the words I could pick up seemed slurred. The other three men were holding six-packs of beer. From the way all of them acted, the six-packs were not their first of the evening.

They went inside. I slipped my gun into my purse and got out of my truck, walking up to the door. I knocked.

My luck: Big-and-Fat answered. Up close he was nutmeg-brown, with fleshy cheeks and thick lips. His teeth were rotten, and he smelled of sweat and beer.

"I'm looking for Martina Cruz," I said in Spanish.

Big-and-Fat stared at me—at my *Anglo* face. He told me in English that she wasn't home.

"Can I speak to José?"

"He's no home, too."

"I saw him come in." It wasn't really a lie, more of an educated guess. Maybe one of the four men was José.

Big-and-Fat stared at me, then broke into a contemptuous grin. "I say he no home."

I heard Spanish in the background, a male voice calling out the name José. I peered around Big-and-Fat's shoulders, trying to peek inside, but he stepped forward, making me back up. His expression was becoming increasingly hostile, and I always make it a point not to provoke drunk men who outweigh me.

"I'm going," I announced with a smile.

"Pasqual," someone said. A thinner version of Big-and-Fat stepped onto the porch. "Pasqual, *qué pasa*?"

Opportunity knocked. I took advantage.

"I'm looking for José Cruz," I said as I kept walking backward. "I've been hired to look for Martin—"

The thinner man blanched.

"Go away!" Pasqual thundered out. "Go or I kill you!"

I didn't stick around to see if he'd make good on his threat.

The morning paper stated that Malibu Mike, having expired from natural causes, was still in deep freeze, waiting for a relative to claim his body. He'd died buried under tiers of clothing, his feet wrapped in three pairs of socks stuffed into size-twelve mismatched shoes. Two pairs of gloves had covered his hands, and three scarves had been wrapped around his neck. A Dodgers cap was perched atop a ski hat that encased Malibu's head. In all those layers, there was not one single piece of ID to let us know who he really was. After all these years, I thought he deserved a decent burial, and I guess I wasn't the only one who felt that way. The locals were taking up a collection to have him cremated. Maybe a small service, too—a few words of remembrance, then his ashes would be mixed with the tides.

I thought Malibu might have liked that. I took a twenty from my wallet and began to search the trailer for a clean envelope and a stamp. I found what I was looking for and was addressing the envelope when Yolanda Flores called me.

"Dey find her," she said, choking back sobs. "She *dead.* The police find her in a trash can. She beat to death. Es *horrible*!"

"Yolanda, I'm so sorry." I really was. "I wish I could do something for you."

"You wan' do somethin' for me?" Yolanda said. "You find out what happen to my sister."

Generally, I like to be paid for my services, but my mind flashed to little dresses in cardboard boxes. I knew what it was like to live without a mother. Besides, I was still fuming over last night's encounter with Pasqual.

"I'll look into it for you," I said.

There was a silence across the line.

"Yolanda?"

"I still here," she said. "I . . . surprise you help me."

"No problem."

"Thank you." She started to cry. "Thank you very much. I pay you—"

"Forget it."

"No, I work for you on weekends—"

"Yolanda, I live in a trailer and couldn't find anything if you cleaned up my place. Forget about paying me. Let's get back to your sister. Tell me about José. Martina and he got along?"

There was a very long pause. Yolanda finally said, "José no good. He and his brothers."

"Is Pasqual one of José's brothers?"

"How you know?"

I told her about my visit with Pasqual the night before, about Big-and-Fat's threat. "Has he ever killed anyone before?"

"I don' know. He drink and fight. I don' know if he kill anyone when he's drunk."

"Did you ever see Pasqual beating Martina?"

"No," Yolanda said. "I never see that."

"What about José?"

Another moment of silence.

Yolanda said, "He slap her mebbe one or two time. I tell her to leave him, but she say no 'cause of the girls."

"Do you think José could kill Martina?"

Yolanda said, "He slap her when he drink. But I don' think he would kill her to kill her."

"He wouldn't do it on purpose."

"Essackly."

"Yolanda, would José kill Martina for money?"

"No," she said firmly. "He's *Evangélico.* A bad *Evangélico,* but not *el diablo.*"

"He wouldn't do it for *lots* of money?"

"No, he don' kill her for money."

I said, "What about Pasqual?"

"I don' think so."

"Martina have any *enemigos*?"

"*Nunca personal!*" Yolanda said. "No one want to hurt her. She like sugar. Es so *terrible*!"

She began to cry. I didn't want to question her further over the phone. A face-to-face meeting would be better. I asked her when was the funeral service.

"Tonight. *En la iglesia a las ocho.* After the *culto funeral,* we go to *cementerio.* You wan' come?"

"Yes, I think that might be best." I told her I knew the address of the church and would meet her at eight o'clock sharp.

I was unnerved by what I had to do next: break the bad news to Deirdre Pollack. The old woman took it relatively well, never even asked about the ring. When I told her I'd volunteered to look into Martina's death, she offered to pay me. I told her that wasn't necessary, but when she insisted, I didn't refuse.

I got to the church by eight, then realized I didn't know Yolanda from Adam. But she picked me out in a snap. Not a plethora of five-foot-eight, blond, blue-eyed Salvadoran women.

Yolanda was petite, barely five feet and maybe ninety pounds tops. She had yards of brown hair—Evangelical women don't cut their tresses—and big brown eyes moistened with tears. She took my hand, squeezed it tightly, and thanked me for coming.

The church was filled to capacity, the masses adding

warmth to the unheated chapel. In front of the stage was a table laden with broth, hot chocolate, and plates of bread. Yolanda asked me if I wanted anything to eat, and I declined.

We sat in the first row of the married women's section. I glanced at the men's area and noticed Pasqual with his cronies. I asked Yolanda to point out José: the man who had come to the door with Pasqual. The other two men were also brothers. José's eyes were swollen and bright red. Crying or post-alcohol intoxication?

I studied him further. He'd been stuffed into an ill-fitting black suit, his dark hair slicked back with grease. All the brothers wore dark suits. José looked nervous, but the others seemed almost jocular.

Pasqual caught me staring, and his expression immediately darkened, his eyes bearing down on me. I felt needles down my spine as he began to rise, but luckily, the service started and he sank back into his seat.

Pastor Gomez came to the dais and spoke about what a wonderful wife and mother Martina had been. As he talked, the women around me began to let out soft, muted sobs. I did manage to sneak a couple of sidelong glances at the brothers. I met up with Pasqual's dark stare once again.

When the pastor had finished speaking, he gave the audience directions to the cemetery. Pasqual hadn't forgotten about my presence, but I was too quick for him, making a beeline for the pastor. I managed to snare Gomez before Pasqual could get to me. The fat slob backed off when the pastor pulled me into a corner.

"What happened?" I asked.

Gomez looked down. "I wish I knew."

"Do the police—"

"Police!" the pastor spat. "They don't care about a dead Hispanic girl. One less flea in their country. I was wearing my work clothes when I got the call this morning. I'd been doing some plumbing, and I guess they thought I was a wetback who didn't understand English." His eyes held pain. "They joked about her. They said it was a shame to let such a wonderful body go to waste!"

"That stinks."

"Yes, it stinks." Gomez shook his head. "So you see, I don't expect much from the police."

"I'm looking into her death."

Gomez stared at me. "Who's paying you to do it?"

"Not Yolanda," I said.

"Martina's *patrona*. She wants her ring."

"I think she wants justice for Martina."

The pastor blushed from embarrassment.

I said, "I would have done it gratis. I've got some suspicions." I filled him in on my encounter with Pasqual.

Gomez thought a moment. "Pasqual drinks, even though the church forbids alcohol. Pasqual's not a bad person. Maybe you made him feel threatened."

"Maybe I did."

"I'll talk to him," Gomez said. "Calm him down. But I don't think you should come to the *cementerio* with us. Now's not the time for accusations."

I agreed. He excused himself as another parishioner approached, and suddenly, I was alone. Luckily, Pasqual had gone somewhere else. I met up with Yolanda, explaining my reason for not going to the cemetery. She understood.

We walked out to the school yard into a cold misty night. José and his brothers had already taken off their ties and replaced their suit jackets with warmer windbreakers. Pasqual took a deep swig from a bottle inside a paper bag, then passed the bag to one of his brothers.

"Look at them!" Yolanda said with disgust. "They no even wait till after the funeral. They nothing but *cholos*. Es terrible!"

I glanced at José and his brothers. Something was bothering me, and it took a minute or two before it came to me. As on the night before, three of them—including José—were wearing old baseball caps. Pasqual was the only one wearing a painter's cap.

I didn't know why, but I found that odd. Then something familiar began to come up from my subconscious, and I knew I'd better start phoning up bus drivers. From behind me came a gentle tap on my shoulder. I turned around.

Pastor Gomez said, "Thank you for coming, Ms. Darling."

I nodded. "I'm sorry I never met Martina. From what I've heard, she seemed to be a good person."

"She was." Gomez bowed his head. "I appreciate your help, and I wish you peace."

Then he turned and walked away. I'd probably never see him again, and I felt a little bad about that.

I tailed José the next morning. He and his brothers were part of a crew framing a house in the Hollywood Hills. I kept watch from a quarter block away, my truck partly hidden by the overhanging boughs of a eucalyptus. I was trying to figure out how to get José alone, and then I got a big break. The roach wagon pulled in, and José was elected by his brothers to pick up lunch.

I got out of my truck, intercepted him as he carried an armful of burritos, and stuck my .38 in his side, telling him if he said a word, I'd pull the trigger. My Spanish must have been very clear, because he was as mute as Dopey.

After I got him into the cab of my truck, I took the gun out of his ribs and held it in my lap.

I said, "What happened to Martina?"

"I don' know."

"You're lying," I said. "You killed her."

"I don' kill her!" José was shaking hard. "*Yo juro!* I don' kill her!"

"Who did?"

"I don' know!"

"You killed her for the ring, didn't you, José?" As I spoke, I saw him shrink. "Martina would never tell you she had the ring: She knew you would take it from her. But you must have found out. You asked her about the ring, and she said she didn't have any ring, right?"

José didn't answer.

I repeated the accusation in *español,* but he still didn't respond. I went on.

"You didn't know what to do, did you, José? So you waited and waited, and finally, Monday morning, you told your brothers about the ring. But by *that* time, Martina and the ring had already taken the bus to work."

"All we wan' do is talk to her!" José insisted. "Nothin' was esuppose to happen."

"What wasn't supposed to happen?" I asked.

José opened his mouth, then shut it again.

I continued, "Pasqual has a truck—a Ford pickup." I read him the license number. "You and your brothers decided to meet up with her. A truck can go a lot faster than a bus. When the bus made a stop, two of you got on it and made Martina get off."

José shook his head.

"I called the bus company," I said. "The driver remembered you and your brother—two men making this woman carrying a big bag get off at the stop behind the big garbage bin. The driver even asked if she was okay. But Martina didn't want to get you in trouble and said *todo está bien*—everything was fine. But everything wasn't fine, was it?"

Tears welled up in José's eyes.

"You tried to force her into the truck, but she fought, didn't she?"

José remained mute.

"But you did get her in Pasqual's truck," I said. "Only you forgot something. When she fought, she must have knocked off Pasqual's Dodgers cap. He didn't know it was gone until later, did he?"

José jerked his head up. "How you know?"

"How do I know? I *have* that cap, José." Not exactly true, but close enough. "Now, why don't you tell me what happened?"

José thought a long time. Then he said, "It was assident. Pasqual no mean to hurt her bad. Just get her to talk. She no have ring when we take her off the bus."

"Not in her bag—*su bolsa*?"

"*Ella no tiene ninguna bolsa.* She no have bags. She tell us she left ring at home. So we took her home, but she don' fin' the ring. That make me mad. I *saw* her with ring. No good for a wife to *lie* to husband." His eyes filled with rage, his nostrils flared. "No good! A wife must always tell husband the truth!"

"So you killed her," I said.

José said, "Pasqual . . . he did it. It was assident!"

I shook my head in disgust. I sat there in my truck, off guard and full of indignation. I didn't even hear him until it was too late. The driver's door jerked open, and the gun flew out of my lap. I felt as if I'd been wrenched from my mother's bosom. Pasqual dragged me to the ground, his face looming over me, his complexion florid and furious. He drew back his fist and aimed it at my jaw.

I rolled my head to one side, and his hand hit the ground. Pasqual yelled, but not as loud as José did, shouting at his brother to *stop*. Then I heard the click of the hammer. Pasqual heard it, too, and released me immediately. By now a crowd had gathered. Gun in hand, José looked at me, seemed to speak English for my benefit.

"You kill Martina!" José screamed out to Pasqual. "I'm going to kill you!"

Pasqual looked genuinely confused. He spoke in Spanish. "*You* killed her, you little shit! You beat her to death when we couldn't find the ring!"

José looked at me, his expression saying: Do you understand this? Something in my eye must have told him I did. I told him to put the gun down. Instead, he turned his back on me and focused his eyes on Pasqual. "You lie. You get drunk, you kill Martina!"

In Spanish, Pasqual said, "I tried to stop you, you *asshole*!"

"You lie!" José said. And then he pulled the trigger.

I charged him before he could squeeze another bullet out of the chamber, but the damage had been done. Pasqual was already dead when the sirens pulled up.

* * *

The two other brothers backed José's story. They'd come to confront Martina about the ring. She told them she had left it at home. But when they returned to the house and the ring wasn't there, Pasqual, in his drunken rage, had beaten Martina to death and dumped her body in the trash.

José will be charged with second-degree murder for Pasqual, and maybe a good lawyer'll be able to bargain it down to manslaughter. But I remembered a murderous look in José's eyes after he'd stated that Martina had lied to him. If I were the prosecutor, I'd be going after José with charges of manslaughter on Martina, Murder One on Pasqual. But that's not how the system works. Anyway, my verdict—right or wrong—wouldn't bring Martina back to life.

I called Mrs. Pollack after it was all over. Through her tears, she wished she'd never remembered the ring. It wasn't her fault, but she still felt responsible. There was a small consolation. I was pretty sure I knew where the ring was.

I'm not too bad at guesses—like the one about Pasqual losing his hat in a struggle. That simple snapshot in my mind of the brothers at the church—three with beat-up Dodgers caps, the fourth wearing a *new* painter's cap. Something off-kilter.

So my hunch had been correct. Pasqual had once owned a Dodgers cap. Where had it gone? Same place as Mr. Pollack's robe. Martina had packed the robe in her bag Monday morning. When she was forced off the bus by José and his brothers, I pictured her quickly dumping the bag in a garbage bin at the bus stop, hoping to retrieve it later. She never got that chance.

As for the ring, it was right where I thought it would be:

among the discards that had shrouded Malibu Mike the night he died. The Dodgers cap on Malibu's head got me thinking in the right direction. If Malibu *had* found Pasqual's cap, maybe he'd found the other bag left behind by Martina. After all, that bin had been his spot.

Good old Malibu. One of his layers had been a grimy old robe. Wedged into the corner of its pocket, a diamond ring. Had Malibu not died that Monday, José might have been a free man today.

Mrs. Pollack didn't feel right about keeping the ring, so she offered it to Yolanda Flores. Yolanda was appreciative of such generosity, but she refused the gift, saying the ring was cursed. Mrs. Pollack didn't take offense; Yolanda was a woman with pride. Finally, after a lot of consideration, Mrs. Pollack gave the ring to the burial committee for Malibu Mike. Malibu never lived wealthy, but he sure went out in high style.

TENDRILS

of LOVE

"Tendrils of Love" falls under the category of "be careful what you wish for," especially in this modern-day age of instantaneous communication via the wireless highway. It is not a smart practice to believe everything you read. In some cases, it can be deadly.

THERE IS AN ARM—LONG AND SINUOUS—stretching across gigabytes of electronic cables, fingers emitting charged impulses that touch, then seize, unsuspecting hearts. And so it was with Ophelia. What started out as a lark to alleviate boredom became a hobby, which gave way to an obsession. Private hours spent on the Net, trapping human discourse. In the end, it was the Net that trapped her. Because when she met Justice, she broke every cardinal rule of proper cyber-behavior—giving him the state where she lived, then the city, and ultimately, her real name.

There were things to consider: her life as it stood. But she made the decision with ease. Not a hard one, but an important one. It ended her ten-year stale marriage, her dead-end job, and her nowhere life. She prayed it was the *right* decision, if not the moral one.

The morning she decided to leave her husband held no special markers. Brian got up as usual, showered and shaved, lumbered down to the breakfast table, tossed her a usual "Mornin'." He slipped two slices of sourdough in the toaster, poured himself a cup of coffee. Ophelia poured her own, remembering a time when Brian not only served her java but ground it fresh. A millennium ago.

She regarded her mate, trying to imagine life without him. Brian had held up nicely. At thirty-five, he retained a head of black hair and wrinkle-free skin with regular features. Good living had rounded his waistline, hiding a once-flat stomach. But at 210 pounds, he still had a muscular and fit appearance. Physicality wasn't the problem. Ophelia found him desirable. It was the slow disintegration of his love and affection until all that remained were pecks on the cheek and pats on the hand.

She hadn't meant to fall for Justice, but they had so much in common. Included was a longing for something more, something bigger. He told her he was in his forties, also unhappily married, in the throes of a crisis. He, like her, had felt that life was passing him by. They both wanted more; both hoped they would find the elusive piece of the pie in each other's arms.

Brian left for work at the usual time, his smile and goodbye as personal as autopilot. Ophelia smiled back. And then she heard the door close.

What would Brian think when he read her note? She supposed he would be shocked, stunned by the betrayal that would pierce like a lance of emotional hurt. A serious wound, not a mortal one. Eventually, he would turn to self-righteous anger and indignation. Take it out on her. Messy times ahead, but who said life was easy.

Alone in the house, she felt her heart pounding with adolescent excitement.

She was really going to do it.

Up to the bedroom, packing her suitcase, throwing it into the trunk of her Camry. The transfer of funds had been completed yesterday—ten thousand dollars squirreled away in a secret bank account. It represented freedom as heady as an aged cabernet.

She drove to work in record time.

Her boss waiting at her desk, foot tapping, scowl on his

face. Shoving a pile of work in her face before she had a chance to take off her coat.

Charles Lawrence Taft. A pig and a petty bureaucrat, thickheaded and small-minded. She waited until he left, then took out the dense manila envelope from her briefcase. It contained a five-page, single-spaced document of every inappropriate move the man had ever made. Also included in the package were secret tapes of his lewd comments, of his racial slurs, and of his callous disregard of his coworkers. It was not only enough to get him fired but enough to ensure an out-of-court settlement with the company. She had decided that a quarter of a million would do the trick.

Extortion?

Hardly.

Just combat pay.

A nice surprise for Justice after it had all worked out.

She slaved until noon, typing in a windowless cubicle on her word processor, sending Justice piles of e-mail love letters. His excitement was palpable and leaped off the monitor. He wrote her that he couldn't wait to hold her in his arms, caress her body, smother her in kisses.

Their union. It had been born, nurtured, and sustained via an underground roadway. Secretive . . . hidden from view. It was now time for them to board the El train.

A group of rough-and-ready scouts taking a sunrise walk found the body in one of the many swollen creeks that snaked through the backwoods. A well-developed, well-nourished white female who wore a now-sodden black wool dress. The hem of the garment was caught on a craggy rock and kept her anchored as she bobbed in rhythm to the ripples in the water. The dress had risen above her hips, displaying colorless legs. Her black panty hose had puddled around her ankles, and there were no shoes on her feet. A black coat had been left about fifty yards to the right, crumpled in a pile of dead leaves. She wore jewelry but not in the normal fashion. A braided gold chain had been wound tightly around her neck, turning her face as shiny and purple as eggplant. No ID on the body. No purse in direct view.

The county coroner—who also owned the Kenton, Missouri, mortuary—took the body's temperature and shook his head when he read the results.

"Been here overnight."

Deputy Jim Schultz rubbed itchy eyes and hiked his pants over an ever-growing gut. An old man's move. Seeing this horror, he felt like an old man. "Overnight as in twelve hours, Cale, or overnight as in six hours?"

"That sounds about right."

"What does?"

"Six to twelve hours." Cale shivered as he clumsily recorded the numbers. Not easy writing with gloves as big as catchers' mitts. At least his hands were warm. "Ain't no local, Jimbo."

"They never are," Schultz remarked.

As he stared at the inflated face, he rubbed his wool-gloved hands on his leather bomber jacket. Why did they always leave 'em on his turf? Something to do with the locale. St. Louis to Kenton was a straight highway ride of seventy-five miles. Made for perfect dumping ground. He called out, "Joe?"

"Yo." Joe was doing squats, trying to deliver warmth to his bony body.

Schultz said, "Someone left a black coat, 'bout hunnerd, two hunnerd feet . . . under the copse of oaks. See it?"

"Yeah, I see it."

"Go fetch it and rummage through the pockets. See if maybe we can find some ID somewhere. 'Cause I can't find a purse."

"Murderer took it?"

"Probably," Schultz said. "Reckon not too many ladies travel without a purse."

Joe shook his head. "I don't recognize her."

Cale said, "Jimbo and me already decided that she ain't no local."

"I heartily concur with that," Joe stated. "Poor thing. Whaddya do to get in a fix like this, sugar?"

"Probably just in the wrong place at the wrong time," Schultz said.

"Want me to run it over the wire, boss?" Joe asked. "See if Medford or Athens reported someone missin' ?"

"First the coat, Joe."

"Ah . . . right." The assistant deputy jogged over to the discarded item, desiccated brush crunching beneath his feet. Picked up the leaf-crusted coat and brushed it off. He checked the pockets, shook his head. "Nothin' so far."

"Bring it here," Schultz said.

Joe walked back. "Nice coat. Better than the usual stuff they sell at Wal-Mart . . . or even Penney's." He read the label. With his bulging eyes, he looked like a preying mantis. "It's got *cashmere* in it, Jimbo. Ten percent."

Schultz took the coat, looked for a department-store label. It had been ripped out. He also searched the oversize exterior pockets and found nothing except balls of lint. Ran his gloved hand over the satin lining, found a small notch. A tiny interior pocket—good for ticket stubs and not much else. He took off his gloves, dipped two meaty fingers inside the smooth material, and came up with a yellow slip of paper.

A credit-card receipt from Macy's.

Schultz said, "Assuming this coat belongs to our lady, we got ourselves a name, folks. Ophelia Wells."

Schultz called it in to the St. Louis police.

No one by that name had been reported missing. A moment later, SLPD had come up with an address and telephone number. Schultz called the number, but no one picked up the phone.

He made it to the Gateway City shortly before noon. The day was cloudy and bitter, the gray sylvan landscape ceding to a lifeless inner-city winter. Ophelia Wells lived in one of the newer suburbs. SLPD had told Schultz to check in with them before he did anything, but he ignored their request. It was his body, he'd do it his way.

He found the house, rapped his knuckles against the door. To his surprise, someone answered the knock. The man looked pissed as hell, though his anger turned to curiosity as he studied Schultz's uniform.

"Mr. Wells?" Schultz asked.

"Yes?"

"Deputy James Roy Schultz from the Kenton County Sheriff's Department." He flashed his badge. "May I come in for a moment?"

"What is it?"

"Mr. Wells, it's awfully cold out here."

"Sorry . . ." Wells backed away from the door. "Come in."

Schultz entered, and Wells shut the door, offering his hand. "Brian Wells."

"Nice to know you, Mr. Wells." Schultz shook hands, then set a plastic garbage bag down on the floor. He made himself comfortable on a sofa printed with geraniums. Wells took an armchair. The men sized each other up for a few moments, then Schultz began.

"We found a body just inside Kenton's city line . . . up in the woods. The victim's a woman. I b'lieve her to be Ophelia Wells."

Brian's eyes grew. He opened his mouth and closed it. His whisper was a hoarse "*Whaaat?*"

Schultz asked, "Was she your wife, sir?"

Wells was mute, stunned.

"Mr. Wells?"

Brian leaned forward. "Yes . . . yes, she's my . . . Oh my . . . I can't believe . . . Are you sure it's Filly? I mean Ophelia. Are you sure it's . . . ?"

Schultz handed him the sanitized postmortem pictures. Brian turned his head away, muttered an "Oh God . . ."

"Is it her, Mr. Wells?"

Brian nodded quickly, tears in his eyes. Then he buried his face in his hands. "I . . . This is . . . Good Lord, what *happened*?"

"Don't rightly know yet," Schultz said. "Any idea what she was doing in Kenton?"

Immediately, Brian's eyes turned menacing, darkening like a tornado sky. "No idea. My wife left me yesterday."

Silence. Then Schultz replied, "Left you?"

"Yesterday," Brian stated. "For another man." He

caught his breath. "I don't know anything about him except his name—Justice C. Flatt. She met him in a chat room on the Internet. Filly has a computer down at work. They've been carrying on for quite a while, according to her Dear John note to me."

Brian inhaled, let it out slowly.

"I guess this bastard Justice must live in Kenton. I mean . . . you don't just wind up in a place like Kenton, do you?"

Schultz kept his face expressionless. "No, you don't. It's a small hamlet." *Not much more than spit on a map.* "Mr. Wells, I know everyone in Kenton, including the pets. Don't know anyone who goes by the name Justice Flatt."

"So what was Filly *doing* there?"

Schultz said, "Tell me more about this Justice Flatt."

"Don't know a thing about him. Don't know what he does, what he looks like . . . if he's even a legitimate person. I mean, what kind of a name is Justice? I'm sure Filly was snowed by this asshole. Even if he is legitimate, he's a homewrecker at best."

"You still got that Dear John note?"

"I . . . I burned it." Brian shrugged. "I was . . . furious. I didn't know that . . ."

"Mind if I have a look around?"

"Not at all."

Cooperative but only up to a point. When Schultz started asking personal questions, Wells pulled back.

"I don't see where my *past* relationship with my wife is any of your business."

"Your wife was murdered," Schultz pointed out.

"But I didn't do it," Wells said. "That's all *you* have to know." His hostility was frank. "You want a suspect, find this Justice guy. Probably some psycho. God, I can't believe Filly would do a thing like that. She was always so . . . reasonable. Must have been some kind of midlife crisis."

He threw up his hands.

"Not that any of this . . . matters . . . anymore . . . God, I'm completely . . . stunned."

Schultz had puttered around the house for the better part of two hours and yet he found *nothing* relating to Justice. Not much pertaining to Ophelia, either. When he asked Wells about the lack of his wife's personal effects, Brian said that she had packed what she had wanted and he had tossed the rest out in a fit of rage.

"Why should she remain a part of the home she left?" Wells seemed to be trying to control his temper. "If I were you, I'd try Filly's work. She probably has stuff in her desk drawers. That's where she probably wrote most of her notes to this bastard."

Schultz nodded. "I hate to ask you about this, but we're going to need someone to identify the body."

Wells closed his eyes. "When?"

"I could pick you up in a couple of hours."

Wells opened his eyes and nodded. "Fine."

Schultz rose, picked up his plastic bag, then took out the contents. A black coat. He handed it to Wells. "Recognize this?"

Wells took the coat, felt it, smelled it. Again tears formed in his eyes. "It's . . . hers. Filly's."

"You're sure?" Schultz asked. "Check it real carefully."

Wells examined the coat, inside as well as outside. Attentively, Schultz watched him.

Finally, Wells handed it back. "As far as I can tell, it's hers. She had a coat just like this. But I can't say beyond a doubt." He made a swipe at the wetness on his cheeks. "I'll see you in a couple of hours, then?"

Schultz hesitated just a moment before he patted Wells on the back. Then he left.

After rifling through Ophelia's desk, Schultz came up empty-handed. There was some flotsam and jetsam, but again, nothing personal. No communications, memos, faxes, e-mails, or notes from Ophelia's elusive cyberlover. Closing the last drawer, Schultz decided to ask the boss a few questions.

Over to the boss's office, the door marked with a gold nameplate—C. L. TAFT. Taft was an abrupt, rude man. His eyes were fierce and his temper was short. He sat behind a desk piled high with paper. He said, "Truthfully, I don't give a damn about Ophelia Wells."

Schultz gave Taft a noncommittal look. "I heard 'bout what she did to you."

Taft's brows raised noticeably. "Good news travels fast."

Schultz said, "Someone did that to me, I'd kill the bitch."

Taft's eyes narrowed. "I would have loved to kill the bitch. But I *didn't*."

Schultz said, "So you don't mind my asking where you were last night."

"I mind your questions, but I'll answer them anyway. I was up all night, poring over these ludicrous charges that were thrown at me . . . by her."

"You're saying they're not true?"

"Most definitely they are *not* true. Ophelia is a very, very sick girl."

She's more than sick, Schultz thought. *She's* dead. Still, Taft's use of the present tense was interesting. Killers usually talked in past tense. "Were you alone all last night?"

"Yes. But I did make phone calls to my lawyer. At around eleven, then again at two or three in the morning. I'm sure you'll verify that."

"Doesn't answer where you were between eleven P.M. and two in the morning."

"No, it doesn't," Taft answered breezily.

Schultz regarded him. "Lucky for you that she died. With no one to press the charges, most likely they'll be dropped."

Taft's smile was owlish. "I don't like your insinuations, and I don't like you. For that matter, I didn't like Ophelia. A goldbrick. Always fooling around on the computer instead of using it. If she had worked more, she wouldn't have gotten herself into this fix."

"You're saying it was her fault she was murdered?"

Taft made a face. "You're twisting my words."

"How 'bout a straight question, then? I couldn't find anything in her desk drawers. Did you go through them, sir?"

Taft tightened his fists. "What are you getting at?"

Schultz said, "You were accused of harassment by this woman. According to her coworkers, Ophelia documented many of the charges. Know what I think? I think you took some pertinent material out of her desk but left behind other things to make it look like you didn't take out pertinent material."

"Get out of here!"

"You want to add a murder charge in addition to your other pile of woes, be my guest."

"Murder charge . . ." Taft turned pale. "I didn't kill her!"

"But you did mess around with her desk."

The boss turned quiet.

Schultz said, "Show me what you removed. Might give me a clue as to who did this."

Slowly, the boss rose, went over to a locked cabinet. He took out a key, opened the drawer, and removed a file. "Here." He gave the papers to Schultz.

Materials documenting harassment. Schultz started to page through them.

Taft said, "I have a meeting to attend. I'll be back in around a half hour."

Schultz nodded. A half hour should give him time to look things over.

All packed up by the time Taft came back. Nothing so lucky as to give them Justice Flatt on a silver platter. But Schultz did find an unsigned fax from Jordon, Missouri, a rustic small burg around a hundred miles south of Kenton. A picturesque place used by campers and tourists in the summer. The letter was graphic, hence the lack of signature. Schultz showed it to Taft. "Do you know who wrote this to Ophelia?"

The boss read it, turned red and indignant. "No, I do not!"

"Then why'd you pull it from the file?"

Taft seemed to stumble. "Because . . . she accused me of harassing her. For all I know, she was planning to use this letter against me. A letter I didn't even write! Look,

Sheriff, I don't owe you anything. I sure don't owe *her* anything. So will you kindly leave?"

"One more thing." Schultz took out the coat, gave it to Taft. "This look familiar at all?"

"This coat? It's a woman's coat."

"Yes, it is. Have you ever seen it before?"

"I couldn't absolutely *swear* to that. But it looks unfamiliar to me."

"Check it out carefully . . . you know, go through the pockets."

Taft made a few perfunctory gestures, handed it back to Schultz. "What? Is it Ophelia's coat?"

"Yes."

Taft shrugged. "Anything else?"

Schultz shook his head.

Dry-eyed, Wells identified the body. "It's her." He turned away. "When are you going to release the body?"

"She's a murder victim, Mr. Wells. An autopsy has to be done."

"What's the point?"

"The point is, it'll give us information as to who might have killed her."

"But she's still dead." Wells heaved his big shoulders.

Schultz looked at him. "Don't you want to know who killed her? Don't you want to see him punished?"

"Justice system's a sham," Wells said. "Justice . . . Justice . . . both of them are bastards."

Schultz said, "You'll have to fill out some paperwork to get the whole ball rolling. Want to start on it now?"

Wells shrugged. "Why not?"

Showing no anxiety. Either Wells was a psycho, or he was numb. Schultz said, "So you don't know anything about this Justice Flatt?"

"I told you, no."

"Well, what did Ophelia say 'bout him when she wrote you that note?"

"She wrote mostly about us . . . about how our passion had died, how our marriage was a shell. That it wasn't good for either of us to go on. Then she said she'd found someone who was impetuous and passionate . . . spontaneous. That she needed to be with him . . ." Wells broke into tears. "Oh God, poor Ophelia. Poor, poor Ophelia."

And he cried with what looked like true grief.

Schultz poured him a cup of coffee, then left him drowning in sorrow and official paperwork. Told him if he had any questions, to ask Cale.

Straight on to Jordon, the Ford passing miles of skeletal forest poking through carpets of compost and detritus. A leaden sky held storm clouds, and the air, though clean, looked dirty. Whipping down the highway, Schultz made it in less than an hour. He managed to get there before the official building closed.

He went through the property tax files, which listed the names of the owners of residences.

No Justice C. Flatt.

A dead end.

Hitting your head against a wall.

A solid, hard, flat wall. As in a solid, hard, Flatt wall.

Justice C. Flatt.

As Wells had stated, Justice Flatt was a weird name. Probably made up by some psycho.

Flatt.

Conjuring up images of being one-dimensional . . . robotic . . . emotionless.

Ironic because Ophelia had left her husband for someone she had deemed passionate, impetuous, spontaneous.

Or was something amiss?

Had Brian Wells found out about his wife's dalliances on the Net? Was he trying to woo her back, using this Flatt character? Or could he have been trying to get even with Ophelia for straying over the wires?

Was Flatt a deliberate play on words?

A husband's final declaration?

You want passion, baby, I'll give you passion. Passion from the man you labeled passionless.

Still, Schultz didn't figure Wells as a killer. The deputy had gone through all the pockets of Ophelia's coat, including the small inside slit. The slit where he had found the credit-card receipt. It wouldn't have made sense for Wells to leave that.

Unless he wanted to be discovered.

Flatt.

Justice C. Flatt.

C. Justice Flatt.

C. J. Flatt.

Now, why did that name look *familiar*?

And then Schultz remembered.

C. L. Taft. Or better yet—C. LTaft. A little anagramming with LTaft, and guess what name popped up?

Quickly, Schultz looked up all the Tafts in Jordon. No permanent resident by that name. Next he called a local Realtor. A brief introduction along with an explanation of the situation.

"Has anyone using the name of Justice C. Flatt or Charles Lawrence Taft rented a house here in Jordon?"

The Realtor informed him of a C. L. Taft. Could that be the man Schultz was looking for?

Yes, that very well could be the man.

Walking out of Fred's Café, Schultz held a Styrofoam cup of coffee in his gloved hands. The day was fiercely cold but less cloudy, the sky thin strips of gauze rather than sheets of anodized gunmetal. Cale was bundled up in a parka. Joe wore a leather jacket and earmuffs. He looked like Barney Fife.

To the boys, Schultz said, "After Ophelia rejected Charles Lawrence Taft, the boss got an idea. If he couldn't get her as Taft, maybe he could get her using an alias. He knew Ophelia was a chat-room fan. Figured he could woo her online if not in person. Hence the name Justice. Because this relationship was the *just* one."

"Or so he thought," Joe said, pointing a finger in the air.

"The man didn't have a clue," Schultz answered. "He thought he could waltz into Ophelia's life as this Justice character and everyone would live happily ever after. He had meant to surprise her. Just show up and say, 'Guess who lover boy really is?' But then Ophelia dumped this harassment thing on him. Taft was completely freaked. He had no idea how much Ophelia hated him as *C. L. Taft.*"

Cale said, "So he had to kill her?"

"He hadn't started out with the idea of killing her, no," Schultz replied. "He showed up at their designated meeting spot. When Ophelia saw Taft, *she* freaked. Spat in his face and told him she never wanted to see him. He asked her to hear him out. She said no. They went back and forth until a physical struggle ensued. He pushed her. She hit her head on something sharp. Taft panicked, dumped her, and left."

"What about his lawyer alibis?"

"They checked out," Schultz said. "He did make the calls but intended to use them as alibis. 'Cause Ophelia was already dead when he made them."

"Then why give himself a three-hour dead period, Jimbo?" Cale asked.

"Didn't want too perfect of an alibi," Schultz said. "Tell you the truth—because it wasn't absolutely perfect, I almost bought it."

Joe said, "All kinda sad, ain't it."

Cale said, "Ain't that the truth."

"Brian Wells was right about one thing," Schultz said. "These chat rooms. Nothing but an electronic Lonely Hearts Club. You don't know who the heck you're dealing with. Ophelia Wells was one naive gal."

The three men sat in silence for a moment.

Cale said, "It's a pi-tee-ful thing." He fidgeted, looked a little sheepish. "You know, I was talking to Mr. Wells . . . 'bout transporting the body back . . ." He blushed. "I suggested he might want to bury her here. Kenton's a heck of a lot prettier than St. Louis."

Schultz said, "You didn't!"

"I did indeed."

"What did he say?" Joe asked.

"He said . . . that he thought it was a very good idea." Cale rubbed his nose. "Now, you two stop looking at me that way. I offered him a super discount rate."

Schultz broke into chuckles, shook his head.

Cale said, "You gotta admit, Jimbo. Kenton is prettier than St. Louis."

Schultz scanned the scenery. The sun had broken through the smoky sky, round patches of brilliant blue peeking through the clouds like sets of azure eyes. He inhaled a breath of sweet, crisp air. He admitted that Kenton was prettier than St. Louis. Threw his cup in a trash container and said, "Okay, Joe. Time to get back to work. Go see Mrs. Dillon. She needs help getting the pilot light lit in her stove."

Joe rolled his eyes. "Suppose it's better than dealing with bodies. Though with Mrs. Dillon, it's hard to tell if she's dead or alive."

Cale said, "Gonna see y'all tonight at Fred's? Thursday-night football."

"I'll be there," Joe answered.

Schultz pondered a moment. "Thursday night . . . Patty's book club is on Thursday."

Joe said, "So you'll be there?"

Schultz nodded. "Yeah, I'll be there."

MALIBU DOG

"Malibu Dog" is one of my first humorous stories. It serves up a nice dish of cold justice.

STUBBORN AND MEAN ARE A LETHAL COMBINATION, a perfect case in point being Conroy Bittune—an old coot of sixty, as skinny and dried up as a stick of jerky. He was a wiry man with small brown eyes, thin lips, and a mouth full of brown-stained teeth. His cheeks were never without wads of chewing tobacco, giving him a stale smell and his scrawny face a pouchy appearance. I've always wondered how he managed to talk and chew without choking. Conroy was retired, having earned modest money doing something for the IRS. He was and always had been short of friends, so no one in the Estates was surprised when Conroy bought himself a companion—a pit bull named Maneater.

I was as close as you could call a friend to Conroy, which meant we were on speaking terms. He and I were next-door neighbors in a condominium complex called the Sand and Sea Estates. The development consisted of one- and two-bedroom boxes built above one-car garages. The units were framed with the cheapest-grade lumber, drywalled with the thinnest plasterboard, and roofed with layers of tar paper. The interiors were equally chintzy. The ceilings were finished with cottage-cheese stucco, and the floors were nothing more than low-pile carpet over cement slab. Who would buy such junk? Fact was, the condos were snapped up faster than flies around frogs.

Why?

Not only did the condos grace the golden sands of

Malibu Beach, but they were also granted *private* beach rights. That meant residents of the Estates could romp in the blue Pacific without mixing with the *public* riffraff. The units sold for six hundred grand and upward, depending on location and size. Of course, Conroy Bittune's little bit of paradise sat on the choicest parcel of land—a corner spot that allowed a view of the famous Malibu sunsets.

Me? I'm a lowly tenant, paying my out-of-town landlord eight hundred a month for the privilege of residing there. I came out to the Estates during one of my college term breaks to visit a friend. I was instantly entranced by the endless horizon, the splashy sunsets, the nighttime sky, sometimes as black as tar winking with millions of stars. Five years later, the ocean still has me under her spell. I earn my living as a handywoman, keeping my rent down by doing free repairs on my unit and a couple of others that my landlord owns.

My connection with Conroy was tenuous. One Saturday morning, his sink pipe burst, spewing water in his face and all over his ultramodern compact kitchen. He came banging on my door at seven in the morning, waking me up, demanding that I do something.

Conroy never asks, he demands.

Being an easygoing gal, I took his harsh tone of voice in stride and went next door. The pipe repair took all of five minutes—a loose joint—and just to show what kind of sport I was, I didn't even charge him. He never did thank me, but from that day on, I was the only one in the complex whom he never threatened to sue. We never became friendly enough to carry on a true conversation—the kind with give-and-take. But I would condo-watch his place when he went away on vacation, which was about four times a year.

One Friday afternoon, Conroy showed up at my door, beaming like a new father as he presented me to the pit bull. The dog was white and black, seemed to be molded from pounds of muscle, and had teeth like razors.

Conroy spat a wad of tobacco into my geranium box. Still chomping his Skoal, he said, "Don't need you no more, Lydia." He spat again. "Meet my new watchdog, Maneater."

The dog was on a leash and, by way of introduction, bared his fangs.

"Lookie at this, Liddy."

Conroy smacked the dog soundly across the mouth with a rolled-up newspaper. The pit bull let out a menacing growl but didn't budge. Conroy hit him again and again. The dog never moved an inch. Then Conroy pried open Maneater's mouth and stuck his nose inside the gaping maw. The dog endured the ordeal but wasn't pleased. And Conroy? He just stood there, smiling wickedly.

"Now you try to pet him, girl," he told me.

Slowly, I raised my hand toward Maneater's scruff. The dog snapped so hard, you could hear an echo from his jaws banging shut. Only quick reflexes prevented me from becoming an amputee. Conroy broke into gales of laughter that turned into a hacking cough, sending bits of tobacco over my threshold.

"Cute, Conroy," I said. "You're going to win loads of friends with this one."

"Don't need no friends," Conroy answered. "I need a good guard dog. One that'll attack anyone *I* say to attack. One that'll protect me with his life no matter how I whop the shit out of 'im."

"That's why you bought a dog?" I said. "To whop the shit out of him?"

"For protection, Liddy," Conroy said. "Now look at this." He looked down at the dog. "Nice, Maneater, let her make nice!"

He turned to me and said, "Go ahead and pet him now."

"Once burned, twice shy, Conroy!"

"Go ahead, Liddy!" His smile bordered on a smirk.

Call me irresponsible, but I reached out for the dog again. This time he was as passive as a baby, moaning under my touch.

"Amazing," I said.

"Now, if *you* tell him to be nice," Conroy said, "it won't mean a thing. He only responds to *my* voice, *my* words. That's what I call a well-trained dog."

"You trained him?" I asked.

"Of course not, girlie!" More laughter mixed with coughing. "I spent six months looking for the choicest breeders, another six sorting through litters to find the perfect pup. *Look* at 'im, girl. Broad chest, strong shoulders, massive forequarters, a jaw as powerful as a vise. Look, *look*!"

I looked.

Conroy spat, then continued. "Before he was even weaned from his mama's tit, I hired the best trainer money could afford. And now he's all mine. Perfect dog for the perfect man."

I gazed down upon Maneater's mug. The pleasure of my company had worn off, and he was growling again.

"I don't know, Conroy," I said. "A dog that mean. He could get you into lots of trouble."

"Bull piss." Conroy spat. "You know how them thieves are. They see Malibu, they think money, money, money.

Well, let them burgle the other condos! No one's gonna touch *my* property unless they wanna be hamburger."

"I don't know, Conroy," I said again. "You'd better keep him locked up during the day or else there's going to be trouble."

Conroy's mouth turned into one of his evil grins. "Liddy, where does a two-ton elephant sleep?"

"Where?" I said.

"Anywhere he wants," Conroy said. "Get what I'm saying?"

I got what he was saying. But before I closed the door, I reiterated my warning. He'd better keep an eye on the dog.

And of course Conroy, being the cooperative fellow that he was, let the dog go wherever he pleased. The dog tore up Mrs. Nelson's geranium boxes, turned over Mrs. Bermuda's trash cans, and peed on Dr. Haberson's BMW car cover. He chased after the resident dogs and cats—terrified them so badly, they refused to go out for walks even when carried by their owners. Maneater should have been called Bird Eater. He ingested with gusto the avian life that roosted in the banana bushes, chased seagulls, spraying feathers along the walkways. Whenever he ran along the shore, he kicked sand and grit in everyone's face.

Since his purchase of Maneater, Conroy had taken many more day trips. When he went away, the dog posted guard in front of the corner condo, not letting anyone get within ten feet of it. Postal carriers stopped delivering mail to neighboring units, leaving letters in a clump at the guardhouse. The gardeners refused to maintain the nearby lawns and planter boxes. Soon the greenery gave way to invading weeds, and the grass dried up until it was a patch of straw.

But the biggest problem had to do with the walkway. One of the two main beach access paths curved by Conroy's condo. Technically, you could pass without getting lunged at if you hugged the extreme right side of the walkway. But pity the poor soul who wasn't aware of this and walked in the middle. Maneater would leap up and scare him to a near faint. Most of us learned to avoid the path whenever Conroy was away. But that wasn't the point at all.

Conroy thought it was hysterically funny. The rest of the tenants were livid. They tried the individual approach, knocking on Conroy's door, only to get frightened away by a low-pitched growl and a flash of white teeth. Every time they were turned away, they heard the old man laugh and hack. One of the tenants finally took the step of calling in Animal Control. Problem was that Maneater hadn't actually succeeded with any of his attempted attacks. Unless they caught him in the act, there wasn't anything they could do.

So the people of the Estates did what they usually do when at wit's end. They called a condo meeting: sans Conroy, of course.

The complaints came fast and furious.

"This used to be a peaceful co-op until Conroy and his dog came along. We didn't pay all this money to have to be scared stiff by a wild beast or have sand thrown on our backs. This is Malibu, for God's sake. People just don't behave like that here. Something has to be done. And it has to be done immediately. Call the City Council. Call the movie-star mayor and ask him to declare Malibu a pit-bull–free zone. Call the Chamber of Commerce."

After living in Malibu all these years, we knew that the local political bodies didn't wield any real power. It was the moneyed ones with their connections downtown who sat on the throne. And since none of us in this development had enough California gold to buy us the ordinance we needed, we were left to deal with the problem on our own.

That left just one recourse. Someone would have to convince Conroy to keep his dog tied up or on a leash. Someone would have to square off with him face-to-face. Someone would be appointed to speak for the group.

That someone was me.

I knocked on his door, identified myself, and Conroy told me to come in.

He was on the floor wrestling with Maneater, baiting the dog with a raw steak. The match was hot and heavy, Conroy all red-faced and panting, saliva and bits of tobacco leaking out of his mouth. Every time the dog would try to get the meat, Conroy would whip him across the back with a blackjack. I hated the dog, but I winced whenever the leather made contact with the rippling canine muscles. Maneater's pelt was striped with oozing red lines, his legs and paws inflamed. The pit bull was *furious,* snapping, growling, digging in with his hind legs as if ready to charge. But he never so much as laid a paw on Conroy. I wondered how long *that* was going to last.

"He's going to maul you one of these days," I said.

"Not a chance."

"I wouldn't be so sure of that," I said.

Conroy stopped wrestling, spat into a bowl, and told

the pit bull to be nice to me. I went over and petted the poor thing. At last Conroy threw the steak to the ceiling and gave Maneater verbal permission to fetch it. The dog leaped into the air and caught it on the rebound.

"I'm telling you," I said. "He's going to get you."

"You don't know a thing, Liddy, so quit wastin' your breath. This dog was well trained. I spent two years finding the right breeders . . ."

He launched into his Maneater pedigree speech. When it was over. I shook my head. "I don't know, Conroy. Seems to me the dog is angry because he's mistreated."

"They need a strong hand, girl."

"But not a cruel one."

"What are you, Liddy? Some kind of dog head-shrinker?"

"I know an angry dog when I see one."

"He's supposed to be angry, girlie," Conroy said. "That's what he was trained to do."

"But it goes beyond that," I said. "He's a menace, Conroy. He doesn't just protect, he destroys."

Conroy spat again. "The condo board must be pretty pissed 'bout him guarding the accessway."

And there it was. The famous Conroy smirk!

"That," I said, "but much more. Maneater charges after the local cats and dogs—"

"If the local cats and dogs come too close, he's gonna chase them," Conroy said. "If *they'd* stay away, Maneater wouldn't do nothin'."

"When he runs on the beach, he kicks sand in everyone's face, Conroy."

"Well, ain't that too bad." Conroy smirked. "How 'bout if I teach him to say ''Scuse me'?" Then he laughed and hacked, laughed and hacked, and finally spat. "They don't like sand, tell them to get off the beach."

"They like the sand, just not in their faces."

"That's their problem, Liddy."

"Conroy, the beach belongs to the whole group."

"They got a complaint with Maneater," Conroy said, "take it up with him. Otherwise, tell them to mind their own damn business."

"You're not going to do anything about curbing the dog's behavior?" I said.

"Girlie, I spent hard-earned money on training him to do what he's doing," Conroy said. "Don't particularly feel like undoing it right now."

I was disgusted. I turned to leave, but before I did, I repeated that the dog was going to get him.

And Conroy? He just laughed and coughed.

No doubt about it. We were stuck with the two of them.

I remember the Sunday because it was such a perfect beach day. The sky was cloudless, smogless, a rich iridescent blue, and full of gulls and pelicans. The sun was strong, shining on the water like a ribbon of gold. The ocean was just right for swimming—seventy degrees with mild waves breaking against the shore in tufts of soft white foam. A saline breeze wafted through the air. Everyone was outdoors building sand castles, reading, or just working on their tans.

We were a funny sight. All of us bunched up on the left side of the beach, tobacco-cheeked Conroy and Maneater owning the right. It didn't seem the least bit fair, but what could we do about it? The inequity had become a fact of life.

Conroy was in perfect form, laughing and coughing, goading us with kissy noises and rude names. We tried to ignore him, but it was getting more intolerable by the minute.

"You guys are lily-livered pussies. Afraid of Maneater. Lookie here."

He took a towel and whacked Maneater on the back. A gasp rose from our group.

"Here he goes again," I said.

"Why does he do that?" Mrs. Bermuda said.

"Because he's a sociopath," said Dr. Haberson. "And that's a professional diagnosis."

"Lookie here," Conroy teased. "You pussies *couldn't* be afraid of a dog like this."

Conroy kicked the pit bull in the stomach. The dog let out a high-pitched squeal, followed by an angry bark.

"Can't we call the ASPCA?" Mrs. Nelson said.

"He'd just deny it," Mrs. Bermuda said.

"Not if we could show marks on the animal," Dr. Haberson said.

"And who could prove Bittune made the marks?" Mrs. Bermuda said.

"Do something, Liddy," Mrs. Nelson said.

"I tried," I said. "He won't listen." I yelled to Conroy, "He's going to get you one day!"

"In a pig's eye, Liddy."

"Yes, he will."

" 'Yes, he will,' " Conroy imitated me. "Just lookie at this, girl."

He punched the dog in the snout. Did it again. The dog started circling him like a hawk around its prey.

I eyed Dr. Haberson. Dr. Haberson eyed Mrs.

Bermuda. Conroy was making nervous wrecks out of all of us. The dog was getting more and more agitated—barking louder, baring his teeth.

"You're a bleeping sadist, Bittune!" Mrs. Nelson shouted. "Any second now, that dog's going to chew you up!"

With that, Conroy doubled over with big, deep guffaws, followed by his spasmodic cough. His face was flushed, beaded with sweat. "You pussies!" he screamed. "Lookie here!"

He grabbed the dog by the neck and yanked him down onto the sand. Then he picked him up by the front paws and swung him around, huffing and puffing from the effort. The dog was all snarls and barks during the ride.

"Watch it, Conroy," I shouted. "Maneater's starting to foam at the mouth."

"Wimps!" Conroy shouted back, spraying bits of saliva and tobacco out of his mouth. "You weak, itty-bitty pussies!"

He put the dog down and doubled over. We expected to hear more derisive laughter, but none came.

We waited a couple of seconds, a half minute, a minute. The dog was still snarling. Suddenly, everyone became aware that no one was talking.

Finally, Mrs. Bermuda said, "What's with Bittune?"

Good question. Even the dog looked puzzled. Conroy's face had turned deep red, and he was jumping up and down.

"A rare Indian rain dance?" Mrs. Bermuda said.

"Figures," Mrs. Nelson said. "Conroy *would* rain on our parade."

"I don't think that's what he's doing," I said.

Conroy was still jumping, his face getting redder and

redder. One hand went to his chest, the other to his neck. He seemed to be gasping for air.

I leaped up and shouted, "He's having a heart attack!"

Applause broke out.

"We've got to help him," I yelled.

No one said a word.

"Dr. Haberson," I scolded, "we both know CPR. We've got to—"

"All right, all right," Dr. Haberson said. He got up slowly, brushed the sand from his legs. Meanwhile, Conroy's lips had turned blue.

I ran toward the old man but was immediately halted by Maneater's growl.

"Nice dog," I tried. "Make nice, nice dog."

I took a step forward and so did he. I took a step backward and so did he.

"For God's sake, Conroy," I shouted in desperation. "Call Maneater off!"

Conroy pointed to his throat.

"You're *choking*?" I said.

Conroy gave a vigorous nod.

His right cheek was empty.

"The tobacco! He's choking on his *tobacco*," I yelled out. "Give Maneater a hand signal."

Conroy flailed his hands in the air. Maneater sat, acting as though the signals meant something. Yet when I tried to approach Conroy, the dog lunged at me.

We were hamstrung. The dog wouldn't let us near Conroy, and Conroy couldn't call Maneater off.

"Hit your chest, old man," Dr. Haberson said. "Try to do a Heimlich maneuver on yourself. Hit your sternum hard! Right here!" The doctor demonstrated the procedure.

Conroy tried and tried again. Meanwhile, he was turning bluer and bluer.

"Give it another try, Conroy!" I said. "Or just hold the dog off physically."

By then Conroy was the color of the sky. He fell onto the sand and blacked out, his body shaking as if he were having a seizure. It was awful. Maneater circled his master, licking his quivering arms and legs, nudging his face. But he snarled at anyone who attempted to come within helping range.

Mrs. Bermuda said, "First time I've ever seen a dog protect his master to death."

We tried to tempt Maneater away with meat. We tried to poke him away. We even tried a decoy method, using me as bait. Nothing would lure him away from his master. By the time Animal Control came with the tranquilizing gun, it was too late.

The dog was well trained.

The BACK PAGE

"The Back Page" comes from one of those urban legends that circulated when I was in dental school way back in the Pleistocene age. No doubt, the story is as apocryphal now as it was then. Then again, with all these UFO sightings, one never knows . . .

HE WAS ALWAYS THE FIRST ONE THERE. Mr. Johnny-on-the-Spot. Radar Robert Roadrunner. The Scoop. No matter how fast the other stringers moved, Biggy Hartley always managed to arrive before anyone else.

No one could figure it out.

Some of it made sense. Hartley worked for the *Chronicle,* and the paper had the largest circulation. Stood to reason that it would have the most sources and the best resources. But even among his fellow reporters at the *Chronicle,* Hartley proved to be the early bird, finishing up when the others began, waiting with the proverbial worm in his mouth.

At first it was annoying. Then it became irritating. Finally, it turned out to be downright frustrating. And Hartley played the part to the hilt. Chomping on a cigar like a catbird-seated character out of a forties play. Arching his fat eyebrows and spitting bits of tobacco into the waste can.

When his colleagues expressed their consternation at his seemingly extraterrestrial sense of timing, Hartley answered evasively.

"I just get this feeling." Chomp. Spit. "Can't explain it. Like a buzz in my head."

"C'mon," they'd insist. "Who are you bribing?"

"You wish it was that simple." Hartley smoothed back thin, ash-colored hair and smiled widely with yellowed teeth. "It'd make you look better to the boss, wouldn't it? Nah, you can't rationalize away my success with money. Some people just got the knack. Can't help it. Just got the knack."

Hartley had grown up in San Diego. None of his coworkers could understand why he spoke with a mid-Atlantic accent.

It wouldn't be *so* bad if the man had an ounce of humility. Instead, each success instilled into Hartley renewed arrogance. He boasted, bragged, and preened like a peacock, spending hours in front of the mirror practicing badass looks.

Narrow the eyes, wrinkle the nose . . . yeah, that's right. Now the sneer, raising the upper lip at the corner. Perfect.

Comical, except that Hartley got results. Which meant frequent raises and invitations to important functions. He would often arrive at the dinners in a rumpled suit with an open-necked shirt and scuffed shoes. His manner was abrasive. He flirted shamelessly with other men's wives. He had dirt underneath his fingernails.

"You can act any way you want as long as you're number one!" he told fellow reporter Carolyn Hislop. They were sitting in Hartley's office. As numero uno ace reporter, Hartley was the only investigative reporter on the paper who had a genuine room with walls and a door that closed. The rest of the plebeians, as he often called them, were stuck with cubicles.

"C'mon!" Carolyn answered. "Everyone knows you've got some kind of card up your sleeve. You're not a warlock. No one can be number one *all* the time."

"I can!" Hartley answered.

A distasteful expression swam across Carolyn's pretty face. For once Hartley decided to pull back. He decided not to spit tobacco into his waste can. He decided not to brag or boast or talk in his mid-Atlantic accent. Because he liked Carolyn. She had big blue eyes and cleavage. He wanted to get into her pants.

"I can't explain it," he said, trying to act very sincere. "I get this feeling, Carolyn."

"What kind of feeling?"

"Like this buzz or this signal inside my brain." As Hartley talked about it, he realized he really couldn't explain it. He took a handful of nuts and popped them into his mouth. Chewing as he talked, he said, "I hear like a shortwave radio. Sometimes I even hear words . . . like the cops are talking to me." He paused. "Plus, I sleep with the news station on. I hear lots of things in my sleep."

"C'mon!" she shot back, doing her best Lois Lane. "We all sleep with the news station on. We all hear the cops talking over the shortwave. We all hear the transmissions as they're going down. Why are you always first?"

"You hear the transmissions that come over the public lines." Hartley took another fistful of goobers. "In my case, I hear the private TAC lines . . . the cops talking to each other before it even makes its way to the RTO. I just hear it in my brain—ah, *shit!*"

"What's wrong?"

"I bit into a piece of shell." Hartley spat into the waste can. Carolyn grimaced. He said, "Friggin' nut can. It says *shelled*. The nuts are supposed to be *shelled*. I'm gonna sue the bastards."

"You do that," Carolyn said. "Claim mental as well as physical distress. By the way, I think you're putting me on . . . all that crap about hearing it in your head."

"No!" Hartley protested. "I'm not putting you on. Why would I put you on? I'm trying to get into your pants."

Carolyn frowned. "Not a chance."

"Even if I shared my byline with you?"

She pondered the offer. "For how long?"

"A month—"

"Nope."

"A year?"

She nodded. "Maybe."

"Wait," Hartley backtracked. "A year's too long. Six months."

"Screw you."

"C'mon," Hartley said. "I'll get you invited to all the parties. Drinks at Mais Oui, dinner at Pretensio's—"

"I don't need your smarmy deals. I can get invited on my own."

"Yeah, so why haven't I seen you there?"

"Because I haven't made *my* move yet."

Meaning she hadn't shown enough skin to their lecherous boss. The man was a total sucker for a big pair of boobs.

"Besides," Carolyn went on, "I'd rather lay him than you. Why eat hamburger when you can get steak?"

"Sometimes a hamburger can be very tasty."

"You're not even hamburger," she said. "You're headcheese."

"Headcheese?"

"Yeah, headcheese. The luncheon meat made from the ears and the eyelids of a pig. That's what you are, Hartley. You're a pig."

"You're just jealous."

"Damn right I'm jealous!"

She stalked off, shutting the door with force. The one bad thing about having a door. People were always slamming it in his face.

He had to be stopped, so they hired someone for the nasty task. He talked over ideas with Hartley's colleagues.

"I'll ice him when he pisses," he said to the others. "His back'll be to the door. He won't see a thing."

"Hartley uses the stalls."

"Even better. Then he definitely won't see anything. I'll shoot him through the door."

"You might miss him. Worse yet, you might hit the crapper. What a mess that would make."

The bathroom was out.

"I'll do it at his house."

So it was decided. At his house, using the old standby ruse. Plugging him with a .32, then masking the pop by tossing the house and making it look like a robbery.

That night, as Hartley turned his twenty-five-year-old red Datsun Z in to his driveway, the hair on the back of his neck suddenly stood on end. Senses heightened, Hartley pulled the keys out of the ignition and tossed them back and forth between his hands.

There it was. The buzz in his brain.

What was it saying to him?

What was going on?

Listen to the buzz, Biggy.

Yeah, it was definitely there.

Buzz, buzz, buzz.

And it felt ominous, although he wasn't sure why.

Figure it out, Biggy. You're the man with the plan.

Buzz, buzz, buzz.

And then he realized what it was.

It was the *music.*

The music from his house.

He couldn't hear it with his ears, but he could damn well hear it in his head.

Yep, it was in his head.

Weird.

Buzz, buzz, buzz.

And it was coming from *his* radio. Instead of the news station, his damn radio was playing music. And *bad* music, at that. Thrash metal. Some junked-up, long-haired pissy little moron in tight pants was screaming something. What was even more amazing was that some idiot thought it was worth recording.

The taste of today's kids.

Mind-boggling.

Of course, that really wasn't the main issue at hand. The main issue was why was thrash metal cacophony coming from his nightstand radio instead of the news station?

Maybe that *was* the news—a new thrash metal band.

He discarded that idea. More than likely, the bad music meant that someone had been inside his house and had changed his radio station.

That made Hartley nervous.

He approached the house with trepidation.

Slowly, slowly.

Come on, Biggy. Give 'im the old sneer.

What would Dick Tracy do in such a situation?

On tiptoes, he arrived at his front door. With great precision while crouching on the sidelines, Hartley deftly inserted the key into the lock.

Quietly, he turned the key.

With force, he pushed the door open while remaining in his hunkered-down position.

Immediately, the stillness broke into the rat-a-tat cadence of machine-gun volley as bullets came flying through the open doorway. Hartley held his hands over his ears, his head bent down to his chest. Like some friggin' cornered cat. He prayed, waiting for the din to die down. It was loud—not as loud as the thrash metal music ringing in his ears—but loud enough to interfere with the buzz.

Then there was silence.

Hartley waited. He heard soft, muffled footsteps. Within moments, a man wearing all black, including a black hood over his face, came out of his door. Either Mr. Black was a hired assassin or the Ku Klux Klan had changed fashion consultants.

Hartley sprang, grabbing the man's legs, and bit him hard in the thigh. The man went down with a thud, landing on his head. The rest, as they say, was history.

And guess who got the scoop.

Once the TV cameras had been set up, Hartley conducted the interviews in his office. With a wheel of microphones surrounding him, Hartley told his story. "I felt that something was off. I *knew* something was off."

"How did you know, Hartley?" someone shouted. "How did you *know*?"

Hartley downed a mouthful of nuts. "I just knew. Just like I know all the breaking action. That's me. Mr. Johnny-on-the-Spot. Radar Robert Roadrunner. The Scoop. I hear all the action in my brain."

More questions as Hartley gobbled more nuts.

"No, I can't explain. It's just like this buzz—ah, *shit*!"

"What?" asked a group of anxious reporters. "What is it? A bomb? A disaster? A mass murder? Another political sex scandal?"

Hartley replied, "I just bit down on a shell. I'm going to sue those bastards!"

The networks bleeped out the cusswords. MTV left them in.

Sitting in the dentist's chair, his mouth numbed and filled with cotton, Hartley breathed in lungful after lungful of laughing gas.

Friggin' nutshells.

It had started out slowly as a dull ache. Within a week, his right jaw had swollen to twice its size until the pain had become unbearable. Without recourse to quell the agony, he finally summoned up the nerve to see the dentist.

"Cracked down the middle," the oral surgeon reported. "The tooth can't be saved. It'll have to come out."

Hartley figured the toothache was penance for all his bragging about his good luck. Well, if this was the worst—although it was pretty bad—he could live with it.

If it didn't happen again.

The gas took the edge off the anxiety, but Hartley's heart still raced when the surgeon entered the operatory.

"How're we doing?" the doctor asked.

Hartley thought, *I'm sure you're doing well, but I'm doing shitty.* Unfortunately, he was too crocked out to say anything.

"Open up," the surgeon said. "It'll only take a minute."

Hartley managed to open his mouth.

With practiced skill, the dentist placed the forceps around the crown of the back molar. He gripped the handles, then paused. "What's that?" he asked.

"Ahhhhh," Hartley responded.

"I hear something." Another beat. "Do you hear something?"

"Ahhhhhh" was Hartley's answer. But he *did* hear something. The buzz in his brain. The *voices,* as always. But how could the dentist hear it?

"Ahhhhhhhhh," Hartley responded, trying to talk louder.

"Can't understand a word you're saying." With care, the surgeon rotated the forceps. Up and down, up and down, back and forth, back and forth, until he could feel the ligaments holding the tooth to the gum breaking. "Ah, well."

Hartley heard the cracking of tooth matter along with the voice. Again he tried to talk, but the gas . . .

"There it is again," the surgeon said. "Like someone's playing a radio inside your head."

"Ahhhhhhhhhhhhh," Hartley tried to scream.

"Now, calm down," the surgeon insisted as he turned up the nitrous portion of the nitrous oxide. "You were doing okay. Just hang in there. It's almost over."

Hartley felt his voice box weaken . . . just couldn't move. But he could damn well hear.

The surgeon chuckled. "You know, you read about funny things in the dental journals . . . about radio transmissions that come through dental fillings. I never believed the stories. But maybe that's what I'm hearing. Has that ever happened to you?"

Hartley couldn't talk.

"There!" the surgeon said triumphantly. He held a bloody tooth aloft. "Got it." Slowly, he turned down the nitrous. "Done. Hartley, I've got you breathing more oxygen now. You should come around in about a minute or two. I'll just let you relax."

The door closed. Again Hartley said nothing. Worse than that, he *heard* nothing.

Absolutely nothing.

No buzz, no voices, no sound.

All of it gone, gone, gone!

Damn those nutshells. He should have sued the bastards.

But what was the point now?

Gone!

No more Mr. Johnny-on-the-Spot.

No more Radar Robert Roadrunner.

No more the Scoop.

No more parties and special invitations.

No more press conferences.

No more office with a door.

Gone, gone, gone.

So what was left for him? Just a life as an ordinary reporter. As these thoughts came into his brain, Hartley became increasingly depressed. As soon as he was physically able, he reached over to the gas tanks, lowered the oxygen tap to almost nil, and turned the nitrous knob on full blast.

Good old nitrous.

He always wanted to die laughing.

MR. BARTON'S HEAD CASE

"Mr. Barton's Head Case" appears here for the very first time in English. It was originally written for a German anthology of short stories that revolved around the biblical theme "Thou Shall Not Murder." I chose the little-known story of Balaam and Balak, and it evolved into a modern-day fable with all the gravitas of the sixties series My Mother the Car, *featuring Jerry Van Dyke. (Strangely, the car in that sitcom not only talked, it spoke in English. Just a step more bizarre than Mr. Ed, the talking horse:* "Oh, Willlllburrrr!"*)*

> And God opened the mouth of the she-donkey and she said to Balaam: "What have I done to you that you have struck me these three times? . . . Am I not your she-donkey on which you have ridden since you have been in existence, until this day? Have I ever been in the habit of doing this to you?"
>
> —*Bamidbar (Numbers) 22 parashat Balak*

IT'S BUSINESS," HE SAID. "NOTHIN' PERsonal. Well, maybe a little personal. Hell, it's a lot personal. I can't stand the son of a bitch! You wanna know why?"

Actually, Billy didn't want to know why. The less he knew, the better. But the man was paying him good money, so he played the game. "Why's that, Mr. Barton?"

" 'Cause he's a goddamn self-righteous son of a bitch, that's why. Comes from nothin' . . . less than nothing. Comes from garbage. And now that he's got a badge, he thinks he's hot shit."

"A badge?"

"Yeah, a badge. He's a Fed."

"Whoa, whoa, Mr. Barton," Billy protested. "You didn't say anything about knocking off a Fed."

"What?" Barton's eyes narrowed to slits, swallowed up

by the thick lids that topped them. "You think I'm payin' you all this money to pop Joe Schmuck?"

"You didn't say anything about a Fed, sir." Billy touched the knot of his tie, a Stefano Ricci. Put him back heavy in the buck department, but only the best. The jacquard silk had been dyed jewel blue, perfectly setting off his crisp white Brioni shirt. His mocha-colored double-breasted suit was Kiton, a cashmere blend and made to measure. His barrel chest necessitated custom clothes. "Feds got protection, sir. Heavy-artillery protection. At this stage in my life, I'm not sure I want the heat."

"What stage?" Mr. Barton protested. "C'mon, Billy. What are you? Thirty-five? Forty?"

"Forty-two."

"You're a young man."

"I've seen a lot of action, Mr. Barton. I've had a good career. You want to go out on a high note, you know what I'm saying?"

"I'm paying for your high note."

"I'm not saying the money isn't good. It's good. Your money is always good, sir. But there are other considerations."

The old don slid back into his leather chair, interlaced his stubby fingers, and set them in his lap. "You gotta do this for me, Billy. I ain't givin' you an option, I'm givin' you an order."

Billy regarded Barton in his flashy silver lamé Valentino getup. Same black shirt and tie—yesterday's statement. The man had no originality, no class. "Sir, with all due respect, and I'm giving you lots of respect 'cause you deserve it, sir. But with all of the respect—due and otherwise—I'm not sure I'm comfortable with this. And if I'm not comfortable, that very much increases the chance of a fuckup. And the one thing you don't want, sir, is that fuckup. So you can order me to do it. And knowing who you are and all that, I'd do it. But keep in mind what I just told you."

"You're gonna fuck this up on purpose?"

"I never fuck up anything on purpose."

"So what's the problem?"

Now Barton was irritated. Not good to get him irritated, especially because Billy knew that Barton had a Heckler & Koch 9mm Parabellum resting in his desk drawer. Probably had other pieces as well. Not to mention those two gorillas outside the office door, and the two gorillas down the hallway. Barton had more gorillas than the Bronx Zoo. Billy felt naked without his piece, but it was part of the process. Whenever he went to see Mr. Barton, the goons outside always copped his steel.

Billy pretended to be thinking about things, busied himself by looking around the office. Barton had come up in the world—from a two-bit bouncer to the head of a very lucrative construction firm. He had punctuated his rise in social status by acquiring things—the big hulking rosewood desk, the new wet bar with the Lalique Scotch tumblers (the clod had left the labels on the bottom of the glasses), and the contemporary artwork that Billy's three-year-old niece could have done in her sleep.

"You ain't answering my question, Billy."

"Look, sir . . ." Billy leaned across the desk. "This is a prime opportunity for some young stud to cut his teeth on. I'm getting old—yeah, I know, I know, I'm only forty-two. But I'm getting out of the business soon. Maybe it would be best if you started breaking in someone with a little more grit."

"You're the best. I want the best!"

Billy said nothing. No sense disagreeing with the obvious.

Mr. Barton laughed, showing off big porcelain-capped teeth. That grin sitting between heavy shadowed jowls reminded Billy of a bulldog. When Barton was younger, thinner, he'd been a dead ringer for Richard Nixon, right down to the ski-slope nose. Now the man was a quintessential crime boss—the gaudy custom suit, the blow-dried gray hair, the collar pin, the gold Rolex, and the flashy pinkie ring. Still, Billy was smart enough to know that although Barton was a caricature, he was no cartoon.

"It's the money, right?"

"I already told you that money wasn't the issue."

"Money is always the fuckin' issue," Barton growled. "I'll make it worth your while, Billy."

"You already did that, sir."

"I'll give you double."

Billy couldn't believe his ears. "*What?*"

"You heard me, kiddo. I'll give you double."

"You must really hate this guy."

"Yeah, I do. He gets in my way."

Again Billy looked around the room, but in his mind, he was already spending the cash. Amber would look dyna-mite parading around the Caribbean, wearing one of those skimpy little things . . . basically tit pasties and butt floss. She had the body, that was for sure, and what Mother Nature had left out, surgery sure helped along. "Yeah . . ." Billy nodded. "Yeah, okay. You want it done that bad, I'll make sure it gets done."

Barton grinned. "See, I told you it was the money."

"You're right, Mr. Barton. You're definitely right!"

"You can smile now, Billy."

Billy felt his lips move upward, then he felt himself beaming. "You are one hell of a crazy motherfucker—"

"Watch your mouth!"

"You've got a file on this guy?"

"Do I got a file on this guy?" Barton leaned back in his chair. "Pshhhh. I got everything you want on this guy, twenty-four/seven. I know when he wakes up in the morning to take a piss, I know how he takes his coffee, I know where he stops to buy his lotto ticket, I know what position he likes best when he fucks his old lady. She's okay, you know. The old lady. You might wanna—"

"It leaves evidence, sir."

Barton laughed. "You never heard of a rubber?"

"As tempting as it sounds, I'd like to get the job done cleanly. In and out."

"Clean, dirty, I don't care. Just so it gets done and it don't come back to haunt me. You wanna know what the beef is, Billy?"

"Anything you want to tell me, Mr. Barton, I'm listening."

"The beef is, he's a self-righteous son of a bitch. Thinks he's better than the rest of us. Makes all of us working stiffs look bad."

Barton was repeating himself. Billy said, "I don't like self-righteous assholes, either."

"He came from garbage. He got above his raising. Such impudence can't go unpunished."

Billy nodded. "I'll take the file whenever you want."

"Go on, Billy. Tell me how you'll do it."

"As soon as I figure it out, I'll let you know." Billy tried out his best smile. "I've got to read the file first."

"Fair enough." Barton leaned forward. "You still ride that piece-of-shit jalopy?"

"I don't need anything fancy."

"Fancy is one thing. But that broken bag of bones? What is it? A Honda or a Hyundai or a Daewoo . . . some small piece of Oriental crap. Don't you need something with accelerated pickup?"

"The engine's modified, sir."

"Why don't you get yourself one of those nifty little two-seater jobs from the Krauts? They really know how to tune an engine."

"Those kind of cars are noticeable, Mr. Barton. What you want for the job is something plain and ordinary. Like Sal."

"Who the fuck is Sal?"

"My car, sir. Her name is Sal."

Barton gave him a strange look. "You name your car, Billy?"

"Yeah. We're like . . . like old friends. She's my workhorse. A mule, actually. That's why I named her Sal, after that song about the Erie Canal from grade school."

Barton looked at him with suspicious eyes.

"You know what I'm talking about?"

"I got no idea what you're talkin' about."

"The mule that helped build the Erie Canal . . ." Billy hummed a few bars. "That don't sound familiar?"

"Not in the least. I went to Catholic school. Only thing I remember about the music was a chance to stare at Katherine O'Neal's tits as she sung in the choir." Mr. Barton shook his head. "Just make sure it don't break down."

"I guarantee you she won't. We've been through a lot together, Sal and me. She's sort of my . . . my good-luck charm."

"Yeah, well, I don't tell you how to do your job. But I *am* saying that she could use a permanent date with the compactor."

"Maybe one day, but not yet."

Barton got up from his chair, signaling Billy to do the same. He handed Billy a black briefcase. "Everything you need is in there."

Billy nodded. The two men shook hands—a gesture of clinching the deal rather than one of trust or friendship. They stood eye-to-eye, locked for a moment in an ocular pissing contest. Then Billy broke it off. After all, the man was paying a considerable sum of cash. He held the rights to being the alpha dog. "Thank you, sir."

"You're welcome, Billy. As always, it's a pleasure doin' business with you."

"Absolutely."

"I do got a question for you."

"What, sir?"

"You keep calling your hunk of junk a mule. And you also keep callin' it a she. Aren't mules males without balls?"

Billy thought for a moment.

The man wasn't educated, but he sure as hell wasn't stupid.

Billy did what he always did before he went on the road. He brought Sal in for a complete tune-up. Harry announced that she—in Billy's mind, Sal was always going to be a she—

was healthy and fit enough to travel anywhere Billy wanted to go. Afterward, he gave Sal a wash. Her bronze coat had faded to peanut-butter brown, and primer was peeking through some of the bigger dents, but Billy loved her more because of her imperfections. To him, the dings and scratches were war medals, emblems of fine service and a job well done. Her interior leather had begun to crack, little spiderweb lines in the seat cushions, but for a ten-year-old baby, she was still soft and supple.

The next part of the routine was the meal: the biggest, baddest, most cholesterol-laden piece of motherfucking cow you ever wanted to eat in your whole life, served specimen-rare—blue, they called it—with blood still running from the animal's veins.

Just hit the beast over the head and put it on a plate.

The waiters knew what he liked, had heard him order like that before. Still, they laughed at his corny joke whenever he told it. They knew a good tip when it bit them in the ass. The eatery he liked best served his cow with a mound of french fries dripping with oil or a baked potato the size of Idaho. Salad, too. Yeah, it was good to eat something green. He called the meal his primary-color dinner—red, yellow, and green—until Amber pointed out that green wasn't a primary color, blue was, and that green was actually a mixture of blue and yellow. That's when he told her to shut up unless she wanted her crème brûlée shoved in her face. (He said it a little nicer, but that was the gist.)

After the meal came the bedroom calisthenics, one for the road, and usually pretty slow after eating all that meat. But Amber was patient and kept up the moans and groans until it was over. Then she'd fall deep asleep, her soft smooth leg draping over his. He'd catnap but inevitably wake up, leaving her apartment as she squeaked and snored with that cute little grunt of hers every time she exhaled. He liked Amber. She didn't cost him a whole lot of money, she wasn't too demanding, and she didn't have a whiny voice. It was sultry—low and hoarse, no doubt from the cigarettes, but still, it was sexy.

Yeah, Amber was all right, he thought as he left her place, walking down the empty streets of the city. But Sal was better. Sal was his true-blue friend who always showed up no matter how tough the going got. The night was warm and muggy, and Billy heard the constant hum of air-conditioning from all corners. Life was decent and would be even better as soon as Billy took care of this business. He couldn't say for sure that it was his *last* job, but he did have other things in mind now that he was older. He had lived within a four-mile radius his entire life, his spectrum of experience limited to the dull city rhythms of his formative years. The same people, the same food, the same girls, the same thugs. He was tired of freezing his bones off in the winter, tired of battling mold and damp walls and wind tunnels and freezing pipes and hissing radiators.

He wanted to try out new things: someplace that was warm in the winter with an ocean nearby. He could picture himself and Sal driving down the East Coast to the Keys to visit his sister, Fiona, who was a big pain in the ass but was the only living relative he had who still talked to him. Her husband was a doofus but played a decent game of golf.

Surely he could do better than Fiona.

How about cross-country? A coast-to-coast excursion,

just Sal and him and the open road. Maybe find some hot little spot in Ma-li-bu!

The heels of his shoes made a clacking sound on the sidewalk as he dreamed about his future.

Trouble was, the Malibu chicks liked those sardine-box sports cars—little two-seater numbers with souped-up motors and ear-blasting boom-box jungle-bunny stereo. No, no, no, anyone who couldn't appreciate Sal didn't stand a chance with him.

He took off his jacket and draped it over his arm and thought some more.

Those Malibu babes were fine numbers. He remembered that bathing-suit special about them on TV, all those luscious asses. So hey, if the girls wanted glitz, he'd get a Harley. He certainly could afford one after this job, that was for sure.

A Fed.

He really didn't want to whack this Fed or any Fed. Feds had protection. Feds had nice families and went to church picnics and taught their kids how to play baseball . . . Well, not all Feds. He didn't know a thing about the Fed Barton wanted him to take out. Maybe this Fed was a monster. Maybe he was that kinda self-righteous prick who would hide under the guise of being a law-abiding citizen, be all prim and proper but would be, in actuality, a secret diddler of little boys.

Billy thought about that as he made his way home. In his mind, he was picturing this guy—this Fed—coming in backdoor on some little six-year-old boy screaming bloody murder.

It always helped to demonize the enemy.

*   *   *

The Fed had a name: Benny Jacopetti. He was middle-aged, average height, average build, average face, just an average guy with nothing that distinguished him from any of the other working stiffs. The guy had a family that included a wife and a slew of kids. He lived in a spanking-new housing development in the middle of nowhere. That was a mixed bag—the city versus the burbs. In the city, Billy was a known quantity; the police were constantly on his ass. Also, town cops were much sharper than their suburban counterparts. But it was also bad, because that far into the burbs, the wilderness, really, there wasn't any cover . . . nowhere to hide. Things got spotted and reported and gossiped about.

That meant the city wasn't the ideal location, but the burbs weren't any better.

He'd clean him on the road.

Mr. Barton hadn't been lying when he said he had Jacopetti's life down to the minute. After a few days of spotting, the guy's routine was as predictable as sunrise. He left the house around seven to get in to work at eight, leaving Billy about an hour of commuter time to get the job done. The route broke down into the following legs.

Trek One:

This portion of the journey—about ten minutes—took Jacopetti from his house to a bypass road, traveling through suburban developments and past a couple of shopping malls. Wide-open spaces, no cover, and other cars on the streets. Meaning it wouldn't serve his needs for the job.

Trek Two:

Tooling down a bypass road: another twenty minutes. This route meandered through the posh houses of the burbs: two-story brick estates sitting on lots of land. Most of the homes were perched on a knoll of lawn, obscured by mature trees and thick clumps of planting. The majority of the area was even devoid of sidewalks. No big commercial developments, only cute little Victorian houses that doubled as offices: One was a real estate agency, another rented to a law firm, and a hairdresser and nail salon took up a third. There were also a couple of small cafés and a Starbucks.

Wherever you went in America, there was a Starbucks.

Four dollars for a cup of java.

And the Feds accused the loan sharks of usurious vigs.

On this pathway, there was better coverage due to the trees. But because it was a bypass road, there was often tons of morning traffic. Plus, the road narrowed down to two lanes, making quick escape in a car damn near impossible. Also, good ole Sal would stick out among all the Mercedeses and Beemers that marched in the early-morning workers' commute.

Billy scratched Trek Two as a possibility.

Trek Four:

Jacopetti's route to his job ended with a twenty-minute ride on the highway. Billy was tempted to whack him while racing down the multilane roadway. Here, Sal would blend into the clump of morning traffic—just another hunk of steel chugging down the pockmarked asphalt. But there were other considerations besides fitting in. Billy would have to make a quick getaway. He'd have to make sure that no one saw him pull the piece.

That was the trick.

On the highway, there was always traffic, and that meant there were always possible witnesses. Also, what if there was an accident that caused vehicular backup? It would stink if he shot Jacopetti only to get jammed because of a bumper-to-bumper tie-up.

No, the highway was out.

Trek Three was the option of final resort:

For a lone ten minutes, Jacopetti turned off the first bypass road, detouring onto a smaller secondary bypass road—*a bypass to the bypass*—that twisted and turned but eventually led to the on-ramp to the highway. Sometimes the lanes got crowded. But at least half the time, traffic was light, almost empty, especially if Jacopetti got an early jump from the house. This small swath of asphalt had only two stoplights and, like the first bypass road, it meandered through large properties but for a major exception.

There was this one spot, a nature preserve that was filled with overgrown bushes and large trees. The parking lot to the forest was hidden behind foliage. It sat at the first of the two traffic light intersections, neither street having any visible road signs. You just had to know it was the first intersection in the bypass to the bypass.

Billy thought this looked promising, so he scoped out the surroundings.

About twenty yards from the lot—twenty feet into the park—stood a tall, lush pine tree next to a thick old cedar, forming a green wall of foliage and needles. Both trees fronted the road. Almost directly behind the cedar and the pine was an old oak that met up with an old sycamore, their branches melting into a leafy canopy. The spot was perfect: nestled and secluded, with a great view of the road and the parking lot. The topper was this little tiny service lane that started at the parking lot, snaked through the park grounds, then ended at the first bypass road across the street from a big mother brick colonial house.

So here was the plan.

Every morning around six-thirty, Billy would drive over to the park and wait, perched in the oak tree, hidden by all the leaves and brush. He'd bide his time, drink a cup of coffee, do the crossword puzzle until it was close to J-time. Then he'd pick up his gun and stare out through the scope, waiting for Jacopetti's station wagon to travel over the second bypass road. Most of the time, Jacopetti would make the light: That couldn't be helped, because the traffic light favored the road, which meant it was green most of the time. But odds had to have it that one time—one itty-bitty time—Jacopetti would miss the light. Then he'd have to wait at the intersection, even if it was just for a moment.

That was all Billy needed: a single moment to clip him.

After the pop, he'd simply scale down from his arboreal hiding spot, jump into Sal, and tear out the back way, dumping the gun while speeding through the park. Then he'd hook up with the first bypass road, which led out to the highway, where he'd be free and clear.

He'd wait a couple days, then pay Mr. Barton a quick visit.

With this final and fruitful score put to bed, he'd be off the radar. It would be retirement from his old life, sunbathing in Florida or Ma-li-bu or someplace with an ocean.

Free and clear with bread falling out of his pockets.

That was the plan.

The first week, Jacopetti made the light, flying through the intersection at high speed. The second week, Jacopetti made the light five times in a row. Third week, same story.

Billy was getting pissed.

To make up for the supreme waste of time he had passed perched in a tree getting needles in his ass, he decided to pack a bender over the weekend, drowning out his bad luck with Scotch and sodas. So it was as hard as hell to wake up Monday morning. Even with the money incentive looming large in the back of his mind, Billy was groggy with a hangover and in a foul mood. He managed a quick shower, then put on a polo shirt, a pair of chinos, and sandals without socks. He packed his gun in the waistband of his pants, locked the door to his apartment, and then went underground to fetch Sal from her parking space.

From the moment Billy fired up Sal's ignition, he was on autopilot. Going through the route without thinking about it until the unexpected happened. At 6:22 on a muggy summer morning, eight minutes before Billy's arrival at the nature reserve, Sal stalled.

"Shit!" Billy proclaimed. "This is all I fucking need."

He tried again.

The engine kicked in, but as soon as he slipped the transmission into drive, it died.

"Fuckin'-*A* shit!" Billy popped the latch for the hood and got out of the car. He stared at the engine block.

Nothing was smoking, and the fluids looked okay. He checked the tubes, then the wires. Everything seemed in working order.

So what's up with that?

He got back inside, slamming the door, and tried the ignition again.

The engine spat out a few helpless coughs and then died.

"Fuck!" Billy pounded the dashboard.

Sal said, "Cut it out!"

Billy's heart started racing, his eyes widening as he sat up and jerked his head from side to side.

What the fuck was that?

Calm down, Billy! You're hearing things.

Okay, okay, try the motor again.

He tried the motor again. It was silent, as dead as his last whack in Jersey.

This time he slapped the steering wheel.

"Ouch!" Sal protested. "Whatcha doin', Billy? Why you takin' out your frustration on me?"

This time Billy sat still, his hands balled up into fists. "Who said that?"

"Who do you think said that?" Sal said. "You think it's the trees talkin' or something?"

Billy's eyes darted from side to side, but he remained motionless. "Who . . . are . . . you?"

"You have to ask?" Sal said. "We only been partners for, like, ten years. I, for one, am insulted. And while I got your attention, stop slammin' the door. Just like you, I ain't as young as I used to be."

Billy swallowed hard. "Sal?"

"Fuckin' bingo! Can we get out of here? We ain't gonna get anything done today."

Billy sat up in the seat. He shook his head several times, knocked on his forehead. "Let me get this right. You're Sal . . . my car . . . and you're talking to me."

"Ain't no one else here."

Throwing back his shoulders, Billy opened and closed his mouth. He checked the CD player. It was empty. The radio was off.

What the H is going on?

If you can't beat it, join it. Billy decided to play along. "Cars don't talk."

"Guess again," Sal said. "Look, Billy, I understand your confusion. Normally I don't talk. But extraordinary circumstances demand extraordinary things. First of all, you're whoppin' me, and I didn't do nothin' to deserve that, so stop, okay? I mean, we've been together for ten years. Haven't I always gotten you from point A to point B without a hitch?"

Billy broke into a sweat. "Yeah. Yeah, you have."

"I've been good to you, right?"

"Right."

"So why you whoppin' me? I tell you, guy, you're losing it."

And that was a true statement. Because here Billy was, having a conversation with a car.

Sal said, "You ain't gonna make it to the park today. Let's just get out of here."

Billy's eyes continued to flit in their sockets. "Why's that?"

"Why's that?" Sal sounded frustrated. "Open your

eyes, Billy. We can't get nowhere with that tree impedin' the roadway. I can talk, sure, but I can't pole-vault. I'm a friggin' car, for God sakes! Just turn me around and let's go home."

Billy looked at the road.

And there it was. The toppled tree had to have been at least sixty feet tall, the five-feet-diameter trunk lying across the asphalt, completely blocking both lanes of the bypass roadway.

"Motherfu— Why didn't I see it before?"

"You know, Billy, you're a good guy, but sometimes you don't trust yourself. When you said you didn't want to clean a Fed because Feds are protected, maybe you shoulda stuck to your guns. Maybe this is the Big Guy's way of telling you to follow your instincts."

Shaking his head, Billy continued to stare at the tree. "I can't understand why I didn't see it before."

"Billy, did you hear what I told you?"

"Yeah, yeah."

"Yeah, yeah, yourself. Go back and tell Mr. Barton that it ain't gonna work with the Fed."

"I can't do that. He already paid me fifty percent down."

"So give him back the money. Givin' up the money is better than sitting in Sing Sing."

Just then the absurdity of the situation dawned on him. He was carrying on a conversation with his car. No, not just a conversation. A debate! An argument! And as far as Billy was concerned, the car was winning.

"Look," Sal said. "There's no sense discussing this here. People are gonna start coming, traffic's gonna be murder. You ain't gonna do anything today with this mama log blocking the street. So go home and do me this one favor, okay? Tell Mr. Barton no. I mean, I've been with you ten years—perfect service—so you owe it to me to just *think* about what I said, okay?"

"Okay," Billy answered. "Okay, let's go home."

He put the key in the ignition, turned it to the right, and the engine fired up as sound and strong as ever. Billy blew out air, did a U-turn, and headed home.

Sal was making perfect sense.

More sense than any other broad he'd ever talked to.

It took Billy three days to fully realize the absurdity of the situation. He was listening—no, not just listening—scratching a lucrative job on the advice of a talking *car*! But knowing he was sane, that he wasn't prone to auditory hallucinations even when piss-drunk, he eventually accepted the ludicrous predicament as real.

Still, he spent time reevaluating his options, which were really only two—to do it or not to do it. Not to do it involved talking to Mr. Barton and telling him *why* he didn't want to do it. When Billy thought about that, it really wasn't an option at all. Though he knew he wasn't crazy, Billy couldn't figure out how to explain a loquacious vehicle to Mr. Barton.

So there was no choice. He *had* to do it. And while it was true that he was fond of Sal—they'd been through lots together—it would be a cold day in hell before he'd let anyone or any*thing* dictate who he'd clean. People talked all the time, and Billy never listened. No way a car was gonna tell him what to do.

It offended the sensibilities.

* * *

"I'm tellin' you, this ain't a good idea—"

"Shut up!"

"Now you're getting nasty," Sal said. "See? Already you're chokin'."

"Don't you come with a mute button?"

"Ten years, we never have *one* disagreement. I open my mouth one friggin' time for your own good, and this is the *thanks* I get?"

"Sal, I love you, but you're sounding like a broad."

"I *am* a broad. You *made* me a broad!"

"I mean a human broad."

Sal let out a cough from the engine in disgust. "Billy, I'm scared. I'm scared it ain't gonna work and they're gonna take me away from you. You know what happens if someone else gets ahold of me?"

"No one's going to take you away from me."

"It's compactor time."

"Nothing's going to happen, okay?" Billy was getting pissed. Sal was sounding more and more like a broad with each passing moment. Billy figured if he wanted to shut her up, he should use a little broad psychology. "Look, Sal. I promise you, it's going to turn out fine. Nothing's going to happen. We still got lots more miles in this relationship, okay? Trust me, baby. I promise you it'll be okay."

Again Sal's engine coughed. "I sure hope you know what you're doing, Billy. 'Cause I'd rather you junk me for parts than . . . than go to the compactor."

"You're not going anywhere, and no one's going to junk you for parts. Don't talk like that."

Sal was quiet.

Billy said, "Hey, baby, just get me to the park and let me take it from there, all right? What the hey. Jacopetti will probably hit a green light, just like he's been doing for the past three weeks, and this entire debate will be for naught."

"I don't know, Billy. I think it's coming to a head."

"Just get me there."

Sal got him there.

"Stay here," Billy whispered to his car.

"Where am I going to go, Billy?"

"Shhhh."

"Be careful, Billy. I love you."

"Love you too, babe." Billy closed the door gently and quietly. With practiced skill, he scaled the pine tree, taking up residence on his favorite branch, which was by now denuded of needles. The day was warm, the skies were clear, and his view was perfect. All he needed was Lady Luck to shine her sweet eyes on him this one last time and he'd be through. Maybe Sal would shut up and leave him alone for good. Because if she didn't—if she persisted in spouting off unasked-for advice—he'd definitely ditch her. There was no way, shape, or form Billy was going to put up with Sal yapping at him when he couldn't even get some sex out of it.

Billy took out his gun, settling it into a V-shaped intersection of branches to help support its weight. He aimed the bore of the weapon at the road.

"This ain't a good idea," the gun told him.

Billy's mouth fell open.

The seconds ticked by. The gun said, "Did you hear me?"

"Et tu, Brute?"

The gun sighed. "If your car's tellin' you it ain't gonna work, and I'm tellin' you it ain't gonna work, then maybe you should start listening."

"This is unreal!"

"Go back to Mr. Barton—"

"Fuckin'-A unreal!" Billy let go of the grip. "I'm going crazy!"

"No, you're just being stubborn as a mule."

"Fuckin' nuts! I'm getting out of here!"

Billy started down the tree. As luck would have it, the light turned red. Jacopetti's wagon slowed, then braked to a stop.

"What about me?" the gun asked as Billy climbed down the trunk of the oak. "You ain't gonna just leave me here, are you?"

"Fuck you!" Billy shouted.

"Don't talk like that to me! What have I ever done but given you good service—"

"Fuck you, fuck you, fuck you!" Billy shouted to his weapon as his feet hit the ground.

"Hey, what's goin' on?" Sal wanted to know.

"Fuck you, too!" Billy screamed.

Jacopetti rolled down his window and stuck out his head. "Hey, buddy, you need some help?"

Billy was frothing at the mouth. When he saw it was Jacopetti, his eyes went wide. He ran over to him, panting and sweating. "You gotta get outta here, mister. They're out to get you."

"It's okay, buddy—"

"No, it *isn't* okay, mister, I'm telling you, they are *really* out to get you. He sent me to do it, but then the car and the gun . . . they told me not to. They both said to me, 'Don't do it, Billy, don't do it.' So when a car *and* a gun start talking to you, you know you better start listening."

"Buddy, I'm going to call someone for you," Jacopetti said. "I'll wait until someone gets here—"

"No, you can't wait. You've got to leave. Just because I didn't do it don't mean that it's not going to get done. He'll just hire someone else for the hit. I'm telling you, you've got to get out of here!"

"I will, just as soon as someone comes to help you!"

A horn honked. Jacopetti pulled the wagon onto the side of the road. "Just stay here. I'll wait with you."

"No, you've got to get out of here!" Billy pounded on the hood of Jacopetti's car. "Out!" Another series of sharp pounds. "Out, *out, OUT!*"

And that was the way the ambulance found him—thumping on the hood of Jacopetti's car, warning him of danger and murder and ranting on about cars and guns that could talk.

The day was beautiful—clear skies with a slight perfumed breeze. The lawn was exceptionally green and sparkling from its early watering with the hose. Almost everyone was outside today, enjoying the wonderful weather. Even Fiona's spirits were lifted as she scraped the bottom of the bowl with a spoon, offering its contents to the man huddled in the rocking chair. As the spoon neared his mouth, his lips opened like automatic supermarket doors.

Fiona smiled as she extracted the spoon from her brother's mouth. "Billy, you ate very well today."

There was no response.

"Ah, Billy, it's such a pretty day. The flowers are blooming, the birds are singing. The sky is blue . . . a perfect day for just lounging around. Maybe we should take a swing on the hammock. You used to love the hammock. Remember at Grandma's, we used to swing on the hammock? And then Daddy would set up the tire and you'd push me high in the sky?"

Billy remained mute.

"So high," Fiona recounted. "I used to feel like I was flying. I felt as light as a bird. You were such a good big brother."

Nothing.

Fiona sighed. "Oh, Billy! If you could just nod or something . . . it would help. It would . . ." Tears in her eyes. "All you have to do is talk, Billy. When you start talking, the doctor says that'll be a breakthrough. Then . . . then there's a good chance that we can get you outta here. You'd like that, wouldn't you? To come back to my house? I got a room set up in the back with a TV and a treadmill."

She punched her brother's arm. "Just in case you want to keep in shape."

Billy continued to stare out through vacant eyes.

"C'mon, Billy. Nod or grunt or fart or do something. You don't want to stay here the rest of your life, do you?"

But Billy didn't answer.

Fiona blew out air. "Billy, I'll be right back. I gotta take a pee. You just . . ." She patted his knee. "You just enjoy yourself. I'll be right back."

The warm sun beat down on Billy's back. In the stillness of the summer morning, if Billy strained hard enough, he could hear the sound of waves lapping on the distant shoreline.

A small smile tickled his lips.

He wasn't going anywhere.

Why should he?

He finally got his place by the beach.

HOLY WATER

"Holy Water" brings together two of my favorite writing elements—humor and religion. When I first heard that the closely guarded secret recipe for Coca-Cola had to be divulged to rabbinic authorities in order to get kosher certification, I knew I had a story that would cross the fine line between the sinister and the absurd.

UNTIL HE FELT THE GUN IN HIS BACK, Rabbi Feinermann thought it was a joke: somebody's idea of a silly pre-Purim schtick. After all, the men who flanked him wore costume masks. The Marx fellows—Groucho and Karl. Two old Jewish troublemakers, but at least one of them had been funny. The revelers spoke in such trite dialogue it had to be a hoax.

"Don't move, old man, and you won't get hurt."

Although he was fasting, Feinermann was always one to join in the festivities, though this prank was on the early side. So he played along, adjusting his hat, then holding up his hands.

"Don't shoot," Feinermann said. "I'll give you my *hamantash*. I'll even give you a shot of schnapps. But first, my two Marxes, we must wait until we've heard the reading of the Megilla—the scroll of Esther. Then we may break our fasts."

Then, as he tried to turn around, Groucho held him tightly, kept him facing forward, pressing his arm uncomfortably into his back. At that moment Feinermann felt the gun. Had he seen it when the two masked men made their initial approach? Maybe. But to Feinermann's naive eyes, the pistol seemed like a toy.

"We're not fooling around here, Rabbi," Karl said.

Feinermann looked around the synagogue's parking lot. It was located in the back alley on a little-used dead-end side street. He was alone with these hoodlums, but he had grown up in New York. Hoodlums were nothing new. Although the masks were a little different. In his day, a stocking over the face was sufficient—a ski mask if you wanted to get fancy.

But times change.

The old man had grown up in neighborhoods where ethnic groups competed for turf—the Irish, the Italians, then, later on, the Puerto Ricans. Each nationality fighting to prove which was the mightiest. Of course, they all tormented the Jews. Pious old men and women had been no match for angry energy and youthful indignation.

No, hoodlums were nothing new. But the gun in the back was a sad concession to modern times. Had mankind really progressed? the rabbi mused.

"Come on, Rabbi," Karl said. "Don't make this difficult on us or on yourself. I want you to walk slowly to the gray car straight ahead."

"Which car do you mean, Mr. Marx?" Feinermann asked. "The eighty-four Electra?"

"The ninety Seville," Groucho answered.

"Oooo, a Cadillac," Feinermann said. "A good car for abduction. May I ask what this is all about?"

"Just shut up and get going," Karl said.

"No need for a sharp tongue, Mr. Marx," the rabbi answered.

Karl said, "Why do you keep calling me Marx?" He pointed to Groucho. "*He's* the Marx guy."

"Your mask is Karl Marx," Feinermann said.

"No, it's not," Karl protested. "I'm Albert Einstein."

"I hate to say this, young man, but you're no Einstein."

"Will both of you just *shut up*?" Groucho snarled.

"Then who am I?" Karl plowed on.

"Karl Marx," Feinermann declared. "The founder of communism . . . which isn't doing too well these days."

"You mean I'm a *pinko* instead of a genius?" Karl was aghast.

"Just *shut up*!" Groucho yelled. To Feinermann, he said, "You can scream, Rabbi, but no one will hear you. We're all alone."

"Besides," Karl added, "you do want to see your wife again, don't you?"

Feinermann paused. "I'm not so sure. Nevertheless, I will cooperate. You haven't shot me yet. You haven't robbed me. I assume what you want from me is more complex than a wallet or a watch."

Groucho pushed the gun deeper into Feinermann's spine. "Get a move on, Rabbi."

Feinermann said, "Watch my backbone, Mr. Jeffrey T. Spaulding. I had disk surgery not more than a year ago. Why cause an old man needless pain?"

Instantly, the rabbi felt relief as the pressure eased off his back. "So you're not without compassion."

"Just keep walking, Rabbi," Groucho said.

"Who's Jeffrey T. Spaulding?" Karl asked.

"*Shut up*!" Groucho said. "Just cooperate, Rabbi, and no one will get hurt."

"Mr. Hugo Z. Hackenbush, I have no doubt that *you* will not get hurt," Feinermann said. "It's me I'm concerned about."

"Hugo Hack . . ." Karl scratched his face under his mask. "Who *are* all these dorks?"

"C'mon!" Groucho pushed the rabbi forward. "Step on it."

As the Marxes sequestered him in the backseat of the

Seville, Feinermann tried to figure out why he was being kidnapped. He wasn't a wealthy man, not in possession of any items of great value. His estate—a small two-bedroom house in the Fairfax district of Los Angeles—would be left to Sarah upon his demise. He and his wife had had their differences, but he couldn't imagine her hiring people to kill him for his paltry insurance policy. Sarah was a *kvetch* and a *yente,* but basically, a good, pious woman. And a practical woman as well. The cost of the hit would greatly exceed any monetary gain she'd receive from the policy.

Karl kept him company in the backseat as Groucho gunned the motor. Then they were off. The men were good-size, capable of doing major physical damage. And they seemed *very* nervous.

Perhaps this was their first kidnapping, Feinermann thought. It was always difficult to do something for the first time. It was then and there that Feinermann decided to make his abductors feel welcome.

"A nice shirt you have on, Karl Marx," he said. "Is it silk?"

Karl looked at his buttercup chemise. "Yeah. You really like it?"

The old man fingered the fabric. "Very good quality. I grew up in New York, had many a friend in the *shmatah* business. This is an impressive shirt."

"Quiet back there," Groucho said.

The old man pressed his lips together. At least his discussion with Karl had produced the desired effect. Feinermann could see the man in the buttercup shirt visibly relax, his shoulders unbunching, his feet burying deep into the Caddy's plush carpeting. The Seville, with its cushy gray leather upholstery and its black-tinted windows, had lots of leg room. It was good that Karl felt at home. He shouldn't be nervous holding a gun.

Groucho, on the other hand, was a different story. His body language was hidden from Feinermann's view. The only thing the rabbi could make out was a pair of dark eyes peeking through the mask with the bushy eyebrows—a reflection in the rearview mirror. The eyes gave Feinermann no hint as to who was the man behind them.

Feinermann sat stiffly and hunched forward, his elbows resting on his knees. Karl reached into his pocket and pulled out a handkerchief.

"Sorry to have to do this to you, old man."

"Do what?" Feinermann felt his heart skip a beat. "You are going to tie me up?"

"Nah, you're not much of a threat," Karl said. "I'm gonna have to blindfold you. Don't want you to see where we're taking you. Be a good man and hold still."

"I always cooperate with people carrying revolvers."

"Good thinking."

Feinermann closed his eyes as they were covered with a soft cloth, the ends of the kerchief secured tightly around his head. Quality silk—very soft and smooth. His abductors had spared him no expense. It made the old man feel important.

"May I now ask what this is all about?"

"Soon enough," Karl answered. "Don't worry. No one wants to hurt you. They just want a little information from you."

"Information?"

Groucho barked, "Keep your trap shut, for Chrissakes!"

"Are you talking to me, Mr. Rufus T. Firefly?" Feinermann asked.

"No, not you, Rabbi. I would never talk to a man of the cloth like that." Groucho paused. "Well, maybe I did tell you to shut up. Sorry about that. I was nervous."

"First time as a kidnapper?"

"You can tell, huh?"

"You don't seem like the hardened criminal type."

"I owed someone a favor."

"It must have been a pretty big favor."

"Ain't they all. Just relax, old man. We're gonna be in the car for a while."

"Then maybe I'll take a little rest." Feinermann took off his hat, exposing the black skullcap underneath, and unbuttoned his jacket. "Is this your first kidnapping as well, Karl?"

"Yep." Karl lowered his voice. "I owed *him* a favor."

Feinermann took the "him" to be Groucho and pondered, "Groucho owed someone a favor, you owed Groucho a favor."

"Yeah," Karl said. "It's kinda like a bad chain letter."

A Hebrew proverb came to Feinermann's mind: *From righteous deeds come righteous deeds. From sin comes sin.*

The car ride lasted over an hour. Afterward, the Marx boys brought Feinermann indoors, eased him into a baby-smooth leather chair, and propped his feet up on an ottoman. Such service, the rabbi thought. After the boys had made him comfortable, they removed the blindfold, then left.

The old man found himself in a magnificent library. The room was about the size of the shul's dining hall but much fancier. The paneling and bookcases were fashioned from rich, deep mahogany, so smooth and shiny the wood seemed to be plastic. The brass pulls on the cases gleamed—not a scratch dared mar the mirror polish. The furniture consisted of burnt-almond leather sofas and chairs, with a couple of tapestry wingbacks thrown in for color. The parquet floor was covered in several places by what looked to be genuine Persian rugs.

Directly in front of Feinermann was a U-shaped desk made out of rosewood with ebony trim. The man behind the desk appeared to be around thirty-five, of slight frame and bald except for a well-trimmed cocoa-colored fringe outlining his nude crown. Over his eyes sat an updated version of old-fashioned wire-rimmed round spectacles. Except these weren't the heavy kind that left a red mark on the bridge of the nose. Mr. Baldy was attired in a black suit, his pocket handkerchief matching the mandarin ascot draped around his neck. He held a crystal highball glass filled with ice, a carbonated beverage, and two swizzle sticks.

"May I offer you something to drink, Rabbi?" The bald man stirred his drink. His voice was surprisingly deep. "I'm drinking KingCola—the only beverage considered *worthy* of Benton's finest imported Bavarian crystal. But we have a full bar—Chivas aged some twenty-five years—if you're so inclined."

"Thank you, sir," said Feinermann, "but I shall be obliged to pass. Today is a fast day in my religion—the fast of Esther. Eating and drinking are prohibited until tonight's holiday."

The bald man stirred his KingCola. "Interesting. And what holiday is tonight, if I may ask?"

"You may ask, and I'll tell you. Tonight is Purim—the

Festival of Lots—when one righteous woman foiled the plans to annihilate the Jews of Persia."

"And you *fast* on such a day?"

"First comes the fasting and praying, then comes the celebration. Makes more sense to feast when you're really hungry. Not to mention it's good for weight control." Feinermann adjusted his hat. "Are you this Benton of the famous Benton's crystal?"

The bald man looked up and chuckled. "No, Rabbi, I am not Mr. Benton."

The old man stroked his beard. "I am trying to figure out why his name rings a bell."

The bald man said, "Perhaps you'd recognize the name in a different form. Benton Hall at the university. Or perhaps you've been to the Benton Civic Light Opera Company. Or read about the new Benton Library downtown."

"Ah . . ."

"Mr. Patrick W. Benton is quite the philanthropist."

"So why does a rich philanthropist need a rabbi with a herniated disk?"

"You are not just a rabbi, you are *the* rabbi."

"I don't understand."

"I realize that. But before we begin, I want you to know that bringing you here was *my* idea, not Mr. Benton's. I work for Mr. Benton, formulating his . . . covert operations."

"Sounds mysterious. Perhaps you're a student of the *Zohar*—our book of mystics?"

"What?"

"Not important. *Nu,* so do you have a name, Mr. Sharp Dresser?"

"Sharp dress . . . you've noticed my couture?"

"I like the touch of orange with the black suit." Actually, Feinermann thought the man looked like a jack-o'-lantern. But hurling insults was not the old man's style. And now was not the time for insults anyway.

The bald man nodded in approval. "Well, I thought it made rather a bold statement."

The rabbi said nothing. To him, a bold statement was splitting the Red Sea. "So, Mr. . . ."

"You may call me Philip."

"Philip it is. Exactly what does your Mr. Benton want from me?"

"It is *I* who want something from you, Rabbi Feinermann. I want something not for myself but for Mr. Benton—for his good deeds. And you, Rabbi Feinermann, are the only one who can help Mr. Benton continue his course of philanthropy. Let me explain."

The old man stroked his beard again. "I *knew* this wasn't going to be simple. Kidnappings are never simple affairs."

Again Philip let go with his pesky chuckle. "Come, come, Rabbi. Surely you don't think we intend any harm to befall you."

"To tell you the truth, with a gun in my back, I wasn't so sure, Philip. But proceed. Explain away."

"Rabbi Feinermann, you may wonder why a man like me would go to such extreme . . . measures to help out Mr. Benton. It's because I truly believe in his work."

"And what does he do besides erect buildings with his name on them?"

"He *cares,* Rabbi. He has built his empire on *caring.* His multibillion-dollar corporation was one of the first to include the *human* side of business. One of the first to offer complete *major* medical and dental care. And if that was not enough, he included in his medical package—free of charge—optometry, orthodontia, and podiatry services. Do you know how many of his employees have availed themselves of braces, eyeglasses, and bunion removal at Mr. Benton's expense?"

"I have no idea."

"Thousands."

"A lot of bunions, Philip."

"Corns are no laughing matter, Rabbi."

"Not at all, Philip."

"It's not just in medical services where Mr. Benton has taken the social lead. His was one of the first major corporations to provide on-site day care, flexible shifts for working mothers, and free turkeys on Thanksgiving, Christmas, *and* Easter." Philip paused. "And kosher turkeys for our kosher-keeping workers, I might add."

"Sounds like a thoughtful man, your Mr. Benton."

"That he is, Rabbi." Philip tensed his body and shook with gravity. "That's why desperate times call for desperate measures. You being here . . . it was a desperate measure that I took. But one that I hope you will truly understand."

"I'm all ears, Philip."

"Do you know how Mr. Benton made his money, Rabbi?"

"I'm afraid I don't."

"I'm not surprised. He is not a grandstander, like your ordinary billionaire."

"I'm not a maven on billionaires, Philip. I wouldn't know an ordinary one from an unusual one."

"Well, let me assure you that Mr. Benton is extraordinary."

"I'm assured."

"He made his money right here." Philip held his highball tumbler aloft. "Right in the palm of my hand."

"In Bavarian crystal?"

Philip frowned. "No. In the soft-drink industry. KingCola. A King, as it is affectionately known. 'I'll have a hamburger, french fries, and a King.' How many times have you heard that, Rabbi?"

"Not too many. But don't go by me. I don't patronize fast-food places, because I keep kosher."

"But even you, as insulated as you are from pop culture, have heard of KingCola."

"Certainly."

"But there's so much *more* to Mr. Benton than KingCola."

Feinermann noticed that Philip was shaking again. "We've been over the wonders of Mr. Benton. May I ask what does *any* of this have to do with me?"

"I can sum that up in two words. Cola Gold."

"Cola Gold? Your chief competitor?"

"Our *enemy,* Rabbi!" Philip started foaming at the mouth. "Not just our enemy in the War of the Soft Drinks, oh no, Rabbi. It's deeper than that. Much, much deeper. If it was only money, do you think Mr. Benton would waste his time on them?"

Feinermann thought maybe Mr. Benton *would* bother wasting his time. From his scant knowledge of billionaires, the old man was under the impression that billionaires—and maybe millionaires as well—spent a great deal of time on the subject of money. But he was silent.

Philip went on, "It's the whole CeeGee mentality, Rabbi. CeeGee—that's our code word for Cola Gold."

Feinermann nodded.

"CeeGee's attitude is Machiavellian—only the *product* counts, not the *people* behind the product. Do you know that last year alone, CeeGee laid off over two hundred people? And what replaced these people?"

"What, Philip?"

"*Machines!*" Philip spat out. "*Machines* took over jobs that had once put bread on the tables of families. How would you feel if a machine took over your job, Rabbi?"

"Not too good."

"Exactly!" Philip pulled the orange handkerchief from his pocket and wiped his face and forehead. "We're not talking about ordinary business competition, Rabbi. We're not just talking about sugar, flavoring, and water. We are talking sugar, flavoring, and *holy* water, Rabbi. What KingCola and Cola Gold have going is an all-out *holy* war."

"I see your point, Philip."

"So you will help, won't you, Rabbi?"

Feinermann stroked his beard, then held his finger up in the air. "Yes, I shall help. Call up Cola Gold and ask for the list of those who've been laid off. I could use an extra man to clean up the shul after Friday-night kiddush."

Philip bristled. "That's *not* what I had in mind!"

"So if you have an alternative plan, tell me."

Philip pointed a finger at the old man. "It rests entirely in your hands."

Feinermann looked at his hands. All he saw was air.

Philip said, "It has to do with CeeGee's new formula. The one they use to appeal to the youth?"

"Ah, yes," the old man said. "I'm aware of it. What is the slogan? 'The new cola for the now generation—' "

"Don't utter those words!" Philip covered his ears and began to pant.

Feinermann stood and quickly handed Philip his glass of KingCola. By now the ice had melted and the drink looked watered down. But it looked pretty good nonetheless, because the rabbi's mouth was dry from fasting. "Philip, calm down and drink."

Philip slurped up the remains of his soft drink.

"I beg your pardon," the rabbi said. "I didn't realize it would cause such a reaction. I won't say another word."

Philip took a deep breath and let it out slowly. "It's not your fault, Rabbi. You couldn't have known."

Feinermann said, "I take it by your reaction that the new . . . youthful formula has been successful."

"Youth!" Philip despaired. "What do they know of Mr. Benton's greatness and humanism?"

"Why don't you tell them?"

"As if they'd listen. As if this generation cares about *humanism.* Did you know that soft drinks are a forty-eight-billion-dollar industry? Did you know that colas—both caffeinated and decaffeinated—comprise a forty-percent market share? And who do you think drinks cola?"

"Who?"

"Youth!" Philip exclaimed. "Youth, youth, youth! Those rats at CeeGee have not only exploited the workers, they've exploited our youth! Did you know that they've signed DeJon Jonson to a twenty-million-dollar ad contract?"

"He's the fellow with the lamé glove?"

"He's the hottest thing in the recording industry, Rabbi. And CeeGee's got him under *contract.*"

"Twenty million is a lot to pay for a fellow with just one glove. Surely you can find a chap with two gloves for a cheaper price."

Philip glared at him.

"What do you *want* from me, Philip?" Feinermann asked.

"I've tried everything, Rabbi. This is my last desperate attempt to gain a victory for *our* side—the side of truth and justice. The key is in your hands because . . ." Philip paused for dramatic effect. "Because *you* are one of the handful of people who know Cola Gold's secret formula."

The rabbi's eyes widened. "Me?"

"There's no use in denying it, Rabbi," Philip stated. "*You* are one of the privileged who know every single ingredient, additive, and flavoring, artificial or otherwise, that give CeeGee's new formula its unique taste."

"Philip—"

"You, Rabbi, have personally checked the formula in an *official* capacity in order to give sanction to the kosher-keeping world that the new formula is as kosher as their original formula. Don't deny it, Rabbi, don't deny it."

"A minute, Philip. Give an old man a minute. Two would even be preferable."

Feinermann needed to collect his thoughts.

He had to think back, because the job had not been part of his regular duties. The assignment had been given to him because Rav Gottlieb, the *mashgiach* for Cola Gold, had come down with a flu named after one of the continents—Asian or African. Feinermann hadn't thought much about it at the time. Gottlieb had been certifying all Cola Gold Inc. beverages as kosher for over twenty years. Still, the corporate wheels hadn't wanted to wait for an old man's recuperation. Gottlieb had suggested Rav Morris Feinermann as a substitute.

As Feinermann recalled it, the CeeGee people hadn't

been happy to deal with him. Only reluctantly had they parted with the formula, and then they'd sworn him to secrecy. At the time Feinermann had thought the management overly dramatic.

He stroked his beard. A mistake on his part to underestimate the competition.

Philip couldn't contain himself. "I *want* that formula, and you will give it to me. You will give it to me because you, like Mr. Benton, are a humanitarian and have the best interest of people upmost in your mind! If we lose our market share, Rabbi, our sales will go down. If our sales decrease, it will be necessary to lay people off from work. And why? Because a cold, heartless manufacturer prefers to use robots rather than *people*. You're a humanist, Rabbi. You will help."

"But I can't give you the formula, Philip. It would be unethical. And there's also a very practical reason. I don't remember it. All the Latin-sounding chemical names they use for flavoring. Very confusing. Perhaps if you had kidnapped me earlier . . ."

"Had we known about the precipitous rise in their market share, believe me, Rabbi, we wouldn't have waited so long. Still, it's never too late." Philip pounded the table. "I'll help you, Rabbi. I have lists and lists of chemicals, the finest hypnotists to help you with memory recall. We will work day and night if we have to. I will do anything within my power, sacrifice myself, because I believe in Mr. Benton."

"I was never a big student of sacrifices, Philip. The bottom line, my young friend, is I will not divulge anything that was given to me in confidence."

Philip's face went crimson, and his eyes became steely and cold. Then his lips turned up in a mean smile. "I can see you'll need a bit of *convincing*." He rang a bell. In walked the Marxes. Red-faced Philip turned to them and, with his irritating chuckle, said, "Take Rabbi Feinermann to the dungeon!"

The Marxes gasped.

"Not the dungeon," Karl exclaimed. "Not the dungeon, Mr. P. Not for a *rabbi*!"

"To the dungeon!" Philip ordered. "And no food and water for him."

That part was acceptable, Feinermann thought. He was fasting anyway.

The old man told them to walk slowly. His back was sore from the car ride, and he was a little light in the head from not having eaten. Then he said, "And just what is this dungeon?"

"Corporate torture, Rabbi," Groucho responded solemnly. "It's better if you don't know."

The rabbi sighed. "I'll survive. Our people have experienced all sorts of adversity."

"Yeah, you guys have sure had some hard knocks," Karl added.

"If you got any personal role models, Rabbi," Groucho said, "you know, people you admire 'cause they're strong—maybe now's the time to start thinkin' about them."

"There is no shortage of Jewish martyrs," Feinermann said. "Take, for example, Channah and her ten sons. A bit of a zealot, Channah was, but righteous nonetheless. She instructed her ten sons to die rather than give themselves over to the Hellenic ways."

"Did they listen to her?" Karl asked.

"Yes, indeed, they did. The youngest was only six, yet he accepted death rather than bow down to the Greek gods and goddesses."

"That's terrible," Groucho said. "A six-year-old kid, what does he know?"

"They were probably more mature in those days," Karl said. "After all, didn't most people kick the bucket around thirty?"

"Still, the kid was only six," Groucho said.

"Surely your corporate torture could not be as terrible as that," Feinermann piped in.

Karl said, "If thinking of this broad helps you along, Rabbi, then more power to you."

"Then I shall think about Channah. And I shall also think about the Ten Martyrs our people read about on Yom Kippur. Our holiest rabbis were tortured to death by the Romans because of their beliefs. One was decapitated, one was burned, one was flayed, and one of the most famous of our sages, Rabbi Akiva, had his flesh raked with hot combs."

"Those Romans were surely uncivilized people!" Groucho exclaimed. "Gladiators, lion pits, and torturing men of the cloth. Even Mr. P. wouldn't do that."

"Comforting," Feinermann said.

"Yeah, Rabbi, that's the spirit!" Karl cheered on.

Feinermann thought: So maybe *this* was his chance to show his faith, like the Ten Martyrs. Always the little Jew against someone of might—the Persians, the Romans, the Spanish of the Inquisition, the Cossacks, and, most deadly, the Nazis. Not to mention Tommy Hoolihan, who beat Feinermann up every day for two years as the small boy of ten with the big black *kippah* walked home from *heder.* His mother thought that the bruises he'd sustained were from falls. She must have thought he was the clumsiest kid in New York.

Twenty-five hundred years of persecution.

Yet the Jews as a nation refused to die. Could he, like Rabbi Akiva, die with the words *Sh'ma Yisroel* on his lips and mean them?

Feinermann thought about that as the two masked men led him to his destiny.

Perhaps he could die a true martyr, perhaps not. But if he couldn't, he wouldn't worry about it too much. After all, how many Rabbi Akivas were there in a lifetime?

He had expected darkness and filth, chains and nooses hanging from the ceiling. And some red-eyed, emaciated rats ready to eat his *kishkas* out. Instead Feinermann was brought into a semicircular projection room. The auditorium consisted of a wide-angled screen and a half-dozen rows of plush chairs, maybe seating for fifty in all.

Not so bad for a dungeon, Feinermann thought.

They placed him in the center row and shackled his feet and hands to the chair. He watched fearfully as Karl took out some masking tape. But all Marx did was tape the old man's eyes open. Not tight enough to prevent him from clearing his eyes of debris, but firmly enough to prevent him from pressing his lids together.

"Scream when you can't take it anymore." Karl stood up. "Nothing personal, Rabbi. I'd like to help you, but I can't." He moved closer to the old man's ear and whispered, "I'm into Elvis for a lot of bread."

"Elvis?" Feinermann said.

Karl swore and hit his face mask, whispering, "That's Groucho's real name. Don't say nothing or we'll both be in deep water. Let's just get this over with."

As Groucho dimmed the lights, Feinermann waited solemnly, wondering why Elvis didn't hide under an Elvis Presley mask. It would have seemed like a natural disguise.

Soon the old man was sitting in total darkness. All he could hear and feel were the sensations his own body provided—the whooshing of blood coursing through his head, his heartbeat, the quick steps of his nervous breathing.

Then the first outside stimulus. A motor running. The room slowly beginning to brighten as shadowy shapes illuminated the movie screen. Sound . . . music . . . bad music. Not only was it sappy but it was old and distorted. It sounded as if it had come from an ancient, irrelevant documentary—the kind they show frequently on PBS.

On-screen was a fuzzy sienna image of a young man digging up potatoes. A voice-over with a reedy mid-Atlantic accent explained that this man was Patrick Benton, Sr., the potato farmer. The shack in the background was Benton's house in County Cork. The film went on to explain the hardships of Irish potato farming, including the great famine of the eighteen hundreds.

A little history lesson never hurt anyone, the rabbi thought. Still, he wished he could blink in earnest. Next on the screen was a boat stuffed with Irish immigrants approaching Ellis Island. He wondered if Tommy Hoolihan's parents were aboard.

Then a cut to a tenement house, not far from where Feinermann grew up. He recognized old buildings that had been razed decades ago. The old clothing, the pushcarts, faces of men and women who still believed in the American Dream. Nostalgia gripped his chest. The film switched to an indoor shot—a frame of a woman with a plump face holding a baby in her arms. She looked like Feinermann's mother. In fact, she could have been any one of a thousand immigrant mothers.

His eyes were watering, and he knew it wasn't because he couldn't blink. The moisture in his orbs represented something deeper.

The baby had been christened Patrick Jr. Feinermann didn't know Mr. Benton's forename, but he was pretty certain he was looking at the great philanthropist himself. As the film progressed, it was clear to the old man that what he was watching was Patrick Jr.'s rags-to-riches story. From the son of a potato farmer to the CEO of one of the biggest corporations in the *world.*

Only in America.

The old man watched with rapt attention.

Philip said to Groucho, "How long has he been in there now?"

"Close to six hours, sir."

"Incredible." Philip paced. "Simply incredible. Most ordinary men would have cracked hours ago. Seeing that same story over and over. Are you sure he didn't puke? Puking is usually the first sign that they're coming around."

"No sign of puke anywhere," Karl said. "It's really amazing. That thing is so corny, *I* almost puked. And I only had to sit through it once."

"Maybe it's because he hasn't eaten," Groucho suggested.

Philip thought about that for a moment. "Did he retch at all?"

"Not even a single *gag,*" Karl said.

"I just don't understand." Philip pulled out his handkerchief and wiped his face. "If psychological torture isn't bringing him around, we'll have to take sterner measures."

Groucho said, "Surely you're not suggestin' *physical* torture?"

"Our market share in the industry is plummeting." Philip wrung his hands. "CeeGee's new formula is wiping us off the map. I've got a five-figure monthly mortgage and a Range Rover owned by the bank. I'm gonna crack that old geezer somehow!"

Over the intercom came Feinermann's voice. "Marxes, can you hear me?"

"Rabbi, it's Philip. We can hear you. What do you want?"

"I think we should talk."

"Are you going to help us, Rabbi?" Philip inquired.

"I will help you, I will help you," Feinermann said.

Philip broke into a wide smile and whispered to his henchmen, "I knew it, I knew it. No one can sit through that much hokey drivel and come out sane." Into the intercom, he said, "I have your word that you will help me, Rabbi?"

"Absolutely, but first I must have your help."

"What do you require from me?"

"I want a few things. First you must call my wife and tell her I will be delayed. She should go hear the Megilla without me, and she shouldn't worry. I'll be home in time to deliver our *shalach manot*—our gift baskets—and our charity to the poor."

"What do I say if she asks questions?"

"Sarah's a practical woman. As long as I can make deliveries tomorrow, she won't care. Next you must get me a *Megillas Esther.* It's nighttime, and I need to read it before I can eat."

Philip said, "I'll find you this . . . Megilla."

"Be sure it's a *Megillas Esther.* There are five *megillos.*"

"Rabbi, I assure you you'll get the whole Megilla," Philip said. "Anything else?"

"I'd like to eat after I read. A kosher meal."

"Done."

"Not so fast, Philip. It is *not* enough to have a kosher meal. I must have a *seudah*—a feast. Not a feast in terms of food. I must have a feast in terms of a party, a gathering." The rabbi thought a moment. "I want to have a feast, and I want it to be in your honor, Philip. You have shown me the light."

"Why, Rabbi, I'm so *honored.*"

"The Marxes can come, too. That will make it quite a deal. And also, you must invite your Mr. Benton as the guest of honor."

Philip didn't like that idea at all. "I don't know if I can do that, Rabbi."

"You want the help?" Feinermann asked.

Philip thought of his five-figure monthly mortgage. "He'll be there. But you mustn't tell him you were—"

" 'Kidnapped' is the word, Philip. But I'm willing to let bygones be bygones. I'm not even angry about it. I think it was the Almighty's way of telling me something."

"You are a remarkable man, Rabbi," Philip said.

"So you will call up your Mr. Benton?"

"Yes," Philip said. "And we will have a feast—to celebrate our new partnership, shall we say?"

"I don't know if 'partnership' is the right word, but if you meet my conditions, I will help you. That's all for now."

Feinermann stopped talking, wondering if his idea would work out. The part about the banquet he'd cribbed straight out of the Megilla. But he didn't feel too guilty about it. If it worked once, maybe it would work again.

Left alone in the library, Feinermann read the Megilla aloud, intoning each word with precision, stomping his foot loudly whenever he came to the name of the evil Haman. According to Jewish law, Haman was so wicked that one's ears were not even supposed to hear his name. Also according to Jewish law, one was required to hear every word of the Megilla, including the name of Haman. A difficult dilemma, Feinermann thought.

When he was done, he closed the Hebrew text, imbued with a sense of purpose. He buzzed Philip, and the bald man came in, a grin slapped upon his face.

"We have prepared a most sumptuous kosher meal for you, Rabbi Feinermann. I've phoned Mr. Benton, and he can't wait to meet the man who will bring KingCola back to its rightful number one position."

The bald man rubbed his hands together.

"Now, don't worry if it takes a little time to recall the formula in its entirety. We have an excellent staff who'll be at your beck and call . . . Tell me the truth, Rabbi. Did they indeed use trichlorobenzoate? I'm not a taste expert, but I swear I detect a little trichlor in their new formula."

"I don't remember, Philip. And even if I did, I couldn't tell you."

"B-b-b . . . but you swore," Philip stammered.

"I swore I wouldn't tell Mr. Benton that you abducted me—a big concession on my part. *And* I swore to help you. I will help you. But I will not give you Cola Gold's formula!"

A buzz came over the intercom. The secretary said, "Mr. Benton's limo has just pulled up, Mr. P."

The bald man began to sweat. Out came the handkerchief. Feinermann noticed it was a new one—white linen, starched and ironed. Philip said, "So help me God, if I hadn't asked Mr. Benton to come personally, I'd tear you limb from limb."

"Not a smart idea, Philip. And against religious law as well."

"Banquet in my honor! This was just a ruse, wasn't it?"

"It worked for Queen Esther—"

"Shut up!"

"Are you going to let me help you, or are you going to sit there like a sodden lump?"

Philip glared at him. For the first time he realized he was working against a formidable opponent. "Just what do I tell Mr. Benton?"

Feinermann held up his hand. "You let me handle your Mr. Benton." He stood. "First we will eat."

The meal started with cabbage soup. The main course was boiled chicken with vegetables, kasha and farfel stuffing, and a salad of chopped onions, tomatoes, and cucumbers. Dessert consisted of apple strudel, tea, and coffee.

Feinermann wiped his mouth with satisfaction while studying the faces of the men who had abducted him, introduced to Benton as chauffeurs. Elvis and Donnie were in their thirties; both had bad skin and little ponytails. Without the masks and the guns, they were not impressive as thugs. But Philip had gotten them for free. You buy cheap, you get cheap. The old man noticed the food was not to their liking. He expected that. But Benton had cleaned his plate.

Everything was going according to plan.

The rabbi asked for a moment to say grace after the meal. While he gave benedictions to the Almighty, he sneaked sidelong glances at the great industrialist/philanthropist.

Patrick Benton had been a tall man in his youth. From the film, Feinermann remembered a strapping man of thirty whose frame easily topped those around him. But now, with the hunched shoulders and the curved spine, Benton didn't seem so tall. His eyes were watery blue, his skin as translucent as tracing paper. What was left of his hair was white. The rabbi noted with pride that most of his own hair was still brown.

Finishing up the last of his prayers, Feinermann sat with his hands folded and smiled at Benton. KingCola's CEO smiled back.

"I don't know when I've eaten such tasty . . . nostalgic food. All these exclusive restaurants I go to, where everyone knows my name and kisses my keister." Benton waved his hand in the air. "Food that doesn't look like food, and the portions aren't big enough to feed a flea. Damn fine grub, Feinermann." He turned to his assistant. "Philip, make a note of where the chow came from. This is the kind of cooking I like."

The bald man quickly pulled out a notepad and began to scribble.

"So." Benton harrumphed. "I understand you have a way to help out KingCola. Philip was sketchy with the details. Give me your ideas, Rabbi."

"Mr. Benton, first I want to say what an honor it is to meet you, even though this was not my idea."

Philip turned pale.

"Not your idea?" Benton questioned.

"Not at all," the rabbi said. "I'll be honest. I didn't know you from any of the other philanthropists with names on buildings until Philip here convinced me to come and meet you. Even so, I wasn't crazy about the prospect. His idea of help and my idea of help weren't exactly the same thing."

Benton looked intrigued. "How so?"

"You see, Mr. Benton, I worked with Cola Gold in a very tangential way. It was necessary for me to learn the formula of their new line of cola—"

"*Good God,* Rabbi! *You* know the formula? That would be worth *millions* to me!"

"I take it you'd pass a few million to me in the process. But that's not the point. I can't give you the formula. That would be unethical."

Benton sat back in his seat. "Yes, of course." He ran his hand through thin strands of white hair. "However, there's nothing . . . unethical . . . about you making . . . suggestions for additives in our competing brand of new-generation cola."

"The problem is, Mr. Benton, I don't know anything about new generations, period. I am from an old generation."

Benton turned to Philip. "So this is why you interrupted me at the clubhouse?"

"Hold on, Mr. Benton," Feinermann said. "Don't be so rude to Philip. The man is not my best friend, but he does have your interests at heart. I don't have any suggestions for your new-generation drinks. But I have a lot of suggestions for your old-generation drinks."

"What old-generation drinks?" Benton asked.

"That's the problem," the rabbi said. "There *are* none. Mr. Benton, I watched your life story many, many times. Not my doing, but be that as it may, I feel I know you quite well. We have a lot in common. We both had immigrant parents, grew up dirt-poor in New York, the first generation of Americans in our family. We were the dreams and hopes of our parents who sacrificed everything so we could have it a little better, *nu*? We lived through the Depression, fought in World War Two, gritted our teeth as our hippie children lived through the sixties. And now, in our waning years, we sit with a sense of pride in our lives and maybe bask a little in our grandchildren. Am I not correct?"

Benton stared at Feinermann. "Exactly! I see you as a man with vision! Philip, *hire* this man on as a consultant. Start him at—"

"Wait, wait," Feinermann interjected. "Thank you for the offer, but I already have a job. And I'm not so visionary. I know how you feel because we're from the same generation. I saw your mother, Mr. Benton. She looked like my mother. She probably knocked herself out chopping meat by hand and scrubbing floors with a sponge."

"Her hands were as rough as sandpaper, poor woman."

"And I bet she always had a pitcher of iced tea in the icebox when you came home from school. Maybe some shpritz from a bottle with the O_2 pellets?"

Benton smiled. "You've got that one down."

"No cans of cola in her refrigerator."

"Just where is all this leading?" Philip asked.

"Shut up!" Benton replied. "We're reminiscing."

Again Feinermann wiped his mouth. "I'll tell you where this is leading, Philip. Pay attention, because it has to do with business."

The bald man wiped his forehead. "I'm listening."

Feinermann said, "You have a multibillion-dollar business that provides beverages to America. And *all* of your products are aimed at the young or the ones who wish they were young. Not that I have anything against the new generation, but I can't relate to them. And I don't drink the same things they drink. I want my glass of tea with a lemon. I want my old-fashioned shpritz without essences of this flavor or that flavor. Whatever happened to tonic water and ginger ale, for goodness' sake?"

"We have ginger ale," Philip protested. "King Ginger."

"Ach!" The rabbi gave him a disgusted look. "Relegated to the back of the cooler. The young people think it's a drink for stomach maladies."

"You have to realize that New Age drinks comprise a measly three hundred and twenty-seven million dollars of market sales," Philip said. "Ginger ale's a drink with no appeal."

"It appeals to me," Feinermann insisted.

"The rabbi's got a point," Benton said. "The New Age drinks do appeal to the older set. And let's not forget the growth rate, Philip—fifteen percent as compared to two percent in the industry as a whole."

"There you go," Feinermann stated. "When are you companies going to wake up and realize there is a whole generation out there waiting for you to appeal to them?" He turned to Benton. "You gobbled up dinner tonight because it reminded you of your mother's cooking."

Benton bit his lip. "I see what you're saying. But, Rabbi, you have to realize that carbonated beverages are still a youth-oriented market."

"Because you *choose* to woo the youth. What about me?"

"The elderly market is tricky," Benton said.

"Even if you convert them to your product, they're just going to keel over anyway," Philip said.

Benton glared at his assistant. "I beg your pardon."

"No . . . I mean . . . not you, Mr. Benton—"

"Calm down, Philip," Feinermann said with little patience. "Yes, we're all going to die. Even your Mr. Benton here. But I see your point. So don't market them as old-fashioned drinks. Make them *family* drinks. Seltzer, tonic water, ginger ale—promote them as new, lighter, less sugary drinks with a history of *America.* Show teenagers and grandpas drinking them at the family barbecues. What could be better?"

Philip said, "I've got the hook, sir—a New Age drink with a touch of nostalgia."

"I like it, Philip," Benton said.

"And what about iced teas?" Feinermann said.

Philip said, "Only a four-hundred-million-dollar share of the market."

Feinermann said, "But combine it with your three-hundred-and-twenty-seven-million-dollar New Age share, Philip. That's almost a billion dollars."

"Man's got a point, Philip."

"Tensel's has a lock on tea, sir," Philip said. "Besides, I

heard Heavenly Brew is coming out with a new line. Lots of teas for such a little market share."

"Ah, Heavenly Brew. That's not *tea.* Not tea the way Mr. Benton and I remember it," Feinermann said.

Benton nodded. "True. We had tea that rotted the gut. How about a new full-flavored tea drink, Philip? It just might work, especially if we get a decaf version."

"Very good, Mr. Benton."

Feinermann said, "We're a lost generation, Mr. Benton, just waiting for someone to sing our tunes. Stop regurgitating old cola recipes and expand your horizons."

Benton exclaimed, "Glad you brought all this to my attention, Rabbi! Philip, make a note to bring all this crap to the board's attention this Thursday. And, Rabbi, you will join us at the meeting, won't you?"

"Thursday I have a funeral to preside over. I'm afraid I must pass. Besides, I've stated my piece. Perhaps now your Philip will leave me in peace?"

"Absolutely! Philip, stop pestering the rabbi."

Philip nodded like a Kewpie doll.

Feinermann stood. "If you don't mind, I'd like to take my leave."

"Certainly, Rabbi," Benton responded. "And anytime you need anything, just ask."

"Thank you, Mr. Benton." The old man shook hands with the philanthropist and bade him goodbye. As he was accompanied back to the car, walking in the cool March air, he reflected on how much he missed his childhood. Not the part about being beaten up by Tommy Hoolihan . . . and he didn't miss the cholera and polio, either. But he did miss his youth—a generation that grew up without TV. And a good glass of ginger ale . . . corporations do forget about the elderly—a reflection of society, he supposed.

Ah well, at least he'd sleep in his own bed tonight.

When they arrived at the Cadillac, Feinermann said to Philip, "You don't have to come back with me. The Marxes know the way."

"The Marxes?" Philip said.

"Private joke, Mr. P.," Donnie/Karl said.

Philip shook hands with the rabbi. "I'm sorry if I inconvenienced you."

"No problem," Feinermann said. "I'll integrate the experience into next week's sermon." He opened the door to the backseat. "By the way, Marxes, what did you do with the face masks?"

"They're in the trunk," Elvis/Groucho said. "Why?"

"Unless you're planning another abduction, give them to me," Feinermann said. "I'll use them in the Purim festivities! Why let them go to waste?"

These last four stories and essays deal less with mystery and more with my favorite subject—family. My husband, Jonathan, and I have been married for thirty-four years, a union that has produced four children and a lot of material for my fiction. I thank them all—husband, parents, children, grandparents, uncles, aunts, and cousins—for my beautiful life.

FREE PARKING

"Free Parking" is a charming tale that addresses the gap between generations. Its origin was a conversation I had with my daughter Rachel. I chose the game Monopoly as a nexus for the story because that was the board game that my mother and her sisters used to play with their *mother. Family lore states that Grandma was so sedentary, her daughters used to move her token around the board for her.*

ALL OF OUR FAMILY TRADITIONS ARE stupid, but at least this one's harmless. And just maybe Great-granny enjoys it, although she never says so to me. At eighty-seven, Great-granny doesn't say much of anything. Not that she's senile. She knows all her children, her grandchildren, and her great-grandchildren, but she just doesn't talk anymore. Mom says she never talked much to begin with, so I suppose the adjustment was an easy one.

Great-granny has been in an old-age home for about six years now. It's called the Golden Years, and it's a nice place, especially in the summertime. It has a fenced back-yard that holds a sweeping lawn outlined with beds of jeweled marigolds. Behind the fence sits Taylor's Woods, full of sweet-smelling leaves and crunchy bark that decays into soft ground that sinks beneath your sneakers. The backyard also has an old swing set off to the side. When I was younger, I used to pass the time swinging. Even back then the seat—a black leather strap—was cracked and dry, and the chains that held it creaked as I rose and fell. The rusty rhythm used to rock me into a trance, making the visiting hours go quickly.

But now I'm twelve and too old to swing, too old to play explorer in the woods. Mom expects more. Not that she makes me come. But if I'm going to come, I have to behave like an adult, whatever *that* means. I never liked the way adults act around old people. They're uncomfortable with them, like being elderly is contagious. They're freaked out by the palsies and the bladder bags, by the toothlessness and drool. None of that stuff bothers me, but maybe that's because I've been visiting Great-granny forever. Besides, it isn't that much different from my schoolmates, with Emma Tolosky munching on her hair, or Sammy Robertson squeezing his zits, or the worst . . . Jason Rathers picking his nose and rubbing it in his history book. I'll take Granny over Jason any day of the week.

My family is considered a good one by the staff. We visit Great-granny with prune-eating regularity. Twice a week my grandma, my two great-aunts, and my mom trudge down to the home. It has become such a routine, it's been ritualized—Tuesday afternoon there are the soaps, Thursday morning is the Monopoly game, and then there's the bimonthly brunch picnic with all the aunts and cousins, weather permitting, of course. I'm only obligated to go to the picnics, because I'm in school. But this particular Thursday, some kind of teachers' conference was called at my school, so I'm off.

Then Mom suggests that I might do a good deed and come with her. In an unusual burst of generosity, I say okay. I put down my book, put on my shoes, and climb way back in the van to make room for Grandma and her two sisters. Since we own a big car, Mom drives carpool.

My great-aunts have daughters, too, but *my* mom is the only one who visits Granny on a regular basis. Which gives my grandma lots of brownie points over her sisters. My great-aunts have tried to disparage Mom's visits, Kate saying things like: "I'm so happy that Allison has so much free time. Connie works so hard as a lawyer."

Or sometimes Great-aunt Renee will say, "Allison is such a caring girl. She should really think about becoming a social worker, like my Judy."

My mom, who takes a very Zen approach to life, always chooses to ignore the barbs. Rather, it's like she never even hears them in the first place. *Nothing* ever bothers her. Not me and my mouth, not my klutzy older sister, not even my hypochondriac father, who has yet to figure out how he got from football hero to middle-aged man. My mom has always been the eye in the swirling storm. All activity centers around her, but she never seems to get caught up by it. Always calm but caring, even if she is a space cadet. It's better than Emma's mom, who yells all the time.

Grandma, on the other hand, is not one to let things pass. Whenever her sisters would throw verbal daggers at my mom, Grandma Lion would get this steely look in her eyes and say things like:

"Your shmocial worker Judy has time for everyone except her family."

Or:

"And your Connie has *plenty* of time to go to the gym but not to visit her own flesh and blood?"

Then Mom would take a deep breath and put on a serene smile and say, "Mom, Connie is Connie, and I'm me."

Then Grandma would add, "Thank goodness for that." Otherwise, Granny would never have any visitors under sixty.

Of course, Great-aunt Kate would have to defend her progeny. "Connie needs a way to burn up her frustrations at work, Ida."

"So let her lead an aerobics class for the people here at the home," Grandma would snap back.

Then Guru Mom would say in a calm voice, "Everybody has their own strengths."

"Your daughter is very wise," Great-aunt Kate would state with authority.

And Renee would agree, and that would be that until the next time. Until the next visit, when Mom would show up again and their daughters wouldn't. And the whole thing would repeat itself in some variation or another.

When *I* show up, well, it's almost too much for them to bear.

How sweet for Christy to come.

Isn't she a special girl.

What a little love you have there, Allison. She must take after you!

Today Grandma wears a pink polyester suit complete with a matching plastic purse. Renee has on a bulky mustard sweater over black stretch pants. Kate has chosen a multicolored caftan and dangling wooden earrings.

Kate has been married three times. Last time she took the plunge, she wanted an alternative ceremony. My second cousin Sandy, her grandniece, played the recorder as Kate danced down the aisle and threw autumn leaves and dried rose petals from a basket she had made in her junior college art class. She and her husband, Hubert, made vows to the Earth Goddess, Ceres, and prayed for the release of the Mother Spirit. My great-granny had raised her daughters Baptist, but if she disapproved of Kate's wedding, she never said so.

This morning both Mom and I wear jeans, T-shirts, and sneakers. My T is red, Mom's is white. Mom made a vow to always wear white in some form or another because she says it symbolizes purity. She got that idea from one of the Eastern religion books on her nightstand. *I* think she wears white T's because they're easy. Just throw on a Hanes special and you're dressed for any occasion.

We arrive at the home around ten in the morning, time for Granny's midmorning snack. Great-granny has her own semiprivate dining room containing four round tables, six chairs per table. Granny is about four foot five and weighs about one fifty, down from her former weight of two hundred plus. She started losing pounds awhile back, and everyone panicked that she was sick. It turned out to be a case of ill-fitting dentures.

Today the snack is ice cream, so Great-granny's in seventh heaven. The dining room's jammed, staff working fast and furious, so we're expected to give a hand. I take to feeding Mr. Zarapata. Carefully, I give him measured spoonfuls of orange sherbet. But he becomes impatient with me.

"You feed me like a baby," he croaks out testily. "Give me more."

I give him a bigger spoonful. Of course, he starts coughing. I wipe spittle off his mouth. "Told you so," I say.

"You little snot," he retorts.

"Yeah, yeah. Open your mouth."

He complies, then complains once again that I'm feeding him like a baby. And on and on it goes until he polishes off his sherbet and snack time's over. By the time I finish wiping his mouth, plumping his pillow, and adjusting the footrests of his wheelchair, Great-aunt Kate has set up the board on one of the cleared tables. Great-aunt Renee wheels Great-granny over, and Grandma pulls up five chairs. Mr. Zarapata asks if he can play, too, but tradition demands that only blood relatives play. He calls us all snots—and worse—until finally, a nurse wheels him away.

"We have enough tokens for eight," I say to Grandma.

"Rules are rules," she answers.

"Yeah, but who makes up the rules?" I contest. "We do. So that means we can change them."

"Rules are rules," Renee answers.

"That's right," Kate agrees. "Rules are rules."

"Rules are a state of mind," my mother interjects. "In the universe, there are no absolutes."

"I want the thimble," Renee states.

"You had the thimble last week," Grandma says.

"No, I had the hat," Renee corrects.

"You had the thimble," Grandma repeats.

"Kate had the thimble," Renee says. "I had the hat."

I reach over and grab the thimble. "Here, Renee."

Renee takes the thimble. "I had the hat last week. You're thinking two weeks ago."

"Who wants to go first?" I say.

"Wait, Christy," Grandma says. "I don't even have my token yet. I think I'll be the iron."

"I was going to be the iron," Kate says. "Why don't you be the rocking horse? You had good luck with that last week."

"No, I had good luck with the shoe," Grandma says. "Okay, you be the iron, I'll be the shoe."

"I'll be the race car," I say. "I'll roll first to see who goes first."

"Wait, wait," Grandma says. "Your mother doesn't have her token. And nobody has any money. Who's the bank?"

"I can be the bank," my mom says.

"Mom, I'll be the bank," I say, picking up a stack of apricot-colored five-hundred-dollar bills. "By the time you count out the money, it'll be dark."

My mom gives me a gentle rap on the shoulder. "Have a little patience."

"You're so impatient, Christy," my grandma chides.

"It's because she's young," Renee pronounces.

"I know she's young," Grandma says. "But she's also impatient. Allison isn't impatient."

"That's because Allison has time," Renee mutters out loud under her breath.

"That's because her husband makes a *good* living and she doesn't have to work," Grandma mutters even louder under her breath.

I start doling out the cash. "Mom, did you choose a token yet?"

"You choose one for me."

I hand her the wheelbarrow. At this point Mom closes her eyes and puts on her Buddha smile.

"You're not going to *chant* first, Allison." Renee turns to my grandma. "Ida, she's not going to chant, is she?"

Grandma reaches out and touches my mother's arm. "Allison, honey, we don't have time for the chant today. Renee has a hairdresser's appointment."

Kate says, "Why are you going to the hairdresser's, Renee?"

My grandma gets a teasing look on her face. "She's got a date tonight—"

"Oh, hush up," Renee scolds. "It's not a date."

My mother says, "I refuse to play without some acknowledgment of the Higher Spirit."

"Oh, for goodness' sakes!" Renee mutters.

Grandma says, "Hush up. How about the hands thing, Allison?"

"The universal hand circle would be lovely," Mom states. "Let's all join together and give praise to our spirits and souls."

We all take each other's hands. I'm sitting next to Great-granny. Her hand is dry, knobby, and liver-spotted. I give it a small kiss, and Great-granny smiles. Slowly, she strokes my face with a crooked finger. I kiss her again and admire her nails. They are clean and manicured—courtesy of her daughters.

My mother closes her eyes and says, "Heavenly Being, we thank You for the opportunity to address You, and for the many blessings You have bestowed upon this family. Please bless the game we are about to play."

Mom opens her eyes and says, "Great-granny, do you want to be the hat?"

Great-granny grunts. Mom picks up the hat and places it on Go.

"I'll roll first," I say. "Just to see who goes first."

"Just go, Christy," Grandma says. "I can see you're very impatient."

I roll the dice. I get a five. I buy a railroad.

Kate says, "Mom, you can be next." She rolls the dice for her and says, "Mom, do you want to buy Oriental?"

Great-granny grunts. Kate buys Oriental. She says, "So, Renee, tell me about this date that isn't a date."

Renee says, "There's nothing to tell."

Kate says, "So tell me the nothing. Who is he?"

"He's William the ex-insurance agent," Grandma says.

"Not ex," Renee clarifies. "He's retired."

"Did I ever meet him?" Mom wants to know.

Renee says, "He insured your house, Allison. Don't you remember?"

"I remember someone." She thinks for a moment. "I'm usually good at faces. What does he look like?"

"It's someone's turn," I state. "Whose turn is it?"

Grandma says, "He's nice-looking. Except for the beard. The beard has to go."

"I like the beard," Renee says.

"It's too white."

Renee says, "He's old, Ida. Of course it's white."

Grandma says, "It looks like someone threw a pie in his face."

"I don't think I know him," my mother says. "But David usually deals with the insurance agents."

"Whose turn is it?" I say in a singsong voice.

Nobody knows. Mom shrugs. "I'll go." She rolls a seven and lands on Connecticut. "I think I'll buy . . . no, forget it. I'll pass."

"Why?" I ask.

"Because if I buy the property, Great-granny can't get a monopoly."

I stare at her. "Mom, that's why you should buy the property. You want to block anyone else from getting a monopoly."

My mom smiles at me and whispers, "Christy, don't you know that Great-granny always wins?"

I frown. "You mean the game is fixed?"

"We prefer to think of it as predetermined."

Grandma says, "You're upsetting Christy's bile, Allison. Buy the property. Trade it to Great-granny later."

"It's okay if I buy it, Great-granny?" Mom asks.

"I don't believe this," I say to myself.

Great-granny grunts. Mom buys the property. It's Renee's turn. She rolls the dice and lands on my railroad. I make her pay me the twenty-five dollars.

"Such avarice," Renee states, handing me five five-dollar bills.

"It's the rules," I say.

"I know it's the rules. It's just that you ask me for money with such relish!"

"She's young," Kate says. "So where are you and William your nondate going to go, Renee?"

"Probably the Submarine Station for a tuna sandwich."

"That's your date?" I say to my great-aunt. "A tuna sandwich at the Submarine Station?"

"I told you, it isn't a date." Renee talks to me like I'm a child.

"Then why are you getting your hair done?" I ask.

"Because she wants to look nice," Grandma says as if I'm a moron. "Why are you going to the Submarine Station instead of the Salad Shop?"

"Because the Submarine Station is closer."

"Two blocks closer," my grandma says.

"Two blocks is two blocks," Renee says.

"Whose turn is it?" I'm dying of boredom.

Grandma picks up the dice and rolls. "I still don't understand why you'd want to go to the Submarine Station. I thought you like plate food."

Renee says, "I do like plate food."

"So do I," Kate pipes in. "I never could understand the breast-of-chicken sandwich. I like chicken on a plate, with a fork and a knife and a nice glass of tea. Chicken does not belong in a sandwich."

"1 can even understand the chicken sandwich," Grandma states. "But meatballs? Meatballs belong on spaghetti—"

"Or on rice," Renee interrupts.

"I'll give you rice," Grandma concedes. "But meatballs definitely do not belong in a sandwich. Like in Gardilucci's on Third. I don't understand these Italian restaurants."

"I agree that meatballs belong on a plate," Kate says. "But that's not true of all chopped meat. Take hamburgers, for instance. I like hamburgers in a sandwich, not on a plate."

"Hamburgers belong in a sandwich," my mom agrees.

I say, "Grandma, you landed on Chance. You're supposed to pick a card."

She picks a card but doesn't read it. "So if you like plate food, Renee, why are you going to a sandwich place?"

Renee says, "Because sandwiches are easier to eat than plate food. I always spill on the first date."

Kate says, "I thought you said it wasn't a date."

"It isn't a date," Renee says. "But I still don't want to spill."

"You can spill with a sandwich," Grandma says. "Especially the big ones they make at the Submarine Station. You take a bite and it comes smushing out the other end."

I take the card from my grandmother, read it, and pay the fine with her money. "Grandma, you've got to roll again. You got doubles."

Grandma looks up. "I rolled doubles?"

"Yes."

"You're the boss, Christy." She rolls the dice absently. She gets doubles again.

"You want to buy State, Grandma?" I ask.

"Certainly I want to buy State! What do you think?" Grandma hands me two hundred dollars. "Give me change, honey."

Kate says, "You don't wrap your sandwiches in a napkin, Ida? I always wrap up my sandwiches. When I eat sandwiches. Mostly I like plate food."

"Except hamburgers," I mutter.

"Exactly," Kate agrees.

I give Grandma change. "You rolled doubles again."

"Christy, hold on," Grandma says. "You're giving me a headache."

"Just trying to move the game along," I say with a strained smile.

"Then what?" Renee says. "We finish and I have to wait three hours for my hair appointment. Ida, roll the dice. You're making Christy antsy."

Grandma gets a ten and lands on Free Parking. "Where's my money? Christy, honey, you forgot to put out the money for Free Parking."

"That's not in the rules," I say.

No one says anything, but I sense hostility. "You guys play with one hundred or five hundred?" I say, taking both bills from the bank.

Grandma smiles. "Now you're catching on. Monopoly isn't life, Christy. In life, there's no such thing as Free Parking."

Kate says, "To me, Free Parking symbolizes stagnation. You don't go anywhere, you don't do anything. You just sit there."

"Or it could be the elusive respite we're all looking

for," Mom says. "The opportunity to meditate without interference."

"To me, Free Parking is family," Grandma says.

"The whole game is a metaphor for family," Kate says.

"It is?" I ask.

Grandma pats my hand. "You'll understand when you have your own children."

I nod as if I understand her.

"In the meantime, I'll take five hundred bucks." Grandma snatches the bill from my hand.

Renee says, "You know, Allison, if Christy hurries up and has a baby, you can have five generations of Hathaway women."

"I'm only twelve," I say.

"Say you have a baby at twenty-two," Kate says. "Not so impossible."

"Not at all," Grandma agrees.

"That means Mom has to make it to ninety-seven," Renee says.

"Mom has longevity in the family," Kate says.

"It would be better to have the baby at twenty," Renee states.

Grandma says, "Mom, didn't your mother live to ninety-two?"

Great-granny grunts twice.

"Ninety-three, excuse me," Grandma says.

Renee says, "So split the difference and have a baby at twenty-one, Christy."

"Thanks for planning my life," I say.

"Oh, Christy." My grandma waves me away. "Can't you take a joke?"

I don't say anything, because I know she's not joking. "Whose *turn* is it?" I say angrily.

"Mom, is it your turn?" Renee says.

"Great-granny had her turn," I say. "She bought Oriental, remember?"

"I'll take a turn," Renee says. "Unless you want to go ahead of me, Kate?"

I blurt out, "How do you guys *ever* finish anything? You move so slowly and talk so much, it'll be Easter by the time we're done."

Five pairs of eyes stare at me. Even *Granny* is looking at me. I suddenly feel embarrassed by my outburst. No one knows what to say, and I mutter an apology.

Renee pats my arm. "Aw, youth."

"It's hard being with a bunch of old ladies," Kate says.

"No, really, it's not," I say. "I'm just impatient." I pick up the dice and give them to Renee. "Your turn."

At first everyone is real quiet, and I feel very bad. But after a few minutes, the chatter starts. I bite my lip and endure it. The rest of the visit moves *slowly.* I try to understand them, I try to be patient, I even try to contemplate the true meaning of Free Parking. But I fidget and squirm and probably make everyone feel uncomfortable. Two hours later, the game is still going. Renee checks her watch and says it's time for her hairdresser's appointment. Without ceremony, we clean up the board, get up, and kiss Great-granny goodbye. They will meet again for the game next week. I'm sure they'll be happy that I'll be in school.

After Mom has dropped off her kin, I turn to her. "How do you stand it week after week?"

"Stand what?"

"The game, Mom. They move so slow. It's so *boring*!"

"It depends on what you want out of the game, Christy. For you, the outcome is important—who wins, who loses. For your grandma and her sisters, it's the process. The game is just an excuse for them to get together and chat."

"So why don't they just get together and chat?"

"Because then Great-granny wouldn't be included."

"She's hardly included now. They move her pieces, they talk around her. All *she* does is make an occasional grunt."

Mom smiles at me and kisses my cheek. "You'll understand when you get older."

"Yeah, just like I'll understand the philosophy of Free Parking."

My mom pauses for a moment. "Some people race through life, Christy. Some people stroll through it. Whatever suits you, suits me. Just remember, whether you walk or run, it doesn't matter much. The finish line is still death."

I frowned. "What a morbid thought."

"Not if you have beautiful children like I do."

I stare at her. "That isn't a hint, is it?"

"A hint?"

"You guys kept saying that I should have a baby at twenty-one. They didn't really mean that, did they?"

"Of course not," she says. "They were just doing some idle talk."

"A lot of idle talk."

My mom kisses me. "Have a little patience, Christy."

"You sound like Grandma."

"I am her daughter. Maybe one day you'll sound like me."

A scary thought. I say nothing.

"After all, we are four generations of Hathaway women." She smiles. "And maybe one day, when you're willing . . . and the Higher Spirit is willing . . . it will be five generations."

"But *not* at twenty-one," I say.

"I agree," Mom says. "No sense rushing things. Besides, it could all be for naught. You just might have a boy."

The LUCK *of the* DRAW

with Rachel Kellerman

and Ilana Kellerman

"The Luck of the Draw" is a sweet story that was commissioned for the anthology Mothers and Daughters, *edited by Jill Morgan. It was cowritten with my daughters, Rachel and Ilana. I wanted this effort to be a true collaboration, not my interpretation of their ideas. To achieve that goal, I had the girls write from their point of view. Rachel and Ilana, now young women, were fifteen and eleven when we wrote this story, and as I reread their words, I find them a touching window into bygone days. What a cherished way to capture my daughters' points of view as children.*

Amanda's Turn

I thought Jack was kidding when he told me the news. But when he pulled the kids out of school, I knew he was serious. He sat them both down to tell them the same thing he had told me. That he had won the lottery.

"Not the big, big money," he explained. "Five out of six on the Scratchers."

I was stunned. Jack hadn't gone into the specifics. Our younger daughter, Beth, clapped her hands and paraded around the room. Our elder daughter, Toni, asked the obvious question.

"How much?"

Jack answered, "The amount isn't important."

We looked at him, dumbfounded.

"Well, put it this way. Not enough for me to quit the firm." He added this with a wink. "But guess who's going to get her own car on her sixteenth birthday?"

Toni leaped up and hugged him with all her strength. I was happy for her but angry with Jack. Money did not give him the right to make unilateral decisions.

"What about me?" Beth asked.

Jack broke from Toni's grip. Again out came the wink. "Well, we might splurge on something special for you."

"Like?"

I said, "No need to go into details right now." I realized

my voice was harsh and softened my tone. "1 need to talk to your father, girls. Right now and alone."

After they had left, he was peeved. "Look, I realize I should have discussed it with you first. But did you have to cut me off in my moment of glory?"

I said, "How much?"

He was clearly irritated. "Two mil."

I gasped. Then I did the mental math. Two million amortized over twenty years came out to about one hundred thousand a year. After deducting for taxes, we now had an additional seventy thousand dollars of disposable income.

Yes, we could easily afford a car for Toni. And a new stereo for Beth. And that small speedboat that Jack had been eyeing. And what about redoing the kitchen?

I broke out into laughter. I gave my husband a bear hug.

On weekends the mall was always crowded. But ritual was ritual, and every Saturday my mother, my daughters, and I trekked through the ganglia of stores and tried to bond. Sometimes these excursions were pleasant. Sometimes they were exhausting. Since winning the lottery, those days had become tedious.

Beth was nagging me. "Why can't I have the dress? We can afford it."

I counted to ten so I wouldn't lose my temper.

That seemingly innocuous phrase.

We can afford it.

And then I launched into my standard explanation. "Just because we can afford something doesn't mean I'm obligated to *buy* it."

Beth was now sulking. My mother tried to comfort her,

which made me angrier. I tried to contain my ire and be rational. "I bought you clothes a few weeks ago, Beth."

"But they didn't have the white dress in my size, Mom. You said you'd buy it for me."

"I said you could wait and I'd buy it when it arrived in your size. *Or,* I said, you could have the plaid dress. You chose the plaid dress. End of story!"

Beth muttered to herself.

I tried to be motherly. "Honey, yesterday I saw a gorgeous suit. It was beautiful and it fit me perfectly. But I didn't buy it. You know why?"

"Here comes the lecture," Beth said. "Because it's not healthy to have everything you want."

Of course, that shut me up.

"Where's Toni?" my mother asked.

"She went into her favorite store. She's looking at some pants."

"You bought Toni pants last week," Beth said. "Why does she get pants this week and last week?"

"I bought her a pair of jeans. Today she's looking at dress pants. Beth, it doesn't matter what Toni has or what Toni does. We're not dealing with Toni now, we're dealing with you. You made your choice, and that's it!"

"You're not being—"

"I don't want to hear this!"

With that, Beth stomped away.

"Where are you going?" I shouted at her.

"I'll be at Body Beautiful . . . *looking* at stuff I can't buy!"

At least she hadn't added "because my mom isn't fair."

My mother tried to he helpful. "They'll get over it. Things'll be back to normal. Once they've . . . adjusted."

I turned to my mother, smiling sadly. "Know what, Ma? Every day I thank God that we didn't hit the big one."

She laughed, then frowned. Instantly, I spotted the reason behind her wariness. Toni had returned, carrying three separate parcels. She gave me a cat-in-the-canary-cage smile.

Wryly, I said, "That must be one large pair of pants."

She showed me what she had bought. I told her she'd have to return everything but the pants. She told me I didn't understand. I said that might be, but she'd still have to take back her purchases.

And then the famous retort.

"We have the *money,* don't we?"

At that point I gave my mother the car keys and elected to walk home.

Toni's Turn

When I was called out of class that Thursday, I thought maybe someone had died. Why else would Mom let me miss school? She was uptight about those types of things. But nothing could have prepared me for the news to come.

"We won *what*?" shrieked Beth, my younger sister.

"Whoa," I muttered under my breath.

The *lottery.*

Of course, my parents wouldn't tell us the specifics, like how much we had actually won. But I was promised a car, so I wasn't about to stage a protest.

So we had finally come into some money. Not like we were hurting financially, but I knew the money would help us out. Mom was always nervous when it came to money, and I thought the extra cash might put her more at ease. And if she was more relaxed, she'd be more inclined to buy her lovely elder daughter more wonderful tokens of affection.

Yes, this new lifestyle was fine by me.

Later that day I overheard Mom talking to Grandma about the whole thing on the phone.

"Yes, Ma, the lottery. One of those Scratcher tickets . . . No, not all six numbers . . . I know—amazing, isn't it? Jack has always had good luck, but still, the odds of winning are so low. But you know what's strange? I have mixed feelings about this. On one hand, I'm thrilled. Who wouldn't be thrilled about winning two million dollars . . ."

So *that's* how much we had won!

Mom continued, "But I'm kind of worried this will go to everyone's head. Jack has already promised Toni a car, and Beth thinks we're millionaires now . . . I know, I know. I just don't want to spoil them."

She didn't want to spoil us? Didn't want the money to go to our heads? Who cares if it does when it means we can live more comfortably?

But I knew how to plan my course of action. Not to complain, not to ask for a lot. I'd have to work my way up slowly and be excessively grateful. I would show Mom that I was not taking the money for granted. And then she'd realize that the money wasn't spoiling us. And she could buy us what we wanted with a clear conscience.

I started my plan Saturday at the mall. At first everything went as planned. With much restraint, I picked out only one pair of pants. One. And they weren't even expensive. Mom seemed pleased.

Good.

A couple of weeks after we had won the money, I was still sticking to my plan.

Beth was a different story. She went psycho when Mom told her no, she couldn't have another pair of shoes and two dresses.

"But, Mom," she complained, "it's not fair. I've wanted these dresses for such a long time. Lisa's mother bought her four outfits last week, and her father didn't even win the lottery."

Grandma tried to cover a smile. I knew my actions would look even better next to Beth's greedy fits.

I separated from everyone to go into one of my favorite stores.

Big mistake number one. Mom had given me her credit card to buy some dress pants.

Big mistake number two. As I looked around, I knew I was losing my self-control.

"Restraint," I muttered to myself. But everything was so cute—and not *that* expensive. Besides, we could afford it.

After a while, eight new articles of clothing now officially belonged to me.

I smiled.

Mom did not when she saw what I had bought.

"Toni, I really expected more from you. You're fifteen. How could you do this?"

She wouldn't even look at me.

I said, "But you just don't understand—"

"I do understand," Mom interrupted. "But maybe you don't understand the concept of self-discipline. You girls are unappreciative. I never would have acted like this. You're going to have to go back and return the items."

Return them? I just couldn't understand why Mom was being so uptight. I know she didn't want us to get into the habit of buying everything we wanted, but I thought she could be a little more understanding. I had to say it.

"Mom, I really don't see why you should care so much. We have the money, don't we?"

Mom looked exasperated. When she stomped off, I didn't know what to think.

Beth's Turn

I guess when I found out we had won the lottery, it made my day. I'm in sixth grade, and that day I had just taken a social studies quiz and a big English grammar test.

I'm the worst at grammar.

Mr. Furling had called me out of class, and I saw Dad. He took me home and told me the big news. We had won the lottery. I didn't care how much. I paraded around the room. When my dad told Toni, standing for Tonia, that she could buy a car, I thought about my own list of things that I wanted: a pair of Steve Madden shoes, a couple of new dresses, and a CD player with a Spice Girls CD to go along with it.

Even though we had won the lottery, I was still frustrated about the tests I had taken. So when we went shopping and the store didn't have the beautiful long, slinky white dress in my size, I almost cried. Mom gave me the choice of waiting for the dress in my size or getting a blue-and-white-plaid dress that was half price. I'm not very good at waiting, so I grumpily told my mom that I would take the plaid dress. My sister, Toni, bought a pair of jeans.

A few weeks later, we took another trip to the mall, and I saw the white dress in size ten—my size! It was just my fit, and I could get great use out of it. So I ran over to ask Mom if we could buy it. She said no. At first I kept saying please, please, please.

Then I got so upset that I yelled, "It's not like we can't afford it."

Mom started giving me this whole lecture about how she didn't buy a suit because she used common sense. Being argumentative, I told her there was no such thing as common sense, because everyone had different genes in their bodies. I also reminded her that she had said she would buy the dress when it came to the store in my size. Mom seemed very agitated, explaining that I had made a choice.

Grandma tried to comfort me, but that didn't help. Then I started to compare Toni to me. I said that Toni got to buy two pairs of pants, why couldn't I have two dresses? Mom told me Toni was not my concern.

Tears streamed from my eyes, but I didn't want Mom to see them. When she asked what was wrong, I told her I was sweating from frustration. I remembered I had five dollars in my pocket and I started to walk away. When Mom asked me where I was going, I screamed that I was going to Body Beautiful to *look* because I didn't want to steal any of her *precious* money.

While I was walking away, I saw Toni coming out of her store carrying three bags.

"You're crazy," I said. "Mom won't allow it."

Toni just glared at me like all snobby older sisters do and walked away. When I got to Body Beautiful, I bought mango-scented bubble bath. I had earned my five dollars washing the neighbor's car.

Then the strangest thing happened. I looked out the mall window and saw Mom stomping down the sidewalk. I felt bad for what I had done and decided to give her the bubble bath.

The Solution

I said, "I called this family meeting because something has to be done!"

My daughters stared at their laps with sullen expressions.

I continued, "Winning the lottery doesn't give you two license to start making demands!"

"So you can continue to be arbitrary," snapped Toni.

"That's uncalled for." Jack leaped to my defense. "Apologize."

"She is being arbitrary," Toni insisted. "You both are. One minute you're both expansive, saying we can afford this and that and taking us out to fancy restaurants. The next minute I find a blouse—*on sale,* no less—and you won't buy it for me. Oh, you have enough to afford a hundred-dollar bottle of wine, but I can't buy a fifteen-dollar blouse."

Jack said, "What *we* do with *our* money is our concern, not yours."

"Obviously," Beth retorted.

"You know what I think?" I said. "I think we were doing just great before this lottery business came up. I think we should . . . give it all to charity!"

Jack smiled. "I'll tell you girls right here and now, if things don't work out soon, we're going to give Mom's idea some real thought."

I looked at my husband. "Jack, I'm serious. Let's give it away—"

"Amanda—"

"Okay. We'll keep enough for the girls' education. Give them some motivation for doing well in school. But beyond that, I think I've hit upon a perfect solution. We weren't hurting before. Why shouldn't we share our good fortune?"

My family was stunned. No one spoke.

Finally, Beth said, "Dad, *say* something."

Jack faltered. "Honey, I admire your nobility. But there's no reason to be hasty. Besides, we've made plans for that money."

"I know we've made plans," I ventured on. "And Toni has made plans. And Beth has made plans as well. So whose plans do we listen to? And you know as well as I do that someone is always going to feel shortchanged. All the money has done is build resentment!"

Again the room fell silent. I could see desperation on my daughters' faces.

Toni said, "Look, I know I've been selfish." Tears were in her eyes. "I'll do better, Mom. I really can do better."

Beth started crying as well. "So can I. I'm sorry I've been so selfish."

Jack winked and said, "I think you got the point across."

But they didn't understand. I wasn't trying to get a point across. "Then you spend the money, Jack. Put it in your wine collection, give it to the girls, I don't care. I don't want any part of it—"

"Amanda, you're being . . ." He looked at the girls, keeping his accusations in check. "As I stated before, I think your idealism is commendable. Giving money to charity is a fine idea. But that's *your* idea. There are other people in this house. As you always said, we don't make unilateral decisions."

Beth said, "How about this?"

All eyes went to her.

"We give away some money . . . even most of the money. But let's keep a *little* for fun." She paused, then her eyes lit up. "I know who we can give the money to. The homeless guy we always see in the park. He could use some money, I bet."

Jack stifled a laugh. "Yes, maybe we could give him a handout." He turned to me. "If you're serious about this giveaway program, what about the National Endowment for the Arts? With all the budget cuts, I'm sure we could fund something."

"Art doesn't feed people, Dad," Toni said. "How about LIFE—Love Is Feeding Everyone? They feed poor people, Dad, including children. Best of all, it doesn't cost them anything. They use expired but good food from supermarkets. All they need is people to collect it and distribute it. We could give them something."

"You really want to feed people, just go downtown to Mission Street," Jack said. "I'm sure we could supply some meals there."

I put in my own two cents. "I like Children's Hospital. So many sick kids. And even the healthy ones. They're very poor. Their parents have to wait hours just to get seen."

Toni said, "I hope we have enough money for all these good causes—and a *little* left over for fun."

No one spoke.

Beth said, "Not that I mean to be selfish. But . . . does

this mean I'm not going to get any new stuff? And what about Toni's car?"

Toni sighed. "You know, I really don't go many places without friends. I suppose I could . . ." Another sigh. "*Save up* for a car . . . like we originally planned."

I said, "A car was promised to you. But it doesn't have to be a new one."

Toni nodded. "I agree. Anything that gets me to school and back is okay. Who needs a Jeep, anyway?"

She was disappointed but trying to hide it.

I said, "In answer to your question, Beth, yes, you will still get new stuff. You always did get new stuff. But we don't have to spend as if we own the store."

"About that fun money, Amanda?" Jack said. "There was this bottle of cabernet . . ."

"Oh, let him buy the wine, Mom," Toni broke in.

"I'm not his mother. He can do what he wants."

Toni said, "He wants your approval. Stop being so withholding and enjoy life!"

She was right. I said, "I love cabernet."

"A bottle a year," Jack announced. "I propose we put twenty percent of the newfound money into our savings, twenty percent in a fund for the kids' education, ten percent for fun stuff, and the rest goes for those who truly need it. A great idea, Amanda."

Toni said, "But Beth came up with the idea of keeping a *little* for fun. And a great idea it was."

Beth beamed golden rays at her older sister's approval. I smiled, too.

There were still things that money couldn't buy.

SMALL MIRACLES

"Small Miracles" was from a best-selling anthology of everyday coincidences that truly seemed directed by divine intervention. My contribution, reprinted here, shows that I'm not only a mama lion when it comes to my children but that I'm also equally protective of my mother, Anne Marder, who's about five feet tall and tips the scales at 100 pounds after a hearty dinner. This story should have been entitled: "You Mess with My Mom, You Mess with Me." In all seriousness, this incident taught me a lot about myself.

UNRELENTINGLY LOGICAL, I HAVE ALways been a math-science person. I graduated from high school in 1970 as a math major and went to UCLA, where I received a bachelor of arts in theoretical mathematics in 1974. Then, being a practical sort who aspired to employment, I entered UCLA Dental School and graduated with a doctorate of dental surgery four years later. At that time I fully intended to pursue a career as a dentist. One doesn't usually attend dental school for self-actualization.

That was twenty-two years ago. And during those past twenty-two years, I've never picked up a drill—euphemistically known as a handpiece—nor have I scraped a single tartar-coated tooth. Instead, I am now a writer of detective fiction, choosing to explore the human condition instead of oral hygiene.

I couldn't pinpoint the metamorphosis, but I am glad it worked out that way. I could list several factors that steered me toward mystery writing—a desire for justice, a suspicious nature, an overactive imagination, and, of course, a penchant for the bizarre. All of the above can be summed up by what transpired the day I nabbed a mugger.

On that particular morning, my then-four-year-old son—now a strapping lad of eighteen—had chosen to come down with a high fever and a burning sore throat. I suspected strep throat. My mother was at the house, lending a comforting hand while caring for my year-old daughter, Rachel. Rather than drag the entire crew to the pediatrician, I suggested that my mother take a walk with the baby to the corner bakery while I ran my preschooler to the doctor's. It was a fine L.A. day—sunny but not too hot. Yes, I thought, a walk would be refreshing for both Grandma and baby. Not to mention the fact that the soft-hearted bakery lady was always good for a couple of extra cookies for my tyke.

Grandma, baby, and stroller left first. I followed a few minutes later, and I could see them easily about a half-block up. As I pulled out of my driveway, I noticed a car near them but on the opposite side . . . slowing . . . then stopping. A young man got out of the front passenger's seat and started walking. And walking. And walking. Across the street from my mother and daughter, about twenty feet behind them.

But keeping pace with them.

I straightened the wheel of my automobile and shifted into drive. The car up the street was still there . . . creeping by . . . slowly.

And the man kept walking. Still across the way from my mother and child, still keeping pace.

That is odd, I thought. When I let someone out of the car, that person usually goes into a house. He doesn't keep walking for a block or two.

I'm being paranoid, I decided. Nevertheless, this was my daughter, this was my mother. I drove down the street, pointedly behind the creeping car. And then it drove away.

Just like that.

And I felt a little better.

Meanwhile, the man across the street kept strolling

aimlessly, not doing anything suspicious. I waved to my mom and she waved back. Then I drove off.

But something nagged at my gut.

I turned the corner, made a series of right turns, and circled around the block. Then I caught up with my mother, who was blithely ambling in the sunshine. Again we exchanged waves, although she did have a puzzled look on her face. It said, *Why did you come back?*

And the man across the street continued to keep pace with my mother.

Too much TV, I chided myself.

Too many detective novels.

I drove off. One block, then another.

But this was my daughter, this was my mother.

Again I retraced my route.

By the time I returned, my mother was down on her knees, her hand gripping her head. The stroller had been tipped over. My heart raced as I pulled over, screaming, "Are you all right?"

"He took my purse," she shouted hysterically. Frantically, she pointed around the corner.

Again I asked if she was all right. Was the baby all right?

Yes, my mother answered. Despite the fact that she had two scraped knees from her fall, she was fine.

Anger coursed through my body. This was my *baby,* this was my *mother*!

With my son firmly ensconced in his car seat, I gave chase. Admittedly, not the brightest decision I've made. But I reacted rather than considered.

The French Connection it wasn't. I was in a car and he was on foot, so I caught up rather handily. Leaning on the horn, I rolled down the window and screamed at the top of my lungs, "Drop the purse, you son of a bitch!"

"Son of a bitch!" my son imitated from the backseat.

But the sucker kept running. In retrospect, I think it was more in fear than in obstinacy. He pumped his legs hard and fast, racing with the wind. *Chariots of Felony.* But even Jesse Owens wouldn't have had a chance against a V-8 engine. I kept honking the horn, shrieking at him to drop the goddamn purse.

"Goddamn purse," my son aped.

Up ahead was a pedestrian. Two of them. I don't remember much about them. Except that they were male and one of them was wearing a yellow plaid sport coat. I don't know why that particular fact registered, but it did. And it was the one in the plaid coat who pulled out the gun . . . pointed it at the runner, and yelled, "Freeze!"

And the man froze.

Just like in the movies.

I jerked the car into a driveway, not really understanding what was going on.

Plaid Coat instructed the runner to drop the purse. "Drop it," he shouted. "Drop it, drop it, drop it!"

The runner had that deer-in-the-headlights look on his face. He dropped the purse.

Plaid Coat told him to hit the ground.

Just like in the movies.

I bounded out of the car, spoke to Plaid Coat. I pointed to the runner, pointed to my mother's stolen handbag, and angrily said, "That's not his purse!"

Neighbors began filing out, offering to call the police. Which was kind of redundant.

Because Plaid Coat turned out to be an off-duty policeman who had been visiting his father, heard me leaning on the horn, and came out to investigate.

Now he took off his belt and began to secure the suspect. At that point I went back to my mother. She was upright and so was the stroller. I pulled the car over, loaded them both inside. Her palms were sore, her pants were ripped at the knees. But, as promised, both she and my baby were all right.

"He took my purse!" my mother sobbed.

"We caught him, Ma," I said.

"You what?"

"We caught him. We have your purse!"

"Oh. That's good," my mother answered. "That's very good."

"Very good," my son coughed from the backseat.

We returned to the scene of the crime, now thick with patrol cars. I explained my story as I held my baby, and my mother explained her story from inside my car. The uniformed police officers were amazed.

"We never catch these guys," one of them told me.

My mother was required to come down to the station to claim the purse. It would be there waiting for her. The police needed only a couple of hours to process the paperwork.

"She can't just take it now?" I asked. "Save us both a trip?"

"Nope. Evidence."

"Fine," I said.

They congratulated me. I took my mother and baby home. We were all pretty shaken, but life does go on.

I loaded my son back into his car seat and zipped him over to the pediatrician. A good move on my part.

Indeed, it was strep throat.

The SUMMER *of* MY WOMANHOOD

"The Summer of My Womanhood" is perhaps the most emotional piece in the anthology. It's about my father, who died thirty years ago at the age of fifty-three, and by the time I finished writing this essay, I was engulfed by a cloud of wistfulness. Dad owned a deli and a small bakery, and I was fortunate enough to work with him as a preteen and teenager. In order to earn spending cash, I often stood for hours behind the counter helping customers. Of course, my ultimate reward was spending time with my dad, and as I remembered him, my heart filled with treasured memories.

MY FATHER WASN'T A DISTANT FIGURE in my childhood, but I certainly didn't know him well. Like many men of the World War II generation, he worked excruciatingly long and hard hours, not for career fulfillment or self-enlightenment but in order to pay the mortgage on a Veterans Affairs–financed three-bedroom, one-bath house in the hot, dusty San Fernando Valley of Los Angeles County. My father was in the retail food business, not by default but by choice. His decision, especially since he came from a religious Jewish background in which education had always been prized, always puzzled me.

When World War II broke out, Dad was drafted. Instead of immediately being sent to Europe, he was deemed smart enough by the army to send to college. After two years of attending classes at Rutgers University, studying subjects that obviously excited him—he spoke about them well into my young adulthood—he was offered officers' training. After declining the chance for advancement because it meant a longer tour of duty, he was shipped overseas and into the infantry. God must have shone His light on Dad, because he spent only two weeks in the front lines, though it probably felt like years. After the brief stint, he was reassigned to the medical corps. Trained as a medic, he desperately tried to save what the enemy was determined to destroy. After the war, Dad's fluency in Yiddish made him invaluable to the army because he understood many of the languages spoken by concentration-camp victims. He would often translate for his superior officers, aiding in placement and relocation of those who'd survived the Nazis' final solution.

When he talked about the war, it was not often and not very much. But I do remember what he told me. Yes, he revealed stories of the human atrocities, but he was much more intrigued by the ability of ordinary people to rationalize those horrors away, by the denials in Polish towns where the stink of the crematoriums could be detected from miles away. It affected his lifelong outlook. How could it not.

Honorably discharged from the army, my father did what most newly married men did back then: They took jobs not for their glamorous titles but because they needed money. Even though Dad had passed entrance exams to local law schools, he decided to skip three years without income in favor of immediate cash. My father became Oscar the Deli Man—following in the footsteps of his father, Judah (Edward) the Butcher.

I'm sure money had much to do with it. But after observing my father at work up until he died, I do think he was happy with his occupation. It was backbreaking toil, which involved but wasn't limited to toting hundreds of pounds of meat, lifting cases of canned goods, shivering in walk-in freezers and coolers during the winter in stores with no heat, and putting in ungodly hours—from dark to dark. Sunlight was something that glared through plate-glass windows. But the money he earned was from the sweat of his own brow, and that was good enough for Oscar Marder.

As a small child, I was often put to bed before Dad

came home. As an older child, I remember watching TV with him. He didn't talk much except to ask me if I had yet guessed the plot of the latest *Streets of San Francisco* or, at the very least, the quarterly subtitles given after each commercial break during the hour show. Heart-to-hearts were nonexistent, but some sort of primordial communication—that of father and young daughter—did exist.

Dad staked out his claim by renting space in independent food markets. Usually, he ran just one operation at a time. Occasionally, he managed two locations. His booth consisted of a fresh delicatessen with all the traditional meats, cheeses, salads, and, of course, lox and pickled herring. He also took on a small bakery that catered and complemented items sold in a deli. His breads included loaves of soft yellow egg challah, caraway ryes, savory onion rolls, kaiser twists covered with poppy seeds, and oh, those aromatic fruit and cheese Danish and coffee cakes. Dad's kiosk had everything needed for the perfect Saturday picnic or the in-law Sunday brunch. I loved the food, and I loved everything that went along with it. Because I loved my father.

When my older brothers reached double-digit age, they worked in the deli on weekends and helped our father out. When I was eleven, no such demands were made of me. This, of course, angered me. If Dad wasn't going to require it of me, I'd simply require it of myself.

When I announced that I was going to work at the deli, Dad said that was fine, although I was sure it wasn't fine at all. But that didn't stop me.

He didn't know what to do with me. Being short and slight, I didn't fit the job description. There was a physical component to the work that called for muscle mass. I had none. The most skilled chores required an adeptness with sharp objects—meat slicers, cheese slicers, knives for trimming and cutting lox. I had small hands and fingers—way too little to handle industrial equipment that could slice a digit as easily as a corned beef.

There was the retail side—the greeting and the waiting on customers—but I was too short to be seen above the countertops. To the consumers on the other side, I was more or less a floating head. My father was constantly dodging me because I was underfoot and the operating space behind the counters was minimal. The starched white apron my father gave me for protection was way too big. It dragged on the baseboards, picking up sawdust around the hemline. Occasionally, I'd trip on it. When that happened, I hiked up the cloth. Eventually, it would fall down again.

I'm sure I was a disaster. I'm sure I got in Dad's way. But he never said anything to me about it.

Dad knew I couldn't remain an ornament. He had to give me something to do. My first assignment was shoveling the three most popular salads—potato, cole slaw, and macaroni (this was prior to the urban elite pasta salad)—from the cooler into pint or half-pint containers. This job was a snap because the salads were priced by the pint. A pint of cole slaw was X number of cents. A half pint totaled X/2. I was a math whiz in school. I had absolutely no trouble figuring out how to halve things.

Having mastered salads, I was given my next assignment—the weighing and wrapping of dill pickles. This, to my surprise, turned out to be a very tricky affair.

I was given a stool in order to see and read the scale.

But first I needed to learn *how* to read a scale. Back then, before the advent of LCD and the digital revolution, watches were analogs, and scales were mean critters consisting of columns of prices and rows of weights—a veritable crisscross of numbers that bounced up and down with a spring weight. To find out how much something cost necessitated finding the correct intersection between price and weight along a skinny red line. I've known adults who never mastered the art of reading this kind of scale, just as I've known those who never got the hang of a slide rule.

It took me some time. For the first week, all my pickle prices magically came out in pounds, half pounds, or quarter pounds because—being a math whiz—I could divide the price by factors of two. Anything in between was rounded off to the nearest whole number divisible by two. In order to please the customer, I usually rounded down. I'm sure I cost my father some pocket change.

If he noticed it, he never said anything.

Eventually, I vanquished the scale. It was a proud moment that should have been worthy of some kind of certification. But knowledge has its own rewards. Reading the scale now allowed me to *weigh* things—items like lox and precut cheeses and meats, fishy pickled herring and the wonderfully oily Greek olives.

With two skills mastered, I was determined to crack another—wrapping. Origami enthusiasts needn't have worried. Still, I was proud of my neatly swaddled packages with just the right amount of sticky tape on them. And when I wrote the word "pickles" or "Swiss" on the white paper in my own handwriting, no one could have been more pleased than I was.

My weighing and packaging skills had been honed to such an extent that Dad took an enormous chance. No, I was still forbidden to use the meat slicers, but he let me try the bread slicers.

For those unschooled in the literature on bread slicers, I shall explain. To slice a whole loaf of bread, one usually places the bread against a back bar, then turns on the machine. With a manual handle—which the operator slowly pulls toward him or her—the bread is advanced and forced between a series of moving parallel blades until it emerges out the other side in neat, perfect slices.

Immediately upon exiting the blades, my first rye fell apart, the slices fanning out like a deck of cards. Spotting the trouble, Dad once again explained to me that as the bread advances between the blades, it is necessary to secure the loaf on the other side with your hand. This must be done with care, as fingers are not supposed to get close to the blades. Was I up to the challenge?

Indeed I was. After a couple of failures, I was finally able to produce a successfully sliced loaf of rye. I was even able to hold it aloft, vertically by the heel, as the experts did.

Alas, it was the next step that tripped me up. I placed the rye *directly* into the white waxed-paper bag. Needless to say, again the rye fell apart.

As I apologized profusely, the customers just laughed it off.

Isn't she cute?

C'mon, guys. I'm trying to do a job here.

Of course, the crucial error was not housing the rye in a tight plastic bag and securing it with a flexible steel tie before I placed the loaf in the white waxed-paper bag. Of course, that step necessitated opening the plastic bag while still holding the rye in the air.

Not an easy task of coordination. A few of my loaves ended up as fodder for the sawdust floor.

More waste.

If it bothered Dad, he never said so.

Eventually I mastered the coordination necessary for packing the ryes. And not just ryes but loaves of challah and wheat bread as well. These were a challenge unto themselves, because challahs and wheat breads are much softer. They required a *delicate* touch with the bread slicer.

Not one to rest on my laurels, I demanded more. Dad must have felt that I was up to the ultimate challenge, because he put the entire bakery under my charge.

The entire bakery, and I was only eleven.

This was monumental.

Faye the bakery lady.

Take a number, please!

There I was, wearing a hairnet, slicing breads, twirling plastic bags with a flourish, and handing out free sprinkle cookies to toddlers.

The coup de grâce came when Dad started taking me to the wholesale bakery to pick out items for our little bakery. We chose the usual rolls and breads and bagels and Danish. But now, since Dad had a genuine bakery lady, he began to invest in more coffee cakes, coffee rings, *babkas*, and cookies.

The smells were incredible. Hot and yeasty doughs laden with sugar, chocolate, nuts, and cinnamon, glazed with thin white frostings. The aromas, more than the visuals, made my mouth water. We chose our fare straight from the ovens, still hot, resting on parchment paper. At first my dad made all the selections. As I got bolder, I began to make a few suggestions of my own. Sometimes he listened. Sometimes he did not.

One week there was a particular coffee-ring cake that appealed to my eye as well as to my nose. It was a typical cinnamon yeast dough topped with circles of cherries, lemon, blueberries, and apple, the fruit swimming in seas of pectin and sugar. I had to have it. Though not particularly aromatic, it appealed to my eye.

"It will never sell," Dad said.

"But it's pretty."

"People buy with their noses, not with their eyes."

"People like fruit rings," I countered. "And if it doesn't sell, we can take it home."

I was the youngest in my family and the only daughter. I batted my eyelashes and Dad melted. Arriving at the store before the opening hour, I set out the coffee cakes, the cookies, the rolls, and the breads. I tidied up the plastic and paper bags. Unplugging the cord to the bread slicer, I cleaned it of yesterday's crumbs and seeds. I plugged in the bread slicer. Then, with my duties done, I waited for the customers to come out of the starting gate.

Our first consumer came in a few minutes after the doors opened at nine. She was a forty-plus woman—Jewish, as many of our customers were—who scrutinized my baked goods. I saw her eyeing my pretty coffee ring. The artificially red cherries, the egg yolk–colored lemon filling, the blueberries, and the apples.

She scrunched up her brow. "I'll take that one," she stated.

My father was looking over his shoulder as I scooped the cake under my hand and placed it in a pink bakery box, tying it with bakery string.

"Bingo, skittle ball in the old pocket," he whispered to me.

I had never heard the expression before. And Dad never used it again. But I never forgot it.

I decided to take on the job full-time during my summer vacation. It was hard work. I was on my feet most of the time, and I worked four- to eight-hour shifts. Halfway through the month of July, I experienced an epiphany. I was not going to do this for the rest of my life, putting up with cranky customers, flaky vendors, the whims of mechanical equipment, and fallen arches. I made a decision to go for an advanced educational degree. Though writing wasn't in my sights at the time—I never had the audacity to dream I could get published—I was still a person with many options. I could be anything I wanted to be. What I wanted more than anything was to do interesting work while *seated.*

One morning right after the store opened, I went to the restroom and realized, after a very startled reaction, that I had begun my menses. Enormously embarrassed, I didn't know what to do. Sneaking off, I called my mother from a pay phone, and she came to pick me up. No stickum pads back then. We girls were inducted into the clumsy world of belts and napkins. After the problem had been secured, Mom took me back to work.

She must have said something to my dad. He came up to me with a perplexed look on his face.

"Are you okay?" he asked with the concern of those men who stayed clear of *female* things.

"I'm fine, Dad."

"You're sure?"

"Positive."

"I think you have a customer."

"Then I'd better go help her."

After that moment there were no more references to female things. We were just two people trying to earn an honest buck.

Publishing History

"Bull's-eye," copyright © 1997 by Faye Kellerman. Previously published in: *Family Circle/Mary Higgins Clark Mystery Magazine* #2 (spring 1997).

"A Woman of Mystery," copyright © 1999 by Faye Kellerman. Previously published in: a) *Family Circle/Mary Higgins Clark Mystery Magazine* #6 (summer 1999); b) *New Idea* Magazine (2000), Pacific Publications (Australia).

"The Stalker," copyright © 1996 by Faye Kellerman. Previously published in: *Murder for Love,* edited by Otto Penzler, Delacorte, 1996.

"Mummy and Jack," copyright © 2000 by Faye Kellerman and Jesse Kellerman. Previously published in: *Mothers and Sons: A Celebration in Memoirs, Stories, and Photographs,* edited by Jill M. Morgan, NAL, 2000.

"Bonding," copyright © 1989 by Faye Kellerman. Previously published in: a) *Sisters in Crime,* edited by Marilyn Wallace, Berkley, 1989; b) *Hard-boiled: An Anthology of American Crime Stories,* edited by Bill Pronzini and Jack Adrian, Oxford University Press, 1995.

"Discards," copyright © 1990 by Faye Kellerman. Previously published in: a) *Ellery Queen's Mystery Magazine* (November 1990, Volume 96, no. 5), edited by Eleanor Sullivan, Davis Publications; b) *A Woman's Eye,* edited by Sarah Paretsky, Delacorte, 1991; c) *Women of Mystery: Stories from Ellery Queen's Mystery Magazine and Alfred Hitchcock's Mystery Magazine,* edited by Cynthia Manson, Carroll & Graf, 1992; d) *Third Annual Best Mystery Stories of the Year,* edited by Josh Pachter and Martin H. Greenberg, Dercum audio, 1993.

"Tendrils of Love," copyright © 1997 by Faye Kellerman. Originally written for publication in: *The Night Awakens: A Mystery Writers of America Anthology,* edited by Mary Higgins Clark, Pocket Books, 1999/2000.

"Malibu Dog," copyright © 1990 by Faye Kellerman. Previously published in: a) *Sisters in Crime 3,* edited by Marilyn Wallace, Berkley, 1990; b) *Year's 25 Finest Crime and Mystery Stories,* Carroll & Graf, 1992; c) *Modern Treasury of Great Detective and Murder Mysteries,* edited by Edward Gorman, Carroll & Graf, 1994.

"The Back Page," copyright © 1998 by Faye Kellerman. Previously published in: a) *Diagnosis: Dead: A Mystery Writers of America Anthology,* edited by Jonathan Kellerman, Pocket Books, 1999; b) *Giallo* (Japanese quarterly), 2002/2003, Kobunsha (Japan).

"Mr. Barton's Head Case," copyright © 2003 by Faye Kellerman. Previously published in: *Du Sollst Nicht Toten: Zwolf Verbrechen aus der Bibel,* edited by Regula Veske, Scherz Verlag, 2003 (German title, "Mr Bartons Spezi").

"Holy Water," copyright © 1994 by Faye Kellerman. Previously published in: a) *Deadly Allies II: Private Eye*

Writers of America and Sisters in Crime Collaborative Anthology, edited by Robert J. Randisi and Susan Dunlap, Doubleday, 1994; b) *Mystery Midrash: An Anthology of Jewish Mystery and Detective Fiction,* edited by Lawrence W. Raphael, Jewish Lights Publishing, 1999; c) *Stellar Audio Volume 20* (with "Inconvenience Store" by Max Allan Collins), Brilliance, Stellar Audio imprint, 1997.

"Free Parking," copyright © 1996 by Faye Kellerman. Previously published in: *Mother: Famous Writers Celebrate Motherhood with a Treasury of Short Stories, Essays, and Poems,* edited by Claudia O'Keefe, Pocket Books, 1996.

"The Luck of the Draw," copyright © 1998 by Faye Kellerman, Rachel Kellerman, and Ilana Kellerman. Previously published in: *Mothers and Daughters: Celebrating the Gift of Love with 12 New Stories,* edited by Jill M. Morgan, NAL, 1998.

"Small Miracles," copyright © 1997 by Faye Kellerman. Previously published in: *Small Miracles: Extraordinary Coincidences from Everyday Life,* edited by Yitta Halberstam and Judith Leventhal, Adams Media Corporation, 1997.

"The Summer of My Womanhood," copyright © 1999 by Faye Kellerman. Previously published in: *Fathers and Daughters: A Celebration in Memoirs, Stories, and Photographs,* edited by Jill M. Morgan, Signet/NAL, 1999.

About the Author

FAYE KELLERMAN is the bestselling author of the Peter Decker/Rina Lazarus thrillers, as well as the novels *Moon Music, The Quality of Mercy,* and *Straight into Darkness.* She has also cowritten *Double Homicide* and *Capital Crimes* with her husband, Jonathan Kellerman. She lives with her family in California and New Mexico.